"Listen to this," Janet said. She pointed to the TV.

". . . 82nd Airborne out of Fort Bragg," the news commentator was saying. "The 101st out of Fort Campbell and the 19th Mountain Division. Marines from the West Coast will be used to help police Los Angeles and San Diego, National Guard and regular army troops in San Francisco. Experts predict that within forty-eight hours, martial law will be declared in all of the nation's larger cities. . . ."

"Jim," Janet went on. "Almost a year ago the intelligence community predicted something like this. Next comes the blockade of food shipments into the city. . . ."

"Why New York?"

"Because the city is eighty-five-percent liberal, that's why. They—you, Jim—have become the enemy." She jerked a thumb toward the outside, where the rumble of military vehicles could be heard. "You see what's happening?"

Before he could reply, a violent explosion rattled the window; pictures fell from the wall. Flames leaped from the shattered windows of the apartment next door. The explosion almost knocked Janet off her feet. Jim jumped up and rushed to her side.

"That was a rocket!" Janet said. "Let's get out of here.

"Rocket! *Rocket?*" Jim shouted. What the hell is this city turning into, Bosnia?"

WILLIAM W. JOHNSTONE
THE ASHES SERIES

BREAKDOWN

William W. Johnstone

Pinnacle Books
Kensington Publishing Corp.
http://www.pinnaclebooks.com

PINNACLE BOOKS are published by

Kensington Publishing Corp.
850 Third Avenue
New York, NY 10022

Pinnacle and the P logo Reg. U.S. Pat. & TM Off.

First Printing: March, 1997
10 9 8 7 6 5 4 3 2 1

Printed in the United States of America

BOOK ONE

Good laws lead to the making of better ones; bad laws bring about worse.

—Jean Jacques Rousseau

Would you realize what Revolution is, call it Progress; and would you realize what Progress is, call it Tomorrow.

—Victor Hugo

Prologue

In Southern California, five men walked into a video store that featured XXX porno films. While one stood watch in front, another began spray-painting religious graffiti on the walls. The other three marched the manager and the two employees on duty into a back room, ordered them to kneel, then executed the two men and one woman with a single pistol-shot to the back of each head.

The five men then exited the store and, according to witnesses, got into an older-model station wagon and drove away.

On the back wall of the video store, in huge, red runny letters, these words had been spray-painted: SET THY HOUSE IN ORDER.

The stolen station wagon was found a few days later, abandoned in a parking lot in Los Angeles. Those responsible for the triple murders were never caught.

In New Orleans, one of the city's most notorious drug pushers walked out of the courtroom grinning, waving his jeweled fingers at his cheering supporters. The jury, after deliberating for only twenty-five minutes, had returned a not-guilty verdict. No one was in the least surprised. It was the fifth time the drug pusher, pimp, loan shark, and nightclub-owner had been tried, and the fifth time he had walked free. That some jurors had been bought off and others frightened off and still others had played the race card in reaching their decision was a foregone conclusion.

Later that evening, outside his suburban mansion, Leroy "Big Baboo" Wilson, along with his bodyguard, Willie "Bonebreaker" Jones, and two women whose intelligence quotient could be accurately compared with that of an oyster, got into Leroy's custom-built stretch Cadillac. The explosion that followed uprooted six magnolia trees, wiped out half of Leroy's mansion, and spread Big Baboo, Bonebreaker, and the two women over several square miles of South Louisiana.

One writer to the *Times-Picayune* observed that it was a damn shame about those magnolia trees.

In Chicago, one week after his release from prison, a known child-molester grabbed a six-year-old boy and sodomized him. He was immediately arrested and immediately released by a judge because one of the arresting officers had roughed him up, thereby depriving him of his constitutional rights.

A few hours later, half-a-dozen men and women wearing ski masks dragged the child-molester kicking and screaming from his parents' home and hanged him from an oak tree in the front yard.

No arrests were made.

In a small town in north-central Missouri, a gang of teenage thugs had been terrorizing the town for weeks, driving around at night and shooting randomly into homes with high-powered rifles. No one had been killed, but several people had been wounded by the gunfire, one woman seriously.

On a chilly late February evening, heavy-metal music blaring from speakers pushed to the max, the carload of teenagers roared through a quiet neighborhood, blasting away at homes on either side of the street, the bullets shattering windows and terrorizing homeowners.

As the car slid around a corner, tires burning rubber on the concrete, the occupants of the vehicle were met with a solid wall of semi-automatic gunfire. State police later counted over a hundred-and-fifty bullet-holes in the car. Since every window in the vehicle was completely shot out, state police estimated it took another one-hundred-and-fifty rounds to accomplish that. None of the rampaging teenagers survived the ambush. All had to be buried in a closed-casket service due to the extensive damage caused by the gunfire.

No one who was interviewed saw anything.

No arrests were made.

Over the relatively short period of three months, an astonishing three-hundred-and-fifty acts of vigilantism were recorded in the forty-eight contiguous United States of America and Alaska and Hawaii, most of which resulted in the very sudden demise of the criminal suspect or suspects. Seventy-five were recorded in Canada. In both nations, most suspects were either shot or hanged. A few were horsewhipped; a half-dozen were castrated. None of the vigilantes was caught.

One network news commentator closed his nightly

news by solemnly observing that all was not well in America.

A viewer, responding by E-mail to the network news commentator's observation, electronically remarked: No kidding?

One

Jim Kincaide looked across the table and smiled at the woman. Even after a half-dozen dates, it was still difficult for him to believe this lovely lady was in the army.

"Dessert, Janet?"

She shook her head. "Better not. I've only been in the city six weeks and already picked up three pounds." She smiled. "You wouldn't know where the nearest obstacle course is, would you?"

Jim chuckled softly. He recalled his own days in the army and that hated obstacle course during basic training. "You really run the obstacle course?"

"Several times a week when I'm on base. It's a great way to keep in shape."

"I hated that damn thing!"

She grinned at him. "I think you hated the army."

"Oddly enough, I really didn't. Oh, I was delighted to get out and put it all behind me. I'll sure admit that. But for a seventeen-year-old who was running wild on the streets of New York, the discipline was just what I needed." Jim signaled the waiter for the check, looked back at Janet. "Want to take in a movie?"

"I feel like a long walk instead. How about it? It's a pleasant night."

"This is New York City, Janet. Remember? Where do you have in mind to walk?"

Her dark-blue eyes darkened further, becoming almost black. It had not taken Jim long to discover that Janet Shaw had a short fuse and her very expressive eyes were the first giveaway. "I'll walk any place I choose to walk, Jim. This is America. Not a damn minefield in Bosnia."

Jim held up a hand. "Okay, okay. Peace. You want to walk, we'll walk." Just, for God's sake, don't suggest the middle of Central Park at nine o'clock at night, he thought.

"We'll take a cab over to the park and walk some, all right?"

Jim sighed, but he knew better than to argue. In the few weeks he'd been seeing Janet, he had learned that when she made up her mind to do something, she was going to do it.

Janet smiled. "We can even hold hands if you like."

"Here?" the cabbie asked, pulling over to the curb.

Jim resisted a sudden impulse to give the cabbie the bird. He turned from the curb to find Janet had already walked to the entrance at East 61st, a block above Grand Army Plaza. He hurried to catch up with her.

"Will you, for Christ's sake, wait up?"

"Relax," she rejoined. "Don't worry. I'll take care of you."

Jim knew she was only kidding; at least he thought she was. The remark still irritated him; but he maintained his composure and, together, they entered the park.

He said, pointing, "This path will take us to the . . ."

"I know where we are. I've reconnoitered this place thoroughly."

"Reconnoitered," he muttered. "I haven't heard that word since 'Nam."

Janet stopped, dug in her purse, and fished out a box of English cigarettes. She only smoked about five cigarettes a day, and Jim wondered why she didn't just quit altogether. He had kicked the habit ten years back, but he still craved a smoke, especially after a meal or when having a drink.

They walked in silence for a few moments. The faint scent of early lilacs drifted to them from the Sheep Meadow.

Jim stole a glance at her as they walked. *Major* Janet Shaw, he thought. United States Army. Mystery lady, for I damn sure don't know much else about you.

Janet was only a couple of inches shorter than Jim's five feet ten and she matched his stride as they walked. Her hair was a dark, dark brown and she wore it short. Jim's hair was a fashionably cut lighter brown peppered with flecks of gray. He was ten years older than Janet's thirty-five. Both were in excellent physical shape—Janet from years of military service, Jim from daily use of his home exercise equipment in his apartment at 72nd and Park. Janet had rented a place over on Columbus Ave. She had been to Jim's apartment several times; she had never invited him to hers.

"You own a gun, Jim?" She broke the silence of midevening, surprising him with the question.

"Why, ah, no. I don't." He smiled. "Do you?"

"Several."

He didn't know how to respond to that, so he said nothing.

They walked along East Drive for a time—the pond and bird sanctuary to their left, the zoo coming up on the right.

Jim finally broke the silence. "Why did you ask me about a gun?"

"Just curious."

He took a chance. "I don't think that was it at all. Why don't you level with me for a change?"

That strange smile moved her lips. "You have my word that I have never lied to you."

"And I never said you did. But there are times when I can't seem to get a straight answer out of you."

"I'm in the army, Jim."

"What do you do in the army?"

"Right now I'm in recruiting, working with several of our offices in and around the city."

Jim had been in advertising for nearly twenty years. He had joined the army right out of high school, pulled two tours in Vietnam, returned home, and gone to college. He had married, was now divorced, with two kids he had not seen in several years . . . at their mother's request. He had left college in his third year to take a position with a fledgling firm, quickly becoming one of their rising stars. He was now a senior account executive. Jim had been around some of the most skillful liars in the world, having worked hands-on with politicians in three presidential campaigns and several senatorial and congressional campaigns. He'd worked on ad campaigns in four mayoral elections and dozens of lesser elections, state and local. He knew when he was being lied to.

"All right, Janet. If you say so."

She laughed softly. "You don't believe me, do you?"

"I didn't say that."

"You didn't have to."

He detected movement behind them and tensed. "We have people following us," Jim said in low tones.

"They've been following us since we entered the park."

Jim cut his eyes to her. Janet didn't seem to be disturbed about the men tagging along behind him. "And we're just going deeper into the park?"

"Why not? It's a free country, isn't it?"

Jim sighed as patiently as possible, certain they both were about to get mugged, possibly killed. Before they had taken another five steps along the poorly lighted walkway, he lost patience. "Goddamnit, Janet!" he whispered. "This is crazy. Those thugs are surely armed."

"So am I," she said. "Legally. So if those pukes back there want to dance, let us rock and roll."

Jim stopped abruptly, not really believing what he'd just heard. Janet kept walking. He hurried to catch up. They were almost even with a young man waiting under the dim streetlamp at the intersection.

Suddenly, headlights cut the night, coming at them along East Drive. The young man on the corner vanished, taking off at a run back toward Fifth Avenue. The two men who had been following them vanished just as quickly.

"Shit!" Janet muttered, disappointment evident in her voice.

Jim looked at the woman as if seeing her for the first time. He didn't understand any of this.

The Park Police unit stopped alongside them, the cop on the passenger side looking at the pair. "You folks better clear the park. We're going to close it in a few minutes. We've had some trouble tonight." He pointed.

"That way back to Fifth. The road forks into 65th and 66th."

"Thank you, officer," Jim said. "I was born in the city."

"Then you should know better than to wander around the park after dark, mister. Go on. Both of you. We'll tag along behind until you reach Fifth."

Walking along—the Park Police unit laying back about a hundred yards, idling along, headlights on bright—Jim said, "You were pushing that back there, Janet. You wanted those thugs to do something, didn't you?"

"Whatever in the world do you mean?"

"What if those cops had searched us? They would have found the weapon you claim to be carrying."

"So what? Big deal. I have a federal concealed-weapons permit."

"Would you really have shot those thugs?"

"Would you rather I patted them on the head and said what good boys they were?"

"Jesus, Janet! I don't understand you at all."

She smiled. "No, Jim. That is one thing about you I'm sure of. You do not understand me at all."

Janet Shaw. Born into abject, grinding poverty in a shack without running water or lights in Florida. Youngest daughter of what in the South is referred to as "white trash." Left a migrant workers' camp at age thirteen and never once looked back. Behaved and physically appeared much older than her years. Bummed around the country for a time. Worked two jobs for a year and then enrolled in a small state-supported college in North Carolina. Joined the ROTC program. Graduated near the top of her class. Went straight into the army and, after basic and AIT, was sent to intelligence schools. Jump qualified. Licensed pilot, fixed wing and helicopter. Became one of the few women ever to graduate from the CIA's infamous training school in Virginia. Expert rifle and pistol shot. Expert in judo. Actual combat experience in Desert Storm and two tours in Bosnia.

Jim was right: He did not understand her at all.

"I'm telling you," one of the ad agency's junior executives was speaking as Jim poured a cup of coffee and snagged a donut, "that news program last night was right on the money. I m surprised you didn't see it." He looked at Jim. "Did you see it, Mr. Kincaide?"

"No. What are you talking about?"

"A nationwide vigilante movement."

Jim winked at the young man. "Have you been watching Charles Bronson movies again, Tom?"

"No, sir! This was a network news program. And very well done."

"Speaking of done, have you finished with the McLeary workups?" There was no rush on that job, but talk of militias and conspiracy theories and the like bored Jim.

"Ah, no, sir. I'd better get right on it."

"Fine. You do that."

As Jim walked away, he paused just outside the door and heard Tom say, "I'm telling you, Dick. It's serious. People are beginning to take the law into their own hands."

"Maybe it's time for that," the other young man said.

"Don't say that too loud," Tom replied in a whisper. "Not around this bunch of weepy liberals."

Jim returned to his office and sat down. He ate the donut and sipped his coffee. Weepy liberals. Is that what this new bunch of young ad execs thought about people his age? He shook his head. He'd always thought of himself as more of a politically moderate Democrat.

He looked up as Bob Waldman stepped into his office and took a seat. Bob had started the company with a few bucks and a lot of chutzpa. Jim had answered an ad in the paper and had been offered long hours and low pay, but a promise of a piece of the action if things worked out. Bob, Jim, and a handful of others had worked like sweatshop employees for several years, and it had paid off handsomely.

"Busy, Jim?"

"As a matter of fact, no. I find myself with nothing to do." He grinned. "For a change. I could have stayed in bed this morning." He looked at the serious expression on Waldman's face and his smile faded. "What's the matter, Bob?"

"Did you watch that TV special last night about vigilantes?"

Jim knew from long years of working with the man that Bob Waldman was one of the most levelheaded people he'd ever met. If that news program had gotten Bob's attention, maybe there was something to it. He shook his head. "No. I missed it."

"I was advised to tape it." He pulled a video cassette tape from his right-hand jacket pocket and laid it on the desk. "I did. Give it a look this evening. It's worth an hour of your time."

Jim put the tape in his attaché case. "All right."

"You can keep it. I made several copies." He stood up. "I'm going to take my vacation early this year, Jim.

And . . . I talked it over with Rebecca, and we've agreed that it's time I thought about retiring—or at least cutting back."

Jim tapped his attaché case. "The contents of this tape have you that worried, Bob?"

Bob waited several heartbeats before replying. At first it was just the nod of his head. Then, "You remember my telling you about Marty Lieber?"

Jim thought for a moment. "Yes. That college buddy of yours who was killed some months ago."

"Shot to death in his study at home. Yesterday afternoon, my friend Norman Feldman was assassinated. Shot to death in his car two blocks from his home."

"I'm sorry, Bob. He lives . . . lived in Chicago, didn't he?"

"In a suburb, yes. Last month, in St. Louis, Harold Stone was shot to death leaving his office. The month before that, it was a man named Stern in Boston. In the past six months, there have been a dozen Jews that I know of killed in the U.S. and Canada, nearly all of them bankers. All of them shot to death. I bought two pistols last month, Jim," he blurted out. "Rebecca and I have been taking lessons at a shooting club."

Jim was shocked, and his expression betrayed that emotion. He knew that Bob Waldman was a liberal's liberal, contributing heavily to a lot of social causes. And he hated guns. "Bob . . ."

Waldman held up a hand. "I know. I know. Big-talking me. All pistols should be banned. Gathered up. No one but the police and the military should be allowed to own handguns. So, maybe I was wrong, my friend. Maybe I didn't have my facts straight. Maybe if my neighbor is going to own a handgun, I should, too. So, who the hell knows who is right and who is wrong? My suggestion to you is get a gun. I'm buying a shotgun this afternoon. A twelve-gauge. Pump. Shoots magnum bullets . . ."

"Shells, Bob," Jim said automatically. "A shotgun chambers shells."

"Shells, then. So what do I know about guns? I'm taking lessons to learn. I was never in the army. I'm legally blind. I can't see my hand in front of my face without glasses." He stared at his longtime friend and colleague. "So, how do you know so much about shotguns?"

"Some of the recon people in my outfit carried them in the bush in 'Nam. And . . . my father was a big hunter. He had all sorts of rifles and shotguns and pistols. I was shooting on a range before I was ten years old."

"I never knew that, Jim. Did you hunt as a boy?"

"Oh, yes. But after 'Nam, I never hunted again. Haven't owned or fired a gun in nearly twenty-five years. Well, the first part isn't really true. The hunting lodge my father built in the Adirondacks was willed to me after his death three years ago. It's looked after by a caretaker. A fund was set up just for that purpose. Dad had a gun vault built in the basement. It's full of guns."

"You haven't been back since his death?"

"I go up once a year to check out the place."

"The guns still there?"

"I guess so. I haven't opened the vault since his death. The caretaker doesn't even know about the vault. I'm the only one who knows the combination. My dad had it very carefully built behind a false wall. It was almost as if he . . ." Jim paused and shook his head.

"Sounds to me like he was preparing for a very uncertain future," Bob finished. "Maybe he knew some-

thing the rest of us didn't." Bob moved toward the door.
He turned to face Jim. "Get a gun, Jim. I think the revolution certain people have talked about for years—people
that we used to brush aside as crackpots—is no laughing
matter. I think the right-wingers have declared war on
the Jews. And in case you've forgotten, you're in part-
nership with a Jew."

Jim brushed that aside with an impatient wave of his
hand. "Bob, what is this about retiring? You're still a
young man. You . . ."

"I'm sixty-one-years-old. I would like to live out the
years ahead of me in peace. But the future scares me."
He shook his head. "These killings of Jews across the
country . . . too much has been going on for it to be
coincidence. You take care of things for a while. I'll be
in and out of the office. Mostly out. And get a gun, Jim.
I think you're going to need one." He stepped out into
the hall and closed the door behind him.

Jim sat for a long time, looking at the closed office
door. He opened his attaché case and looked at the box
containing the video tape. He finally blurted out, "What
in the hell is going on?"

Two

"Well, now look at this," Janet muttered after receiving and reading a copy of the military records of James Edward Kincaide. "Instead of a tame house-cat, I've been petting a real live tiger."

Janet sat in the Manhattan offices of the Central Intelligence Agency, where she was working as liaison between military and civilian intelligence. This was the company's "dark" office; the public office could be found in the phone book, under U. S. Government. The gold lettering on the hall door read *Carson Imports*. She had requested a full report on Jim, but the first page of the second report revealed little that she did not already know. Jim was straight-arrow: excellent credit, did not belong to any subversive groups, did not drink to excess, was not homosexual. The second page was a bit more interesting: James Edward Kincaide had been born with that proverbial silver spoon in his mouth. The third child of wealthy parents. One sister—married and divorced four times; a socialite who drank herself to sleep every night, now living in Miami. One brother, whose sexual orientation was highly questionable; a lawyer/gay-rights activist who lived in San Francisco. Jim did not get along with either brother or sister.

He had never mentioned either one to Janet.

Jim's mother had died of cancer while he was in Vietnam. The father had never remarried and followed his wife to the grave nearly twenty years later. The family's wealth was divided equally among the three children. None of the three had contested any part of the will.

Jim had also never mentioned the hunting lodge he owned in the Adirondacks, the lodge specifically left him by his father.

There were a number of things Jim had not mentioned to Janet, including the Silver Star, the Distinguished Service Cross, two Bronze Stars, and two Purple Hearts.

"Interesting," Janet said, closing the folder and leaning back in her chair. "Most interesting."

Of course, there were also a few things Janet had never mentioned to Jim.

"I didn't know you were a conspiracy freak," Janet said, looking at the tape Jim was about to slip into the VCR.

"I'm not. But my partner asked me to watch this. He thinks some sort of civil war is about to erupt."

"So do a lot of people." She spoke from the large window overlooking the still-busy street below. "Why so high up, Jim?"

"It isn't fashionable to live close to the street. Too much noise."

When she didn't immediately respond, he turned from the expensive entertainment center to look at her. He couldn't read her faint smile. "What, Janet?"

"Not fashionable." She spoke softly. "Well," she said, clearing her throat. "We wouldn't want that, now, would we?"

"Do I detect more than a hint of sarcasm in that remark?"

"Oh, no. Not at all."

"Ummm." He punched the *play* button and took a seat on the couch.

Janet sat down beside him. She made no mention of it, but she and the others at the agency had viewed this news program several times only hours before.

They watched in silence until the first commercial break, Janet occasionally stealing a glance to check the expression on Jim's face. It was usually one of dark amusement mixed with incredulity.

"You find the threat of violent civil disobedience amusing, Jim?"

"Oh, come on. You have a few thousand nuts—spread out over fifty states—running around in the woods on weekends shooting off semi-automatic weapons, playing soldier-boy and scaring bird-watchers. Many, if not most, of those militia-joiners are racist to the core. They're night-riders, Janet. Cowards and malcontents, with connections to the KKK and other groups of that ilk. I cannot believe they pose any real threat to the public safety."

"You don't think these groups are strong enough or organized enough to make any real attempt to knock over the government?"

"Are you joking? Good Lord, no!"

The commercials over, they settled back to watch the next segment of the report. Janet pretended to be interested. She would have liked to level with Jim Kincaide, for he was a nice guy and the first man she'd allowed herself to get close to in years, but he was a typical liberal. His world was surrounded by a huge bubble, penetrable only by certain news reports—print and broadcast—and utterances from liberal politicians. Everything else was either a lie or a gross exaggeration. Conservatives (and that certainly included all Republicans) were racists, war-mongers, and hardhearted, unfeeling monsters when it came to the needs of others less fortunate.

That type of thinking amused and often disgusted Janet, but she believed that every American citizen had a right to a point of view and the license to voice his convictions, no matter how repugnant.

She left Jim sitting on the couch, muttering under his breath, and fixed them drinks from the mirrored wet bar: scotch and water for Jim, bourbon and water for her.

She paused by the window for a moment, looking down at the street. Far below, a police car roared by, siren shrieking and lights flashing.

Stay out of the way when the shit hits the fan, people, she thought. You are not the enemy.

The Arizona deputy cut on his emergency lights, and the late-model station wagon ahead of him veered to the side of the road and stopped. He reached for his mic, then pulled his hand back. No point, he thought. He wasn't going to give them a hard copy, just a warning. They hadn't been traveling that fast, just a few miles over the speed limit. He got out of his unit, hitched at his gunbelt, and began walking toward the station wagon. Quiet out tonight, no headlights showing in either direction.

Halfway to the station wagon, the driver's side door opened and a man got out. The deputy stopped cold in his tracks as he spotted the sawed-off pump shotgun in the man's hands.

"Now, just hold on, mister," the deputy said, a cold numbness settling in the pit of his stomach.

"I'm sorry about this," the shotgun-wielding man said. "I truly am. You are not the enemy."

"Hell, I know I'm not your enemy!" the deputy retorted as another man stepped out of the station wagon. The second man held what appeared to be some sort of machine pistol. An Uzi or MAC, the deputy thought. Not that it made all that much difference. Either one of them could blow a full magazine of rounds in about two seconds.

"Do you believe this nation is heading down a godless path?" the second man asked in a low voice.

"Ah . . . you bet!" the deputy said. "Sure is. I was tellin' my wife that this afternoon."

"You have children?"

"Two. A boy and a girl. Boy is five; the girl is eighteen months." He wondered if he'd ever see them again. Suddenly he had to go to the bathroom real bad.

"Are they being raised in the church?"

"Yes. We go to church every Sunday . . . when I don't have to work, that is."

A third man got out of the station wagon and walked to the deputy's unit, opening the door and getting in.

"Religion is very important in a child's life," the second man said. The deputy figured he was the leader of this . . . whatever the hell it was.

The man who had done something in the county unit got out and fished the deputy's wallet out of his pocket.

"I'm sorry I don't have much money," the deputy said. "But you're welcome to what I have."

"We are not interested in your money," the spokesman said. "Just your soul and your cooperation."

"My soul belongs to God." And my ass. That disrespectful thought popped into the young man's head. Why did I think that? he questioned silently. "If you'll tell me what you want, you can have my cooperation."

"Then you'll live," the spokesman said. "We have your name and address. If you betray us, we'll be back and you will pay with your life. Do you understand that?"

"Yes, sir. But what am I not supposed to betray?"

"You'll know when the time comes. See to your family and lay in a supply of food and water. Now get in your car and head back in the other direction."

The deputy wasted no time in complying. Soon his taillights had faded from view.

"We might have made a mistake with him," the driver said.

The spokesman smiled. "Or we might have made a convert."

The news program over, Jim began making dinner. Janet did not offer to help.

"Overall, what did you think of the program, Jim?"

He looked up from the chopping board. "The program was well done. The content was lacking in credibility."

She turned her head to hide her amusement. "Didn't believe anything about it, right?"

He resumed his chopping of onions and peppers. "Very little. If the FBI ever shows up at the doorstep of those people, they'll collapse like a house of cards."

Janet took a stool at the open snack bar dividing the kitchen from the living room and sipped her drink as she watched him work. "How long were you in Vietnam, Jim?"

He did not reply immediately. He scraped the onions and peppers from the board to a bowl and set that aside. "Two tours. I didn't finish the last tour because I got hit."

"And haven't fired a weapon since you left the service."

"That's right."

"Did you ever do any hunting, Jim?"

"As a kid. Deer, duck, geese, quail. I haven't hunted in years."

"Not since Vietnam." It was not a question.

"That's right."

Jim sighed, a strange look suddenly shining in his eyes.

"What's wrong?"

"Are you free this weekend?"

"Sure."

"If we can get clear of the city by three o'clock, we can be there in a few hours."

"Be where?"

"I need to check on some property my father left me. It's upstate. We can spend Friday and Saturday nights there and come back Sunday afternoon. It's a nice place. Rustic. Very peaceful."

She met his gaze for a few seconds. Nodded. "All right. We can take my truck. I need to run it. It's been in a parking garage ever since I got here."

"Your truck?"

She smiled at the expression on his face. "Yes. It's a Ford F-150, extended cab. Four-wheel drive on demand. We might need four-wheel drive, don't you think?"

He arched one eyebrow, a trick she'd always wanted to master but never could. She couldn't wink, either. Every time she tried, she closed both eyes. She'd been told by more than one person she looked like an idiot.

"Yeah. I guess we might, at that. I haven't bounced around in a truck in years."

"I think you'll be surprised at how comfortable they are. How about I pick you up at two outside the building?"

"All right. Sounds good. Can you mix up this sauce and put it on to heat while I fix the garlic butter?"

"Not unless you have a fire extinguisher and a death wish."

"You're not at home in the kitchen, eh?"

"No. But the last time I qualified, I fired expert with rifle and pistol."

"That's . . . certainly something every lady should know."

Three

President Arthur Evans—Art to his friends—read the report again and looked across the desk in the Oval Office at his national security advisor, Richard Guy—Dick to his friends. "This report seems to lend some credence to that news report last evening."

Richard nodded in agreement.

Evans cut his eyes to the director of the FBI, Kevin Brewer. "And you concur with this report and the news broadcast?"

"Yes."

The president drummed his fingertips on the desktop. Shifted his gaze to the attorney general of the United States, Stella Newton. "And you?"

"I believe the report is accurate. We've been seeing a steady buildup of militia membership over the past few years. And we've grossly underestimated their nationwide strength."

"But you, none of you, had any inkling of this vigilante movement?"

"Not until about three months ago," Director Brewer replied, speaking for all present. "But we don't believe it is *one* nationwide movement. We believe it's a number of small groups operating independently. No centralized leadership."

"It's also our opinion that was done deliberately," Richard Guy said. "Some years ago. Then those who met returned home, made their plans, and remained dormant until recently."

The president was silent for a moment. Then he asked, "And where is all this leading?"

The three officials exchanged glances. Stella Newton answered for the three of them. "God only knows, sir."

The comfort of the twin front seats in the Ford F-150 surprised Jim when he got in and buckled up. Then the ride brought a smile to his lips. "This is really nice. It just surprised me when you said you had a truck."

"They're handy."

Janet had picked him up before the rush-hour traffic began, so they cleared the city without a lot of difficulty and headed north. Jim had called the caretaker and arranged for the lodge to be aired out and to make sure the electricity was on. Phil LaBarre had been a cranky bastard ever since Jim first met him, twenty-five years back, and time had not improved his disposition. Now, he seemed worse.

"You ain't givin' me much time, Mr. Kincaide," he had complained.

"Two days, LaBarre. Just do the best you can."

On the ride up, Jim laughed about the caretaker's cantankerousness and Janet asked, "How well do you know this Phil LaBarre?"

"I've known him since I was fifteen-years-old."

"How old a man is he?"

"Oh . . . he's in his early sixties, I'd guess. Hard to

say, really. I don't know much about him. His family came down from Canada years back."

"Is he happy with his station in life?"

He glanced at her as they drove north along the interstate. Early spring, the trees just beginning to bud. "What an odd question. Hell, I don't know. I guess so. Why?"

"Just curious."

They left the interstate and headed in a northwesterly direction. Daylight savings time, a system that Jim liked and for some reason Janet professed to hate, had not yet kicked in, so it was full dark when they pulled into the parking lot of a small grocery store in the nearest town to the lodge. Jim bought steaks, bread, milk, potatoes, and salad makings—enough for the evening meal—and they hit the road once more, this time with Jim behind the wheel.

"It gets a little complicated from here on in," he explained, glancing at her in the dim light from the dashboard. "Why do you dislike daylight savings time?"

"Just another example of big government attempting to run people's lives."

"What do you think the function of government should be, Janet?"

"To protect our shores and borders from foreign invaders and deliver the mail."

He laughed aloud. "Isn't that somewhat of an oversimplification?" He cut off onto a county road. The night seemed to close in on them as the landscape changed, with timber on both sides of the road and no homes.

"Certainly. How big is this park?" She abruptly changed the subject.

"Six million acres, about half of it wilderness. Toward the end of the last century, the state of New York, which owns about half of the Adirondacks, declared the area to be forever wild. And much of it is that."

"Not many roads, right?"

"Not many. And nearly all lead to Lake Placid. I think there are twelve-hundred miles of streams and eleven-hundred miles of roads in the park. It's a wonderful place to get away from it all. I've missed it, truthfully."

"I can see why." It's also a dandy place to train small groups of militiamen in the art of guerrilla warfare and silent killing, Janet thought.

The lodge was built of native stone, with a covered porch that extended all the way across the front. The front-porch light was burning as they drove up.

"Phil's done his job," Jim said. "Albeit grudgingly and complaining the entire time, I'm sure. I'll give him a nice bonus, and that will make him happy. Or as happy as he ever gets."

There was a note stuck between the screen door and jamb. I DID WHAT I COULD IN THE TIME YOU GIVE ME. ENJOY YOUR STAY.

It was unsigned.

"Mr. LaBarre?" Janet asked.

"Sure. Phil got the last word. He always did. Even with my father. And that was no mean trick."

Jim opened the door, fumbled for the switch, and flooded the huge front room with light. "Go on in. I'll get the groceries."

The living room was enormous, stretching from one side of the house to the other, taking up at least a third of the square footage of the first floor of the two-story lodge, with a fireplace large enough to roast a whole cow. The furniture was old and had seen some wear, but it was of good quality; couches and chairs were scattered about the huge room. Stuffed birds and the antlered heads of trophy deer hung on the walls. A wet bar had been built into one corner of the room.

"Mother wouldn't allow any animal trophies in our place in the city." Jim spoke from the doorway. Janet turned to take one of the sacks of groceries. "So, Dad spent as much time here as he could. He'd stay up here for weeks during hunting season. Kitchen's over there."

Groceries put away, Jim retrieved the luggage from the truck and then led Janet on a tour of the house. "You take that bedroom. I'll take the one down the hall."

She stood for a moment, smiling at him. "Why don't we just find the linen closet and make up one bed, Jim?"

"That, ah, would be the practical thing to do, wouldn't it?"

She laughed. "I've heard sex called a lot of things, Jim. But this is the first time I've ever heard it called *practical.*"

"They're both city people," Phil LaBarre told the gathering of men and women. "We got nothin' to worry about with them. Jim's a candy-ass and he always has been. Takes after his mama. His daddy was a real man." He grimaced. "Right up to the end."

"How long will they be here?" a woman asked.

"The weekend. He comes up once a year to check on the place. Then he's gone come Sunday."

"Do you have to see him again this trip?" a man asked LaBarre.

"No. I never do."

"Make it a point to avoid him. All right, then. We don't meet or train while Kincaide and the woman are here. All of you go home. Mark, Richard, you two stay for a moment; I want to talk to you."

The hunting camp emptied. When the sounds of cars and trucks had faded into the night, Dr. Tom Durant poured a cup of coffee and sat down at the table, looking at the two men who had stayed behind. "The report just came back from our people in Washington. Got it this morning. It's confirmed. Pat Monroe is working for the feds. They planted him in here several years ago, when the militia movement was really getting started. We think he's regular FBI." The respected medical doctor shook his head and frowned. "The second phase of the push starts a week from Monday morning. No way to delay it. Sunday night, kill Pat Monroe and bury his body deep in the woods."

"What about his wife?"

"We'll have to kill her, too. We can't afford to be squeamish; it's too late for that. The green light is on and the forward momentum cannot be halted now."

"I think she's still downstate, visiting friends."

"Then wait until she returns and take them out together. It's a shame, for we really don't know whether she's involved in this or not. I can't see Claire being aligned in any type of filthy allegiance with the government. I think she's a good woman. A moral woman. She really doesn't share her husband's views." He shrugged his shoulders. "Kill her anyway." He looked closely at each man. "We don't meet again until a week from tomorrow night. After that, there is no turning back. God bless you both."

"Power to the righteous," both men said.

* * *

They were awkward with each other the next morning. Neither one of them knew exactly what to say or how to say it. Janet was not a promiscuous woman; and with AIDS so prevalent, Jim did not sleep around. This was the first sexual liaison in over a year for either of them.

Finally, Janet said, "This is ridiculous, Jim. Did you sleep well?"

"Like that proverbial log. You?"

"Like a baby. I don't know about you, but I'm starving!"

"Breakfast coming right up. Country ham, scrambled eggs, home fries, and toast sound all right to you?"

"Just put it on the table and watch me go."

After breakfast, they cleaned up the kitchen and then went for a walk. No hunting season was open at this time, so they weren't in any real danger of being shot by that simpleminded brand of hunter who makes "sound shots," shooting at anything that makes a sound.

They were no more than a quarter of a mile from the lodge when a glinting flash on the ground caught Jim's eye. He knelt down and picked up the brass shell-casing.

"That's a .223," Janet said.

"Yes. The civilian equivalent to 5.56. Awfully light for deer." He handed the brass to Janet and seemingly thought no more of it.

Janet said nothing; but she had a hunch the person who fired this round was not hunting deer. She put the brass into her windbreaker pocket and they walked on, following a vague path through the woods.

Janet began to notice some trees that had small areas of bark knocked off them, just about belly-high to the average person. Once, while Jim was looking in the other direction, she inspected one of the scarred areas. She could clearly see the mangled remnants of what were once jacketed bullets. .223s. She was certain.

She began to search the ground around her more carefully, and she picked up numerous boot tracks in the soft areas. They had all been made recently.

They walked on until they stepped out into a small clearing. "Old logging road," Jim said. "The area is dotted with them."

Janet wondered if all the old logging roads were as well used as this one appeared to be, but she made no mention of it.

She also made no mention of what she had picked up on almost immediately: Jim did not really *walk* through the woods; he moved noiselessly, never stepping on even the smallest of fallen branches, never breaking any low-hanging living branches or disturbing the natural look of bushes. He left no trace of his passing.

The hard-taught lessons from his father had refused to die. Jim was a woodsman, and always would be. It was something he did without thinking, and she was sure he was completely unaware of the skillful way he moved through the timber.

Janet had an unfailing sense of direction and was at home in the woods. She was by no means as expert as Jim, but she could move silently.

Unknown to Janet, the skillful way she moved through the brush was something Jim had already taken note of. It came as no surprise to him for he had strongly suspected there was a great deal about herself that Janet was holding back.

Several weeks back, he had risen early, grabbed a taxi, and told the driver if he wanted to earn a hundred-dollar tip, to just do what he told him to do and not ask questions. It was still something that he didn't fully understand, but he had done it—feeling a bit foolish all the while—and it had served only to deepen the mystery about the woman. He had ridden over to Columbus Circle and followed the cab Janet hailed over to her "recruiting station." Jim had checked the directory in the lobby and there was no army-recruiting station in that building— and none within miles of its location. Janet had taken the elevator to the fifteenth floor and gotten off. . . . That was the only stop the lift had made on its ascent. She had left an hour later in the company of three men, all civilians. Jim had no idea who the men were, but they sure as hell weren't military types.

Jim had toyed briefly with the notion of hiring a private detective to find out what he could about Janet, but quickly dismissed that as being grossly overmelodramatic. He felt there was a logical explanation for Janet's going to that building and certainly it was none of his business.

But still . . .

Vice President Potter sat in the Oval Office, read the file, then closed it, tossed it back on the president's desk, and said only, "Told you."

That cavalier remark irritated the hell out of President Evans, but he sighed, ground his teeth in frustration, and kept his temper. He took several deep breaths. "Damnit, Fred! I cannot, will not, believe this nation is on the verge of an armed insurrection. The FBI would have picked up on it. God knows, we've got enough people under surveillance."

"And have had for years," the VP added sourly.

Evans held up a warning hand. "Let's don't get into that again. Please."

Less than six months into his second term, Evans knew he was a very unpopular president. Forty-five percent of those eligible to vote had not exercised that right. Evans was very much aware that he had been elected by liberals, minorities, and much of the labor movement, and also helped by several million votes cast to candidates belonging to obscure, off-the-wall parties.

He also knew that he was more than unpopular among conservatives, especially the gun-owners of America. He was hated. Many of those popularly referred to as right-wing considered him a socialist. Others just called him a no-good son of a bitch. The Secret Service worried constantly that someone would put a bullet in him; and on several occasions, snipers had come awfully close to doing just that.

Of the two men present in the Oval Office that morning, all cameras and tape recorders turned off, VP Fred Potter was the moderate, politically speaking. Many times, on many topics, Evans and Potter did not see eye to eye. That they could manage to get along at all was nothing short of a miracle for they had never been friends.

The present mood of the country was one topic on which they were almost diametrically opposed.

Fred pointed to the folder he had just tossed on the president's desk. "The country is ready to explode, Art."

"Bullshit, Fred."

And so it went.

The men traveling cross-country in the station wagon reached their destination without further incident. Because of that, they knew the deputy sheriff had made no mention of their "meeting" on the lonely highway.

After a brief rest, the spokesman left the house and traveled to a nearby service station to make a few long-distance calls, speaking no more than a few seconds to each person. Back at the safe house, rented for them by a local person, he sat down in a recliner and smiled.

He looked at each of the people who had traveled across the country with him and said, "It starts in eight days."

"Power to the righteous!" the others said in unison.

Four

Janet watched in silence as Jim locked the front door, sliding the heavy wooden bar into place, preventing entry even if one had a key. He had done the same to the back door.

Very cautious man, she thought.

Then they walked down a flight of steps to the basement. The basement of the lodge was a huge game room, with a Ping-Pong table, a billiards table, and a card table. A wet bar was built into one corner. Heads of trophy deer hung on the walls, their glass eyes forever fixed, staring at nothing.

Janet looked all around her, then folded her arms under her breasts. "This place is spooky."

"I agree . . . although I didn't used to think so." He sighed in remembrance. "I understand that Dad used to have some pretty wild parties down here."

"He was unfaithful to your mother?"

"Every chance he got. In a great many respects, Dad was a prick. But on the other side of the coin, he was a good provider. He gave mother anything she wanted, whenever she wanted it. Same with us kids."

"Except love, perhaps."

"Oh, he loved her. And us. In his own strange way." Again, he sighed, almost painfully. "I guess he loved me the most. I was the black sheep. I would stand up to him while the others would cower. I actually hit him once. Right here in this very room. He laughed his ass off, wiped the blood off his mouth, then knocked me against that wall over there. . . ." He pointed. "And told me never to try that again."

"How old were you?"

"Oh . . . fifteen, I guess. I damn sure never tried to hit him again."

"He was a big man?"

"Like a bull. Self-made man, too. Took incredible chances in business and made a lot of money. Come on."

Jim opened a closet door, turned on the lights, then moved a panel aside, exposing a steel door. He first used a key, then carefully worked the combination lock and pulled the door open. He stepped into the darkness and clicked on the lights, flooding the room with illumination.

Racks filled with guns lined both walls, a thin sheen of oil still shining on the metal. Shotguns and rifles, pump, bolt action, and semi-autos. Cases of ammunition were stacked on the floor.

"Good Lord!" Janet exclaimed.

"Yeah, my Dad believed in being prepared," Jim said, his tone martini-dry. "Some of these weapons are custom-made, worth thousands of dollars. A few are collectors' items. That cabinet there—" He pointed. "—is filled with pistols. Just a few weeks before he died, Dad told me he was getting ready to order several months' supply of food. MREs, I imagine. I guess he never got around to it."

"Your father was expecting trouble, and when it happened, he was going to hole up here."

"I suppose. Dad got slightly paranoid in his later years."

"Maybe he wasn't paranoid at all," Janet suggested.

Jim turned and met her level, serious gaze. "What are you trying to tell me, Janet?"

Janet took a Colt AR-15 from the rack—the civilian version of the M-16. She inspected the weapon, then returned it to the rack. "The nation is in trouble. It's becoming fractured. All the symptoms have been visible for several years. More so, over the past several months. Certain . . . ah . . . intelligence-gathering agencies have tried to warn the president. He won't listen. Says it can't happen."

"Janet, you of all people should know that the military will handle anything like that, should it occur. Which I doubt that it will."

She walked out of the gun room and into the game room, taking a seat at the card table. Puzzled, Jim followed her. He picked up a deck of cards and began shuffling them to keep his hands busy.

"The military will *attempt* to handle it, Jim. But if this insurrection movement is as large as we think it is, spread out all over the United States, we won't be able to contain it. And . . . the military will be facing problems of its own, largely along racial and political lines."

"You said *we,* Janet."

"That's right, I did."

"You're not in recruiting, are you?"

She said nothing. Toyed with a handful of poker chips.

"I . . . followed you to work one morning Janet. You weren't in uniform. I watched you leave the building with several non-military types. I told you several weeks ago I felt you weren't leveling with me."

"You followed me?" She was smiling.

"That's right."

"Then you're pretty good at it, Jim. Maybe you missed your calling."

"My dad was teaching me how to hunt and track and stalk before I was six. Yes, I'm pretty good at it."

"And your conclusion about me?"

"I haven't reached one."

She nodded her head. "I'll level with you if you'll do the same with me."

"I don't know what you mean. You know who I am and what I do. I'm as open as a book."

"A book missing the first few chapters."

Jim laid the deck of cards aside. "What are you talking about?"

"You came back from 'Nam with a lot of medals, Jim. You were even nominated for the Congressional. That's pretty heavy stuff for a man who professes to be a bleeding-heart liberal."

"You pulled my records."

"Yes."

"You're military intelligence."

"Yes."

He nodded his head. "I should have guessed. Those civilian types I saw you with are spooks, aren't they?"

"You know the drill, Jim. I can neither confirm nor deny that."

"CIA, probably. All right. It's no big deal. My company was out on patrol. We had just lost our CO and a First John was leading. It was a screwup. He was brand new to the field and didn't know shit from shoe polish. He'd been in 'Nam for a while, but he'd spent all his time in country as an REM. . . ."

She knew what REM meant: Rear Echelon Motherfucker.

". . . I was in the middle of my second tour. A nineteen-year-old experienced combat veteran. The lieutenant split us all up, and my platoon got lost with him leading. Son of bitch couldn't even read a map. He panicked. We were deep in enemy territory. Several miles deep. Suddenly we walked right into an ambush. We got cut to pieces. Half the platoon was lost within the first two minutes. We were facing hard NVA regulars. Radio was gone; walkie-talkies wouldn't work. I don't know why. I was on high ground with our sniper. He took a round right through the head. Something . . . snapped within me. I didn't get mad; I got all cold inside. I took his rifle, got into good position, and went to work. He had all his ammo. Eighty-five rounds, I think it was. I don't remember exactly. But before it was over, I had forty-six confirmed kills. And probably ten more that couldn't be confirmed. I was hit three times before we got out of there."

"But you kept shooting."

"I kept shooting. We were pinned down a day and a night and most of the next day. I got credited for keeping what was left of the platoon alive. That's all there was to it. I was sent home."

"And you've never picked up a weapon since then?"

He shook his head. "No. I haven't. Don't intend to. At the range I was working, that 'scope pulls them in close. You can see a pimple, a smudge of dirt, a runny nose, fear in their eyes. But I was a machine, a human killing machine. Just me and that rifle. Like siamese twins joined at the shoulder." He looked at her. "That's it, Janet. I have no more secrets. Now it's your turn."

She stared at him for a very long moment before slowly nodding her head. "All right, Jim. I'll tell you what I can, which isn't much. But it will have to do. Okay?' "

"Fine."

"I've been on loan to the agency for about a year. I may be bending the rules a bit by telling you that, but I'm not divulging any classified information. Really what I am is liaison between MI and CIA. Before I arrived in New York, I spent several months crisscrossing the country. We have, well, contacts here and there who listen, take notes, and report to us."

"Americans spying on Americans," Jim said, a flat tone to his voice.

"Well . . . yes. You could put it that way."

"I've heard about citizens who got behind in their taxes or got into some minor trouble with the government. The government makes deals with them to clear their records if they'll spy on friends and neighbors. Are those reports true, Janet?"

She toyed with the poker chips and said nothing. But she refused to meet his eyes.

Jim laid the deck of cards aside. When he spoke, his words were soft. "I see."

"I don't like that aspect of my work either. But I don't make policy. We can debate governmental ethics later. Jim, this country is about to explode." She held up a warning hand. She wore no rings. Jim had asked her about that once. She'd said they got in the way. He had not asked in the way of what. "I know how you feel about this issue. But you're wrong."

"I'll take your word for that."

"I hope you do; I can't tell you very much more. But maybe I can have more luck with you than my bosses have in convincing the president."

"He dismissed all this insurrection talk?"

"Without hesitation."

"Then?" Jim's expression was one of exasperation mingled with confusion.

"Jim, the president doesn't know horseshit from hog jowls about what is going on in this nation. Neither did his predecessor, and neither do most members of Congress. What do you think people are going to do? Walk up to their senator or representative and say, 'If you don't do something about taxes or jobs or crime or whatever, me and a bunch of others guys are going to blow your head off.' Of course not. One has to be able to read all the little signs and put them together. That's what we've been doing for some time now; and when they're all assembled, they spell vigilantism and insurrection."

Jim riffled the cards. "It's very difficult for me to accept this, Janet."

"Of course it is. It's going to be impossible for most people to accept until it's too late. That's what the insurrectionists are counting on."

"But the military?"

"They won't be able to do much because they'll be spread so thin. The president will order them into the cities, and that's exactly what the rebels—we'll have to call them something—want him to do. To hell with the cities. Seize the heartland, the heartbeat of this nation. Control the food supply, the gas, the oil, the coal, and you control the country."

Jim stared at her, then he flared. "Call them something?" He questioned, considerable heat in his voice. "Good God, Janet. You're talking about people who are dedicated to the overthrow of this nation. Why not call them the enemy and have done with it?"

"Some of them will be just that, Jim: racists and bigots and anarchists and worse. But others will be good, solid Americans who have worked hard and obeyed the law and paid more than their share of taxes for years. People who have seen their jobs go overseas; people who have lost their jobs due to corporate downsizing. And all the while, they were arguing for a change and getting only a lot of hot air, at best, from Washington; at the worst, they were ignored by politicians and ridiculed by the press."

"Whose damn side are you on in this, Janet?"

"I just don't know," she replied. "And there is something else you'd better know: According to our intel, there are millions of Americans who feel the same way."

Five

The elder Kincaide had installed a television satellite system for the lodge, but the services had gone unpaid since his death.

"I would suggest you bring all that up to date," Janet said, pointing at the electronic gear lying dormant in the entertainment center built around the television set.

"So it can be used once a year?" Jim questioned.

"You never know when you might want to be informed as to what is happening across America."

"I brought fresh batteries for the portable radio. We have a huge generator out back. LaBarre keeps it up."

"Do you test it each time you come up?"

Jim shrugged. "Janet, what is the matter with you? LaBarre says it works; I believe him. Why shouldn't I?"

"Just curious," she replied without emotion. "That's all."

Reminded of his married days, Jim knew he would get no peace until he responded with positive action. "I'll test it. I will make you happy, and I'll test it."

The generator worked just fine. He checked the 55-gallon drums of diesel fuel. Full.

"Are you happy now, Janet?"

"I was never unhappy. But I would change the lock on the generator-room door."

"Why?"

"So only you can have access."

Jim stared at her, then glanced at his watch. Midmorning. The nearest town of any size was about sixty miles away, to the north. He had a hunch this was going to be a busy day. "Do you want to take a ride, Janet?"

"I'd love to!"

"Before we go, would you like for me to activate the satellite system?"

"Well . . . if you want to."

"It's all up to me, right?"

"Of course," she said sweetly.

Jim took a credit card from his wallet, and fifteen minutes later, the system was up and running.

"We might be up here again sooner than you think," Janet said. "It would be nice to have some news, don't you think?"

"Oh, absolutely. I'd hate to think of spending an evening without Dan Rather."

"I personally like Tom Brocaw. He's cuter. I like the way he wriggles when he stands up to give the in-depth report."

"I really haven't noticed," Jim said sourly.

Jim stood patiently as Janet loaded up both buggies with canned goods. He'd finally gotten it through his head what she was doing: She was preparing for a prolonged siege at the hunting lodge. He said nothing, but thought it was nonsense.

On the way out of town, the bed of the truck filled with cases and sacks of canned food, she stopped at a sporting goods store. "I'll only be a minute. Would you like to come in?"

"No, thanks. I'll wait in the truck. I know what you're doing, Janet. The thought is inconceivable. It's bullshit."

"I hope you're right, Jim. But I think you're wrong."

They were back at the lodge an hour and a half later, unloading the supplies. Jim installed the new lock on the generator-room door and returned to the lodge. Janet was watching a special report on television. Jim sat down in an overstuffed chair.

There had been minor confrontations between FBI agents and local militia units in Texas, Montana, and Florida. In all three incidents, the bureau had wisely backed away before any shooting started. In each case, according to the commentator, the federal agents had been greatly outnumbered.

"That's not the reason they backed off," Janet said. "They backed away because they didn't want to be the ones to light the fuse."

Jim was beginning to believe there was at least a modicum of truth in the conspiracy and insurrection theories being bounced around, but he did not believe it was nearly as serious as Janet thought it was. It would take more than a few news reports to convince him that the threat to overthrow the government was anything except pure hyperbole.

The news special over, Janet stretched out on the couch for a nap and Jim fixed a cup of coffee and went out to sit on the front porch. The land where the lodge sat had been purchased around the turn of the century, before restrictions had been placed on how much acreage could be cleared in the park. The front and one side of the lodge were cleared and landscaped for about a hundred yards, the rear and other side for about seventy-five yards. A few trees had been left standing for shade, and various decorative shrubbery had been planted all around.

Jim was startled when he found himself speculating that the lodge would be easy to defend. "Oh, for God's sake!" he muttered, angry that he would think that. He shook those thoughts away and did his best to keep them out of his head. "You're becoming as bad as some of these militia whackos," he mumbled.

At noon Sunday, Jim locked up the lodge and they headed back to the city. A thunderstorm had passed through the area during the night, dumping heavy rains. Now, under gray skies, a slow, steady drizzle would accompany them all the way back.

"LaBarre was snooping around the lodge last night," Janet said, breaking the miles-long silence between them.

"LaBarre?"

"Yes. The storm woke me up about one o'clock, and I went downstairs for a glass of water. I stood in the kitchen and watched him for about ten minutes. You slept right through the storm. The lightning was fierce, put on quite a show. For seconds at a time, the grounds were illuminated as bright as day. It was LaBarre. He prowled all the way around the house. Wrote down the license number on my truck. Then he stood for a time at the generator building, looking at the new lock. He tried his old key and became very agitated when it didn't work. I'll tell you something else: LaBarre was wearing a holstered pistol on his belt. Looked like a Beretta 9mm."

"What the hell?" Jim muttered.

"I'll run Mr. LaBarre when we get back. See what I

can come up with. But I'll tell you now, I don't trust him. There's something about him that's bogus."

Jim shook his head. "LaBarre's been the caretaker at the lodge since I was a kid. His father worked there before him. I m not disputing your word, Janet. Not at all, if you saw him, he was there. I'm just curious about what he was doing and why he was wearing a gun."

Janet said nothing. But she had a pretty good idea why LaBarre was at the lodge in the middle of a dark and stormy night.

While Jim was sitting at his desk on Monday, doodling on a legal pad, and Janet was running the name of Phil LaBarre through various state and federal computers, in a courthouse in a small Iowa city, the first of several scenes that would forever change the face of justice in America was about to take place.

The judge had polled the jury. The defendant and his attorney stood up. "The jury has ruled in favor of the plaintiff," the judge said. "The amount of damages is set at five-hundred-thousand dollars."

"Fuck you," the defendant said in a loud and clear voice.

The judge lowered his gavel. "I beg your pardon, Mr. Harrison."

Harrison's attorney looked about ready to have a heart attack.

"I said *fuck you*," Harrison repeated. "I'm not paying that thieving son of a bitch over there one penny."

There was a look of astonishment on the judge's face. His face reddened in anger. He wrestled his temper under control with a visible effort and said, "I find you in contempt, Mr. Harrison. And I order you to serve thirty days in jail. Perhaps, during that time, you can contemplate your words and learn some respect for this court."

"I have no respect for you, this court, or the present system of so-called justice in America," Harrison said. "And you can take your ruling and your contempt citation and stick it where the sun don't shine—your honor."

This case had received a lot of publicity in the local papers and on TV. A noise had awakened Gene Harrison from a sound sleep late one night. Picking up the shotgun he kept propped in a corner by his bed, he slipped through the house to his garage. He found a young man helping himself to his collection of very expensive tools.

"Just hold it right there, boy," Gene ordered.

The young man whirled around, a wrench in his hand. He grinned. "You won't shoot me, dude. I ain't armed. You'd go to prison."

"Call the police!" Gene yelled to his wife. "Stand still," he told the thief.

"Fuck you!" the thief said. Then he threw the wrench at Gene. The wrench struck the homeowner on the forehead, knocking him down; and blood poured from the gash.

The thief laughed and picked up two toolboxes. "Stupid motherfucker," he told Gene.

Gene cut the legs out from under him with a load of double-ought buckshot. The thief was still squalling and thrashing around in his own blood when the police arrived.

A few months later, Gene Harrison, wearing a scar on his forehead where the punk had hit him with a wrench, found himself in court, being sued by the thief for several million dollars. A lawyer decided that Gene had used excessive force in dealing with the thief.

That was the last straw for Gene Harrison, a hard-working, law-abiding taxpayer, a man who had never so much as received a parking ticket. The local police had a jacket on the thief about two-inches thick, everything from car stealing to assault to dope peddling.

When the judge recovered from his shock, he yelled for the bailiff to take Mr. Harrison into custody.

As the bailiffs moved toward Gene Harrison, fifteen men and women stood up, some with pistols in their hands, others with sawed-off, pistol-grip shotguns they had hidden under their coats.

The two bailiffs stopped their forward movement—abruptly.

For a time it was a mystery how the men and women had gotten the guns past the metal detectors at the courthouse entrances and into the courtroom. After the second American revolution was over, it was learned that the janitors had been members of the local resistance groups and had brought the weapons in at night, hiding them in storage rooms.

Gene Harrison was not much of a cusser; but on this day, he set records for the profanity directed at the jurors for bringing back such a verdict. And on that day, Gene Harrison became two things he never dreamed he'd ever become. A racist, for the makeup of the jury was overwhelmingly black, as was the thief. And a revolutionary, dedicated to the overthrow of the government of the United States, a government he had proudly served in Vietnam.

After venting his spleen at the jury, Gene turned to the judge. "None of us who have chosen to rebel against this joke of a justice system may make it out of this building alive, Judge. We've talked that over and we all understand that. But if that is the case, I can assure you—and that piss-poor excuse for a so-called fair and impartial jury of my peers, which is a joke in itself—that none of you will leave alive either." He directed his gaze toward the lawyer who represented the thief. "And you, you sorry son of a bitch, I'll take great pleasure in killing you personally. You have bankrupted me with legal fees, torn my family apart, and cost me my job."

The lawyer sat ashen-faced, speechless and numb with fear.

The judge kept a .45 autoloader on the bench, but he made no move toward the weapon. The judge, and he was a good and fair judge, had great respect for the law; but he—and a lot of other judges nationwide—had seen this coming. To his mind, what was happening in his courtroom this day had been inevitable. The judge was fully aware that the system wasn't working.

"We're leaving now, Judge," Mr. Harrison announced. "If you want a bloodbath in the streets of this little city, just pick up that phone you have on the bench and try to stop us. There are two hundred armed militia members within a one-block radius of this building. We're ready for a fight, Judge. We've made out our wills, said our goodbyes to loved ones, and settled our affairs." He stood tall. "We're ready to start dumping another load of tea, if you get my drift."

The judge nodded his head. "Oh, I get your drift. Loud and clear. But you're going about changing the system in the wrong way."

"Could be. But it seems this is the only way we can get anyone's attention."

"You certainly got mine," the judge said, a sarcastic edge to his words.

Mr. Harrison and his friends exited the courthouse building and got into waiting cars and pickup trucks and rolled out of town without incident, even though after only a few blocks, half the police force knew what had happened in the courthouse.

"I'm not tangling with those people." A police lieutenant summed up the feelings of most of the department personnel. "Let them go. We are not the enemy."

"We could lose our badge if we don't do something," a sergeant reminded him.

"Which would you rather lose—your life or your badge?"

The sergeant nodded. "Good point."

"These people are primed and cocked and spoiling for a fight, and I'm damned if I'll be the first casualty in this war."

"If we're not the enemy, who is?" a young patrolman asked.

"That's a good question, son. I'd have to say this war is against the government. The system, if you will."

"You really think there's going to be a war between Americans, Lieutenant?"

"Yeah, I really do. And I'm thinking it's gonna be a nasty, dirty little war."

"But the government is invisible," the sergeant pointed out.

The lieutenant shook his head. "Liberal politicians aren't invisible. Federal buildings aren't invisible."

"What do you want us to do, Lieutenant?" the young patrolman asked.

"Stay alive."

* * *

The warden at the county jail in a small California town looked up, then put his hands in the air. "You'll get no fight here, people," he told the group of heavily armed men and women who had crowded the lobby of the jail. "We're jailers, not heroes."

"Stay away from the radio and send someone to get Bobby Wilson," a woman said. The muzzle of the Mini-14 she held was pointed at the older man's belly. Her voice was calm and the muzzle was unwavering.

"You got it." The man nodded to a young and very scared jailer. "Go get him. Louise—" the warden turned back to the woman. "—we've known each other since high school. You don't have to point that thing at me."

"Would you rather the feds think you're a part of this?"

"In the end, is that going to make any difference, Louise?" the warden countered. "When this . . . mess is over, will there even be a country?"

"It'll be different, that's for sure."

"For the worse or better?"

"That depends on which side you're on, Larry."

Bobby Wilson was led out of the lockup and into the reception area. He smiled at the group of men and women. "Let me get out of this damn prison uniform, and I'll be right with you."

"No hurry, Bobby," Louise told him. "The locals aren't going to interfere." She handed him clean street-clothing.

The chief of police and the four city officers who worked the seven-to-three shift were being held at gun-point at the city hall. The deputies assigned to this part of the county were all part of the local militia; when they were informed of the time of the breakout, they made themselves scarce.

"Shit, Bobby!" the warden called. "Think about this, man."

"I've had several weeks to think about it, Larry," Bobby called from an interrogation room. "Believe me, I've thought of little else."

Bobby had farmed, until recently, several hundred acres just outside of town. He grew melons. But the government declared about half of Bobby's property as wetlands. Now Bobby was in danger of losing his farm; he couldn't make a living farming half his acreage. He was filling as much of the "wetlands" as he could when the feds arrested him. Sometimes it doesn't take much to push a good person over the edge.

Louise had been accused by the feds of spreading sedition over the Internet. They had seized her computer equipment and files, which also included the computer and files she used in her in-home business. In effect, she was put out of work for expressing an opinion.

Bobby came out of the room. He wadded up the orange-colored jail-jumpsuit and tossed it into the garbage. A man handed him a Colt AR-15 with a thirty-round magazine.

"You ready?" Louise asked.

"Let's do it."

Half a minute later, the revolutionaries had cleared the jail. Larry reached for the mic, then withdrew his hand. "Fuck it!" he said. He stood up and shrugged into his jacket.

"What are you going to do, Larry?" the young jailer asked.

"I'm going home. Keep my head down. It's about to bust loose, boy." He tossed the young man a ring of keys. "It's all yours, Donnie. The best advice I can give you now is to stay the hell out of the way of these people. And we will be seeing a lot more of them. Believe it."

Six

Janet looked at the information faxed to her on a secure line from intelligence law enforcement agencies in and around Washington. Phil LaBarre had never broken any laws—other than a few traffic tickets—and he paid his taxes on time . . . albeit grudgingly and always with a letter outlining his views on the IRS and the people who worked for that agency. LaBarre had been a vocal critic of the tax system and the U. S. Government and hadn't given much of a damn who knew it . . . until about five years back. Then he'd suddenly shut up, and paid informants reported that he'd never made another critical comment about the IRS in particular and the government in general and never sent another letter with his tax return.

Janet read on. Approximately five years ago, just about the time LaBarre ceased his caustic remarks concerning the government, reports began coming in about a large militia group training in the Adirondacks. It had taken the government a year to get an informant inside their ranks, and for nearly three years his reports had been disappointingly sketchy; then the reports had become fuller.

The informant was certain the group LaBarre was associated with was a part of a much larger organization, one that was nationwide in scope, and very secret. They trained in small groups, usually squad-size, and always trained to hit hard, then seize and hold. They never trained defensively, but always offensively. They never wore military clothing. The members professed to be deeply religious and attended a variety of churches in the area. Their training sessions in the timber were not only military in nature, but also were steeped in religious studies.

The informant could only guess at the overall strength of the unit, for the group never met en masse. LaBarre was a senior member of his twelve-person squad. The members were trained along the lines of the army's special forces units: Each member was cross-trained so each member could do another's job if need be. He did not know the name of the commander; he could report only that he believed it was a man and a highly educated and respected member of the community.

The group was well-armed and considered by the FBI to be very dangerous.

Neither the President of the United States nor the attorney general considered the group to be any threat to the security of the United States.

"That figures," Janet muttered, closing the file folder. "One is a political dimwit and the other is a socialistic dickhead."

Jim read again the articles he'd circled with an accent pen in that morning's newspaper. A gay bar had been bombed last night on Long Island: Two dead and a dozen injured. A young man—a known purse-snatcher and mugger with an arrest record about half-a-mile long— was found dead, hanging from a tree limb in Central

Park. A black gang had been ambushed two nights ago: Four dead and several dozen wounded by semi-automatic gunfire. The attackers shouted vulgar and demeaning racist remarks before they opened fire. Another synagogue had been defaced with profane language and Nazi symbols, spray-painted on the outside. Five hundred pounds of dynamite stolen from a construction site. Persons unknown had backed trucks up to the rear entrance of a half-a-dozen sporting goods stores, all within a fifty-mile radius of the city, professionally bypassed the alarm systems, and cleaned out the stores of nearly everything, including dozens of weapons—rifles, pistols, shotguns, and cases of ammunition.

What the hell was going on? Jim mused. Or have things like this been going on all the time and I just didn't notice them?

He looked up at a tap on his door. "Come."

Don Williams, who worked in the art department, stuck his head into the office. "Busy?"

"No. Come on in. Sit down."

Jim leaned back and waited until the black man had taken a chair. Jim had personally interviewed and hired the man over fifteen years ago, and he had proven an invaluable asset to the company. Don was Jim's age, if Jim recalled correctly, maybe a couple of years over, married to a lovely lady, Shirley, a schoolteacher. They had twins, a boy and a girl. He thought they both were now in their second or third year of college. Don and Shirley lived out of the city in the suburbs.

"What's going on, Don?"

"I was hoping perhaps you could tell me."

"I'll try. Ask away."

"Well, Shirley came home Friday all upset. One of her

brightest students is dropping out of school for a time. Finals are coming up in about five or six weeks, and this boy is going to blow his chances for a scholarship if he misses them. I've told you how attached she gets to students. It really upset her. She went to see the boy's parents. Now, this man is an accountant, a good one, makes plenty of money. Levelheaded sort of man. But Shirley told me she never saw so much outdoors gear in all her life. Scattered all over the living room. Tents and sleeping bags and blankets and cases of emergency rations. Shirley said she saw half-a-dozen guns. Four long guns, as she called them, and a couple of semi-automatic pistols. Boxes of ammunition. Camp axes and machetes. Rope. Camp stoves. Camouflage hunting clothing. Shirley said she asked the man why he was going camping now, when he had to take his son out of school? She said the man gazed at her intently, then said, 'Mrs. Williams, my boy likes you. And I appreciate the interest you've shown him. I'm going to tell you something: You be careful. Things are not what they seem. And that's all I can say. Best you leave now before you're seen here. You just remember what I said and be careful.' That's a direct quote, Jim. Now, is that weird, or what?"

Jim experienced an odd sensation in the pit of his stomach as Janet's words came back to him. *It's going to blow, Jim. This country is coming unglued. Hundreds of thousands of people are ready to take up arms against the government.* "It's strange, Don." He found his voice. "It's certainly that."

"Did you see that news report on militias the other night?"

"Ah . . . yes. I did. What about it?"

"Did you take it seriously?"

Jim hesitated. "To tell you the truth, no, I didn't. But that isn't to say there might not be some truth to it. Did you take it seriously?"

Don dropped his gaze. When he again met Jim's eyes, Jim thought the man's expression held a mixture of sadness and concern. "Yes, I did. I have relatives scattered around the nation. We talk occasionally. Nearly all of them have expressed some degree of concern about the growing militia movement. I think it's a hell of a lot bigger than we think, and a hell of a lot more dangerous."

"Do you own a gun, Don?"

Don was startled at the question. "Why . . . no. Do you?"

"No." That was not a lie. He didn't keep a gun in the city. "You think this father's pulling his son out of school has something to do with a militia?"

"I don't know. But coming right on the heels of that news report, I have to say it's a damn strange coincidence. Why did you ask if I owned a gun?"

"Just curious, that's all. Were you ever in the service?"

"No. I was sure my number would come up and I'd get sent to Vietnam, but it never did."

"You didn't miss a damn thing."

"I never even knew you were in the service, Jim. You never talk about it."

Jim shrugged. "Not that much to talk about."

Don stood up and Jim saw that he was still in good physical shape. "You work out, Don?"

"I run five miles every day. Work out in the gym every Saturday."

"Pays to stay in shape."

Don gave him an odd look. "You bet,' he agreed, then left the office, closing the door.

Jim glanced at the clock. He had about an hour before he was to meet Janet for lunch.

"Here is ten percent of my gross income for last year and the year before," the man said, holding out a check to the IRS agent. "If ten percent is good enough for the Lord, it should be good enough for any government."

The IRS agent smiled. Treasury agents had not descended upon Gary Scott in force, guns drawn and ready for action. This slightly overweight midwestern-based minister was not considered dangerous. Intelligence reports stated that he did not own a gun, had never been in the military, had never belonged to any subversive group, did not subscribe to any magazine or newsletter that regularly featured anti-government rhetoric, did not listen to Rush Limbaugh or G. Gordon Liddy, was a registered Democrat and a respected member of his community. Gary Scott was an all-around nice fellow. He just hadn't paid his federal income taxes for several years.

The agent took the check and tucked it away in his briefcase. "That's very nice, Reverend Scott," he said gently. "But I'm afraid it just doesn't work that way. According to our figures, you owe twenty-nine-thousand-four-hundred-and-fifty-eight dollars. This check—" He tapped his briefcase. "—will be applied to that, of course. But it still leaves a considerable balance. When may we expect to receive that?"

"When hell freezes over, pigs fly, lions lie down with lambs, and Jesus returns to this earth to heal the sick and feed the multitudes," the minister said softly.

The agent's smile slowly faded with considerably less

grace than the hues of the last rose of summer. "I do not find that amusing, sir."

"It wasn't meant to be amusing."

"You are stating your refusal to pay your federal income tax?"

"That is correct."

"You can be arrested, sir."

"I am well aware of that."

The agent cut his eyes to the woman who entered the den of the small house beside the church, an attractive lady in her forties. What really got his attention was the shotgun in her hands. "Put that gun away, ma'am," the agent told her.

"Not likely, sir," she replied. "Now get up and get out of this house."

"You're making a mistake, ma'am."

"You're going to make a worse one if you attempt to arrest my husband."

The treasury agent cut his eyes back to Gary. They widened at the sight of the pistol in the minister's hand. "I am not a violent man, sir," Gary said. "But I believe the time has come for revolution. I do not know whether or not the majority of American citizens will support this uprising. But enough of us will to make an impact."

"Mr. Scott, you know I'll be back. What will you do then? Fight us?"

"Just remember this, sir," the minister said. "And please pass the word to your coworkers: You are not the enemy. Now leave, quickly."

As soon as the door closed behind the man, Gary turned to his wife. "Call the others, dear. It's time."

* * *

As Jim walked the few blocks to the restaurant where he was to lunch with Janet, he found himself looking for bearded and robed men holding placards reading: REPENT, THE END IS NEAR.

Then he realized he was being silly and smiled. His good humor faded as he paused in front of a department store with a dozen TVs in the show window, tuned to an all-news channel. The newscaster told of some of the bizarre events that had taken place that morning across America: The confrontation in the Iowa courtroom, the jail-break in California. There had been a near-shootout in Louisiana between federal marshals and local militia people before both sides backed away and a near-riot in South Carolina involving the KKK, the local chapter of skinheads, and a black group staging a peaceful march.

Shaking his head in bewilderment, Jim crossed the street to the restaurant. Janet had arrived a few minutes earlier and had been shown to their table, a quiet spot in a corner where they could talk.

She stood up, kissed him on the cheek, and said, "I ordered drinks for us. I thought you could use a very dry martini."

"I sure could. Thanks. Been waiting long?"

"Only a few minutes. Heard any news?"

"Yes. On the walk over. It was . . . somewhat distressing. You?"

"I'm still tying news reports together."

"You really believe they're all connected?"

"Oh, yes. Jim, should we have to leave the city in a hurry, do you have any close friends you want to bring along?"

Jim downed half of his martini before replying—and

then only after giving her a long hard look. "I really don't think it's that serious."

She paused while the waiter took their lunch orders—a salad for her, fish for Jim—and then replied. "All the signs indicate we're on the brink of an extremely violent time. Now, I'm going to tell you again: The government won't be able to contain it. How about your kids?"

"They have nothing to do with me. Their mother remarried not long after the divorce and requested that I stop sending money. She's turned them solidly against me."

Janet decided not to pursue that, at least for the time being; but it was something he was going to have to face before much longer. She reached across the table and touched his hand. "Jim, when I call you and tell you that it's time to leave the city, don't argue with me. Just stop what you're doing and meet me. Okay?"

Might as well humor her, he thought, nodding. "All right. But we're going to have to discuss this further. You want another drink?"

"No. Take this seriously, Jim. I mean it. You're a part of the New York liberal crowd, and that means you don't know what in the hell is going on outside this city. You think these militia people are a bunch of harmless good ol' boys. You re wrong. Jim, I've been waiting for years for someone like you. We've got a good thing going, and I don't want to lose you."

She knows a lot more than she's told me, he thought and found himself reassuring her. "I promise you that whatever happens, we'll see it through together. Okay?"

Her expression was somber. "I hope you aren't just saying that to placate me."

"I mean it. Every word."

Janet slipped one shoe off and rubbed her foot against the calf of his leg. "Wanna play footsie until lunch arrives?"

Seven

"Does anybody have any explanation as to what is happening in this nation?" President Evans asked, breaking an uncomfortable silence in the Oval Office.

Vice President Potter gave the president a pitying look and shook his head in disgust. Before he could speak, the AG said, "I don't think it's anything to be alarmed about, sir. We have no intel that points to this morning's events being related."

Evans had just about reached the long-overdue conclusion that his AG was not the brightest person he could have picked for the job. The president had no law-enforcement experience, and even he could see that a pattern was developing. No—*had developed.*

FBI Director Brewer said, "With all due respect to the attorney general, I think we are seeing the first tentacles of civil war emerging in this nation."

VP Potter said, "With all due respect to everyone in this room, it is my opinion that an uprising among a certain segment of American citizens is already underway and has passed the point of being contained."

"I agree," National Security Advisor Guy said.

All eyes turned to General Robert Coplin, Chairman of the Joint Chiefs. He sat quietly, saying nothing, eyes fixed straight ahead. He had been dreading this moment for months. He had suspected for some time the country was on the verge of tearing itself apart through civil insurrection. He had watched these and other feather-headed civilians in Washington ignore the blatant indications for several years. And he had known for a very long time it was too late to do anything. His own intelligence people had accurately read all the signs months ago. Coplin had discussed this at length with his fellow members of the Joint Chiefs. To a man, they had all finally admitted that they had been contacted by leaders of militia groups and each had been given a clear warning: Stay out of it, for you are not the enemy. The president will order troops into the cities. Protect the cities. Fine. Send them in. I promise you, we will not fire on American troops unless fired on first. The president will order you to man roadblocks and checkpoints on major highways. Go right ahead; we'll stick to the back roads to avoid coming in contact with your troops. When we take power, the spokespeople had said, the military will not be touched by any cuts in federal spending; your role will not change. Another reason for you to stay out of it.

The meetings had been few, but lengthy. And General Coplin had been amazed at the highly professional intelligence network of the revolutionaries. He had suspected for some time that all branches of the military had been infiltrated by men and women sympathetic to the coming uprising, and he had been correct in that assumption. The revolutionaries had people in key positions in all levels of the military. The Joint Chiefs strongly suspected that about twenty-five percent of all enlisted personnel and anywhere from eight- to twelve-percent of officers were sympathetic to the revolutionaries cause. Those sympathetic included spec-ops personnel in all branches, fighter and bomber pilots, intelligence personnel, and infantry troops.

The Joint Chiefs agreed that to commit their people against fellow Americans would cause a revolt within the ranks. And that was something they wanted to avoid at all costs.

Chief of Staff David Waymon quietly stepped into the room, laid a sheet of paper on the president's desk, then took a seat. Evans quickly scanned the paper, sighed heavily, and removed his glasses. He rubbed his temples with his fingertips. "A nice, gentle minister from Michigan, a man well-thought-of in his community, just hours ago ordered an IRS agent from his home at gunpoint, announcing that it was time for the revolution to start. When the agent returned with several other agents to place the tax resister under arrest, Reverend Scott and his wife were gone. Now it has been learned, much too late, that Reverend Scott was the chaplain of the local militia. And those members have now disappeared from the community. Just . . . vanished. Their families say they have no idea where the men and, in some cases, women might be . . . Shit!" the president yelled, startling everyone in the room.

President Evans rose from his chair and paced the room. His face was flushed and he was breathing heavily. When he had calmed himself, he sat down and looked at General Coplin. "I want troops placed on low alert, ready to move into the cities on my orders."

General Coplin carefully hid his smile. Exactly what the revolutionaries thought you'd do. "All the cities, sir?"

"The major cities, General. Now then, what about the National Guard?"

"We suspect that many units have been heavily infiltrated with militia members," Director Brewer said.

"The militia movement should have been stopped cold long ago," Evans muttered.

"We should have disarmed the American people long ago," AG Newton said.

At that, General Coplin stood up. "Will that be all, Mr. President?"

"Yes, General. You have your orders." Evans flapped his right hand in a gesture of dismissal.

Coplin left the Oval Office.

Evans watched him go. When the door had closed, the president said, "It's all in the hands of the military now."

"God help us all," Chief of Staff Waymon said, no fan of the military. Marine Corps General Max Jordan had once made the statement that guns frightened Waymon almost as much as a penis frightened AG Newton.

"Gene Baronne's our man," the director of the FBI was told. "He has definitely been fingered as head of the anti-government group that call themselves the Sword of the Righteous."

"Where is he now?"

"We don't know. We only learned this day that the man our people have had under surveillance is a look-alike. Baronne might have been gone two hours; he might have been gone a week. The SAC in San Diego pulled in the look-alike. So far, he's maintained a wall of silence."

"Prognosis?"

"Not good. We've never been able to crack one of these people."

"Do we have any idea where this Baronne might be?"

"No, sir."

"All right." The director loosened his tie, leaned back in his chair, and picked up the thick folder on the group called the Sword of the Righteous.

The *Righteous,* as the members called themselves, was a hard right-wing religious organization whose estimated membership—no one knew for sure how many people belonged to the group—numbered in the thousands. The bureau knew the Righteous had cells in all of the lower forty-eight, for they'd been watching the group for several years. They had only recently gotten an agent inside.

He picked another folder and read, cursing as he read. Field agents had begun to report that it was their belief that dozens of right-wing groups had aligned themselves with Baronne's organization, swearing allegiance to Baronne's movement; and that made the Sword of the Righteous a very large and very dangerous group.

"I was wrong," Director Brewer muttered. "Many of the groups have come together."

He picked up another folder. The Sword of the Righteous took a hard right-wing view, all mixed up with the Bible. They were opposed to abortion, believed that homosexuals should be rounded up and placed in detention camps and tested for AIDS and that any found to be carriers should be quarantined or executed, whichever action was more expedient. Should it be the latter, they advocated that their bodies be burned and that those who were free of the disease should be placed into reorientation camps until they repented of their sins and suitable female mates were found for them, preferably former lesbians who were now free of the devil's grasp and willing to take on a proper woman's role and station in life.

"Good God!" the words involuntarily bolted from Brewer's mouth.

The director suddenly felt sick at his stomach. What in the name of God kind of people were they dealing with?

"Some of the members of these groups are real whackos," Janet said. "Especially the ultra hard-line, right-wing religious groups. They're dangerous, Jim. Really dangerous. And we believe they make up about fifty percent of the movement. Others are just plain ordinary people who are fed up with government interference in their lives. They've decided that since this nation was born out of gunsmoke and blood, it can be reborn out of gunsmoke and blood."

"Reborn to their specifications, of course."

Janet turned away from the window. "Jim, let me see if I can get through to you on some points. Discounting the ultra-religious and lunatic fringe, many of these people aren't ogres. And their demands are not that many or unattainable. One: They want government out of their lives. Two: They want the right to protect what is theirs by any means at hand without fear of arrest, prosecution, or civil lawsuit. Three: They want the sheer size of government drastically reduced. Four: They want programs that are proven ineffective to be stopped. Five: They want a complete overhaul of the criminal justice system. That's just about it."

"Is that all?" Jim asked sarcastically. Then he softened that with a smile that Janet did not return. He stared at her for a few pulse beats. "What's the matter?"

"Jim, how many people know that you're such a bleeding-heart liberal?"

"What the hell kind of question is that? Just about all my friends are liberal. Why?"

"When we leave this city, Jim, you keep your mouth shut about your liberal views. I mean it. For your own good."

Janet could tell that made him mad. It was the first time she'd ever seen him really lose his temper. He rose from the chair, his face tight with anger.

She held up a hand. "Just calm down and listen for a moment, Jim. There was a time when liberals were viewed by the other side of the political spectrum as friendly political foes. Probably, most conservatives still feel that way." She shook her head. "But not this bunch who are now rising up to be heard. The government may be invisible, but liberals aren't. You people are now the enemy."

"For God's sake, Janet, that's insane. Why would anybody in their right mind think that? We're talking politics, not guerrilla warfare."

"That's what you think. The chickens have come home to roost. Did you and the rest of the lace-on-your-drawers, take-a-punk-to-lunch bunch think you could continue to flaunt your liberal agenda in the face of hardline right-wingers and not have to pay for it someday? Which political party voted for massive funding for unpopular social programs such as welfare, SSI, the Great Society—which pissed off a trillion taxpayer-dollars? Which political party poured billions and billions of dollars into public housing, which promptly turned into centers of crime and dope-dealing? Which political party was soft on crime and criminals? Which political party was constantly screaming for gun control and the disarming of law-abiding American citizens? Which political party literally threw open our borders and allowed a million legal immigrants a year into the country, plus another million or so illegal immigrants, and allowed them to promptly go on welfare and receive free medical care—at the expense of taxpayers—when people born in this country were losing their jobs and those who managed to hold onto their jobs were seeing their quality of life diminish and their taxes go up every goddamn year?"

Jim faced her, and both of them just barely held onto their tempers. "Are you through?"

"Hell, no! It's time you turned around and looked at the truth. You namby-pamby liberals have legislated this country into near bankruptcy. Every social program you can get your fat little greedy fingers into you turn into a monumental cluster-fuck! You've allowed what was once the finest educational system in the free world to disintegrate into a bureaucratic nightmare. Kids are promoted who can't read or write. Many kids can't even point out their own state on a road map. Do you realize that the military had to put instruction manuals in comic-book form so recruits could understand them? There is no discipline in school. But let's don't allow teachers to bend little Johnny over a desk and paddle his arrogant behind. Oh, heavens, no. That might traumatize him and scar him for life. Horse shit! Punks are attacking teachers and, in some instances, killing them! And all you goddamn liberals have done for years is wring your hands and make excuses. 'Oh, dear me.' Janet put her hands together, held them close to her breasts, feigned great consternation, and spoke in a whiny voice. 'I think there is entirely too much violence on TV.' "

Jim's eyes widened in shock as Janet balled her right hand into a fist and gave him the middle finger. "All that is liberal crap! Have you ever seen Japanese TV? That's some of the most violent programming on earth, and yet they have one of the most progressive, educated, and civilized of all societies. Ahh, to hell with it!"

She shrugged into her coat and headed for the door. There, she paused and faced him. "Wise up, buddy boy. You're the enemy now, and you'd damn well better make up your mind how you're going to cope with it." She jerked open the door.

"What about dinner?" Jim asked, then realized how lame that sounded in the face of her tirade.

Janet smiled sweetly. "You really want me to tell you what you can do with dinner?"

"Well, fuck you then!" Jim flared.

"You wish. Why don't you invite all the homeless in off the streets and give dinner to them? Of course, seventy-five percent of them would still be living in a reasonably comfortable environment, clean and dry and fed and medicated if the goddamn liberals hadn't opened all the doors to mental institutions and turned them loose to fend for themselves."

Jim chose to ignore that since he had no defense. "If you're so sure your views are correct, Janet, why is the women's movement so pro-Democratic Party?"

She closed the door and stepped back into the foyer. "That bunch of man-hating battle-axes? Hell, they're so scared of a stiff dick, they eat a banana as if it were an ear of corn."

Jim tired to keep his anger hot, but with the mental image of her last remark in his brain, he could not sustain his ire. He suddenly burst out laughing.

The laughter was infectious and soon spread to Janet. Then both of them were on the couch, howling and sputtering. One thing led to another, and soon a trail of clothing marked the path to the bedroom. . . . Dinner was served late.

Eight

"Cynthia?" Jim asked. "Ah . . . it's good to hear from you. No, I'm not lying; it *is* good to hear from you. It's been a long time. How are the kids? You *what?* I . . . didn't know that. I understand that you are under no obligation to tell me anything. But I do like to send the kids presents on their birthday and at Christmas. I . . . Cynthia . . . I . . . Okay. All right. Yes. I . . ."

Jim looked at the buzzing receiver and frowned. His ex-wife had abruptly hung up.

"Let me guess," Don Williams said with a smile. "Your ex-wife?"

"Yeah." Jim sighed. "First time she's spoken to me in, well, since my father died. She just called to tell me she and hubby and kids have moved to Albany. Let me rewrite this address and phone number before my handwriting gets cold." That done, Jim looked up at Don. "Cynthia doesn't like me very much."

"I never would have guessed."

Jim frowned. He had carefully rehearsed what he was going to say but at the last minute felt it sounded just that—rehearsed. "Ah . . . Don. I've been thinking about what you said yesterday, about trouble brewing. You may be right. Maybe we should make some plans."

"To do what?"

"To get the hell out of the city."

Don leaned forward and placed his coffee mug on the desk. "You know something I should know?"

"No," Jim lied. "I just have a feeling, that's all."

The art director slowly nodded his head. "Am I the only one in the office you've talked to about this?"

"Yes, so far. I thought about talking to Bob. Then he made the announcement this morning that he and his wife were leaving the country on an extended vacation. I thought about talking to some of the others, but I don't want to start a panic around here . . . if you know what I mean."

"I guess so. You sure changed your mind in a hurry."

"Yeah, I guess I did at that."

"Well, that's the reason I came in here. Did you watch the public-access channel last night?"

"No."

"Revolution was all the people were talking about. Blacks talking about whites planning a war against them. Whites talking about blacks staging a violent uprising. Then this . . . person got on and started yelling about an ultra-religious, right-wing plot and this white-supremacist woman—I guess that's a nice word for Ku Klux Klan—got on camera and talked about something called ZOG and how the Jews were controlling all the banks. Man, it was crazy. What the hell is ZOG?"

Jim shook his head. "I don't know. But I'm not kidding about making plans to get out."

A neatly dressed man in Atlanta took a sip of water, set the glass down on the desk, sighed deeply. He looked out at the gathering of black men and a few black women. "All right, people. We've all got jobs, and we're late for work, so let's get this said and get out of here. We've all suspected this day was coming. Well, it looks as though it's here." He smiled. "We have always had a better intelligence system than the CIA. For centuries, our people have worked as cooks, maids, yardmen. We've listened to the white people talk and then reported back. Too many have now reported that this country is only days, perhaps hours, away from civil war. We can't sit back and hope it won't happen. We've got to be prepared. We know there are white-racist groups who want to annihilate us. That's not going to happen. It isn't going to happen here or in New Orleans or New York or Detroit or Los Angeles or anywhere else. I got the word last night, called you people within the hour. But we have got to use restraint: We cannot, must not have a hand in starting this. And we have got to keep in mind that the majority of whites are not our enemy. This planned uprising—and it isn't just talk any longer; it's fact—is going to take millions of whites by surprise. So we've got to not only help our brothers and sisters, but help the innocent white people as well. Many of them have stood by us in hard times and helped us at considerable risk to themselves. These people don't even know what end of a weapon the bullet comes out of. They're going to be easy targets, so we must not forget that they are our friends and need our help. Our people within police and sheriff's departments have pointed out those officers whose allegiance lies with the racist, militant, white groups." Again he sighed heavily and rubbed his face. "When the fighting starts and those known racist officers approach you, we have no choice but to put them down." He was expecting a murmur of alarm and protest, but the group remained stoic and silent. God help us all, the spokesman thought. God help us all.

A man in South Dakota held up a hand, fingers splayed. "Five days, people. Five days until we strike. I know you've all heard the reports about some of us around the nation being forced to take action before they were ready, but they had no choice. Government agents or turncoat local authorities forced their hand. It's regrettable but was anticipated. Howard Jennings?"

"Right here," a man said, standing up.

"You've made your last report to the FBI, you traitorous son of a bitch. We've known all along that you were an informant. You weren't in our group seventy-two hours before the word came down on you. We've been feeding you bogus information for six months."

Howard knew he'd had it. He took a chance and bolted for the door. He didn't make it. The man standing behind the rostrum lifted a Colt Combat Commander in .45 caliber and shot him in the back. Howard pitched facedown to the floor and was still.

The spokesman carefully lowered the hammer and tucked the autoloader behind his belt. "He isn't due to meet with his contact until Monday at noon. By that time, the revolution will be well underway. Wrap the body in a tarp; you know where to take him for disposal." He stood, looking at the large gathering of people. Then he shouted, "Power to the Righteous!"

There was a meeting on Tuesday afternoon in the War Room of the White House.

"The growing threat of civil insurrection will be the lead story on all the networks this evening," Chief of Staff Waymon said. "They're going to milk it for everything it's worth."

"Same with the overseas press," National Security Advisor Guy said.

"Why don't we declare a national emergency and turn the military loose on these damn lunatics?" Senator Eleanor Donahue demanded.

The president stared for a moment at the senator from California. Drummed his fingers on the table. "And where would you send the military, Senator? The United States encompasses millions of square miles of land mass. Hundreds of towns. Where is the enemy? *Who* is the enemy? For all I know, my neighbor and your neighbor back home might be a part of this: my barber, your hairdresser, the man who works on my car, the woman who checks us out at the supermarket, the repairman from the phone company, the lineman from the utility company, that friendly clerk at the hardware store, the cop on the beat, the crossing guard at school. Who do we arrest and what proof do we have they've done anything except join a militia? As we speak, most militia members are just sitting back doing nothing except smiling at our people as they come around to check on them. Granted, they are smug and condescending smiles, but that isn't against the law."

"We should have smashed these damn militias," Eleanor groused.

"And disarmed the American citizens and raised their taxes to fund more social programs and bugged more phones and spied on more Americans and interfered further in their lives?" Vice President Potter questioned, a grimace on his face. "Yes, Eleanor, we all know where you stand." Idiot, he thought.

"That's enough." President Evans spoke sharply. "Bickering among ourselves won't bring us any closer to solving this problem." If there is a peaceful solution, he amended silently. He cleared his throat. "So far, none of these dissident groups has contacted us. So we don't know what they want. . . ."

"Horse shit!" Vice President Potter interrupted. "We all know exactly what they want. We've known for years and blatantly ignored them and dismissed them as fanatics. But we did so realizing all the while that a full thirty-five to forty percent of the American public agreed with at least some of their objectives." Fred held up a hand. "Don't worry, people, I'm not going to belabor a point and give you a lecture on civics. I know only too well that in my position I'm virtually powerless. Well, I'm about to become even more so." He stood up. "To tell you the truth, I really don't know how to go about this; I don't know if any VP has ever done it . . . although I would imagine that most have entertained the thought—some more seriously than others. So I'll just go back to my office and sit this one out. I might even go back home for a long vacation. I want no part of whatever it is you people are cooking up."

"Oh, sit down, Fred!" President Evans said. "You don't mean that."

"The hell I don't. You just watch me. And as they say in the media, stay tuned. My press conference in about an hour is going to be a real eye-opener."

"You want to talk about this, Fred?" Evans asked.

"No. My mind is made up. I'm going back to Kentucky. Some of these groups that are rising up, Art, plan to kill you." He looked at Senator Donahue. "And *you,* Senator." He cut his eyes to Director Brewer. "And *you,* Kevin. They're going to kill anybody who stands in their way. So I'm stepping aside while there is still time."

"Nonsense!" Senator Donahue snorted.

"You're an arrogant, socialist bitch," VP Potter told the woman. "And you and your damned Marxist colleagues who walk around with their noses up your ass can go straight to hell."

"That's enough. Sit down and shut up!" the president barked.

Fred cut his eyes to the man and smiled. "Fuck you, Art!"

Nine

"Are you resigning because of all this talk about civil insurrection?" The question was thrown out from the crowd of reporters that evening at Blair House.

"No," Fred Potter replied. "I'm not resigning at all. I'm just taking a vacation from the politics, government programs, and legislation in general that forced American citizens to resort to civil insurrection in order to be heard."

"Would you care to elaborate, Mr. Potter?"

"As a moderate Democrat in the Senate I am on record as being opposed to raising taxes in order to fund social programs. I was and am opposed to gun control. While in the Senate, I voted against the recently passed crime bill that does little to fight crime. but gives the government broad new powers to spy on American citizens, to harass law-abiding gun-owners, to label any group a terrorist organization, and to make illegal wiretaps admissible in court. That crime bill is nothing more than another instrument enabling the government to legally strip American citizens of more rights."

For fifteen minutes Fred Potter stood before the knot of reporters and threw verbal bombs at the government of the United States of America. He blasted the Presidency, the House and Senate, called for a massive downsizing of government, including the abolition of HUD, BATF, IRS, and Commerce, and the complete revamping of the FBI and CIA.

It's difficult to shock Capitol Hill reporters, but Fred managed to do it. He stunned them all by saying, "Civil insurrection is inevitable in this nation. I've seen it coming for years. I believe it is probably only hours away; and furthermore, it is my belief that government will be powerless to stop it."

"What do you suggest the average American citizen do, Mr. Potter?" a young reporter asked.

Fred leaned closer to the microphone. "If you are a known and vocal liberal who has loudly advocated higher taxes to fund unworkable social programs, more government interference in the private lives of law-abiding citizens, gun control, and the pampering of criminals . . . if you have criticized the growing movement of the religious right and ridiculed citizen militias, I would suggest you bend over and kiss your ass goodbye."

"I can't believe someone as respected as Fred Potter would actually say that!" Jim exclaimed as he sat beside Janet on the couch, watching television.

Janet, however, was not surprised. Fred was wisely playing the old Washington game of CYA—Cover Your Ass—putting as much distance as possible between himself and President Evans. Fred would not linger in Washington; Janet suspected he would be on the road back to Kentucky within hours. And once there, he would maintain a very low profile. She knew that Fred had many friends in the intelligence community and probably had been listening carefully to them for several months.

"Pack a small bag, Jim," she told him. "Keep it handy and be ready to go at a moment's notice. We're coming down to the wire."

Jim used the remote to mute the TV set. "I am not in the least ashamed to say that you are scaring the hell out of me, Janet."

"Good. Believe me, I'm just as scared as you. We both stay scared, we'll come out of this all right."

"I have a friend that I've confided in—a man who works at the agency with me. We discussed the advisability of leaving the city today."

"Fine with me. It's a big lodge. I suppose he's another one who doesn't know shit from shinola about guns."

Jim no longer paid any attention to her raw expressions. He knew that as a military officer she had fought her way up in an almost exclusively man's world. "As a matter of fact, Don told me he has never fired a gun in his life."

"What a bunch of happy warriors we'll be," Janet said drily.

"I still can't believe an insurrection is going to take place . . . but then, it never hurts to be prepared."

She reached over and patted his cheek. "You're a real Boy Scout, darling."

"Wanna help me earn another merit badge?"

"Now, how can I do that?"

He whispered in her ear and she giggled. "I'd love to. But I didn't know they gave merit badges for *that!*"

It had not taken him long to claw his way out of the shallow grave, even though he could dig only with his right hand: the .45-bullet had broken his left shoulder blade and shattered his collarbone as it exited. After he had dug his way clear, he passed out on the ground beside the disturbed grave and lay unconscious on the cold ground for hours. When he awakened, it was very cold and cloudy and he did not know where he was. The cold had helped coagulate the blood, front and back, and stop the bleeding, but each movement brought intense pain. He stumbled around for hours before finally collapsing in a ditch from pain and exhaustion.

The sunlight woke him.

Howard managed to crawl out of the ditch and take a long look around him. He knew where he was, and he was miles from the nearest road and phone. Gritting his teeth against the pain caused by the grinding of the broken bones, he stumbled on. He knew he must get to a phone. He also knew there were a couple of deputies that he must not allow to find him, for they were part of the Righteous and they would not hesitate to kill him. The resident state-patrol officer was also a part of the Righteous, a fact he had uncovered only a few hours before he was shot and had been unable to report to his contact.

It was nearly dark when he finally staggered onto a dirt road. About a mile ahead, he could see the stark outline of a darkened farmhouse. He stumbled on. Half-way to the house he fell heavily, rolled into a ditch, and passed out. He would be unconscious for many hours.

On Wednesday morning, Jim awakened several hours earlier than usual. He did not try to get back to sleep, for he knew from past experience that was a totally use-less endeavor. He got out of bed, made a pot of coffee, and turned on the TV, tuning it to an all-news station.

All vestiges of sleep immediately left him as the screen filled with the sounds and scenes of gunfire and grim-faced helmeted federal agents, state police, and local deputies. They were easily identified in the glare of TV lights by the lettering on the back of their jackets: ATF, FBI, SHERIFF, STATE POLICE.

An armed confrontation was taking place, and it was clear that whomever the authorities were facing was not going to surrender.

Jim punched out Janet's number, and a sleepy voice answered. "Get up, Janet. Turn on your television. It looks like its starting . . . some part of it, anyway."

She said she'd call him back in a few minutes. Jim poured another cup of coffee, made some toast, and settled back to watch the action unfolding live on the wide-screen TV in his den.

A federal agent who had infiltrated a militia group in the Dakotas (the town was named, but Jim was unclear whether that was North or South Dakota) had been shot and badly wounded. Before he went into the operating room, he had named the people responsible, and the authorities had moved in quickly and in strength.

"Four members of this local militia group are confirmed dead," the reporter on the scene said. "A well-respected dentist, two farmers, and a farm-implement dealer. Two federal agents are confirmed dead, and several more have been wounded. Those militia members inside have sworn they will not be taken alive. The situation here is . . ."

His voice was drowned out by gunfire. Several federal agents standing nearby spun and jerked and went down under the impact of in-coming, high-powered rounds fired from somewhere behind the line of defense. Blood and bits of bone and brain sprayed the reporter as several rounds struck an agent in the head, and the head exploded like an over-ripe melon.

"Jesus Christ!" the reporter shouted as the picture suddenly went topsy-turvy and both the reporter and camera-operator hit the ground.

Now the federal agents were facing unfriendly fire from front and back and were taking some hard hits. Jim, two thousand-miles away and watching the events on TV, could see that the agents were badly outnumbered.

A machine gun began yammering from the darkness surrounding the circle of light around the brick home. Jim recognized the unmistakable heavy sounds of a .50 caliber. The federal agents had no chance at all against the superior firepower and took the only reasonable course of action left them: They got the hell out of there.

The gunfire stopped. The area grew quiet, except for the moaning of the wounded.

"You federal sons of bitches want war?" The voice sprang out of the darkness. "You've got war, goddamn you!"

Jim's TV screen went dark, the sound also terminated.

"Oh, shit!" Jim whispered.

The TV screen suddenly filled with color and sound as control at the flagship station took over and a worried-looking commentator's face filled the screen. It was obvious he was winging it.

"I . . . ah . . ." He cleared his throat. "To bring you up to date . . . an FBI agent, his name was . . . is Howard Jennings, infiltrated a cell of an ultra-secret and militant sect called the Righteous. About twenty-four hours ago—we're not sure of that time frame—he was shot. We assume he was presumed dead and buried in a grave out in the

Badlands. The agent managed to escape from the shallow grave and make his way to a farmhouse, where he called a local FBI office. Shortly thereafter, agents from federal, state, and local law-enforcement branches, surrounded the house of the alleged sect-leader. You, ah, witnessed the events that followed. Wait a minute! We have the reporter on the scene on line. He's all right, thank God. Dick, are you there?"

"I'm here, Chuck. We have sound but no picture. The camera took a round. I don't know how long I will be able to continue broadcasting. What appears to be several hundred heavily armed men and women are moving toward my location. . . . I'm friendly!" Dick shouted, a great deal of urgency in his voice. "I'm not armed. Don't shoot!"

What followed was too muted for the words to be clearly understood, but definitely threatening in tone. "Okay." Dick's voice was suddenly clear; he was still holding the microphone. "We're out of here, people. We're not filming. The camera's busted. That's it right there. We're going to get in the satellite truck and leave—okay? Whatever you say. We won't stop until we hit the state line. We're gone."

The screen went black, then Chuck at the flagship station came back on. The man was badly shaken. "There you have it." He paused, shook his head. "Ah, a live report from the shooting scene. We're going to break for a moment, then be right back."

A commercial featuring talking brassieres came on, and Jim muted the sound. He was reaching for the phone when it jangled under his hand.

"Pack a small bag, Jim," Janet said. "Call your friend and tell him to do the same."

"The government can't just sit back and let something

like this slide under the table," he protested. "They've got to make some sort of move."

"It's too late. The situation is out of control. The militias aligned with the Righteous have got to go for the big casino. They'll adjust their timetable and go now. They have no choice in the matter. They just killed a dozen or more federal agents. One more thing, Jim: Stay away from federal buildings today. Don't get near one."

Jim hadn't thought about that. "All right. I'm going to start calling my gang at six. I'll catch most people at home. But I'll have to go to the office to shut it down and tell the others."

"I'll see you this afternoon. Say . . . about two o'clock at your place. I'll be busy until then. Take care." She hung up.

Jim slowly replaced the receiver. He picked up his address book and found Don Williams' number. Just as he put his hand on the phone, it rang again, startling him.

"Jim? Don Williams here. I'm up watching the news. I took a chance you'd be up, too."

"I was just about to call you. You and Shirley get a bag packed and get your car filled up with gas and serviced. Don't come in to the office today. I'm shutting it down indefinitely. Don, as soon as it's light, go to your supermarket and get canned foods and bottled water. There is a chance we'll get sidetracked on the way up to the lodge, and we'll need food and water. Pack blankets, too. I'll call you later on."

"All right, Jim. I . . . saw the VP on television. I think the nation is coming apart."

"So do I, Don. So do I."

* * *

By mid-morning, Jim was alone in the empty office complex, watching the news. He had gotten in touch with every employee. They had all seemed surprised that he was closing the office, and no one was in the least bit alarmed by the shoot-out in the Dakotas. A couple of the men had seemed more upset by the poor showing at the Yankees' training camp the day before.

Bob Waldman and his wife had left for Europe.

Jim stood up, stretched the kinks out—he'd been sitting for more than two hours—and left the office, carefully locking the outer door. He took the elevator down to the lobby and cut across the street to his bank. There, he withdrew several thousand dollars from his savings account, requesting the money in tens and twenties, as Janet had instructed. Back on the street, he felt uncomfortable carrying that much cash.

Jim looked at the page he'd torn from the phone directory before leaving the office. He hailed a taxi and gave the driver the address. Miraculously, this driver spoke understandable English. Jim leaned back in the seat and said, "What do you think about the news this morning?"

"What news, buddy?"

"That big shoot-out in the Dakotas."

"Oh. That. I didn't pay much attention to it. The government will send the Marines or the paratroopers in, and they'll take care of it. Be old news by afternoon, you just wait and see."

"I hope."

"Oh, it will."

Jim stood in front of the sporting goods store which boasted the largest selection of Army-Navy surplus in the city. He pushed open the door and was immediately assailed by odors he had fought to forget for years: gun oil, leather, canvas, rope. He walked around the huge store for several moments, until a clerk stopped him.

"Let me guess," the man dressed in military fatigues said. "To start with, you want about three sets of BDUs, two pairs of boots—right?"

"How'd you know?" Jim asked, surprised.

"Been a hell of a run on battle-dress the past month. I never seen so many men—ladies, too—wanting to dress up like soldiers. Must be a new trend in style. Suits me. I stocked up plenty." He paused. "Curious, though. Must be a trend that don't interest the blacks. Haven't had a single black person come in for that stuff. Oh, well. Had plenty of whites. But what puzzles me is how in the hell they're gonna wear pup tents and hunting knives and entrenching tools. Now then—" He smiled. "—let's get you outfitted."

Ten

To save his cash, Jim put all his purchases on plastic and then took a cab back to his apartment. He engaged the cab driver in conversation—this one also thought the shoot-out in the Dakotas was no big deal.

"The Feds'll probably burn 'em out like they done them whackos down in Texas a couple years ago," the cabbie opined.

"Right," Jim agreed. He was beginning to feel like a fool for believing a war was about to break out in America—between Americans.

"However," the cabbie said, just as they pulled up to Jim's apartment building, "from what I read, I think the government's been pushing them militia people pretty damn hard—infiltratin' them, you know. I'm not sure that's right. They're Americans, and they got a right to hold an opinion like anybody else. You start pushin' Americans long enough, and they'll pick up a gun and fight. You know what I mean?"

Jim nodded his head. "Yes. Yes, I do."

In his apartment, Jim stuffed his washer full of camo BDUs and white cotton socks, quick-washing the load twice to get the stiffness out of the shirts and pants, then tossed them into the dryer. Changing into casual clothes, he packed the rest of his purchases into the new overseas bag. Then he fixed some lunch and sat down in front of the TV, using the remote to click it on.

FBI and BATF agents, along with federal marshals, were engaged in a nationwide sweep of militia and survivalist leaders. But they were coming up zero. Anyone known to be even remotely connected with any militia or survival group had vanished; their school-age children were all staying with grandparents or cousins or aunts and uncles or friends. Agents reported that those they interviewed were very uncooperative.

"Why don't you go on back to Washington and kiss a liberal's ass?" a film crew caught one elderly man in a small Montana town telling an FBI agent.

The agent showed great patience and restraint. "And you have no idea where your son might be, sir?"

"If I did, I damn sure wouldn't tell you."

"We just want to talk with him, sir."

"That's crap and you know it. Now either show me a search warrant or get the hell off my property and leave me and mine alone."

Hundreds of parents and grandparents and close friends of suspected militia and survivalist members were exhibiting a great deal of hostility toward federal agents.

"I've never seen anything like it," one agent, who insisted on anonymity told a reporter, "We've had seventy-five- and eighty-year-old men and women meet us at the door with shotguns and order us off their property. What are we supposed to do: get into a fire-fight with elderly people who have worked and paid taxes all their lives?"

Director Brewer was reported to have said that if he ever found out who'd made that statement he would fire him.

* * *

All federal trials were halted and postponed to a later date, some stopped right in the middle of a summation. Federal troops, beefed up by quickly mobilized national guardsmen, were moved into the nation's airports to prevent acts of what the government called *terrorism*.

By one o'clock on Wednesday, federal workers all over the nation were receiving phone calls at their offices telling them they were not the enemy and to go home before something happened to them. The callers were warning the government-workers that any who stayed at their jobs would be considered government stooges and collaborators and their safety could not be guaranteed. Many government-workers took the threats seriously and left, telling their supervisors to go straight to hell.

At two o'clock on Wednesday, IRS regional offices and other federal buildings in Shreveport, Louisiana; Little Rock, Arkansas; and a dozen other small cities came under attack by small arms fire and grenades. No one was killed, but dozens suffered injuries ranging from minor cuts and bruises to major trauma. The president immediately ordered all federal buildings to be evacuated and the offices closed indefinitely.

The FBI did not make the report public, but privately estimated that fewer than a hundred-thousand well-trained and highly disciplined and motivated men and women, waging a guerrilla-type hit-and-run operation were effectively bringing the government to an abrupt halt and creating chaos throughout the United States.

"Told you," Janet said as she stood by a window in Jim's apartment. "And it's going to get a hell of a lot worse."

"How about your, ah, coworkers? What do they have to say about it?"

"The office has shut down. Moved out of Manhattan."

Jim thought about that. He had never had much use for the CIA. He'd rubbed elbows with a few spooks in Vietnam and thought them some of the weirdest people he'd ever met. "Getting out while they can, huh?"

"Something like that."

Jim pointed to the TV. A newsperson was wrapping up an interview with a panel of men and women. "Those government spokespeople seem to think the worst is over. They just said so."

"They're wrong." She cut her eyes to the TV. "They're government eggheads. And they're liberals to boot. I've met very few liberals in my life who had a firm grasp on reality."

"Does that include me?"

"Yes," she said without hesitation, then softened her tone. "But I believe there is some hope for you."

"Thank you for that much."

Janet was quiet, looking down at Park Avenue. "Jim," she said, "come look at this."

Jim rose from the couch, walked across the room, and looked down at the street. Military HumVees, deuce-and-a-halfs, APCs, and tanks were rumbling up the street. He sighed. "I never thought I'd see this in America."

"I didn't either until about five years ago," she replied, her eyes on the soldiers in the backs of trucks. They all carried M-16's.

Jim did not pursue that line of thought. "Wonder where those people are from?"

"Fort Drum, probably."

"They don't look happy."

"I'm sure they're not. Would you be if you were being asked to open fire on fellow Americans?"

The nation's top military brass weren't admitting it except to themselves, and then in hushed tones and in private; but mixed in with their dismay at what was taking place in America was a certain amusement. They had known and tried to convince the powers-that-be for years that a dedicated group of disciplined and highly motivated men and women waging a hit-and-run guerrilla war could wreak havoc on the government, and do it in a very short time. To a person, they were students of history's many wars, veterans of the Vietnam War who knew firsthand how devastating guerrilla tactics could be. After all, Castro had come down from the hills with no more than a handful of fighters, and look what he had done.

Meeting in emergency session at the Pentagon, the Joint Chiefs were anything but optimistic about America's immediate future.

"We're going to have unfriendly nations looking for any weak spot," General Coplin said. "We can't afford to show the first one."

"I don't want my people having to open fire on Americans," Marine Corps General Pete Knowles said. "This whole business could have been avoided if the goddamn Democrats had stopped their insidious invasion into the rights of American citizens. I will agree to beef up local police and prevent looting, but I will not commit my people into a civil war."

"Is that firm, Pete?" Admiral Rutherford asked.

"Tight as a virgin's pussy."

Coplin cut his eyes to Air Force General Ashcroft. "Dickie?"

"Hell, Bob, I don't know who's loyal and who isn't. Our stats are running about the same as yours. We could easily have rebellion in the ranks. I sure as hell don't want that. We've all been told that we are not the enemy. All right, fine. Let's play a waiting game and see if that's really the case."

"I don't trust these ultra-religious types," Coplin said. "They always go too far to suit me. History bears that out. There have been more people killed in the name of God than for any other cause. But . . ." He sighed. ". . . I'll play along with the rest of you."

"This recently passed so-called *anti-terrorism* bill pushed them over the edge," Admiral Rutherford said. "That thing contains more shit than a barnyard. Bob?"

Coplin nodded his head. "My father used to say the function of government should be to protect our borders against foreign invasion and deliver the mail on time. Well, we don't have any control over the mail, but we can damn sure protect our borders against foreign invaders."

"And not against fellow Americans," the admiral said. "Many of whom have valid gripes."

"We'll take some heat for this decision," Dickie observed.

Pete Knowles chuckled. "Verbal heat is all we'll take from Evans because, without us, he's shit out of luck."

Jim stilled the ringing of the phone, and the first words out of the mouth of an excited Don Williams were, "I bought a shotgun from a neighbor. I was amazed at how heavy it is. Also several boxes of bullets."

"It's shells, Don, not bullets. Didn't you tell me you've never fired a gun?"

"I haven't. But I can learn. These things kick a lot, don't they?"

"Some of them. What gauge is it, Don?"

"Ahhh . . . twelve-gauge, I think he said. It's a double-barrel. But it's brand new. Still in the box."

Jim glanced at Janet, who was standing by the window looking at him, an amused expression on her face.

"Don, put it back in the box until I can go over it with you, okay?"

"Sure. I just wanted to tell you about it."

"What does Shirley think about your buying a gun?"

"She . . . ah, hasn't come home from school yet. She hates guns. I don't want to think about what her reaction is going to be. Jim, what about my kids? They're both in college."

"I . . . think this might be their last day for a while, Don. The government has closed all federal buildings and the mayor has shut down everything but essential services here in the city. We have federal troops moving in right now."

"Really? Jesus! Uh-oh, I hear Shirley's car pulling in the drive. Wish me luck."

"Talk to you later."

"Listen to this," Janet said as Jim hung up the phone. She pointed to the TV.

". . . 82nd Airborne out of Fort Bragg," the news commentator was saying. "The 101st out of Fort Campbell and the 10th Mountain Division. Marines from the West Coast will be used to help police Los Angeles and

San Diego; National Guard and regular army troops will be used in San Francisco. National Guard units all over the nation have been mobilized and are swiftly moving into the cities. Experts predict that within forty-eight hours, martial law will be declared in all of the nation's larger cities. . . ."

"We leave the city no later than Friday morning, Jim," Janet said. "Call your friend and advise him to be ready."

"What if there is martial law by then?"

"New York City won't stop functioning, except for a dusk-to-dawn curfew that will probably be in effect. But food is going to be at a premium very soon."

"What do you mean?"

"Jim . . . almost a year ago, the intelligence community predicted something like this. We began running various scenarios through computers. So far, everything is running on schedule, just as we predicted. Next comes the blockage of food shipments into the city. . . ."

"Why New York?"

"Because the city is eighty-five-percent liberal, that's why. And those staging this uprising don't give a damn what happens to liberals. Liberals are no longer viewed by the insurrectionists as friendly political adversaries. They—you—have become the enemy."

"Janet, that is absurd! We live in a democracy. I can vote for whomever I damn well please."

"Yes, but when your party's platform begins to infringe upon what is viewed by the other side as their constitutional rights . . . well . . ." She jerked a thumb toward the outside, where the faint rumble of military vehicles could be heard. "You see what's happening."

Jim sat down on the couch, his mouth hanging open in disbelief. He cleared his throat. "Let me get this straight: You're blaming all this . . . this bombing and shooting . . . on the liberal wing of the Democratic Party?"

"I think you people certainly have to accept your fair share of it."

"I do not believe *any* of this!" Jim protested. "But *you're serious!*"

Before she could reply, a violent explosion rattled the windows; pictures fell from the walls. Flames leaped from the shattered windows of the apartment next to Jim's. The explosion almost knocked Janet off her feet. They both began to smell smoke. Jim jumped to his feet and ran to her side.

"That was a rocket!" Janet said. "Are you packed, Jim?"

"Yeah . . . everything I was going to take."

"Get it and let's get out of here. The apartment next to this one is on fire. Can't you smell it?"

"Rocket! *Rocket?* What the hell is this city turning into, Bosnia?"

"Probably," Janet replied, grabbing her purse. "Get your bag, Jim. We're outta here!"

Eleven

In the few minutes it took for the fire trucks to arrive, the fire had spread to the apartments on either side of the target and jumped across the hall. Jim's floor was engulfed in flames.

Jim and Janet stood across the street—well out of the way of the trucks, the hoses, and firemen—and watched as the building was safely evacuated.

"Who lives in that apartment next to yours?" Janet asked.

"A lawyer. A man who specializes in civil rights cases. He just won a large settlement from a construction company . . . took it all the way to the supreme court. Millions of dollars were involved."

"What was the case about?"

"Discriminatory hiring practices." Jim looked at the smoke and flames pouring from his floor. "Everything I own is in that apartment."

"Some people have strong views about the government telling them who they can hire."

Jim turned his attention from the fire to Janet. Her face was expressionless. "Are you saying . . ."

"Someone put about ten pounds of explosives into the man's apartment, Jim. Draw your own conclusions. Come on. Let's get out of here."

"Won't the police want to talk to us?"

"In seventy-two hours, one apartment fire will be the least of their worries. *Come on.* We'll walk a few blocks and then grab a cab. Is that duffle heavy?"

"No. It's clothing. I, ah, went to a sporting goods store this morning and bought several sets of BDUs."

She grinned. "Do I call you Jim or Sergeant?"

"Very funny. I got hit and sent home before I could sew the stripes on. I would have made a lousy sergeant anyway. Look, when we get to your place, I guess I'd better call my insurance company."

"I'm sure they'll send an adjustor right over."

Jim suppressed a sigh. Sometimes Janet's sarcasm could be a bit wearing. He paused and looked back at the smoke-filled street. "That rocket had to have come from the building across the street. Probably from the roof, don't you think?"

"And five seconds after it was triggered, those responsible were gone, blending in with the others in that building. This is going to be a dirty little war."

Before Jim could reply, Janet had spotted a cab, whistled as loud as a football referee, and waved it to the curb.

At her apartment, a third-floor walk-up, three small and very spartan rooms, Jim called Don and brought him up to date.

"A rocket?"

"Yes. I'm over at Janet's apartment. Did you get your car serviced and gassed?"

"I'm ready to go. I couldn't get the shotgun hidden quickly enough. Shirley hit the ceiling. Now it's a wall of angry silence around here. Before she turned clam on me, she said she thought what you and I are planning is childish nonsense."

"So did I, at first. But no more. She'll come with us though, right?"

"I'm sure. This rocket business might be what it takes to convince her. Oh, the kids will be coming in later on today. Classes dismissed indefinitely."

"We'll talk every few hours, Don."

"Hopefully, Shirley will, too," Don said drily, then hung up.

Jim was slow in replacing the phone. Janet studied his face for a moment, then asked, "What's wrong?"

"Oh, I just recalled something Don told me about his son several months ago. He said the boy was becoming militant . . . and flirting with Islam. Don and Shirley are devout Baptists. Don told the boy—I can't think of his name—that if he didn't straighten up his act and forget this Islam business, he could damn well hit the road and not look back. Shirley stood solidly beside her husband on that issue."

"And?"

"Don said that outwardly, at least, the boy straightened up. But he thinks it's just a front for his benefit."

"The girl?"

"I haven't seen her in a couple of years, but I remember her as being sweet, soft-spoken, a talented dancer. Don told me she's studying ballet."

Janet nodded her head, being careful to hide the frown she felt. A militant young black, scarcely more than a boy, she thought, carrying a load of contempt for the Christian faith, plus a wide load of hate for whitey and the years of oppression.What a joyful little trip this was going to be . . .

If Jim took note of her noncommittal expression, he made no mention of it. "I'm still holding out some hope that this can be resolved without any more violence."

"I truly wish it could be, Jim. But I'm afraid it's gone too far for that." She smiled. "I missed lunch. You hungry?"

"Yes, as a matter of fact, I am." He grinned. "Are you going to cook?"

"God, no!"

Jim laughed at her expression. "Show me where to stow my gear and we'll go get something to eat. There are some marvelous restaurants in this area."

By Thursday morning, according to the TV news commentator, it was as if the revolutionaries had dropped off the face of the earth. Not one incident had been reported overnight. But a list of demands had been received at the White House. A panel of government "experts" was about to be interviewed concerning the content of those demands.

"This should be interesting," Janet said, coming out of the bathroom, rubbing her short wet hair vigorously with a towel. She poured a cup of coffee and sat down beside Jim on the couch. "But pull your socks up before they start, for the crap is about to get deep."

"Don't you have any faith at all in this government's ability to act in the best interest of the people, Janet?"

"No."

Jim returned his attention to the panel.

"We are overreacting," one "expert" solemnly intoned. He had been introduced as a professor at an eastern university. "This massive show of force is not necessary. We are dealing with a very small group of malcontents. By overreacting we are succeeding only in needlessly frightening the American people."

The four men and two women on the panel began squabbling among themselves, and the moderator couldn't shut them up. Janet laughed. "Professor Jonathan Willis has thus spoke. And as usual, he doesn't know what he's talking about. None of them do. There isn't a single person on that panel who has rubbed shoulders with the real world in thirty years. They go from campus to Washington to think tank and back to campus. If they're not talking with kids, most of whom get their political views from "Saturday Night Live" or MTV, they're huddling with other college professors who are just as misinformed as they are. Every so-called government expert should be forced to go into a different country honky-tonk around the nation at least two weekends a month to drink beer and speak with real folks."

The moderator finally got the panel quieted and asked, "What about the demands received last evening by the White House? Will you divulge the contents of that letter?"

"Right-wing raving," a woman said.

"Professor Susan Sparkman," Janet said. "An acid-tongued, vicious, man-hating dyke . . ."

Jim held up a hand, stilling her. "How come you know so much about this group, Janet?"

"We've been building dossiers on these people for years," she replied evenly. "Just as soon as we learned that Evans was going to appoint them as advisors. There isn't a conservative drop of blood or an ounce of common sense in that whole bunch."

"You were spying on Americans?"

"Not spying on them, Jim, not the way *you* mean it. We didn't tap their phones or bug their bedrooms or intercept their mail. All you have to do is read their papers or go to some of their lectures or classes and you'll know everything you need to know about them—or can stomach. Don't look so shocked. Every administration does it. But Evans's regime has been the worst—by far."

"Worse than Nixon?"

"You'd better believe it."

"The demands being made upon this government are unreasonable," a panelist declared, his voice carrying above the squabbling of the others.

"Well, what *are* the demands?" the moderator asked, showing just a bit of temper.

The panelists fell silent and assumed wise and scholarly expressions.

"Looks like a bunch of chipmunks up there all studying the same nut," Janet muttered, and Jim could not contain his grin; to be fair, he agreed with her on that point.

"They are ridiculous," another panelist said.

The moderator sighed . . . patiently . . . and Jim and Janet could tell that the reporter did not place much credence in the panel's ability to tell time, much less discuss the present situation with any kind of intelligence.

"These . . . people . . ." Professor Sparkman spat out the word. ". . . have called for the complete dismantling or drastic downsizing of various government departments and agencies. Of course, that will never happen."

"What departments?" the moderator asked wearily.

Professor Sparkman gave him a dirty look. "Department of Housing and Urban Development; Bureau of Alcohol, Tobacco, and Firearms; Commerce; Internal Revenue Service; EEOC; Labor . . . among others."

That started the panel scrabbling again. The moderator looked as though he would have liked to turn a fire hose on the whole lot of them. Someone stepped up and handed him a sheet of paper, which he quickly scanned, then held up a hand for silence. The panel ignored him. "Be quiet!" he shouted.

That got their attention. The crème de la crème of liberal academia, politically correct to the core, was not accustomed to being spoken to in such an abrupt manner.

"Thank you," the moderator said, with more than a touch of satisfaction. "Ladies and gentlemen, I have just been handed this bulletin. The revolutionary group who call themselves the Righteous and who claim responsibility for the recent wave of terror across America have ordered their people to stand down for thirty-six hours, the countdown beginning at 6:00 A.M. today, EST. According to this bulletin, they have done so in order to give the president and members of Congress time to study and act on their demands. We have no word, as yet, on any reaction from the White House. Perhaps our panel could comment on this recent development."

The members of the panel all began talking at once, and Janet clicked off the set. Jim looked at her, questions in his eyes.

"The members on that panel don't know anything, Jim. They don't have a clue about the people behind and in the Righteous movement and simply cannot grasp the reasons for their actions. Anything they say would be pure guesswork. The only thing those eggheads are going to accomplish is getting a bunch of civilians killed."

Jim rose from the couch, picked up both cups, and

poured fresh coffee. He sugared his and sugared and creamed Janet's. He sat down beside Janet, who was staring at the wall while she brushed her hair. "Start from the beginning, Janet. Tell me where it all began—all this hate, I mean."

"It probably began when one group of cavemen had fire and another didn't. The latter couldn't figure out how to produce the spark it took to make fire, so they grunted around and decided to steal the source from the former. That's probably where it all began."

Jim sighed patiently. "You know what I mean."

She laid the brush aside, picked up her coffee cup, and took a sip. "Just right," she said, nodding her approval. "I might decide to keep you around."

"I hope so," he said drily. "Now where did it all begin? Give me the Gospel according to the CIA."

"The CIA is not allowed to operate within the United States, Jim, not without congressional approval. Of course they do and always have, but very carefully. Some eighteen months ago, just about the time the anti-terrorism bill was gutted in Congress and President Evans, Attorney General Newton, and several lace-pants liberals in both houses nearly went ballistic about it, the various intelligence agencies, military and civilian, came together in an unprecedented move to share intel. What we found out shook us down to our collective socks. The FBI's estimate of membership in various militias nationwide fell drastically short of the real mark. The FBI also believed that the old Posse Comitatus was no longer a threat. We found out it was a real threat. It had gone hard underground and become huge. The Posse had joined hands with factions of the Aryan Nation, the skinheads, the KKK, neo-Nazi groups, and dozens of other smaller but just as dangerous organizations. They'd gotten smart, too. They had an intelligence system that was really good and sophisticated polygraph and psychological stress-evaluator equipment. They had doctors skilled in the use of pentothal, injectable Valium, and other drugs useful in bringing out the truth in a subject."

"I didn't know Valium was a truth serum."

"Oh, yes, if given in massive doses. But it has side effects. In male patients it produces long-lasting erections. Some of the kinkier female members of these groups had fun with that, so I'm told. Anyway, ninety-nine percent of our informants were ferreted out and either killed or kicked out." She looked down at her coffee cup. "In most cases, we believe they were killed and their bodies carefully buried. We've been able to find only a few of the bodies. Practically overnight, the group became known as the Righteous and took on hard right-wing, back-to-the-Bible, overtones which appealed to a great many ultra-religious types and people with racist views; people who can point to Scriptures which they claim back up their slanted opinions." She paused, taking another sip of coffee.

"Most militias refused to join the Righteous. Most militia members aren't bad people. They just want a downsizing of government, less taxes, no gun-control. Basically, that's what the majority of militias are about.

"Well, as I said, the government 'experts' were wrong about membership in these off-the-wall groups. Including the people in militias and various survival groups, we estimate membership at about two million . . ."

"Two million?" Jim interrupted her.

"That's active and inactive. About three hundred thousand of them are well-armed and trained and highly disciplined and motivated and will actually take to the field and fight. The rest are, well, call them reservists. They run the safe houses and bunkers and maintain the vehicles and buy the food and print the newsletters and so forth."

"You said the majority wouldn't join with these Righteous people."

"That's correct. But when the Righteous make their move, so will the militias, albeit in a different direction. Military commanders know their ranks have been infiltrated. In thirty-six hours, the public will see just how heavily that infiltration is. You're going to see racial tensions explode. Originally, the government planned to deploy the two airborne divisions, the 82nd at Bragg and the 101st at Fort Campbell, along with the 10th Mountain Division at Fort Drum and contingents of Special Forces and Rangers to use against civilians—which is, I might point out, in direct violation of the Federal Posse Comitatus Act, which forbids the use of federal troops against U. S. citizens. Well, all that was scrapped when the military learned that the ranks had been heavily infiltrated by militia sympathizers. The military will be used to beef up local police in the city, and not much else."

"So the intelligence community knew about the rapid buildup of these Righteous kooks, and did nothing about it?"

"That's not exactly true. Actually, what we did was attempt to buy the government a little more time in the hopes of convincing somebody to listen to the grievances of the militia people—really *listen*, not just pay them lip service and then do nothing, as happened when that one hearing was held last year."

"So what was the result?"

She shrugged her shoulders. "Nothing. Even the conservative hard-liners on the hill know they didn't have the votes to even begin to downsize government and cut taxes. The moderates won't even think about touching these precious social programs. If they did, they'd never get re-elected. The head-up-their ass liberals throw a hissy fit anytime anybody wants to cut anything except the military. So . . . the national debt keeps right on growing, social security is facing certain bankruptcy, taxes are sure to be raised—probably drastically—and more liberties will be taken away from Americans while they watch their buying power shrinking. The militias finally said to hell with it and joined, to some extent, the Righteous. Now, the nation is facing real revolution."

"I still believe if the military would swing in behind the president, they could put this down in no time."

"You know better, Jim," Janet said softly. "Not a guerrilla war in a country the size of America. Not a hit-and-run, blow-up-this, ambush-that, assassinate-this-person-or-that-person-and-then-vanish-like-a-puff-of-smoke war. You, especially, should know how dirty a war that can be."

Jim tasted his coffee. It was still warm enough to be drinkable. "I guess the nation is in for a pretty rough time of it, then."

"A lot of innocent people are going to suffer," Janet said grimly.

Twelve

If any New Yorker were taking the threat of revolution seriously, Jim couldn't see it. According to the Friday morning news, few Americans in the nation's major cities were taking it very seriously.

"Cities are traditionally liberal," Janet pointed out. "And New York is about eighty-percent democratic. Home of political correctness," she added sarcastically. "The scourge of the '90's."

"Big Brother will take care of everything," she added as she turned off the TV. "From womb to tomb, never fear; Big Brother is here." When Jim didn't comment, she went on. "I'm certain it will come as a great surprise to some mechanic in the Midwest, a small businessman in Texas, a nurse in South Carolina, a bus driver in Tennessee, and a lumber mill operator in Washington who have worked and obeyed the law and paid taxes all their lives to learn that they are now branded fascists."

Jim said nothing, but his suspicion that Janet's sympathies were tilted to the right were growing decidedly stronger.

"I'm waiting to see a T-shirt that reads LIBERALS—WALKING ADVERTISEMENTS THAT ABORTION SHOULD BE LEGALIZED," Janet said.

Jim laughed aloud at that and checked his watch. "We

should get ready. Don and Shirley said they'd be here right at noon."

"They bringing their kids?"

"Don was sure his daughter was coming along. Lori, that's her name. He and his son Donald had another fight last night. He said the boy stormed out of the house and, at the time we spoke, had not returned."

"Is he expecting him to come back?"

"He hopes he will."

The five of them had lunch at a restaurant a block from Janet's apartment. Lori Williams was shy and soft-spoken; but when she did speak, her words were intelligently offered. Shirley and Janet hit it off almost immediately, much to Jim's relief. He was still not entirely certain how Janet felt about blacks. She was much more complex than he'd first thought. She never talked about her youth or her parents, and Jim did not push the issue.

Shirley was the daughter of Jamaican immigrants and Jim knew she had not had an easy time of it in her youth. She and Don had met while both were working full-time jobs and taking night courses at college. Six months later they were married. The twins, Lori and Donald, Jr., had been babies when Jim hired Don to work for the Waldman Agency.

"These soldiers all over the city convinced me to go along with Don's plan," Shirley said after the lunch dishes had been cleared away and dessert and coffee had been served. "At first I thought it was the wildest thing I had ever heard of." She looked down. "I still think it's very strange."

"No word from Donald?" Jim asked.

"No," Don said. "He's probably hanging out with

some of his hoodlum friends." He smiled. "To borrow part of a line from the Coasters."

"Yakky-Yak, don't look back," Jim filled in almost automatically.

The two women looked at one another, shared a smile, and shook their heads.

Shirley's smile faded. "Don, what about Donald? What if he isn't back when we're ready to leave?"

"I warned him about that. He's a big boy now. When Jim calls and says it's time to pull out, we go. With or without Donald."

Janet cut her eyes to the twin. Lori's eyes shifted away quickly. "You know where he is, don't you, Lori?"

Lori toyed with what was left of her carrot cake. "Yes."

"Where is your brother, Lori?" the mother asked, a hard note behind her words.

"Over at LaShana's house," the young woman said softly.

The father's eyes flashed with anger. "Why didn't you tell us this, girl?"

"You didn't ask me."

Jim and Janet chuckled, and the parents' anger slowly faded away. "We'll swing by there and pick him up on the way home," Don said. "What about your kids, Jim?"

Jim shook his head. "I don't know. I called this morning and left word on the answering machine. Cynthia may or may not return the call. I suspect she won't. For what it's worth, and it isn't worth much, my kids have turned against me, solidly turned, thanks to their mother. I would say they borderline hate me, and I don't know what else I can do. Listen, people, Janet and I have withdrawn several thousand dollars in cash from the bank.

We're using our ATM cards to withdraw more every time we see a machine. I suggest you do the same."

"We have," Shirley said. "We've also stocked up on food and bottled water. I resisted doing that until I saw the soldiers. Then it hit me that the worst-case scenario just might be unfolding. We're ready to go when you give us the word."

"We should leave early in the morning," Janet said. "No later than eight o'clock. Preferably even sooner. Maybe tonight. We'll see. I'm sure that Jim will want to head first to Albany to check on his kids. He's worked up a map that is easy to follow. If we get separated, we'll meet you at the lodge."

"It's all gone crazy," Lori said, her eyes filling with tears. "And it's never going to be the same again."

No one had anything to add; any words of comfort would have rung false, for, to a person, they believed she was right.

"And finally, my friends and fellow Americans," President Evans said, looking grim and staring straight into the camera, "we do not negotiate with terrorists. God bless America, for she will persevere. I thank you, and good night."

"In other words, screw you all," Janet said. "Evans is dumber than I thought."

Jim glanced at his watch. "It's six forty-five, Janet. Thirty-six hours and forty-five minutes since the Righteous issued their deadline. Nothing has happened."

"Give it fifteen more minutes. This speech was ballyhooed from coast to coast for the past twenty-four hours. The revolutionaries just wanted to see what that nitwit in the White House would say. I have a hunch the Righteous will put on quite a show before much longer."

Although Janet was no hand at creative cooking, she was throwing together a salad when the network program was interrupted by a flustered-looking member of the local news team. "The federal building in Nashville, Tennessee, has just come under attack by rockets and mortars," he blurted. "At the same time, federal buildings in a dozen other cities have come under heavy attack by hit-and-run teams, presumably from the movement called the Righteous. All this less than a half hour after the conclusion of the president's speech, during which he refused to even discuss the demands recently submitted by the Righteous in a formal petition, saying that America does not negotiate with terrorists." He looked up as someone off-camera handed him a sheet of paper. "Ah . . . this just in. Several towns in the Midwest have reportedly been taken over by militia members. Taken over?" he repeated, confusion on his face. He glanced away from the camera, held up the copy paper, and asked, "What the hell does this mean?"

The station went to a commercial.

"Let's go," Janet said. "Right now. Call Don and tell him to mount up. Things just shifted into high gear."

"Janet . . ."

"Damnit, Jim, don't argue with me! This city could well turn into a battleground within the hour, troops or no troops." She took a deep breath, and when she spoke again, her words had lost their sharpness. "I'll get our gear while you phone Don; he knows where to meet us. The last thing we want is to be trapped in the city."

Jim rose from the chair and faced her. "You still know more than you've told me, don't you? You haven't leveled with me."

"I told you all I could. What I didn't tell you is moot. Most of it. The most important thing now is getting the hell out of the city as fast as we can. The Big Apple is about to get peeled."

Jim continued to stare at her. "You people knew all along this was going to happen. You want this. My God!"

She shook her head. "You're wrong. We didn't want it; we were powerless to stop it. When enough people band together demanding change, the best thing a government can do is listen carefully to their grievances and negotiate. This president refused to do so, as we knew he would. Jim, this is not the time to argue. I'm leaving the city. Are you coming with me?"

"I'll phone Don." He put his hand on the phone. Paused. Looked at the woman. "What's it going to be like when all the gunsmoke blows away?"

"I can't answer that." She turned from him and added softly, "It's going to be . . . different."

Thirteen

Don's line was busy for nearly half an hour. While Jim waited, Janet dressed in her class-A uniform, complete with all her decorations, which included jump wings and aviator wings, showing that she was qualified in both fixed wing and rotor. "There'll be roadblocks," she explained, "manned by soldiers. This way I can get us through a lot easier. You tell Don to get across the East River ASAP and head north. Don't stop until he reaches the designated rest area just south of Albany. We should be there before him, but if we're not, he should wait for us."

When Jim finally got through, Don assured him the family was together and leaving immediately, Donald driving his own car. They'd meet them at the rest area.

"Good luck," Jim said.

"They're going to need it," Janet muttered under her breath.

They made it to the Henry Hudson Parkway without incident and there they hit their first roadblock, manned by troops from Fort Drum. Several vehicles had been pulled over to the side of the road, and the occupants lay face down on the shoulder. Standing off to one side were crying women and children.

"What the hell happened here?" Jim questioned.

"They probably found guns in the cars and trucks. They're under orders to detain anyone found with a weapon."

"We have weapons," Jim reminded her.

"Several of them." Janet smiled. "But they won't search my truck." She pulled up to the roadblock; the officer in charge had already taken note of the Fort Meade sticker on the front bumper.

"Heading for Drum, Lieutenant," Janet told the young officer, as he looked at her I.D. "We're closing up shop in Manhattan."

The lieutenant wasn't sure exactly what that meant, but he wasn't about to debate the point with an officer from MI, especially one wearing as much fruit salad as Major Shaw. He waved them on through.

"That was easy," Jim remarked.

"We got lucky. Lieutenants don't like to argue with majors."

Jim twisted in the seat to look behind him. Traffic was building as people attempted to leave the city, but they weren't having much luck. The troops were turning most of them around and sending them back.

"Why aren't they letting them leave?" Jim asked.

"Orders. They want to keep the roads as clear as possible for military and emergency vehicles."

"I thought this was a free country," Jim said, an edge to his voice.

"Not anymore. This is martial law. The same thing is happening in all the major cities. President Evans doesn't realize it, but all he's done by sending troops in is toss gasoline on a fire."

"But what else could he have done?"

"Actually, nothing," Janet conceded. "And it really

wouldn't have made any difference who won the last election for the presidency: Democrat, Republican, or independent. Millions of people wanted change, and they were tired of waiting for it. Every graph we worked up pointed in that direction."

At each on-ramp, Jim glanced to his right: Traffic was backed up and cars and trucks were being turned around—or the troops were attempting to turn them around. Soon, he reasoned, the lines would be so long they would stretch for several miles and there would be so much confusion it would be no more than a monumental jam-up. He said as much.

"That's all part of the plan," Janet said as they rolled north, staying with the speed limit. The day had slipped silently into night and the city, off to their right, was blazing with light, much of it coming from headlights, as people attempted to flee the city . . . with no luck. Some of the light was coming from network news crews catching history on film.

"You seem to know quite a lot about this plan, Janet."

"Most of it is guesswork. But so far, it's been right on the money. Those behind this budding revolution want the troops to fire on Americans. Nothing will swing people behind their cause faster than that. They want the network news to show Americans being forced face-down on the ground at gunpoint by heavily armed and helmeted and camoed and flack-jacketed federal troops . . . especially black troops. They want the news to show crying wives and frightened, hysterical little boys and girls as husbands and fathers are led off in handcuffs, under arrest simply because they had a pistol in the glove box or on the floorboards or a shotgun or rifle on the back seat. You see, Jim, a great many people, and I include myself on that list, believe it's every citizen's right to have a weapon in their vehicle, if they choose to do so. The Supreme Court has ruled that your vehicle is an extension of your domicile, and the constitution guarantees every citizen the right to be safe and secure in their homes against unreasonable search and seizure. No, it's all part of the plan, and it's working like a fine Swiss watch."

"Safe and secure in their own homes," Jim muttered.

"That's correct. And if keeping a gun in their vehicle makes a law-abiding person feel safe and secure, that is his or her right."

"And if the majority doesn't agree?"

"That is their right."

Jim changed the subject. "This plan wasn't dreamed up overnight, was it?"

"No. This was all very carefully thought out."

They rode in silence for a few moments, making good time, for the parkway was almost deserted. The lights of Washington Heights lay off to their right, bright pockets in a night that was becoming increasingly gloomy for Jim.

"What if Don and his family can't make it, Janet?" he asked.

She hedged, replying, "That's the problem about living on a damn island. You're easily boxed in."

Jim got it then. "Manhattan is going to be completely cut off, isn't it?"

"More than likely," she said softly. "We theorized that would be part of the plan."

"Why? What purpose will it serve?"

"New York City is eighty-five-percent liberal. And nobody on the other side gives one hoot in hell what happens to a damn liberal."

Jim sighed and returned his attention to the parkway. "I guess that answers that question." It was going to be a long silent ride through the night.

Shirley and Lori rode with Don; Donald followed in his own car, his girlfriend LaShana with him. Lori did not like LaShana, but because she loved her twin, she kept her silence about it. Her mother sensed the dislike because she felt the same way: LaShana was a spoiled, arrogant brat. Pretty, but lazy, with a tendency to whine.

Don and family were lucky in getting past the road-blocks; due to a mix-up in orders, the soldiers manning the Triboro Bridge were letting people through. The bridge was closed ten minutes after Don and family were waved past the blockade. Don set the pace north, driving just under the speed limit.

Janet had insisted that Don and his son buy CB radios with removable magnetic antennas; Janet had a CB radio in her truck in addition to a shortwave radio capable of both scanning and broadcasting on several bands. She had both of them constantly scanning, and to Jim, the racket was incomprehensible. But Janet seemed to be able to pick out what she needed to hear.

Don and Donald had their CB's set on channel 39 and were able to maintain contact as they headed north through the night.

"I'm glad Donald has LaShana with him," Don said. "She's a nice kid."

"Just wonderful," Shirley said.

"I'm thrilled," Lori spoke from the back seat of the Ford Explorer. Behind her, the luggage area was packed to nearly overflowing with gear.

Don picked up on the flatness in the voices of his wife and daughter. "Is there something I'm missing here?"

Shirley reached across the console, and patted him on the leg. "Not a thing. Must be your imagination, dear."

"Right," Don said, only a tiny bit of sarcasm creeping into his tone. "I'll just drive the car."

"Good, dear. You do that. You're doing splendidly."

Before Don could retort, a pickup truck passed them, then slowed and let Don pull alongside. A young man leaned out of the passenger-side window and hollered, "You're headin' in the wrong direction, nigger! All the monkeys are in Africa!" The truck sped on past and exited off the New York State Thruway.

"I wish I had a gun," Lori said. "I'll kill people like that."

"Lori!" Shirley spoke sharply, twisting in the seat to glare at her daughter. "You know you don't mean that. Those types of people are ignorant, that's all."

"Don't jump down her throat," Don said. "Not when I'm beginning to feel the same way."

"Thank you, Father," Lori said tightly.

Shirley stared at her husband. "Is that why you bought that shotgun, Don? So we can all revert to barbarism?"

Don reached under the seat and took out a heavy black auto-loader, showing it to his wife.

"Is that thing loaded?" Shirley questioned fearfully. "What is that?"

"It's a .45 and yes, it's loaded. I haven't shot it yet, but I know how it works. Randy Phillips gave it to me last evening."

"Put it away, Don. Put it away!" The pistol out of sight under the seat, Shirley asked, "Gave it to you? Where did he get it?"

"He bought it at a gun show. He's got a whole arsenal of guns and stuff in his basement. Rifles, shotguns, and pistols. Cases of ammunition."

"Randy? Our neighbor Randy?"

"Yes. I never knew about his gun collection either until he waved me over yesterday. Told me the country was about to go to shit and we needed to be prepared. If those punks in that pickup truck come back, I'll show them what this monkey can do. I'm tired of taking crap from white trash. No more."

Shirley stared at her husband. She had never seen this side of him. "White trash, Don?"

"That's what my grandmother used to call those types. She was right."

"What else did your grandmother used to say, Don?" Shirley asked, very much aware of Lori, listening attentively in the back seat.

"That a person didn't have to be black to be a nigger."

"I . . . see," Shirley said. "I think. Well! This trip is certainly going to be a real learning experience for us all, isn't it?"

"In more ways than one, dear." Don replied.

In more than five hundred locations all over the United States, the revolutionaries swung into action. There were no cells within the confines of the nation's large cities. Those who were followers of the Righteous or members of the various militia groups had left the cities hours before the troops arrived. The cities were, for the most part during the first few days, ignored, for all knew they would self-destruct despite the presence of federal troops. What arsonists, professional criminals, and roaming gangs of street punks didn't accomplish, the food riots would when the supermarket shelves began to run bare . . . and the Righteous and their allies had plans on how to achieve that goal. The residents of several of the nation's larger cities were in for a rough time.

Washington, D.C., became an armed camp as troops ringed the city and patrolled the streets. The White House resembled a fort under siege, circled by tanks.

But the revolutionaries had absolutely no intention of attacking the nation's capital. There was no need for that.

"When we gain control of the Heartland," Gene Baronne had told his commanders, "we shall control the nation."

Jim set the mobile phone back into the bag on the floorboard. "It's no use. They're just not at home. That guy she married—what's-his-name—has taken them somewhere until this, ah, situation blows over."

"It isn't going to blow over," Janet reminded him for about the fiftieth time.

"Is *gets resolved* a better way of putting it?"

"Yes. Is your ex's current husband close to the governor?"

"Hell, I don't know. I would guess so. Why?"

"The governor probably pulled his closest friends and advisors into the capital or a summer residence for safe-keeping . . . surrounded by New York State Police and national guardsmen. When we get closer to Albany, we'll tune in a local station for news."

Manhattan lay miles behind them. Just north of the city, Janet had cut west on a secondary road that connected with Interstate 87. Traffic was light and darkness lay oppressive and uninviting on either side of the highway.

Jim again tried to raise Don on the CB. There was no reply other than the crack and hiss of static.

"Those things have a range of only a few miles," Janet pointed out.

"You folks better hunt a hole." The male voice jumped out of the speaker. "It's about to get real hairy out here."

Janet took the mic. "I'm scared to death. I don't know what to do. What's happening in this country?"

"You got the Bulldog here, little lady," the voice came back. "What's your twenty?"

"Interstate 87. I cleared Manhattan about an hour ago."

"You got lucky then, ma'am. I just got word that New York has been shut down tight. Couple of days, that city's gonna be a real mess."

"There are soldiers everywhere."

"You bet. Soldiers all over Albany, too. National Guard boys and girls. And they're all totin' live ammunition. I didn't even wait for a load 'fore I cleared out. I'm deadheadin' back to Georgia to look after my family. Don't even try to get into Albany. Stay on 87 and bypass the city. Don't pick up no hitchhikers, neither. Folks is really runnin' scared and they're liable to hurt you for your vehicle. Good luck to you, ma'am. Bulldog sayin' bye-bye."

"Thank you, Bulldog."

Another voice came busting through. A female voice. "Bulldog's tellin' you right, ma'am. You got the Lucky Lady here. Me and my old man been pullin' up in Canada. We're headin' back to Texas now and hopin' we can make it 'fore the shit really hits the fan. . . ."

"Watch that filthy mouth, Lucky Lady," a man's voice cut in. "There is nothing nastier than a profane woman. Under the new order, you can be punished for vulgarity. Read your Bible for guidance."

"Screw you and the horse you rode in on!" Lucky Lady told the interloper bluntly. "Militias is okay in my book—we need them; but the rest of you people are all nuts!"

"You have been warned," the man told her. "The lady who just left New York City—you sound like a decent sort. Are you traveling alone?"

"I have my husband with me. But he's not feeling well."

Jim arched an eyebrow at that.

"Are you a Christian?"

"As if that's any of his damn business," Jim said.

"Just a sampling of what part of the country is in for," Janet replied, then keyed the mic. "I'm afraid I'm a back-slider."

"Too bad. The sword of the Righteous will offer sanctuary to God-fearing men and women."

"Stay away from those nuts, ma'am." Lucky Lady came back on. "They're dangerous."

"Godless road-whore!" the man popped back.

Lucky Lady then proceeded to tell the man where he could stick his righteousness, his sword, his narrow-mindedness, and anything else that might fit.

Janet reached over and turned the volume down on the CB. "I pity the residents of any community where that group takes over . . . no matter how short their reign might be."

"I can't believe any of this is happening. I know it is," Jim was quick to add. "It's just . . ." His words trailed off into silence, broken only by the heated argument on the radio—Lucky Lady was still cussing out the man from the Righteous—and the hum of tires on concrete.

Another voice came on the CB and Janet turned up the volume. "You folks don't have anything to fear from the militias," the man said. "At least not the militias who have joined with us in this fight for freedom."

Lucky Lady and the militiaman got into a discussion about lost rights and lost liberties and freedoms and gun control and overtaxation.

"Relax, Jim," Janet said. "It's always calm after the storm."

"Yeah. Providing we live through the storm."

Fourteen

Janet had stopped alongside the interstate and changed into jeans and denim shirt, carefully packing away her class-A uniform. A half hour later they pulled into the last rest area just south of Albany. The parking lot was nearly full with cars and pickups and eighteen-wheelers, the drivers and passengers gathered together in animated groups. Stationed around the lighted reception area, Jim and Janet could see a dozen or so men and women dressed in military camo and armed with AR-15s or Mini-14s, twenty- or thirty-round magazines hanging from the belly of each weapon.

"Militia members," Jim said.

"Yes. So keep your liberal views to yourself, Jim."

Jim ignored her comment, pointing out two New York State Police units parked in front of the building.

"They might be part of the movement," Janet told him, parking as close to the on-ramp as possible so Don would spot her truck when he pulled in. "Or they might be just standing around listening and staying alive. Come on." She opened her door. "Let's go see what's happening."

The two New York State Policemen did not appear to be terribly happy about being surrounded by armed militia members, but they were doing their best to maintain their composure and field questions.

Jim and Janet stood quietly near the back of the crowd and listened.

"Folks," the man who appeared to be the senior of the two state policemen said, "I'm sorry, but I don't know the answers to most of your questions. The best advice I can give you is to stay put right here until we can get some things sorted out. . . ."

"The police are no longer the central authority figures," a militiaman said, stepping up to stand beside the highway cop. "The militia is in charge."

"Oh, shit!" the other highway cop muttered.

"You have a problem with that, Officer?" the militiaman asked.

"Yeah," the highway cop replied. "I have a big problem with that. Are you people going to work the wrecks on the highways? Are you going to take the calls and handle the criminal investigations? Are you people going to work the domestic disturbance calls, the prowlers, the thefts, the 911 calls? Somebody better tell me what the hell is going on."

"You received a written outline from us," another militiaman said. "All that was made perfectly clear."

"Wait a minute. Just hang on here. We didn't receive jackshit from you people," the senior state policeman said. "Our brass might have received it, but it wasn't passed down to any of us in the field."

The same scene was being played out in dozens of locations throughout the United States.

"Just do your jobs the way you normally would," the militiaman told the highway cop.

"There's going to be lots of people out here on the highways carrying guns," the other cop said. "What about them?"

"What about them?" the militiaman asked. "We don't have any problem with law-abiding citizens keeping arms in their homes or cars . . ." He grinned. ". . . as long as they're good, conservative Republicans."

The highway cop's smile was thin. "What if they're liberal Democrats?"

The militia members standing around the reception area laughed. "Oh, well," the militiaman said with a chuckle. "You can shoot them."

Both highway cops joined in the laughter, thinking that surely the militiaman was joking.

They were wrong.

A prerecorded tape had been played immediately after President Evans' adamant and, to some, arrogant refusal to sit down and discuss the demands of the revolutionaries. The tape was played on shortwave and picked up at dozens of Sword of Righteous and various militia cell locations around the nation. The originating point for the broadcast was Iowa, to throw the Feds off in their electronic efforts to pinpoint the Righteous leader while Baronne himself was settling in at a safe house in upstate New York, about twenty-five miles from the Kincaide lodge.

"To all loyal God-fearing Americans who have joined with me in our crusade to restore this nation to its former greatness: In the name of our Lord God, welcome. The battle has begun. We are now locked in a war for freedom, friends. Freedom from government interference in our day-to-day lives. Freedom from overtaxation without representation. Freedom to send our children to the schools of our choice and know our children are receiving the best education our tax dollars can buy or to exercise our right to educate them at home without government stooges snooping about, telling us what we can and cannot do. Freedom to go about our daily business with the knowledge our children are safe in public schools, free from the dangers of near-moronic street savages wielding guns and knives in the classrooms, often with impunity. Freedom to defend our loved ones, ourselves, our property without fear of arrest, prosecution, or civil lawsuit from the criminal element whose 'constitutional rights' the left-wing extremist elements of the Democratic Party have embraced over the years. Freedom to mete out swift and proper punishment for drugdealers, child-molesters, killers, rapists, and other Godless scum without years of liberal interference, financed by hard-working taxpayers, the efforts of which often results in little or no punishment for those so deserving of society's scorn and justice. We desire, no, we *demand* freedom from those who maintain that homosexuals—those degenerates who twist God's word to suit their own disgusting habits—have the same rights as normal, heterosexual couples and flaunt their Godless perversion in the face of easily manipulated children; those immoral beings who gave this nation the dreadful AIDS disease and now mince and prance about insisting that normal human beings use their hard-earned tax dollars to find a cure for the punishment that God surely imposed upon them for their disgusting debauchery. We are in a battle for our very existence, my friends, indeed, for the survival of the human race!

"My friends," Baronne's voice lowered, assuming a conspiratorial note, "this is a war we must win. We must win it for the sake of our children and for the children of future generations. Indeed, we must win it for God! If we must, we must not hesitate for one second to sacrifice our own lives for the cause. Be brave, be strong, persevere, keep God in your hearts at all times, and we cannot lose. My thoughts and prayers go with you all. Power to the Righteous!"

Don and his family pulled into the rest area about an hour behind Jim and Janet. Shirley and LaShana immediately headed for the rest rooms. Donald was introduced, and it was a silent and mutual I-don't-like-you-either all the way around.

Trouble, Jim thought, releasing the young man's hand. The boy's got a chip on his shoulder the size of a boxcar.

Somebody's going to shoot this punk before it's all over, Janet thought. We not only have a real authority-hater here, but a white-hater as well.

Donald wandered off to the men's room and his father said, "I never saw such a drastic change in a person. When he was in high school, he had as many white friends as black. Had a good outlook on life. Then he went to college and everything changed."

"Maybe he's beginning to see the world as it really is," Jim said.

"I know what you're trying to say, and for the most part, it's crap," Don replied. "A black person has a hard-enough time in this society without developing an attitude. All an attitude is going to do is hurt him. I'll take an upfront bigot anytime over a hypocrite. At least with a bigot you know where you stand. Donald is heading for a fall, and I'm afraid I'm going to be the one to bring him down. He's raised his fists to me a couple of times, and I'm not going to put up with that much longer."

"He's a pretty good-sized young man," Janet observed.

Don smiled. "I boxed in high school, Janet. Then turned pro at eighteen. I had twenty fights as a middle-weight. I won nineteen of them, fifteen by knock-out. That money helped me through college and made life a lot easier for my parents."

"I never knew that, Don," Jim said.

"Well, I had enough sense to realize that I was never going to be a real contender. I quit the ring just before I met Shirley. If Donald lays down another challenge to me, I'm going to teach him a hard lesson."

Don raised his fists, and for the first time, Jim noticed how big and flat-knuckled they were. Fighter's hands, he thought. And the man is definitely in good shape.

Janet smiled. "I think you just might be the one to teach your son how the cow ate the cabbage."

"Interesting expression," Don said. "Southern collo-quialism, right?"

"Deep south. Born and reared. Excuse me. I'll be back in a minute and we'll head out." Janet walked off toward the ladies' room.

"She's worked hard to remove all traces of an accent from her speech," Don said.

"You've found out more about her in two minutes than I have in three months," Jim replied. "And I've found out more about you in two minutes than I did in all the years you've worked in the office."

"I guess most of us have something in our past we don't talk about. For one reason or another."

Two pickup trucks came roaring past, and a burst of automatic weapons' fire coming from the beds of the trucks sent both men to the ground and the small groups of people standing around the rest area scrambling for cover.

"Shit!" Don muttered, spitting out grass and dirt. The pickups had sped on past and the night became quiet. "Until this minute I guess I never really believed any of this was true."

Jim rose to his knees and, in the dim light coming from the reception building, looked at the grass stains on his hands and then at the people who were getting up from the ground and stepping out from behind whatever cover they could find. No one appeared to be hurt. "I wonder what that was all about?"

"Punks," Don said, pushing himself off the ground. "Goddamn punks with guns."

"Those weren't our people!" one of the militiamen shouted. "Our people wouldn't do anything like that."

"Probably a bunch of goddamn niggers," someone said in the darkness. The hate in his voice was clear.

Jim and Don exchanged glances.

"Or a bunch of goddamn yankee rednecks," another voice countered. The accent was mid-south and probably came from one of the dozen or so truck drivers who had sought sanctuary at the rest area. "Down where I come from, we call those type of people *white trash*."

"I will certainly agree with that," Don said in a voice loud enough to carry to several other groups of people who had bellied down on the ground.

Most of them laughed and nodded their heads in agreement.

Janet returned with Shirley just as the men were getting up from the ground. Donald and LaShana were walking behind them. "Everybody all right?" she asked.

"Damn racist whites," Donald said before either of the men could speak, his voice thick with ill-concealed anger. "I think it's time for our own revolution to begin."

"You'd better get your head screwed on straight, boy," Don told his son.

"Maybe it's you who doesn't have his head on straight!" the young man popped back at his father.

"Damn right, bro!" A voice sprang out of the night. Several young black men stood off to one side.

"Who the hell asked you?" Don snapped at them.

"Nobody, brother. But it's time for all African-Americans to stand up and be counted. Unless they're Uncle Toms or oreos. Which one are you?"

Don balled his fists. "Why, you goddamn punk! I . . ."

Shirley touched his arm. "Come on, honey. Let it alone. We've got to get out of here. Come on."

"She's right, Don," Jim added. "Let's roll. We've got a long way yet to go."

"Right," Donald spoke. "Let's run off and avoid the real fight. We'll certainly get a lot accomplished doing that."

Don whirled around, facing his son. When he spoke there was menace in his voice. "Get in your car and don't you ever lip off to me again. Move!"

Father and son faced each other in the recently gunfire-shattered night, both trembling with anger. Donald wanted to say more, but he had never seen his father quite this furious. He turned and slowly walked to his car, his girl-friend beside him. At his car, he paused and said to his father, "It's not over."

"Get in the damn car!" Don shouted.

For a few moments, it looked as though father and son might physically tie up right there in the semi-darkness of the rest area. Finally, with a sigh of resignation, Donald got into his car and slammed the door. LaShana hurried to jump in the passenger side.

With Janet and Jim in the lead, the three-car caravan headed out.

"Do we really know what we're doing and where we're going?" Shirley asked once they were back on the road and heading north.

"We're doing the right thing," Don replied, his voice somewhat calmer. "As to where we're going, well, we're not alone in that."

"What do you mean?"

Lori sat silent in the bask seat, listening.

"The entire nation is racing toward the unknown," Don said. "And now I've got a stranger for a son."

Lori wept silently, mist-filled eyes staring out into the darkened landscape as they swept past.

Fifteen

There were no more incidents on the way to the Adirondacks, and it was midnight when the caravan reached the Kincaide lodge. The strain of the past eight hours had taken its toll and the group was not long in hitting the beds. Jim had tried calling LaBarre from the small town not many miles from the lodge, but had not been successful in reaching the caretaker.

"I wonder why, if this plan is so carefully thought out," Jim mused, "they haven't disabled the phone system?"

"Too many people have cell phones now," Janet told him. "What would be the point?"

"Always one jump ahead of me, aren't you?" Jim observed.

"Only in some areas, baby," Janet responded.

Shirley was furious about LaShana's brazenly sleeping with her son, but Don told her to cool it. The situation was tense enough without her adding to it.

Jim was the first one up the next morning. After showering and shaving, he put on a pot of coffee to drip and then stepped outside in the murky light between night and day to do a walkabout on the edge of the cleared land. It had not rained since the last time he'd been up—less than a week back—and he could tell that several people had been prowling around the lodge. Jim was well aware that it was not only his tracking skills that were rapidly returning to him, but all his skills as a woodsman. He was somewhat amused at the thought, for he had been certain he had put all that behind him.

Standing at the edge of the timber, looking about him in the quiet mist of early morning, he became aware of something else, too: The thought of people skulking and snooping about on the property infuriated him. He was sure it had been LaBarre and some of his friends—Janet had told him she was certain that LaBarre belonged to a local cell of the Sword of the Righteous—but if she were correct in that assumption, what were they doing? LaBarre had a key to the lodge, so why snoop like thieves in the night?

Jim inspected the concrete-block building that housed the power generator: The new lock was still in place and everything was as he had left it.

He was sitting down in the den drinking his first cup of coffee and listening to the occasional faint sounds of the lodge when Don ambled in, yawning and stretching. Jim pointed him toward the kitchen and while his friend was pouring a mug of coffee, Jim clicked on the TV and positioned the satellite for a New York City station.

A harried newscaster who looked as though he'd been up all night was reporting that conditions were rapidly approaching chaos in the city. Several looters had been shot and killed by troops; a dozen more had been wounded. New York was now sealed off, no one entering or leaving; the only vehicles allowed in were trucks transporting food; the newscaster didn't know it, but that was about to come to an abrupt halt.

Janet walked into the room, coffee cup in hand, just

in time to catch the last bit before the station went to commercial. "Now we'll see just how terrible a guerrilla war is," she said, sitting down beside Jim. "If everything goes as we theorized, the tunnels and bridges will be next to go."

Jim set his cup down on the heavy, rustic coffee table, scarred from many years of cigarette and cigar burns. "If you people knew all along what was going to happen, why didn't you warn the government?"

"We tried. They wouldn't listen." Janet took a sip of coffee, grimaced, and rose to go into the kitchen for more sugar.

The announcer cut into a commercial. "I've just received word that several bridges connecting Manhattan have been rocked by explosion. We have our Eye-in-the-Sky helicopter over one of the bridges now. What's going on, Chick?"

"The Williamsburg, Brooklyn, and Manhattan bridges have sustained some structural damage from heavy charges of explosive," the airborne reporter said. "Even from as far up as we are, I can tell the bridges have been weakened. Wait a minute! Thick smoke is pouring from the Manhattan side of the Brooklyn-Battery Tunnel. The tunnel may have also sustained some damage. We're going to set down at the Manhattan Heliport and work our way over there. We'll get back to you. Jesus Christ!" the reporter hollered. "I can see smoke pouring from the Holland Tunnel, and there is smoke drifting up from the vicinity of the Lincoln and Queens-Midtown tunnels. Hold on. I'm getting a lot of chatter. Yes. Damnit, get down lower." A few seconds passed. "My radios are going nuts. My God!" he suddenly exclaimed. "Oh, my God. We've just been told that the police are closing both the Lincoln and Queens-Midtown tunnels due to explosion-damage. Yes. The Brooklyn-Battery Tunnel is being closed as well. Look, we're being waved away by Army units. We've got to get out of this area. Those people mean business. We'll get back to you."

"Right on schedule," Janet said.

"I wonder how they got the explosives planted on the bridges?" Don mused.

Janet shrugged. "Oh, construction crews, painters, bridge-repair crews, cops, all members of the Sword of Righteous movement. They probably planted the charges weeks back. The explosives were detonated electronically."

"But why?" Don persisted.

Janet sipped her coffee, her face impassive. After a few heartbeats, she said, "To create confusion and panic and just to show the government the revolutionaries can operate with near impunity. The very best, or worst, depending on your point of view, of the tactics of the IRA, the Viet Cong, the Hamas, and a dozen other guerrilla groups have now reached America's shores."

"So what's next?" Jim asked.

Janet looked up from her coffee cup. "For a time we were all in disagreement on that. Then it came to us like the turning on of a light bulb. After the revolutionaries have had their fun . . ." She waved at the muted TV set and the frantic New York City news commentator. ". . . fun being relative to one's state of mind, of course, the small- to medium-sized towns will be next. They'll disarm the police and enforce their own laws. It's about to get real tough on the criminal element. If the government wants to send troops in to reclaim the towns, then it will turn into a game of cat and mouse."

"What do you mean?" Don asked.

"Hearts and minds," Jim said. "Win the hearts and minds of the people, and the rest is easy."

Janet slowly nodded her head. "Exactly. It won't work as easily here as in Southeast Asia, hut enough Americans will go for it to tip the scales." She held up a hand. "It's going to be interesting. But you wait and see, gentlemen: Before this is all over, the bulk of the militia will be fighting against the members of the Sword of Righteous and other small, off-the-wall, super-religious groups that will begin to surface. The militia won't be fighting for the government, but rather against the strict Biblical dictates of the ultra-religious right. If our leaders are smart—which they aren't—they'll keep control of the cities and let the various factions fight it out among themselves. But they won't do that. They'll send troops in; the small teams of revolutionaries will pull out, and the troops will find nothing—classic guerrilla warfare. While the troops are trying to sort things out in the town that managed to sound the alarm, another team of insurgents, fifteen or twenty strong, will be striking at a town a hundred miles away and the first team will have gone hard underground. Big governments, using conventional warfare tactics, just can't win guerrilla-type war. And the troops are going to get very weary of it, very quickly. After all, these are Americans they've been ordered in to fight: Cousin John and Uncle Ralph and Brother Bill and Aunt Myrtle and men and women they grew up with, friends and neighbors, classmates and people who sit next to them in church and high school football and basketball games—and don't forget brother against brother, sister against sister, and father against son." She looked out the front window of the lodge at the peaceful woods.

"In a way, I'd like to be out there right now, just watching it all happen."

She wouldn't have had to travel far, for every town within a fifty-mile radius of the Kincaide lodge had been taken over by members of the Sword of the Righteous and militia members working with them. Most of the towns had only a small police force, and in nearly every locale, the militia or the Righteous had members already on the police force or in the sheriff's department. In every case, take-over was accomplished without a shot being fired.

By noon of the first full day of the second revolution on America soil, from Maine to California, Michigan to South Florida, hundreds of communities—almost all of them towns with fifteen-thousand population or less— suddenly found themselves policed by para-military groups.

And with the exception of the nation's larger cities, life went on pretty much as usual: Stores opened for business and people reported to work. Why not? That was Don Harris or Bill Smith or Jim Perkins or Mattie MacClusky or Jane Simpson standing there on the corner holding that assault-style weapon. Known 'em all my life. Hell, they damn sure can't do any worse in runnin' things than that mess we've had in office for fifty years. Give 'em a chance to show what they can do.

Not everyone was all that happy to see the militia take over. It was guess-timated that approximately fifty per-cent of the American people, while perhaps not happy with the system of government in place, still thought it was the best going on the planet. But those people who didn't like the militia's taking over didn't have much choice in the matter now: The militia and their supporters were heavily armed, well organized, and ready to fight and die for what they believed in.

By noon of the second day, it was clear even to the most optimistic that the government was rapidly losing control. Radio and TV stations in nearly all the small- to medium-sized markets had been seized by the insurgents; any op-ed pieces written by left-leaning columnists were deleted from newspapers and editors were warned to be *very* careful as to what they printed.

Military leaders, while not stating it openly, were impressed by the organization and discipline of the revolutionaries. It was, so far, a bloodless coup. Not one person had been killed . . . and that was nothing short of miraculous in a nation the size of the United States.

"It proves that God is on our side!" Dr. Gene Baronne—as he was now being referred to—proclaimed in a nationwide radio broadcast on the evening of the second day.

"God has chosen us to lead this nation out of the smoking evil pits of debauchery and immorality and degeneracy. God has, indeed, smiled on us. He has touched us all with His approving hand. And this victory proves to me there is no clearer sign that we are His chosen people.

"We have been forced to wander in a stinking wasteland not of our choosing for decades while the Godless in power jeered and heaped scorn upon us for our beliefs. Just as His Son, we the faithful have worn a crown of thorns and suffered for our faith; we endured.

"But the fight has just begun, my friends. We must now begin the purge of government; we must search out and destroy the Godless who have brought this nation to the edge of Satan's abyss. We must now seek out and obliterate all vestiges of Sodom and Gomorrah.

"Burn the filthy books and movies, seek out and lock the doors to the raucous dens of lust and overindulgence.

"Those who lust after their own sex and who carry the curse of Satan must be found and confined. They must be kept from contaminating our innocent young.

"To gather strength for the next phase of the battle, my friends, we must swell the temples of God. We must all lift our voices and let songs praising His glory fill the skies with a joyful noise. Victory is not yet ours, but it is close. Join with me now in a moment of silent reflection before we once more gird our loins and prepare to do battle with evil . . ."

"That guy," Jim said, after finding his voice through near total astonishment, "is nuts!"

"Nuts he may be," Janet replied, "but he's got hundreds of thousands of people throughout America and Canada on a holy crusade. That's not bad for a man who never finished the eighth grade."

"I thought he was a Ph.D," Don said.

Janet shook her head. "He paid twenty-five dollars for his minister's diploma. He got the advertisement from the back of a men's magazine back in the early 1960s. But . . ." She held up a warning finger. ". . . he knows the Bible from Genesis to Revelations. Don't sell him short on that."

Jim grimaced. "His own, ah, peculiar interpretation of the Bible, one should say."

"Of course. I'm told the Good Book is open to dozens of interpretations. I mean, what the hell? Do you know of anyone who ever plucked their own eye out?"

Sixteen

By noon on the third day, the government had still not determined how to deal with the revolutionaries. Both houses of Congress and about fifty percent of the American public agreed that the military should be used to bring about an end to this insurrection, but the questions that begged to be answered were how and where to use the troops.

Hundreds of towns across the nation were now under the control of militia members and citizens sympathetic to one degree or another with the militia movement. The active militia members were arming any adult American who so desired as fast as they could procure arms.

Train and truck traffic were blocked into the nation's largest cities with the exception of food for children and food specifically earmarked for nursing homes and Red Cross centers, the centers ordered to deliver the food to the elderly.

Everybody else could go to hell . . . especially in New York City, that bastion of liberalism and home to the American Civil Liberties Union, so despised by many militia members—although they would have been surprised to learn that the ACLU would have come to their defense on many of their beliefs, had they but asked.

Every National Guard unit in the nation was ordered

mobilized, but many members refused to show up for duty. Many of those who did report to the local armories were adamant in their refusal to take up arms against friends and neighbors.

But there was developing one small hitch in the take-over: Now that the militia members had control of much of the United States, they didn't know what the hell to do with it.

"You sure you know how to use that pistol buckled around your waist, James?" the caretaker asked Jim.

Jim was standing on the porch of the lodge, LaBarre on the ground. Several members of the local cell of the Righteous stood with him.

"I know how to use it, LaBarre," Jim told the older man. "Don't worry about that. What do you and your . . . ah . . . friends want?"

"We're lookin' for a couple of people. Thought they might be here."

"I have several of my friends from the city here with me, but I don't think you're looking for them."

"Yeah. We got eyes everywhere, James. We seen the nigger family drive through town. That's another reason we're here: To tell you them folks ain't welcome in this part of the country. If you know what's good for you, you'll get 'em out of here."

Jim let that sink in for a few seconds before he blurted out, "Phil, that is about the dumbest goddamn thing I believe I ever heard of. But it's certainly on a par with what I now know is your level of intelligence." Ignoring the flush that suddenly sprang up to color LaBarre's face,

Jim asked, "Any other group of people included in this, ah, purge of yours?"

"Jews and queers. You probably know a bunch of them perverts."

Jim stood looking down at the man—in more ways than just from the height of the porch. "These people you're looking for . . . who are they?"

"Man and his wife. Pat and Claire Monroe. He's wounded. They give us the slip. They're in these woods somewheres. If you know where they are, you best tell us."

"Wish I could say I'm sorry, Phil, but I'm really not. I can't help you. I don't know who they are or where they are. Are they black or Jewish?"

"Neither. Worse. Government spies."

"FBI?"

"That's right."

"You shot two FBI agents?" Jim could not keep the astonishment from his voice.

"Claire wasn't an agent. But she's married to a government informant, so that makes her just as bad."

Before Jim could reply, a car turned off the gravel road and onto the driveway, pulling up and stopping in front of the lodge. Behind him, the screen door opened and Janet joined him on the porch, followed a few seconds later by Don and Shirley. Jim watched as Dr. Tom Durant, a long-time friend of his father and one of the most respected men in the area, stepped out of the car and stood beside LaBarre. The doctor was dressed in camo BDUs, a 9mm holstered at his waist. Jim did not know the two men with him.

"James," the doctor greeted him. "Good to see you. You're looking well. You got out of the city just in time;

conditions are getting desperate in there—so I'm told. It's a good thing you decided to listen to Major Shaw."

Janet's eyes narrowed at that, the only visible sign the man's words had shaken her.

"Dr. Tom," Jim said, greeting the man with the only salutation he'd ever heard anyone use.

The doctor turned his attention to Don and Shirley for a few seconds, then returned his gaze to Jim. "If your friends would like to leave now, James, I can guarantee their safety clear of this area. If they wait much longer . . ." He shrugged his shoulders.

"They're my guests. When we decide to leave, we'll all leave together."

"That's your decision to make, of course," the doctor replied. His smile was gone and his voice had turned flat. "Most of the Africans in this area have already been persuaded to leave. I'm sure that before long those few remaining will see the futility of staying and leave as well."

"Where are they going, sir?" Shirley asked.

"They're just leaving," the doctor told her, his tone decidedly unfriendly.

"What about their homes and businesses?" Don asked.

"A small price to pay for their safety, don't you think?"

"Dr. Tom," Jim said, "you can't just drive people from their homes. This . . . ah . . . situation can't last forever. The people will return. What happens then?"

"If they are stupid enough to do that, they will return to nothing, James. There is nothing for them to return to. In a week, if they return, they will find only a vacant lot. They . . ."

The screen door slammed open, banging against the

outside of the lodge. Donald stormed out onto the porch, a pistol in his hand. "You white son-of-a-bitch!" he screamed at Tom. He leveled the pistol at the doctor.

Jim jumped at the youth, knocking the pistol to one side. He hit Donald once, a hard, short right fist to the jaw that addled the young man and put him down to his knees on the porch floor. The pistol discharged, the bullet hitting nothing but air as it screamed off into the timber. Jim twisted the pistol from Donald's fingers and straightened up.

Janet had jerked a 9mm from behind her belt. She stood facing the men, the muzzle of the Beretta steady on Tom's chest.

"The Negro race is emotional," the doctor said, his voice calm. "Whenever they are faced with crisis, they will invariably revert back to their jungle heritage. I have always maintained it will take another three or four centuries of intense education for them to reach the mental stability of the Caucasian. I believe what just occurred proves that."

"The only thing it proves," Jim said, holding the snub-nosed .38 he'd taken from Donald, "is that you are a bigoted fool. Now get off this property and stay the hell off of it."

"Even though that young Ubangi there just tried to kill me, James," Durant said, "my offer of their leaving safely still stands. Until this time tomorrow. Then we will escort them off, and you and Major Shaw with them. You've been warned."

Tom Durant spun around and walked back to his car. He got in the back seat. The two men with him got into the front and the car faded down the road.

"Get out of here, LaBarre," Jim told the caretaker. "And don't come back."

"Oh, we'll be back," LaBarre said. "You can bet on that." He looked at Janet. She had lowered the big Beretta, taking it off cock and holding it to her side. LaBarre's smile was not pleasant. "I'll deal with you personal, you godless whore!"

"Carry your mouth and your skinny ass on out of here, mister," Janet told him. "Right now."

Phil LaBarre and his friends walked slowly back to their vehicle and pulled out, but not before giving those on the porch some very dirty looks.

Jim turned to Donald. "You just about got us killed, boy."

"Don't call me *boy!*" Donald snapped back.

"It's just a figure of speech, Donald," Jim said. "Nothing racial was meant by it."

Don's fuse was hard to light and slow burning, but his temper had reached critical mass. "Goddamn you, Donald!" he yelled at his son. "Where in the hell did you get that gun?"

There was no back-up in Don. He faced his father nose to nose. "I bought it from a guy at school. Somebody in this family has to have the courage to be proud of being black and to stand up to this racist, oppressive government—you damn sure don't!"

Don's eyes narrowed dangerously. "You think I'm ashamed of being black, boy?"

"You want to be white so bad you stink of it!"

"I refuse to listen to this," Shirley said, and walked back into the lodge. Lori, standing by the open door, followed her mother into the den. The door slammed behind them.

"Donald," father said to son, "you are a damn fool!"

"Don't call me Donald. I've converted to the Muslim religion. My name is Ali Muhammed Akbar."

Don laughed at his son, a sound totally without mirth. "Not and stay a part of this family."

"That is easily rectified, Father!" Donald, or Akbar, spat the words at his father.

Don seemed to relax. He took a step back, a faint smile on his lips. "All right, go ahead. I won't stand in your way. But know this: When you leave here, rejecting the family name, you are forever turning your back on us. Now, knowing that, if you still want to leave, then get gone!"

Before the rift between father and son could widen, Jim called, "Something is moving at the edge of the timber. Looks like a man and a woman."

Don glared at his son. "We will continue this."

"Anytime," the son popped back.

Janet was off the porch and running toward the couple just exiting the deep timber. The woman was struggling to support the man, who was obviously badly hurt. Jim and Don were right behind Janet.

"Got to be the couple Durant was talking about," Don said, running alongside Jim.

"Yeah," Jim replied. "Now we've really drawn a line in the dirt."

Both the injured man and his wife collapsed just as the trio reached them.

Kneeling down, Jim could see the man was conscious. "Take it easy, we're friendly."

"That would be . . . a welcome change," he gasped.

"Are you really FBI?" Don asked as Jim opened the

man's shirt and looked at the wound. It was low on one side, and the exit hole was ugly but was not a bleeder.

"Yes. I am. My wife . . . is on loan from the state department."

Jim helped the man to his feet while Don and Janet gently lifted the exhausted woman to her feet and they slowly made their way toward the lodge.

"I know who you are, Mr. Kincaide," Pat whispered. "Your father was up to his eyeballs in the militia movement."

"That doesn't surprise me," Jim said. "But for him to be involved in something like the Sword of the Righteous sure does."

"Oh, he wasn't involved with them in any way." Pat signaled for a stop and looked at Jim. "He found out about them and was going to come to us with that information. They killed him."

Seventeen

The noon deadline set by Dr. Tom Durant passed and no action was taken against those in the lodge. There had been no more harsh words between Don and his son—no words of any kind had passed between them—but the young man had not left the lodge and he had wisely made no further mention of his converting to the Muslim faith.

Janet had produced a first aid kit that would have been the envy of any medical doctor and had skillfully cleaned out the bullet wound on the Bureau man. She had him taking antibiotics several times a day to fight any infection.

"Where did you learn about medicine?" Jim asked her.

"Fort Sam Houston," she told him. "Pat was lucky. The bullet didn't hit anything vital; and if we can keep infection from setting in, he'll be all right. If that had been a .45 round, he'd be dead."

Jim checked his watch. "I think I'm going to take a look around in the woods."

Her eyes were steady on his face. "You know they're out there, waiting for us to make a move."

"I know it."

"Have you finally accepted the seriousness of the situation?"

"Yes," he said softly. "Took me awhile, though."

"And you're still going out there?"

"Yes."

"Get a rifle for me out of the gun room, Jim. One with a scope on it."

He handed her the keys to the outer door and told her the combination to the gun vault. "You pick the one you like. I'm going to change clothes."

By the time Jim had changed, Janet was sitting by the sliding doors at the rear of the lodge. She had chosen a Remington bolt action in .30-06 caliber. She looked up at him. "I'm going to assume this thing was sighted in at a hundred yards. You stay close to the edge of the timber so that red-and-black checkered shirt of yours will stand out. If you get into trouble, anyone wearing anything else is going down."

Jim smiled. "I feel better already."

She met that with a frown. "I still think it's a dumb move on your part."

Jim checked the Beretta 9mm and stuck it back into the holster attached to a web belt. The others stood in silence in the huge den and watched him pull out a long-bladed hunting knife and gently test the edge with a thumb, then carefully slip the razor-sharp knife back into leather.

"Why are you doing this, Jim?" Don asked. "It's dangerous and unnecessary."

"Nobody orders me off my own property, Don. I've got that much of my father in me." He looked at Janet. "I'll be back in about twenty minutes."

"I'll be here."

As Jim slipped out the rear of the lodge, he heard Don say, "This is so out of character for him. . . ."

The rest of Don's statement was lost as Jim strode away from the lodge toward the timber. He did not hear the snick-snick of the bolt as Janet chambered a round. His eyes caught sudden movement just at the edge of the timber and knew it was no animal. "Assholes," Jim muttered, his temper rising. He carefully fought back the anger and let a coldness wash over him, a coldness he had not felt in a quarter of a century.

Different terrain, pretty much the same situation, he thought as he approached the timber.

Except now I'm much older, a full step slower, and should be a lot wiser, he added silently.

He had pinpointed where the movement he'd detected had stopped: A man wearing cammie BDUs. Jim suddenly leaped forward in a burst of speed and ran into the timber and into the startled watcher, who was just rising up from a crouch. He knocked the man sprawling. Jim reached down, picked up a wrist-thick branch that had fallen to the ground, and whacked the guy on the head. The branch was rotten and exploded on impact, not doing much damage to the guy's noggin. But the unexpected attack did catch the man off-guard.

"Help!" the cammie-clad man hollered, trying to scurry away, much like a big bug.

Just for a few seconds, Jim entertained the thought that the man resembled a huge, land crab . . . and was just about as ugly.

Jim reached down, closed a hand around another fallen branch, and gave the man a good solid whack across his ass. The man let out a bellow of fright and some pain, Jim was sure, for this branch was not nearly as rotten as the first one. Jim smacked him on the back of the head and the man fell forward on his face, addled.

Jim turned and saw a second man come charging through the timber, weapon held high across his chest. Jim stepped to one side in the tiny clearing just as the man came within swinging distance.

He let him have the branch right across the face. The blood spurted as the branch broke cartilage and flattened nose. The man dropped his assault rifle and hit the ground, both hands to his bleeding, busted beak and hollering in pain.

A third man appeared, his face dark with anger. Janet's rifle barked from the rear of the lodge. Bark was bullet-torn from a tree, the tree fragments splattering into the man's face. He howled in pain and put one hand to his suddenly bloody cheek and jaw. Jim stepped in and jammed one end of the branch into the man's belly. The air whooshed out of him and he doubled over in agony, dropping his rifle.

Jim picked up the Ruger Mini-14, checked it, and backed up. "All right," he told the three men. "Get up. And don't think I won't shoot."

"Your ass is in deep shit now, Kincaide," the first man sputtered.

"Shut up and move toward the house," Jim ordered.

"I don't think so, candy-ass," a voice said from off to one side. "I think you're a dead man."

Jim turned and fired without even thinking, pulling the trigger several times. The .223 rounds took the man in the belly and chest, knocking him backward, a surprised look on his face. He sat down heavily and died, his mouth open and his eyes staring in utter disbelief that this could happen to him. It was a look Jim had seen many times in 'Nam: Death always happens to somebody else. It can't happen to me, never does in the movies.

Jim's world suddenly lost nearly all hues, becoming almost entirely black and white, with only a slight tinge of gray around the edges. He stared at the dead man for a moment, who stared back at him through unseeing eyes, and fought back a wave of nausea that threatened to explode from his stomach. He remembered with vivid clarity, and in startling, sickening color, the first man he'd killed close up and personal in 'Nam. He hadn't recalled that ugly memory in years.

Jim leaned against a tree, closing his eyes for just a second before the puking of the man he'd jabbed in the stomach brought him back. All the color had returned to his world. He took several deep breaths and calmed himself.

"I'm coming out with three prisoners!" Jim yelled. "If any try to run, shoot them!"

"With pleasure!" Janet returned the shout.

"Don!" Jim shouted. "Come out here and gather up these weapons, will you, please?"

"On my way."

Jim heard running footsteps. "Get up, goddamnit!" he told the men.

"I think I'm hurt bad," the man with the busted nose managed to say.

"No, you're not. You have a broken nose, that's all. I assure you, you will live. Unless you piss me off further," he added, putting a deliberate touch of menace in his voice.

"LaBarre told us you were a pussy," one of the men said, looking at Jim.

"LaBarre was wrong."

"Obviously," the youngest of the trio said. "And that

probably isn't the only area in which he'll be proven incorrect."

Jim and Don exchanged glances, Don arching one eyebrow at the statement. The speaker did not come across as a wild-eyed fanatic, but rather as a man who had completed some level of higher education.

"Get up," Jim told the men. "Move toward the house. And don't even think about running."

"Your ass is gonna be in deep shit for this, Kincaide," the man with the busted nose said.

"Right now, you worry about moving *your* ass, mister," Jim warned him.

The younger man smiled at that. He stood rubbing his sore stomach where Jim had hit him with the stick. "Certainly," he said, and started out of the woods toward the house.

"Steve Malone, Frank Booner, and Will Garrnet," Claire said as the group entered the house. Her husband had slept through the entire episode, slowly regaining his strength from the gunshot wound.

"Bitch!" Will hissed at her.

"Whore!" Frank bellowed.

Claire ignored them and looked at the third man. She shook her head in disgust.

"Claire," Steve said. "I was hoping you and Pat would survive the assassination plan. I didn't know anything about it until it was all over."

"I believe that, Steve," Claire said. "I never could understand why you became a part of this . . . insanity."

"It isn't insanity, Claire," Steve countered. "Sometimes you just have to shake hands with the devil and hope you're ahead of him at the finish line."

"I don't agree with that," Claire said, then turned away.

Jim trussed up Garrnet and Booner, checking the knots carefully. He looked first at Claire, then at Steve, sitting quietly in a chair, keeping his hands in plain sight.

"Make him give his word, Jim," Claire said. "And make him swear with his hand on the Bible. He won't break his bond then. He's a Presbyterian minister."

New York City was running out of food.

Trucks carrying produce were being stopped a hundred miles out by the insurgents. Unless the supplies were earmarked by the Red Cross for the elderly and the very young, food and medical supplies for hospitals, pet food, or food for the animals in the zoo in Central Park, the vehicles were diverted.

Chicago, L.A, Detroit, Atlanta, and half a dozen other larger cities were also beginning to feel the food pinch due to roadblocks set up by the reactionaries.

There really was no need for the food cutoff. People in the cities, the vast majority of whom were unarmed, posed no real threat to the insurgents. But the revolutionaries wanted to show the government how easily they could manipulate the country and display their spite, against urban liberalism and political correctness; they were determined to show those in power that once the nation's Heartland was seized, the cities could quickly be forced into compliance.

Slowly, the cities ground to a halt as all fuel shipments were cut off. The revolutionaries had warned the government in Washington that as long as federal troops were not used against them, military convoys would not be bothered.

Naturally, President Evans, acting on the advice of certain members of Congress and his own advisors, many of whom still did not take the insurrection very seriously, ignored the warning. He ordered the National Guard and those federal troops who would follow his orders (in direct violation of the Posse Comitatus Act, passed by Congress just after the first civil war, which bars federal troops from enforcing domestic laws) to clear the roads and deal with the reactionaries.

Bloody civil war was about to splatter crimson all over the lower forty-nine.

Militia commanders, in many areas now acting independently from those members of the Sword of the Righteous, sent urgent messages to Washington. "We are in control and have virtually stopped the crime wave that prior to our intervention had threatened to strangle this nation. We have harmed no innocent people. If you send federal troops in against us, we will be forced to resort to violence against them."

Units of federal troops—those that would go—and National Guard units were ordered to retake the nation.

The second revolutionary war to be fought on American soil was only heartbeats away.

"What about the body in the woods?" Don asked. "Shouldn't we . . . ah . . . do something about him?"

"Ross Pelley," Steve said. "The second team was due to relieve us in an hour. They'll take care of the body."

"Why don't you shut your big mouth, Malone?" Will snarled at him from across the room.

"You open your mouth again without being asked, and I'll gag you," Jim warned the man.

"A car just turned off the road and is coming up the

drive," Shirley said. "Looks like three . . . no, four people in it."

"Now what?" Jim asked, walking to the window. "Oh, boy." He frowned as the car stopped in the circular drive and the passenger-side door opened.

"Do you know that woman?" Shirley asked.

"Yes. Unfortunately," Jim said. "That's my ex-wife, Cynthia. And the kids, James and Pam. And that's Cynthia's husband behind the wheel, I suppose."

Janet, still carrying the rifle, took a look. She smiled at the expression on Jim's face. "My, my! It's going to be old home week, Jimmy."

"Very funny. Remind me to laugh about it when this is all over." Jim opened the door and stepped out onto the porch. "Cynthia. You're looking well."

The woman frowned up at him. "James, I want you to know these past few days have been horrendous. We're all simply exhausted. There are people with guns all over the place. Horrible people. What is going on, James? Well, get out and say hello to your father, kids! Louis, don't just sit there like a statue, get out and see to the luggage. . . ."

"You were married to that?" Janet whispered from the open front door.

"She's changed." Jim's reply was defensive.

"From what to what?" Janet asked.

Jim sighed.

"Mother," sixteen-year-old Pam Kincaide said, pointing at Janet. "That woman has a gun!"

"I hate guns," Louis said, popping open the trunk.

"Maybe they're only here for a short visit?" Janet whispered.

"Knock it off," Jim said.

"What are we supposed to do out here in the boon-docks?" James, Jr. complained, standing by the car and making no effort to help his stepfather with the luggage.

"Definitely takes after his mother," Janet said.

"I'm sure they've all been under quite a strain," Jim said, feeling obliged to defend his first family.

"And we haven't?" Janet questioned.

"They're . . . well, they . . . Oh, fuck it!" Jim said. "Nothing changes. They're all still a big pain in the ass!"

Janet giggled, an odd sound coming from her. "Gonna be a fun time in the ol' woods tonight."

"You, there, in the house!" a voice shouted from the edge of the timber. "You'll pay for killing Ross!"

"Oh, my God!" Cynthia shrieked, looking wildly all around her. "What was that?"

"It ain't the Welcome Wagon, lady," Janet said.

"Who are you?" Cynthia asked.

"Well . . ." Janet stepped close to Jim and slipped her free hand around his waist. "Introduce us, dear."

Jim closed his eyes and slowly shook his head. This was definitely not going to be one of his better days.

BOOK TWO

They were going to look at war, the red animal—
war, the blood-swollen god.

—Stephen Crane

One

Louis, Cynthia, and the kids had just been introduced all around when the first shots from the woods shattered the glass in windows, exploded the dried heads of stuffed animals on the walls, and sent nearly everybody in the lodge scrambling to the floor.

Don grabbed his rifle and moved to a window. Jim roared at his ex-wife, "Now stay down, goddamnit!"

Jim had given a Ruger Mini-14 in .223 caliber to Don earlier. The man had looked at it dubiously.

"When the time comes, just point the muzzle—that's the little end—in the general direction you want the bullets to go and start pulling the trigger," Jim had told him.

"I know which end the bullets come out of!"

"Let's hope," Jim had replied with a smile.

The bullets hummed and whined and slammed into the walls of the lodge for a full minute, the fusillade causing no physical harm, but doing a good job of rattling everyone's nerves. The wide-screen TV took several rounds, the picture tube exploding.

Don stuck the muzzle of his Mini-14 out the bullet-shattered window and uncorked a full twenty-round magazine in the direction of the woods, cussing under his breath with each pull of the trigger.

During the confusion, Will Garrnet and Frank Booner,

bound hand and foot, hunched and scooted and crawled out of the room and out of the lodge. They fell off the back porch and slowly made their way toward the woods, moving like two crippled bugs.

"Hold your fire!" a voice yelled from the edge of the timber. "Here come the boys!"

"Booner and Garrnet are getting away!" Claire shouted.

"Let them go," Jim said. "It would have been a pain in the butt keeping them here anyway." He glanced at Steve Malone, hunkered down in a corner of the room. "What about you?"

The minister shook his head. "I support the militia movement, but not the Sword of the Righteous. That bunch is too radical for me. I'm glad to be out of it."

"They just dragged Booner and Garrnet into the woods and it looks as though they're pulling out," Janet called. "I think maybe they've had it for this day."

"What in God's name is going on?" Cynthia squalled, sitting up in the middle of the floor. Her face was coated with dust from the exploding animal heads and her hair was disheveled. "What is happening?"

"Revolution," Jim said, his voice seeming unnaturally loud after the din of battle.

"Why isn't the Army in here doing something about this outrage?" Louis demanded.

"Professor Dunlap says the military complex is far too costly to maintain and is vastly overrated." James, Jr. stuck his mouth into it. "He argues that the money would be much better spent on social programs. He says only basically ignorant people join the military anyway."

Jim cut his eyes to Janet. She looked at the butt of her rifle, then studied Junior, several different emotions crossing her face in the course of a few heartbeats. Jim held his breath, certain she was about to butt-stroke his mouthy son . . . and he really couldn't have blamed her had she done just that. He expelled air slowly after she glanced over at Jim and then shrugged her shoulders.

"I want to go home," Pam said. "I don't like it here. I've never liked it here. I hate this place. And I'm hungry, too."

"Spoiled bitch," young Donald muttered, just loud enough for Jim to hear him.

"Let's get the place cleaned up," Jim said, ignoring Donald's words. "Then we'll see about fixing something to eat. I'm a bit hungry myself."

"We're all going to die!" LaShana sobbed. "We're all going to be killed."

Donald put his arm around the girl's shoulders and spoke quietly to her.

"We got you hemmed in now!" A voice sprang out of the woods. "You people ain't goin' nowhere."

"I think that tonight," Jim said after a moment, breaking the shocked silence in the large room, "I will go collect some ears."

"Whatever in the world do you mean, James?" Cynthia asked.

"It means I go out there," Jim replied, jerking a thumb toward the timber that surrounded the lodge.

"Who do you think you are," his ex asked with a grimace. "Rambo?"

Janet smiled sadly. "You never even told her, did you, Jim?"

"No. I never saw the point."

"Told me what, James?" Cynthia demanded.

Jim waved that off. "It isn't important. Look, I suggest

that except for the guards, the rest of you take bread and cold cuts and whatever else we have in the kitchen down to the basement. It's a fortress down there and you'll be safe. . . ."

"Told me *what,* James!" Cynthia insisted, her voice shrill.

Jim turned to her. "I killed a lot of people in Vietnam, Cynthia. I won a lot of medals for killing a lot of people. Most of them I killed from long distance with a sniper rifle. Some of them I killed up close and personal. I killed several with a knife, and one with my bare hands. We were on a silent op—a night mission—and observing noise discipline. So I had to kill him silently. I couldn't get to my knife so I choked the little son of a bitch to death while we were struggling in about a foot and a half of water in a goddamn rice paddy. I can move very quietly at night, Cynthia, and I can kill silently—which is what I intend to do tonight. And when those woods are clear, Janet and I will rig man-traps to kill and maim more people. I don't intend for us to be trapped here for very long. Now, do you have any more questions for me?"

Cynthia's mouth opened, then closed. She shook her head.

"Good," Jim said. Then, remembering how his ex hated to be told what to do, he added, "Now, go help out in the kitchen."

While Jim and his friends were waging their own deadly little war in the woods, the rest of the nation was finally beginning to grasp the enormity of what was taking place around them. Those who were opposed, both politically and philosophically, to the goals of the militia and the followers of the Sword of the Righteous, had begun to realize what a horrible mistake they had made by refusing to compromise with those who leaned to the political right. Had their voices not been so unyielding, so strident, so demanding, and in many instances so sneering and contemptuous, there probably would have been no civil uprising.

At least, that was the opinion of many analysts, sitting in their think-tanks and ivy-covered classrooms, far removed from life's reality. Still others, who occasionally left their lecterns to rub shoulders with Joe and Josephine Six-Pack held to the consensus that due to the makeup of the population, some type of revolution in the United States had been inevitable.

Political pundits and cartoonists and columnists found the right wing great fun to ridicule and caricature and belittle, not knowing (or perhaps caring) they were only adding fuel to the fire. Testosterone levels have a tendency to rise when the views of a certain type of individual are not taken seriously. To many people, ten weapons constitute an appalling number of guns; but to many other people, they do not an arsenal make, and they simply could not understand why others were making such a big deal out of a closetful of guns, none of which had ever spilled a drop of human blood.

Opinions as to what happened raged on, and would for decades, while the dirty little war, as some were calling it, gained momentum.

Jim had dressed in dark clothing and smeared his face and hands with dirt. He had taken everything out of his pockets that would rattle. He had secured his boot laces so they could not snag on anything. There were a few unworldly people in the lodge who thought he was being overly dramatic, but they kept their thoughts private, for even they had witnessed a startling change in Jim Kincaide. The quiet and thoughtful advertising executive was gone, and Don wondered if that person would ever return.

"A lot of those men out there are basically good, decent people." Steve Malone broke his hours-long, self-imposed silence. "I didn't say *all,* but a lot of them."

Jim waved a hand at the bullet-scarred walls of the lodge. "You couldn't prove that by me, preacher."

"My name is Steve. I gave up the ministry last year."

"Why?"

"I lost my faith, my calling."

Janet was standing guard at the rear of the huge den, Don at the front. Shirley was upstairs, at the south end of the lodge; Pat Monroe had insisted he be propped up in bed to watch the north end. Junior and Pam and Lori were in the basement, listening to a radio; Donald and LaShana stayed close together on a couch in the den. Claire was taking a break; Shirley had just relieved her at watch. Louis and Cynthia were sitting in the den, dumbfounded.

"Before I became involved with the militia, then with the Sword of the Righteous," Steve said, "I attended open meetings around the state. My wife and I."

"Where is your wife?" Jim asked as he watched for the sun to sink and the land to darken. As he waited, he slowly sharpened a long-bladed hunting knife.

"She . . . left me last year . . . after I decided to quit the ministry."

"So these . . . meetings convinced you to join others in plotting against the government?" Louis asked, leaning forward.

Jim was not sure exactly what Louis did for a living, other than being involved in some sort of work on the state level.

"Not at first. Because at first most of us thought it was a dandy and quite harmless way to vent our spleens."

"What happened?" Janet asked.

"At first we met openly and were quite vocal in our complaints about the government. Taxes, restrictions, quotas, the whole nine yards; the same things most people gripe about. Then a few months later, a militia organizer came and spoke to us, and most of us liked what he had to say. A militia was formed; they needed a chaplain, and I volunteered."

"Militias should have been outlawed from the very first," Louis said. "Then none of this . . . awfulness would have happened."

"You're wrong," Steve told him. "It might have taken longer, but it still would have happened. As it is, the main body of the militia movement still had to go underground to escape the snooping of the government." The minister looked back at Jim. "We didn't do a thing wrong. We just met and talked—griped mostly. But the government snooped and spied on us. It was infuriating. There wasn't a deadbeat or a bum in the entire organization. We all worked and paid taxes and most of us, at least, were faithful to our wives and good to our kids. We were just ordinary guys. About half the men had served honorably in Vietnam, several were highly decorated; and yet the FBI and the ATF and the IRS were investigating us as possible subversives. At first it was humorous, then it became annoying, and finally we all became determined to stick it out and the devil take the government."

"Grown men running around playing with guns," Louis said, disgust in his voice.

Steve frowned. "Mister, I don't know you, but you're way off base with that kind of thinking. This nation was going to hell in a handbasket and we were determined to stop the downward slide. Or at least try to stop it. That's when a representative of Gene Barrone's Sword of the Righteous entered the picture. . . ."

"And he fed you people a line of crap," Janet interrupted.

Steve nodded "Yes. Spoon-fed us and sucked us right in. He was a talker, all right. He even had me convinced—at first. He spoke of the moral decay of the nation. The disintegrating values. The breakup of the family. He showed us examples of books and music lyrics and actual printouts of conversations taken from chat boards on the Internet and pictures of the filth available to anyone with a computer and a modem. It was . . . disgusting. That's when most of us left the organized militia and joined the Sword of the Righteous."

"Any militia people left in this area?" Jim asked, an idea forming in his head.

"A few. Maybe ten or twelve." He shook his head. "I wish I had stayed with them. Gene Barrone is a huckster, a snake-oil salesman. You can't believe what he has planned for this nation."

"You mentioned something about the militia, Jim," Janet said. "What about them?"

"They just might be our ticket out of here if we could get in touch with them."

"Well, I can give you the phone number of several of them," Steve said. "Terrance Warden was the commander of the local chapter. Still is, I guess."

"What kind of man is he?" Jim asked. The name was vaguely familiar to him, but he couldn't put a face to it.

"He's a nice fellow, but he doesn't have much use for the government. However, he hates Gene Barrone and practically everything the man stands for. And he has even less use for left-wing extremist liberals."

Louis sighed and Cynthia's expression showed her fear.

Jim glanced at Janet. "What do you think about it?"

"It's certainly worth a shot."

Jim looked out the window. The day was fading quickly, the shadows of dusk thickening, and it was a spectacular close of day: The sun was the color of blood. It would be full dark in a few minutes. "See if you can use your cell phone to get in touch with this Warden person. Bring him up to date on all that's happened." He stood up. "I'm going out." He winked at Janet. "I'll be back."

"I'll hold you to that."

Jim sheathed his knife and stood up. "Count on it."

Two

The night brought to light more of Gene Barrone's twisted plans for his concept of a Christian America. Mosques and synagogues were put to the torch all over the nation.

"This is a Christian nation," 'Doctor' Baronne told his followers. "The mumbling of savages and the chanting of greedy moneylenders have no place here."

Baronne had no way of knowing it at the time, but the orders to burn mosques and synagogues further widened the schism between his loyal Sword-of-the-Righteous followers and many of the militiamen who had, most against their better judgment from the outset, joined his movement.

The night also brought massive government troop movement under orders to wrest control of the towns from the insurgents.

Those troops that would go, that is.

As soon as Baronne was notified of the decision to move troops into the smaller towns, he went on the air.

"The government is sending nigger troops against us, just as I told you they would. Team leaders know what to do, do it!"

Of course, the troops being sent in were not solely

black; but at night, with the troops wearing helmets and body armor, it was difficult to tell.

"Our people are going to get bloodied" was the consensus among the military's top brass.

"Those that obeyed orders, that is," came the reply.

The convoy leaders soon found that if they could average five miles an hour, they were doing quite well, for they were having to run a gauntlet of sniper fire every mile of the way. After meeting with disastrous results at the first few overpasses, the commanders had to halt the convoys, send recon people in to secure each and every overpass, making sure there were no snipers, grenade-tossers, dynamite, or Molotov cocktail-throwers, and then move the trucks forward. When the troops did reach their objectives, they found the militiamen were gone, having faded into the night. As soon as the military pulled out, heading on down the road for the next town, the militiamen returned. It was classic guerrilla warfare, cat and mouse.

And it was driving President Arthur Evans nuts.

Evans had never served in the military and knew nothing about strategy or tactics. He could not understand why brute force would not work against these para-military people.

His top brass could have told him why—but Evans never listened to them, except when sending the military all over the world to act as peacekeepers or police in countries the average American had never heard of.

Before the very early evening was over, many of the troops sent into the field were going to become even more disillusioned about fighting other Americans . . . and so were their top brass.

* * *

Steve had told him that many of the men solidly aligned with Gene Baronne's Sword-of-the-Righteous movement were well trained, highly disciplined, and intensely motivated. But some of those in this area who had joined late, although holding strong convictions and believing one-hundred-and-ten percent in what Baronne preached, were poorly trained. The twelve or fifteen New York State militiamen under the command of Terrance Warden, who had become disgusted with Baronne's rantings and ravings and undisguised bigotry and had left early in the game, were highly trained.

But, Steve had warned, Warden's people held the present administration in open contempt, and that was putting their feelings toward President Evans and left-wing liberal extremists mildly.

Jim pushed all those thoughts from his mind as he moved into the timber around the lodge. And again, for about the fifteenth time since leaving the lodge, he questioned why he was doing this. True, his skills in the woods had returned, if indeed those intangibles had ever really left him, but he had to remind himself that he was forty-five years old, not a twenty-year-old in the youthful peak of physical conditioning.

But, he thought, I'm committed, and it's too late to turn back now.

Jim was scarcely fifty feet into the woods, moving quite well, he thought, when the voice reached him.

"Mister, if you had been moving against my people, you would have been dead the instant your boots left the back porch of the lodge."

Jim froze, belly down on the cool ground.

"You probably don't remember me, Jim," the disembodied voice drifted out, "but we played together some as kids. My dad was Bill Warden, the hunting and fishing guide."

Memories came flooding back to Jim, and he pressed his forehead against the ground and smiled. "Guess I'm not as good in the woods as I thought I was, Terry. Steve referred to you as *Terrance*. That threw me off."

"Oh, you're still pretty good in the woods . . . for a city boy. How is Steve?"

"He's all right." Jim crawled to his knees, being careful to keep a tree between himself and where he believed the voice to be coming from. "We were going to call you, Terry. See if you and your people would side with us."

"So I saved you a dime. We've been watching the lodge ever since you arrived. That's a real mixed bag you've got with you, Jimmy."

"I think they're a good bunch. Where are the people who shot at us?"

"Disarmed and tied up and very unhappy with me. Do we step out and shake hands, Jimmy?"

"Sure. Why not?" Jim moved away from the tree to stand exposed, a silhouette in the dark. A cammie-clad man, carrying what appeared to be an M-16, moved out of the brush and began making his way toward him. As he drew near, Jim recognized him immediately, even though it had been years since they were carefree boys, hiking and swimming and hunting together.

The two men shook hands and stood in silence, sizing each other up.

"You're in pretty good shape," Terry said again. "For a city boy."

"I try. You married, Terry?"

"Big time. Five kids. I sent the wife and the two kids

still at home up to some of her relatives in Newfoundland just before the trouble started. You?"

"Divorced. That was my ex-wife and our kids you saw pulling in earlier. And her new husband."

"He didn't look like much."

"You may be right. I think guns frighten him."

"I used to talk to your daddy a lot, Jimmy, 'fore he died." The man frowned. "That's a stupid expression, isn't it? *I talked to him 'fore he died.* How the hell do you talk to someone after they're dead? Anyway, he told me you had turned into a liberal's liberal. I guess he was wrong about that."

Jim shook his head. "Not really, Terry. I vote the liberal democratic ticket. Have for years. But that doesn't necessarily mean a person won't fight when he's pushed."

"I guess it doesn't. Least not in your case."

"You want to call in your men and come on up to the lodge for some conversation?"

"Yeah. I think we better. Sort of clear the air, you might say. I have ten men with me. That's all I could muster on short notice. The rest have scattered to sit things out." Again, he frowned. "That damn Gene Baronne really threw a monkey wrench into matters. He sure had us fooled . . . at least for a long-enough time to foul things up."

Jim decided to let that alone for the moment. "Come on. Let's head for the house and have some coffee and sandwiches."

"Sounds good. Johnny!" Terry called into the darkness. "You pick five men and stay out here. Keep an eye on those Righteous assholes. I'll send relief in a couple of hours."

"OK, Terry," the voice came back. "Will do."

Terry laughed and moved toward the lodge, Jim walking along beside him as the timber permitted, falling behind when brush got in the way. At the timber's edge, Jim shouted, "It's all right, Janet. I'm with a friend. Hold your fire."

"Janet?" Terry questioned.

"Major Janet Shaw. U.S. Army Intelligence. She's all right, Terry. Tough as a boot and good-looking, too."

"Hell of a combination. I guess you trust her?"

"All the way and more."

"All right. That's good enough for me."

In the house, Jim realized then just how tough Terry looked. Like his father, Terry was an outdoorsman, strong on hunting and fishing, and his tan was burned deep and permanent. He wore a .45 caliber autoloader in a leather flap holster, right side, and carried a long-bladed hunting knife on his left side. Terry gave Steve Malone a cool look. "Preacher," he said.

"Terry," Steve acknowledged.

"You trust this hypocritical Bible-thumper?" Terry asked Jim.

Jim waggled his hand, palm down, from side to side.

"Keep it that way," Terry urged.

Terry and the men with him were introduced all the way around, and Shirley and Lori brought out mugs of coffee and a tray of sandwiches. After Terry assured them the outside was safe and secure, the group sat down.

"I'll give you the bad news first," Terry said. He looked at Louis, staring wide-eyed at him. "You got in here just under the wire, mister. The roads were closed shortly thereafter. The park is under hard control of Baronne's people. And you can forget about the Army helping out—at least for a time. The 10th was sent to Albany, Buffalo, and New York City. You're an assistant attorney general, aren't you?"

"That's right," Louis said, surprise on his face. "How did you . . . well, never mind. But let me tell you militiamen something: What you're doing is treasonous. You . . ."

Terry waved him silent. "You won't tell me a damn thing, mister. If I were you, until this mess is cleared up, I'd keep my mouth shut about working out of the attorney general's office. Someone just might decide to shoot you."

"How strong is Baronne, Terry?"

"Thousands of followers, ol' buddy. The Back-to-the-Bible bunch, many of the anti-abortionists, the ultra-hard-right-wingers who want to ban everything that feels good. They are definitely a force to be reckoned with. Baronne's got more kooks and flakes in his organization than the Democratic Party." Terry shook his head. "Well, almost."

"Careful, Terry," Jim said with a smile.

The commander of what was left of the local militia chuckled. "Oh, I just had to say that. It's not often I'm in a room filled with knee-jerk liberals. Tell you the truth, for a couple of years, I had high hopes for the GOP. But as it turned out, there wasn't fifteen cents worth of difference between the two parties. I guess a politician is a politician."

"So what's the plan?" Janet asked.

Terry smiled. "Oh, that hasn't changed at all. We bring the government down, then start all over."

* * *

As night deepened across the nation, mosques and synagogues blazed in mindless fury as Baronne's followers went on a rampage, determined to destroy any house of worship not devoted to Baronne's narrow concept of what that represented. Although Baronne was no lover of the Catholic faith, he knew better than to turn the Catholics against him. Catholic churches were left strictly alone.

When the military convoys started taking unacceptable casualties, they were first ordered to a halt, then ordered back, as the generals realized they were up against a much larger and much more organized resistance force than they had first thought.

To a person, the generals cursed the politicians in Washington who had brought millions of Americans to the point of being forced to take this type of action against their own government.

But they had all suspected it would take something like this to finally open the politicians' eyes.

Army and Marine Corps generals ordered their troops to protect federal buildings, federal property, and federal installations. Navy and Air Force went on high alert against any foreign powers who might decide this would be a good time to launch terrorist attacks against the Great Satan called America.

The consensus among the military leaders was the politicians brought this on, let them handle it. We will not use federal troops against American citizens unless they fire on us in an attempt to seize federal property or attack cities where we have troops stationed. *But you have to give us something in return,* the generals told Baronne's people in secret communiqués. *Let food and fuel shipments into those cities you have sealed off.*

Baronne got the message and agreed. The sniping at military convoys stopped almost immediately, and the food and fuel embargo on the major cities was lifted. A jubilant Baronne canceled all further plans to attack federal buildings.

"We've bought some time," General Coplin told his fellow Joint Chiefs. "If our analysts are reading this right, the militia movement will turn on Baronne's people in a few weeks and this entire operation will shoot itself in the foot."

"At least history won't paint us as the bad guys this time," Admiral Rutherford said. "The idea of firing on Americans is repugnant to me."

"We should have iced Baronne a long time ago." General Max Jordan spoke quietly.

"And let the militia make their move unopposed?" General Pete Knowles jibed.

Max laughed heartily. "Your words, ol' buddy. Not mine."

"Well, it's in motion and working out and we can't stop it now," Admiral Rutherford said. "Even if we wanted to. I had my doubts there for a time. I felt sure that idiot Arthur Evans was going to fuck it up royally. All we can do now is dog the hatch down tight and keep our people clear of it."

"And pray," General Coplin added. "And do so like we mean it."

"It wouldn't hurt for all of us to ask for help from a higher power," General Ashcroft agreed. "This plan could easily backfire."

"Do we have a shooter on the inside?"

"Yes," General Coplin said. "A woman."

"A woman!" Max repeated. "Goddamn!"

"We've used her before," Coplin said. "She's good. She's got balls of brass."

"Try tits," Max said. "To be anatomically correct." Amid the laughter, the Marine shook his head. "God help us all. A damn woman!"

We returned her to Dr. Coblin with ... has been a bit better already. ...

... by the ... Max said. ... 'It ... carefully.' ... and the ... the ... space for what ... Coblin ... us all. A damn weapon.'

Three

Only a few seconds had passed since Terry had calmly spoken about bringing the government down. Those in the den were still staring in open-mouthed shock when Terry's walkie-talkie crackled.

"We've got company, Terry! Half-a-dozen carloads of Durant's men. Dickie reports them coming up fast. One of the men must have gotten away during the firefight here and hoofed it back to town."

"Kill the lights!" Terry said, lunging to his boots. Jim ran to the bank of switches by the front door and plunged the huge room into darkness.

"Let's take the fight to them this time!" Jim called. "We don't want to get trapped here in the lodge."

Terry grinned in the darkness. "OK, Jimmy. You're on. Major Shaw, you don't know these woods, so you ramrod things here in the house, all right?"

"Fine."

"Everybody not at a post start packing up and get ready to move out. You won't be able to stay here any longer. Let's go, boys. Follow us, Jimmy."

"This is insane!" Cynthia shrieked, her voice cutting through the darkness. "This is America. This is not supposed to be happening in America. . . ."

Whatever else Cynthia had to say, if anything, was lost

in the pounding of boots as the men rushed out of the house and hit the ground running for the woods.

"Stay close to me, Jimmy," Terry panted as they ran. "We've got to hit Durant's people hard enough the first go-round to buy us some time."

A man suddenly leaped out of the timber and into the clearing, screaming one word over and over. "Traitors!"

Terry shot the man without hesitation, pulling the trigger on his Colt AR-15 three times. Durant's man stumbled, staggered to one side, then fell backward heavily into the brush.

"Parsons," Terry said. "From over near Potsdam, I think. He was a real jerk."

"Terry!" a voice called from the night. "Defensive line is right where you're standing. They're comin' straight at us. Parsons was about a minute ahead of the pack. He got too anxious, I guess."

"I just solved his anxiety problems, Robbie. All right, pass the word. Let's make their first charge their last one and then get the hell out of here."

"Will do."

"If we get separated, you guys know where to meet."

"Right, Terry. See you in a few minutes."

Bellied down on the ground beside his old friend, Jim said, "I expected a *good luck* or *God Bless America* or something like that before the fight, Terry."

"We'll make our own luck. And America let us down. Heads up. Here they come."

Cold, Jim thought. My childhood friend is all ice inside. And he really feels that his country let him down. Jim knew that a lot of 'Nam vets felt that way, but he doubted that was the reason behind Terry's statement.

Jim glanced at Terry; even in the dark he could detect

a faint smile on the man's lips as he lifted his AR-15. "And here we go," Terry whispered.

Whatever else Dr. Tom Durant's people might have been, they were not fighters. They ran straight into an ambush, and it was a slaughter. Terry's people had formed a U-shaped pocket that quickly became a closed killing circle when all of Durant's people were inside. Jim recognized the guerrilla tactic.

For a few seconds, Jim thought Terry's men were going to kill the wounded and captured. "Relax, Jimmy," Terry told him. "None of us have reached the firing-squad level yet. Although these people," he gestured with the muzzle of his assault rifle toward the prisoners, "would not hesitate to line us up and cut us down."

"Stooges of the government!" a wounded man yelled. "Nigger and Jew-lovers!"

Jim stared at the man. "Do you know these people, Terry?"

"Know them? Hell, yes, I know them. I grew up with them. Went to school with a lot of them. Baronne's people have been brainwashing them for three . . . four years. Now you can see firsthand how effective it's been. You don't yet understand just what Baronne's people are doing and have planned for America. As soon as we get into town, you'll see what I mean."

"Town?"

"Right. We're going to retake the town just down the road and give it back to the people . . . compliments of the militia. With just a few changes," he added grimly.

"Fifteen of us are going to retake an entire town?"

"That's all it's going to take. You'll see."

Every weapon was taken from the captured Righteous members—along with magazine pouches. While Jim was gathering up his people and loading them into vehicles, the prisoners were hauled away in the back of pickup trucks. Jim did not ask where they were being taken.

"How professional are Terry's people, Jim?" Janet asked.

"One hundred percent." He paused. "They've been preparing for this for a long time. You were right, Janet: The militia people are turning against Baronne."

Janet chuckled.

"What?" Jim asked

"Can you just imagine the expression on President Evans' face when he learns that the militia, the very groups he despises so, will be the ones to restore stability to America?" She laughed aloud as they waited for the others to stack their luggage in the trunks of their cars.

"Lady, you have a very weird sense of humor."

Janet did not respond. Instead, she said, "You know, if someone could get close enough to put a bullet in Baronne, I think his organization would fall apart."

Jim had no reply.

"I wonder if Terry knows where Baronne is." Janet mused. "No. I already asked him. He doubts that more than ten people—if that many—in the entire Righteous movement know Baronne's location. Terry said if he knew where Baronne was hiding, he'd kill him himself."

Janet surveyed the grounds from the porch. "Did he now?" she murmured in the darkness.

Jim was the last one to leave the lodge, then only after removing a few more articles from the gun vault. He carefully secured the door to the huge fireproof gun safe, carried the new additions to his personal arsenal out to the front porch, then reached inside and turned out the last lights still burning. He locked the front door and stowed his gear in the truck. Both Terry and Janet had watched him with interest.

"That looks suspiciously like a rifle in that hard case, Jimmy," Terry remarked.

"It is. It's a Weatherby. .300 magnum. Leupold scope."

"Going to do some long-distance shooting?"

Jim looked at his childhood friend. "I just might, ol' buddy. You never know."

"Well, well," Terry said. "The New York liberal has a set of balls after all."

Before Jim could come back with the heated retort that boiled quickly on the tip of his tongue, Terry walked off, chuckling.

"I seem to recall that even as a boy, Terry could get on my nerves at times," Jim said after taking several deep breaths to calm down.

"He certainly doesn't appear to have lost his touch," Janet commented drily, motioning for Jim to get in the truck. "Well, come on. Let's go retake a town."

Jim grimaced as he climbed into the cab and closed the door. "Are you sure you're not related to Terry?"

Laughing at the expression on his face, Janet slipped the automatic transmission into drive and pulled in behind Terry's Bronco.

As Janet drove out of the circular drive to the lodge, Jim said, "I wonder what Terry did with those men he took prisoner."

Janet shook her head. She wore a camo field cap, her short hair tucked up under it. "I'm not so sure I want to know."

"You don't think . . ." Jim let that trail off into silence.

Janet chose not to reply. She shrugged her shoulders and clicked on her CB radio, setting the channel on 39. She glanced at the dash clock. "Did Terry tell you anything about this op?"

"No. But I'm sure he discussed it at length with you."

"I'm military, Jim. He knows I'm going to report in to somebody, and he wants a favorable accounting. Besides—and don't take this the wrong way—he still is not certain which side of the road, so to speak, you're standing on."

"I must remember to thank him for his trust."

"Oh, smooth your feathers down, Jim! Put yourself in his place and think about it before you get all ticked off. You show up here with a bunch of kids and crybaby-adults who don't know which end of the weapon the bullet comes out of. You told him not two hours ago you vote the straight liberal democratic ticket. He's trying to do the right thing—in his mind, at least—all the while knowing he could easily face treason charges no matter what he does."

Jim rode in silence, then nodded his head. "OK. Point taken, Janet."

"This push is coordinated with other militia groups nationwide. At ten o'clock this evening, a hundred towns all over the nation will be wrested from Baronne's Sword-of-the-Righteous movement and returned, more or less, to normal."

"It's the 'more or less' that bothers me."

"Make up your mind, baby," she said flatly. "You can't have it both ways. You're either going to fish or cut bait. Now, goddamnit, which is it?"

There was an edge to her voice that Jim had never heard before. The dark landscape rolled slowly by as the caravan of rebels made their way toward the town. "You want the truth, Janet?"

"That would be nice."

"I'd like for things to be as they were."

"That's not going to happen. Conditions won't ever be as before. This nation is in for a political and social upheaval the like of which its citizens have never before witnessed. Ready your mind for that."

"And pick a side?"

"Very definitely you'd better pick a side. I warned you before about shooting your mouth off concerning your left-wing political views."

"Goddamnit, Janet! I am not a left-winger!"

"You are to the people in the militia movement."

Jim expelled a frustrated breath. "Whole country's gone nuts!"

"The roller-coaster ride has just started, Jimmy. And it's going to be a twisty one, so hang on. Besides, you just want me to reassure you. If you hadn't made up your mind which way you were going to jump, you wouldn't have brought that rifle with you."

"Maybe so," Jim said. He watched as Terry's right-turn signal came blinking on and he pulled off the road. Janet pulled in right behind him and they both got out and joined the crowd gathered around Terry.

"Jump-off time coming up, gang," Terry said. "The town is five miles ahead. Now, all we know for sure is there are about twenty-five of Baronne's people active in the town. I don't know how many converts he's got, but I would guess that surely his people have pulled some over to their side. And it's a pretty good bet we'll have some shooting. When they see us, they'll know that the group sent out to the lodge blew their assignment. So don't take any chances. There are too many of them and too few of us. Roy, you take your bunch and swing around, come in from the north. We'll hit the town from the south and meet at the police station. Good luck. Let's go."

The men who had attacked the lodge the second time had not been carrying radios, so their friends in town would have no way of knowing whether the attack had succeeded or failed. And the attackers, to Jim's mind, had also been very poorly trained. He did not believe, however, that would be the case nationwide.

So, don't worry about nationwide, he thought, as the small convoy neared the town. Worry about your little corner of the world. But there were aspects about this insurrection that bugged Jim. Where was the FBI, some twenty-thousand strong, he suspected? Why weren't they being heard from? And agents from Alcohol, Tobacco, and Firearms, where were they? And federal marshals? Were they all gathering en masse somewhere, planning an attack?

The answer to that was no. The FBI, ATF, and federal marshals were spread out over fifty states. From small three- or four-agent offices to big city offices with a hundred or more agents. But with militiamen and Baronne's people surfacing all over the nation, all organized and heavily armed, the agents could do little except watch and wait. They weren't being paid to engage in suicide missions. The Bureau, the AFT, and, to a lesser degree, the Federal Marshal's service knew that among many militia members, they were not the best-liked people. Most agents decided to sit this one out; besides, there would be plenty to do once the smoke settled and an agreement was worked out between the insurrectionists and the government.

Terry signaled them off the road just outside the city limits. "My informants in town have pinpointed the locations of Baronne's people," he told those gathered around him.

"Why in the hell haven't the people in town, those not affiliated with either group, taken up arms against Baronne?" Jim demanded. "That question has been bothering me ever since this mess started."

"Well, my friend," Terry said, glancing at his watch. "We have a few minutes, so I'll answer your question. Quite simply, the liberals aren't armed; they have no way of fighting either side. They don't like guns. Guns frighten them. If the Jews and the Gypsies in Europe had been armed and organized, Hitler's master plan would never have gotten off the ground and the holocaust would never have happened. Some group of Jews or Gypsies would have shot the little paper-hanging bastard and his vicious circle of friends and that would have been the end of it. Now, that is an oversimplification and I know it, but basically that's it. On the other side of the coin, the conservatives in the towns all over the nation, those that have rifles and pistols and shotguns, are looking at us and saying, 'What the hell? Fifty years of the Democratic Party's fuck-ups sure haven't worked. The nation is in the toilet when it comes to morals, honor, and decency. Crime is running unchecked. Drug-dealers are on every goddamn corner. There is nothing but filth on the television and in the movies. Kids are fucking before they even know what the word means. There is no discipline in the schools; teachers can't teach. Hell, many are in fear for their lives. I'm being screwed out of more money every day when it comes to taxes, and every day I see people who are using my tax dollars to do nothing

but lay up in public housing and breed like rabbits.' "
Terry laughed, a laugh totally void of humor. "You see,
Jimmy, when millions of people are caught between the
devil and the deep blue sea, they want relief. And they
really don't give a damn who provides it."

"We're in position." The metallic words popped out
of Terry's belted walkie-talkie.

Terry clicked the key button twice; a prearranged signal, Jim supposed. "All right, people," Terry said. "Let's
do it."

Four

The main street of the town was deserted. All the streetlamps were burning brightly, but not a store was open for business.

"They know we're coming," Jim said, standing beside Terry in the center of the street.

"Good guess, Jimmy. You got your old in-country instincts back working, eh?"

"All I want is for this crap to get over with and to get back to my office."

Terry glanced at his watch. Two minutes to go. "You make lots of money, Jimmy?"

"Well . . . yes. I do."

"You have tax-deferred retirement plans and smart stockbrokers and all that?"

"Yes, I do," Jim replied, a defensive tone behind the words.

"Average American working stiff doesn't have those advantages. You can go take a client out to lunch and have three martinis and oysters Rockefeller and a juicy steak and tax laws be damned—you'll figure out some way to take it all off your income tax. The rest of us can't do that. Then you can take a cab back to your nice apartment—avoiding whenever possible that mumbling bum on the sidewalk who got his mind all fucked up in

'Nam or in Desert Storm or in Bosnia or some other shitty-assed place where we had no business being." Terry raised a hand and waggled it back and forth. "Aw, Jimmy, the why of what we're doing will be obscured a few years after it's all over. Just like the Civil War. Most people believe it was fought solely over slavery. But those of us who are history buffs, we know that isn't true." He glanced at the luminous hands of his watch. "Talking's over." He raised his voice. "Team B to the left, Team A follow me. The rest of you, stay here and be quiet."

"I can't believe I'm a witness to this armed insanity," Louis said in a hoarse whisper.

"It's kind of exciting," Pam said.

"You're an idiot!" Donald told her. "I hope all these racists kill each other."

Don caught Terry's eye in the semi-gloom and shrugged his shoulders apologetically.

Terry smiled as they walked away, weapons at the ready. "Forget it, Don. I was Seventh Special Forces in 'Nam. My two oldest boys, to use their word, think the military sucks."

"I didn't know you were a green beanie," Jim said.

"Three tours. I got hit on my last one, and that ended my military career. I was there when you won the Silver Star."

They were on the sidewalks now, on both sides of the long and seemingly deserted street. But Jim could feel eyes on him—hostile eyes. He sighed. What the hell am I doing here? A middle-aged man all dressed up in cammie BDUs and carrying a loaded weapon . . .

Movement on the roof of a building across the street

caught his eye and Jim automatically yelled, "Sniper on the roof! Two o'clock!"

The man fired just as Jim went into a crouch, the bullet howling over his head and whining off the brick of a building. Jim brought his AR-15 up to his shoulder and pulled the trigger twice. The dark shape stumbled backward and dropped his rifle. It clattered on the rooftop. The man-shape fell soundlessly out of sight.

"Good shooting, Jimmy," Terry said.

"Yeah." Jim waited for the sickness to flood him. But no nausea came. The town in upstate New York had become a village in Southeast Asia. The man he had just shot was not an American, that was Charlie. Jim really wasn't forty-five-years-old; he was nineteen and full of piss and vinegar. He'd just come back from some R & R in Saigon where he'd spent part of a drunken night dabbing his dauber in a cute little Saigon whore; his ass still hurt where he'd convinced his buddy in the medics to ram both cheeks of his ass full of the Magic Bullet called penicillin as soon as he got back to fight the black crud she might have been carrying around. He couldn't recall the girl's name; hell, he couldn't even recall what she'd looked like. Tiny body and big round eyes and hair as black as night.

"Oh, I love you, Joe. You want me be your number one? I wait for you. I promise. Good girl. You buy me Honda to get 'round on 'til you come back?"

"Jimmy," Terry's voice brought him back. "You and Walt watch the buildings across the street—OK?"

"All right," Jim said in a voice he could not recognize as his own.

"Traitors!" The hard voice sprang out of an alleyway across the street.

"Down!" Terry called just as the artificially lighted night ripped and sparked and flashed with gunfire, the lethal little chunks of lead bouncing and screaming strange songs off the concrete and bricks.

Terry and Jim and the others in their team poured return fire into the dark alley. A long wail of pain greeted the silence after the gunfire had ceased, and only the faint echoes lingered as a reminder of the sudden and violent death that waited in the night.

"Oh, God!" The cry drifted out of the dark alley. "Damn you people to hell! It hurts, it hurts!"

"Shaffer," one of Terry's men called from a doorway where he had taken cover.

"Sounds like him," Terry agreed.

Gunfire suddenly split the night from the other end of the long street. Jim could hear the sounds of yelling.

"Roy's team is mixing it up," another of Terry's team said, no excitement in his voice, and Jim wondered about the lack of emotion.

"Nobody seems to be real excited about this shooting, Terry."

"We've all been gearing up for this for several years, Jimmy. We've known it was coming. What we didn't know was when."

That reply annoyed Jim. "How the hell could you have known civil insurrection was coming?"

Terry laughed. The gunfire at the other end of the street had stopped. "Too many lost liberties for it not to happen, Jimmy. We'll really go into it sometime. But not tonight, not here."

"Terry!" The shout came from across the street and above them. "Is that you out there?"

"Yeah, Cecil! It's me. You all right?"

"I'm OK, Terry. I got Paul with me. Those nuts killed Harry."

"Shit!" Terry whispered. "Harry Webber. One of the city patrolmen. Damn, I hate to hear that. I'm sorry about Harry, Cec. How many men can you muster up?"

"Just me and Paul for now." Terry had spotted the man's location. He was yelling out of a second-story window over a clothing store. "It's a long story, Terry. But I 'spect you know most of it."

"Yeah. I do. OK, Cec. Hang on. We're going to clear this town of Baronne's people."

"The hell you will, you traitor!" The angry voice sprang out of the darkness.

"That's Hal Sweet," the man right behind Terry said. "I got him spotted over there in Barrett's Drug Store."

"Can you take him out, Toby?" Terry asked quietly.

"No problem." Toby's rifle cracked three times. "Shit! I know I got him, but I think I hit him in the throat."

"Breaks of the game." Terry's reply was cold.

"Did Vietnam turn you this hard, Terry?" Jim asked.

"No." Terry answered without turning his head. "This goddamn country of ours did."

Before Jim could reply, a new voice was added to the night. "All right, Terry. You got us boxed. We don't want to lose any more people. We're coming out."

"Come on out, Otis," Terry called. "Just be careful. I'd rather not have any more shooting, but that's your call to make."

"Just take it easy, Terry. Slack off on those trigger fingers. We're packing it in."

"Me and Paul are coming out, Terry!" Chief of Police Cecil Brocato called. "We're armed."

"OK, Cec. Come on. We're both on the same side."

The chief laughed. "More or less."

Terry chuckled. "Yeah," he called. "I hear you, Cec."

The first man to step out into the wide street held his hands high in the air. "Otis Gibson," Terry said. "Big church worker and big shot in the town. He was one of the first to get suckered in by Baronne's bullshit." Terry pointed. "There's Chief Brocato and Paul."

"Where is the county sheriff?"

Terry smiled. "Oh, he's part of Baronne's movement. Baronne's slick, Jimmy. It's taken him years to build his organization and plan all this. And he almost pulled it off."

Chief Brocato and his officer walked up. There were bruises on the chief's face. The men shook hands and Jim and Janet were introduced. Terry studied Brocato's battered face.

"What happened to your face, Cecil?"

"A couple of the Righteous members worked me over some. Phil LaBarre and a guy from over Glens Falls." The town's top cop smiled grimly. "I will settle the score, Terry."

"Be my guest. What's the story here in town?"

"Ed Simpson got killed right off the bat. He come charging out of his house with a deer rifle, yelling and cussing Baronne's people. Tom Durant shot him. Then Frank Stafford holed up in his house for a few hours. They flushed him out. I don't know what happened to him. But I can guess. Mitch Barrow was killed fighting Baronne's bunch. All the fight seemed to go out of the townspeople after that. Then Baronne's people grabbed those two fairies, Guy and Johnny, and hauled them off. God only knows what happened to them. There isn't a minority left in town . . . or a fairy. From what I can gather, the same thing is happening all over America . . . in pockets, that is. Not everywhere."

"Fairies?" Jim asked. "You mean homosexuals?" He was very conscious of Janet's disgusted look aimed at him but chose to ignore it.

"Yeah, Mr. Kincaide. Homos. Queers, swishes, queens. Whatever the hell you want to call them. They're being rounded up and hauled off. I understand from the shortwave radio those that manage to escape the roundup are heading for the cities for sanctuary . . . just as fast as their little footsies can take them."

"How about the blacks in town?" Jim asked.

"Gone. Like I said. But, hell, that started some weeks ago. And before you get up on your New York City liberal high horse, Mr. Kincaide, it was done in a way where the law couldn't touch anybody. I'd have stopped it if I could have found a way."

"I wasn't criticizing, Chief. And my father was Mr. Kincaide. My name is Jim."

Chief Brocato smiled. "All right, Jim. Knew your daddy well. Fine man . . . the rumor is that some Righteous members killed him."

"Yes. I learned that only a few days ago." Had it been days? Jim pondered. Or hours? Jim couldn't remember. Time had gotten away from him.

"All the rest of your force with Baronne, Cec?" Terry inquired.

"Yes. One of my own men, Tony Cornell, shot Harry. Assassinated him as cold as can be while Harry was sitting in his patrol car. Then they took over the police station and sheriff's substation. I think they killed a couple of deputies, but I'm not sure. Hell, I'm not sure of anything anymore. People have been, well, just disappearing around here. It's . . . eerie, is what it is." The chief shook his head. "You warned me something like this was going to happen, Terry. I'm sorry I didn't listen to you. But at the time, I thought it was just wild, anti-government talk. I am sorry I doubted you."

"Forget it, Cec. There were a number of militia groups around the country doing a lot of very foolish things about that time. Everything was disorganized, and all of us were pulling in different directions. None of us really knew which way we were going to move at the time."

Chief Brocato took off his hat and ran blunt fingers through his thick gray hair. "Water under the bridge, Terry. Look, I'll lock these yahoos down and then meet you over at City Hall. Baronne's people have taken over damn near every town in the park and on the fringes. Hell, more than that, Terry. Word I get is that they've taken over hundreds of small towns all over America. We're outnumbered like maybe a hundred to one or more and we've got to do some serious planning."

"For a fact, Cec. All right. See you there in a few."

The chief walked off toward the knot of prisoners in the middle of the street, many of whom were men he used to call *friend*.

"What happens now?" Jim asked.

"Well, Jimmy," Terry replied. "I guess we're in the middle of a war."

Five

President Evans sat in a darkened Oval Office and stared out the window. There was a time he had enjoyed watching the traffic moving up and down the street; the sight had soothed him. Of course, that had been before the street had been closed for security reasons . . . real or imagined.

He swiveled in his chair, turning away from the window, placing both elbows on the polished surface of his desk and putting his face in his hands. Earlier in the day, he'd overheard one of his aides saying the whole country had turned to shit. Not a phrase he could incorporate into the speech he was due to deliver to the nation in a few hours, but it certainly summed up the situation.

Evans was not a stupid man; regardless of what many believed, no successful politician could be stupid. Not and keep getting reelected. But any politician can surround himself with advisers giving lousy advice. And that, Evans thought, is exactly what I did.

"I badly misjudged the mood of the nation," he muttered, his words muffled against his hands. "I didn't think it would come to this."

The chief of the White House staff entered the darkened office without knocking and stood by the door. "Art," he called softly. "You all right?"

"No, I'm not," the president said, lowering his hands from his face and sitting up straight in the chair. He clicked on the desk lamp and waved his long-time friend and confidant to a chair.

"You want me to call the doctor?"

"No. What I want is for the good people of this nation to rise up and kick the hell out of these right-wing whackos and gun-nuts and ultra-religious goofballs and get this nation back on some sort of even keel." He shook his head. "But that isn't going to happen, is it, David?"

"No, it isn't. But I have just received word that many of the militia groups have risen up and are fighting Baronne's people."

"The militias! Good God, they're just as bad as Baronne. We haven't gained anything there."

"That may not be true. We badly misjudged the militia. We mishandled the whole situation."

"The rest of the staff agrees with that, of course."

"You know they don't."

"And you think I should . . . do what?"

"Talk to the leaders of the groups. Really *talk* with them, Art." He held up a hand as the president opened his mouth to speak. "I know what you're going to say, but the military is out of it. They've got their hands full. We have rumblings coming in hourly. Terrorist groups all over the world are talking about striking at America. Mass invasions, missile strikes, and every other type of scenario you might care to mention. Just put using the military out of your mind. Forget it. The time has come to speak."

"To speak of many things," the president recited. "Of shoes and ships and sealing wax, of cabbages and kings."

His long-time friend chuckled. "I'm glad to see you've still got a sense of humor."

The president did not smile. "Not much of one, I'm afraid. I'm still having difficulty accepting all that's happened. It's . . . well, I keep hoping it's all a bad dream and pretty soon I'm going to wake up and the sun will be shining and everything will be all right."

"Things were never *all right,* Art. They haven't been *all right* in years. And in your heart you know that. We all forgot just how diverse this nation is in its makeup."

"What the hell does that mean?"

"You know damn well what I mean. We've been friend's since childhood, so stop playing the political game with me. We all share an equal blame in what happened." He shook his head. "We fucked up."

"Oh, wonderful, David. I can just see me going before a hundred-million people in a few hours and saying, 'We fucked up!' " He pointed to a wastebasket overflowing with wadded-up sheets of paper from a legal pad. "Give me something I can use."

His chief of staff lifted his eyes and stared directly at the president. "How about, 'I'm sorry.' "

"Sorry for *what?*" The president lost his temper. "For doing my best?"

"Doing your best for whom, Art?"

"For the *people,* goddamnit!"

"You're talking about the people who elected you, Art. But how about the people who didn't vote for you? There are millions of good, decent, moderate-thinking Americans out there who don't share your views. We pushed many of them right into the ranks of the militia and the ultra-right and the fringe groups. Maybe they didn't join any active group, but we pushed them so hard they turned against us—at least to some degree. We overtaxed the people; we jammed social programs they didn't want down their throats; we overregulated them; we swamped them with needless paperwork; we spied on them. . . . Jesus Christ, Art, we fucked up! Big time."

"With one side, it was religion," the president said softly. "With the other, it was guns. Religion and guns. What a hell of a combination."

The chief of staff felt that was not only a gross over-simplification but didn't come anywhere near to touching the truth. However, he said nothing in rebuttal, for he had known in his guts for some time his life-long friend had never really understood the feelings of millions of Americans. And not just the president, but Congress in general—both parties. Now everybody was paying for it. And would continue to pay for it for years to come.

Provided that the nation survived this uprising. . . .

Jim yawned and stretched and looked at his watch. 0230 hours. He'd been asleep for about three hours, sitting in a chair in a darkened office at City Hall. He rose stiffly then paused; he was forgetting something. He grimaced and looked around for his AR-15. Picking it up, he walked out into the hall. He was accustomed to picking up a briefcase, not a rifle.

Stepping over sleeping forms, he made his way toward the front of the building. He paused for a second by an office door that was cracked open a few inches. Janet was on the phone, saying a lot of *yes, sirs* and *no, sirs.*

She was reporting in to someone.

Jim walked on, stepping out into the dimly lighted front reception-area. He nodded at a young man sitting at a secretary's desk. One of Terry's men. Jim struggled to recall his name. Al! That was it. Al Milner.

Al smiled at him. "Did you come to relieve me, sir?"

"Sure. Why not. I've got to start pulling my weight around here. Where's the coffeepot?"

"I just made a fresh pot and Miz Osborne brought in some donuts she baked fresh." He grinned boyishly. "I ate three of them. They're good."

"Mrs. Osborne?" Jim asked.

"Yes, sir. She's an older lady. Retired. Used to work here at City Hall. Her husband's too old for active militia work, but he's volunteered to stand sentry duty at the edge of town. They're fine people."

"They're in sympathy with the militia movement, then?"

"Oh . . . I guess so. To some degree, at least. Miz Osborne says we're gonna win and it's always best to be on the winning side."

"Most of the people in town think along those lines?"

" 'Bout half of them, I'd guess. Hard to tell about the others. But at least they're not shooting at us. I'll see you, sir. Thanks for relieving me."

"No problem."

Al paused at the hallway entrance. "Sir? Did you really win the Congressional Medal of Honor?"

"Yes, I did. A long time ago."

The young man nodded his head. "Walkie-talkie's on a shelf behind the desk. We're Eagle One and you're Major Kincaide. See you in a few hours." He turned and disappeared down the hall.

Jim poured a cup of coffee, snagged a couple of home-baked donuts, and returned to the desk. *"Major* Kincaide?" he muttered. He picked up the walkie-talkie and studied it. It was not a model he was familiar with. He pressed the talk button and said, "This is Kincaide. I'm on the dog watch. Everything quiet out there?"

"Yes, sir," voices began reporting in. After the fourth voice, there was silence, so Jim assumed there were four sentry posts.

"Hell of a way to run a war," he muttered, placing the walkie-talkie back on the shelf. Then he ate his donuts and drank his coffee.

Janet strolled in, looking fresh, as usual, and tossed him a very sloppy salute. "Mornin', Major," she said.

"Very funny," Jim replied and watched as she pulled a mug of coffee and grabbed a donut. He waited until she had taken a seat in the dimly lighted reception-area. "Whose idea was this *major* business?"

"Your childhood buddy, Terry's. Personally, I think it's a good idea. It will get you off the fence, so to speak. Did you get any sleep?"

" 'Bout three hours. You?"

"Same."

"I heard you speaking on the phone as I walked up the hall. I didn't pause long enough to eavesdrop. What does the nation's brass have to say about the situation?"

She watched him from across the room. "They're on full alert against possible terrorist and/or missile attack from foreign powers hostile toward the America way."

"In other words, *mind my own business.*"

She chuckled. "No. I'm telling you the truth. Really. But they are staying out of this civilian insurrection."

"What about the FBI, the DEA, the BATF, Federal Marshals Service—what are they doing?"

"Staying out of it, for the most part. They're protecting the nation's senators and representatives and federal judges and so forth. Hell, Jim, they don't have a death wish. Many of the nation's governors got the jump on the Feds and called out the National Guard to protect state office buildings and judges and state senators and reps and so on and so forth. It's all coming together just as most of us in the nation's intelligence community predicted."

"Can't the president override any governor's decision on how to use the guard?"

She shrugged her shoulders. "I'm sure he could. But he isn't. Or hasn't, as yet. He's scheduled to address the nation at 1000 hours this morning." Her eyes twinkled. "You know, Jim, as XO, you don't have to stand a watch."

"Yes, Major Shaw. I am well aware of that."

She laughed. "You have any orders for me, sir?"

Jim grinned as lewdly as he could at her.

She shook her head. "Here? Now?"

"It would certainly give the boys something to talk about, wouldn't it?"

"And the girls," she added, reminding Jim that there were several capable women among the ranks in Terry's militia.

"Oh, yes. Must not forget the ladies. Karen, Judy, and Rose. I got their names right, didn't I?" Before she could reply, he said, "Janet . . . there is no way I'm going to be Terry's XO. So you and everybody else can forget this *major* business."

"I think it's a little late for that, Jim. The word's already gone out to other militia units aligned with Terry."

"Without my permission."

"Jim," she said patiently, sitting down on a couch in front of the street-side window of the office. "What's it going to take to convince you there is a war on? There are several dead bodies stretched out on the sidewalk and covered with blankets right now. You killed one of them." He opened his mouth and she held up a hand. "No, be quiet for a minute and listen to me. You're an experienced combat veteran and a natural leader. You're a take-charge person. I knew that after talking with you for five minutes. Terry knows it. So does everyone else around here. Jim, there are really only two sides in this conflict— Baronne's whacky group and a lot of widely scattered and poorly organized militia units around the nation. The United States military is going to sit this one out. For a while. Oh, they'll step in to pick up the pieces when the smoke settles; you can bet on that. They're not going to see this nation fall. The brass is working right now, frantically, putting together small units on every base in the nation, units they know they can count on to stand firm and take orders and carry them out. I'm telling you things I shouldn't be telling you, Jim, because I need you to assume this position of authority Terry has handed you. Now this is going to sound corny and sort of Ronald Reaganish, but your country needs you right now. Again, you might say . . ."

Slow applause interrupted her, the lone applause coming from the archway of the darkened hall. Jim looked up. Terry stood there, clapping his hands. "God, country, and Mom's apple pie time, Jimmy," the militia leader said. "All we need now is John Wayne to give us a pep talk."

Jim's temper boiled over. "You are still a sarcastic motherfucker, Terry!"

Terry walked into the coffee room, returning with a cup and a donut. He sat down by the side of the desk

Jim was using. "And you still have a slow temper, Jimmy-boy. That's good. I need people like you." He assumed a Nixonish expression and waggled his head from side to side. "Your country needs you."

"How long had you been standing there in the dark, listening?" Janet asked, a note of menace in her voice.

"Relax, Major Shaw," Terry told her. "We know what the brass is doing. And I don't really have to go into the why or how we know, do I?"

Janet stared at him, offering no reply.

"But she's right, Jim," Terry said, sobering his tone. "We need you and your country needs you. You're a stabilizing force in a situation that desperately needs that right now . . . and in the months to come. You see, you've been in a business for a good many years that convinces people to buy things. When the shooting is over, we might need your selling skills. Right now, we need your organizational skills. OK, partner?"

Jim stared and then slowly nodded. "I don't have much choice, do I, Terry? I don't want any part of anything Baronne is offering. So what does that leave me?"

"Us," Terry said with a smile. So . . . welcome aboard, Major Kincaide."

Six

Dawn cut the eastern sky, the new day bringing a warm, humid, and windless morning to upstate New York.

Jim watched the town wake up, the residents, going about their daily routine as if nothing exceptional had happened. Cafes began opening early for business and customers started walking and driving up for breakfast.

"Amazing!" Jim exclaimed, standing on the sidewalk outside City Hall.

"Life goes on," Terry said. "What you're seeing now flies directly in the face of what both our main political parties have for years, in a subtle way, tried to convince each other would not happen."

Jim cut his eyes to his friend. "What do you mean?"

"There are millions of American citizens who really don't give a damn who runs the country, as long as they're left alone." He waved a hand carelessly. "Hell, see for yourself. Most of the citizens passing by us are giving no more than a cursory glance. Their lives have not been affected by the shooting last night. Nobody kicked in their front door, invading their privacy and ransacking their home. Their thinking is let's pretend nothing happened and go on. They see Chief Brocato going into the cafe for breakfast, right across the street. He's wearing his sidearm, so everything must be all right. We're not bothering these people in any way, so they're not going to bother us." Terry chuckled. "Here comes Mrs. Horszowski. Now you're really going to see what I mean."

"Terry Warden!" an elderly lady marched up and addressed Terry.

"Yes, ma'am!"

"Why are you standing on the sidewalk, all dressed up like some Army person and carrying that gun?"

"Helping to keep order in the town, ma'am."

"Is that right?"

"Yes, ma'am. And this is Jim Kincaide. You remember his father, I'm sure. He's come up all the way from New York City to help us."

Mrs. Horszowski gave Jim a good eyeballing. "Well, I certainly don't blame him for leaving that awful city. It's nothing but a cesspool. And watch where you point that gun. It's liable to go off and hurt somebody."

"Yes, ma'am. I sure will."

She walked off without another word.

"Horszowski," Jim muttered. "I knew I'd heard that name before. Her husband was mayor of this town for years, right?"

"That's right. And she taught music for fifty years. Private lessons at home. She was a concert pianist living in New York City when she met Mr. Horszowski. A real nice lady. Taught my youngest girl piano up until her hands became so arthritic she couldn't play."

"Two State Police units coming into town, Terry," one of his men called. "Rolling slow and looking around."

"Okay. Put on a fresh pot of coffee and make sure we have some donuts left."

There were two uniformed state policemen to a car. The four of them got out and looked around. Cautiously, Jim thought. They were careful to keep their hands away from their holstered pistols.

"Morning," Terry called cheerfully. "We have coffee and donuts inside."

"Morning," a man wearing the bars of a lieutenant said, stepping up to the curb. "I'm Mueller." He stuck out his hand and Terry took the peace offering.

"Jim Kincaide," Terry began the introductions just as Janet stepped out of the city hall building. "And this is Major Janet Shaw, United States Army."

"Really?" Mueller asked, open surprise in his eyes.

"Affirmative, Lieutenant," Janet said. "I was TDY in New York City when the lid blew off. I couldn't get through for orders, so I came up here with Kincaide. I have now been instructed to stay put and report."

"That is . . . interesting, Major," the lieutenant of state police admitted. "And what is your current assessment of the . . . ah . . . situation?"

"The militia has stabilized the situation in this town and restored order. I have been instructed to give them my full cooperation and expertise . . . if they ask for the latter."

"That's even . . . ah . . . more interesting, Major," Mueller said. He turned his attention back to Terry. "Have there been any casualties here?"

"Several. Most of them followers of the movement called the Sword of the Righteous. The county sheriff is part of the movement. One of Chief Brocato's men was killed. The chief is all right and working with us. He's having coffee over there at the cafe."

A sergeant of state police standing beside the lieutenant muttered, "This is the goddamnest situation I've ever encountered."

Lieutenant Mueller cleared his throat and looked around him. "So the . . . ah . . . situation is . . . ah . . . well in hand, that's what you're telling me?"

"That's right. No crime happening here, Lieutenant Mueller. And should it occur, we'll take care of it."

"How, Mr. Warden?"

"If the criminal lives until the proper authorities arrive, all of his or her constitutional rights will go into play at that moment. If the victim of the crime shoots the criminal dead, the case will end right there—after an investigation, that is."

The highway cop sighed wearily. "Ah . . . right. That's the way it seems to be shaping up all over the state."

"That's the way it's going to be all over the nation. People have had a bellyful of crime and criminals." He smiled. "Don't get in the way, Lieutenant. You are not the enemy."

"I will bear that in mind," Mueller replied with a slight smile of his own. "Now, if you all will excuse us, we'll walk over to the cafe and have a chat with Chief Brocato."

"Have a nice day, Lieutenant . . . boys," Terry said.

As soon as Mueller walked in, the chief left the stool where he'd been sitting and joined the highway cops at a table. The waitress followed him and filled coffee cups and took orders from the state cops. After she had left, Brocato said, "Statewide, how are things looking?"

"Grim," Mueller said. "If I were a man bent on any type of criminal activity, I would hunt a hole and get in it."

"What is the governor doing?"

"Hiding behind platoons of heavily armed National Guard and regular army troops. But the word has gone out that some militia units and nearly all of the units supportive of Baronne plan to assassinate all liberal-voting state- and federal-level elected officials."

The chief's coffee cup hand paused halfway between table and mouth. "Are you fucking serious?"

"Very. But the networks and wire services have agreed to sit on that information. That is the reason the Bureau, the Secret Service, and the Marshal's Service haven't been seen. They're stretched thin protecting hundreds of representatives and sixty senators around the clock. What do you know about Terry Warden, Chief?"

"Good, solid, steady, hard-working, and law-abiding man. I've known him all his life. He just got tired of high taxes, low morals, federal giveaway programs, and the whole goddamn mess in Washington and Albany. I'd bet my life he is not involved in any plan to assassinate elected officials."

"That's exactly what you are betting, Chief," Mueller said. He put tired eyes on Brocato. "Just thought I'd remind you of that."

"Don't you think the president looked tired," Jim asked after watching the presidential address to the nation.

"Maybe he'll do the nation a favor and drop dead," Terry replied, then stepped out of the room.

"Evans wasn't that bad," Jim said.

"You used past tense," Janet reminded him.

"Oh, Evans is through. I can't imagine any president surviving after something like this. Fred Potter will be the party's nominee and he'll win, probably. Potter is a conservative Democrat who knows how to compromise." Jim shrugged his shoulders. "Hell, Janet—what am I saying? There might not even be an election. Who knows what is going to happen after all this?"

"There won't be as many changes as you might believe, Jim. At least that's my thinking. Not if men such as Terry succeed in defeating Baronne. But there will be some changes. There will be changes in how justice is administrated . . . welfare and income tax. Some federal departments will be abolished."

"Did your computers tell you all this?"

"All you had to do was listen to the people to know what was surely going to happen, sooner or later. The problem was, the politicians didn't listen."

"What departments?"

"HUD, the IRS, as it's currently structured. The Bureau of Alcohol, Tobacco, and Firearms will go; that is a department hated by hundreds of thousands of gunowners. Criminals are going to lose some of their so-called rights. Punishment will be harsher and much swifter—and a lot of it will come from the intended victims. . . ."

"How did you people in the intelligence community come up with all this?"

"We listened to the people. We spent months monitoring the electronic chat and newsgroup boards on America On Line, Compuserve, Prodigy, and all over the Internet. We recruited several thousand active servicemen and women from every state in the Union to talk to people when they went home on leave and then report back to us on what they heard. Much of intelligence work is slow, Jim, but we get results in time; and what we got scared the hell out of us. We saw revolution coming straight at us but couldn't convince the president or Congress. Every time we'd bring it up, we would get these glassy-eyed stares. Only a few senators and representatives believed us. They were the ones who constantly tested the waters, so to speak. They listened to the people. Privately they agreed with us. Publicly, they wouldn't even whisper it."

"But the news media? . . ."

"That pack of whimpering liberals? It didn't help matters when they began referring to genuine militia organizations as hate groups. Men such as Terry don't hate the government; they realize that without government we'd have nothing but anarchy. They hate what the government has become. Or had become, I suppose I should say. It will certainly never be the same after this. But now comes the hard part, Jim. Revolution is easy. Rebuilding and stabilizing is difficult."

"But the military is staying out of it! Damnit, they could have . . ." He trailed off with a sigh and a slight shake of his head.

"Now you're finally getting the big picture, Jim," Janet said, conscious that several of Terry's people had entered the room and were listening intently. "The military didn't want to tear this country wide open with a war that would have lasted for years. Our military leaders of today are a different breed from those of forty or fifty years ago. They don't want to see this country under military rule. They'll do everything they can to prevent that . . . and that includes allowing a limited war among its citizens."

"You mean," a woman that Jim and Janet knew only

as Karen said, "the military knew this was going to happen and did nothing to prevent it?"

"In a manner of speaking," Janet replied. "We did what we could, and that was advise the president and Congress of our findings. Other than that, we could do nothing without the approval of Congress."

Young Al Milner held up a hand as if he were still in school and asked, "But now what, Major Kincaide?"

The question startled Jim. He glanced at Janet, who was looking at him, open amusement in her eyes. "Yes, Major." She was the first to speak. "Now what?"

"We negotiate," he answered.

"With who?" Al asked.

"Whom," the woman standing beside him automatically corrected.

"I ain't in school anymore, Judy," Al told her.

"You should be," she came right back.

Al ignored her. "I mean, you don't want us to try to, well, make a deal with Baronne and his fruitcakes, do you, Major?"

"We may have to."

"No way," the group of men and women replied very nearly in unison. The woman who had corrected Al's grammar added, "And we're firm on that, sir."

"And we're paying no more than ten percent of our income to the state and federal government . . . total," another said. "And we're firm on that, too."

Jim had to ask, "Where is the money going to come from to keep on providing all the services the American people have grown accustomed to receiving?"

"They can get unaccustomed to receiving many of those," Karen said, no small amount of coldness in her voice.

Jim had early on concluded that Karen was one tough package. It had startled him to learn that she was a child psychologist who'd been fired from her job for her unyielding stance on corporal punishment. Karen believed in spanking when it was necessary and had said so to her local school board.

She had lost her job over that.

Judy, about Karen's age, was a high school teacher. Her husband had shot and killed a man he had caught in their home when the burglar had whirled around in the darkened room, a shiny object in his hand. The object turned out to be a candlestick that was a family heirloom. A jury had sent Judy's husband to prison for that. Subsequently, Judy had joined Terry's militia.

The woman named Rose operated a successful daycare center and was the oldest of the three women in Terry's immediate group. Jim guessed her age in the mid-forty range. Rose didn't have much to say, but when she did speak, the others listened. Rose looked at Jim, a slight smile playing on her lips.

"There are going to be some rather drastic changes in this country, Major Kincaide," Rose said. "The government is either going to go along with those changes or else face a civil war that will continue far into the next millennium and tear this country apart."

Terry entered the room just as Rose began to speak, and stood listening, wearing that slightly sarcastic expression that Jim remembered well from their boyhood years. "How about you, Al? You want to tell the Major your story?"

The young man shrugged his muscular shoulders. "My daddy was a gun collector, and a very outspoken man. He had no respect for the present administration—Evans,

I'm talking about. Somebody turned his name into the FBI as a dangerous radical. One night two years ago, agents from the state police, along with agents from the Bureau of Alcohol, Tobacco, and Firearms, busted into my mom and dad's house. No warning; they just kicked in the door about one o'clock in the morning and started ransacking the house looking for illegal weapons. Well, there weren't any illegal weapons; most of my daddy's guns were black powder rifles and pistols. My mother, who was sixty-five at the time, slapped one of the federal agents. He didn't hit her, but he did shove her down hard and she hit her head on something. Knocked her out. My dad went crazy and grabbed for a .38 he kept in a drawer. Two of the men shot him dead; I guess they really had no choice. My dad would have killed them all if he could have. Anyway, when my mom come to, she suffered a stroke. The agents tried to help her; I don't really blame the federal or state agents for what happened. They were following orders from the goddamn justice department. They called for an ambulance and cared for her as best they could until the EMTs got there. But," he sighed deeply, "my Mom died a few months ago in a nursing home."

"Jesus Christ!" Jim whispered.

"I know who turned my dad in, who told those lies about him to the feds. The man is hiding right here in this town, right now. I'm going to find the son of a bitch, and I'm going to kill him. And nobody is going to stop me. I'm going to shoot him in front of his puky-looking wife and his whiny kids. And you can chisel that in stone."

Jim didn't doubt a word of what Al had just said—not for a minute.

"The others have their reasons for joining an anti-government group, Jim," Terry said. "But few of their stories are as dramatic as Al's. Anyway . . . that isn't why I came in here. The state police have gone, and I just learned that a large group of Baronne's people are on their way here to reclaim the town. Chief Brocato is spreading the word now for all noncombatants to clear the area. We'd better get ready for a fight."

Seven

"How large a force?" Jim asked.

"Oh . . . they've got us outnumbered probably seven or eight to one," Terry replied. "Baronne's man in this area, Dr. Tom Durant, knows the militia groups all over upstate are behind me. If he can kill me, he thinks the battle is won."

"Ambush the convoy." The words popped out of Jim's mouth.

Terry's lips twitched. "Now that's why you got promoted, Jimmy. You're a great idea man. OK. Let's do it."

The ambush was textbook classic, and Baronne's men drove straight into it with their eyes wide open. Thirty seconds after the shooting stopped, Jim crawled to his knees in the brush by the side of the road and vomited up his breakfast. If any of the others on either side of Jim noticed, they tactfully did not mention it.

Chewing on a piece of gum to get the bad taste out of his mouth, Jim walked down to the road in time to hear one of the badly wounded men, hanging half in-half out of the back seat of a car, hoarsely whispering the Lord's Prayer. Jim paused by the man and looked down at him. The man's shirt-front was soggy with blood. Jim watched the light in the mans eyes fade as they became dull with death.

Jim walked on, his AR-15 at the ready.

About half the men in the convoy had been killed. The wounds of the others ranged from slight to mortal.

Jim stopped beside a young man, no more than twenty-one-years-old, stretched out on the side of the road, a bloody bandage on his head. The young man opened his eyes and stared at Jim for a moment before speaking.

"You're making a mistake," he told Jim, his voice firm. "God must be brought back into American life. Without God, this nation is doomed to the pits of hell."

Jim said nothing in reply. He had a hunch the young man was not yet through with his sermonizing.

"Dr. Baronne is the only hope left," the young man continued. "His way is the only way."

"I suppose you believe you are one of God's warriors?" Terry spoke from behind Jim.

"Of course," the young man said without hesitation.

"Barrone did a good job of brainwashing them, didn't he, Jimmy?" Terry said.

"It would seem that way. How many dead?"

"Twenty-two. Five of the wounded are certain not to make it. Two . . . three others are iffy. The rest, like Billy Pendleton here, aren't badly hurt."

"You know this young man?"

"Sure. I coached him in Little League. Used to take him camping when I was assistant scoutmaster. We attended the same church until Baronne got his hooks into him. Billy stopped going to church on Sundays and started listening to Baronne's bullshit on shortwave radio. . . ."

"His is the only true word!" Billy almost yelled the rebuttal.

"Dream on, Billy," Terry said coldly.

"The state cops are coming back!" one of Terry's men called out.

"Stand easy!" Jim shouted the words before Terry could reply. "They are not the enemy."

"You catch on fast, Jimmy," Terry said.

The same four men who had been to town earlier parked their units on the side of the road and got out. As before, they were careful to keep their hands away from their guns as they walked up to Jim and Terry.

"Terry," Lt. Mueller greeted him, after glancing down at Billy. "Jim. You boys played hell here, didn't you?"

"Won a skirmish, that's all," Terry replied easily. "One step closer to getting rid of Baronne's nuts."

"I suppose that is one way of looking at it. Do you . . . ah . . . object if my men and I make out reports on this . . . ah . . . skirmish?"

"Not at all, Lieutenant. My XO here will be more than happy to answer all questions. I've got to check on another unit over 'cross state, Jim. Take over here."

"Gee, thanks, Terry."

"Think nothing of it, ol' buddy." Terry walked away.

"Mr. Kincaide," Mueller said. "Everything else might be in a state of chaos, but our computers are still up. We ran you after leaving town. What in the hell is a self-made man, a highly successful advertising executive, a man who inherited millions from his father, doing in a goddamn militia?"

"It's a long story, Lieutenant."

Mueller's reply was dry. "I can hardly wait to hear it."

Baronne's followers had taken a beating. Nearly every militia nationwide had turned on the followers of the

Sword of the Righteous and had done some righteous ass-kicking of their own.

Not that it was any consolation to President Evans. It only drove the president into a deeper depression. But what really drove him into a deep, blue funk was the certain knowledge that he was through as the chief executive of the United States. He didn't need any adviser to tell him that. He was finished. Even if he managed to hold onto the White House, once the militias defeated Baronne—and they would, in time, Evans was sure of that—he would be nothing more than a figurehead. The militia leaders despised him and would never trust him, even if he agreed to their demands while standing in the middle of a Bible factory.

Evans looked up as his friend and confidant, David Waymon, entered the office without knocking. Evans pointed to a chair.

"What good news do you have for me this morning, David?"

"I wish I did have good news," the chief of staff replied, sitting down. "But I do have some interesting news."

"Oh?"

"A new name has surfaced in the militia movement. James Kincaide. He was just named executive officer of the newly revamped New York Volunteer Militia."

Evans shook his head. "The name means nothing to me."

"The Waldman Agency . . . advertising. New York City. Both Waldman and Kincaide are long-time Democrats, heavy contributors to the party. Both were on the guest list the last time you were at a fund-raiser in New York City. Both attended the dinner—a thousand dollars a plate. Kincaide sat at the table to your left. Both Wald-man and Kincaide are known liberals."

"That doesn't make any sense. What the hell is a lib-eral doing mixed up with some racist, anti-semitic right-wing militia?"*

"There's more. Kincaide is a Medal of Honor-winner out of the Vietnam war. Quite a hero. And, if the short-wave broadcast can be believed, the Army has a Major Shaw advising this particular militia group."

The president cursed. "I knew it. I knew those bastards were involved in this all along." He pointed a shaky finger at his chief of staff. "I told you they were, didn't I?"

"Yes," David said with a sigh. "You did."

"And you didn't believe me, did you?" Evans persisted, glad to have even one small victory.

"No, I didn't, Art. But this report has yet to be confirmed. Bear that in mind."

"Kincaide was a spy, wasn't he? *Wasn't he?*" he shouted.

"We don't know that," David replied in a soft tone. He looked closely at his old friend.

Evans's eyes had taken on a strange light. His hair was mussed and his face an odd, pale color.

He's losing it, David thought. He's on the edge and he's losing it.

For a full thirty seconds, Evans pounded his fists on the desk top like a petulant child in the throes of a temper tantrum. When he finally spoke, his face had changed from a sickening pallor to a deep flush. "The country is on the

---

*Many militias are racist, but an equal number are multi-racial. A few all-black militias also side with the so-called right-wing.

the verge of falling apart and I'm getting the blame!" he shouted. "I was a good president. I was, damnit. I did the best I could. I stayed true to my beliefs even though everybody was against me right from the start. That goddamn lard-assed Limbaugh made fun of me every chance he got. That fucking loud-mouthed Liddy called me names. I should have sicced the FBI on them just like I did that right-wing, son-of-a-bitch writer down in Louisiana. Goddamn every Republican to hell!"

"Get a grip on yourself, Art," David urged.

"Fuck a grip! I want the Secret Service and the FBI and the Federal Marshals to go after these goddamn militias and wipe them out! Kill them all. Where's a piece of paper? I'll write out the order personally. Then, by God, they have to obey it. Here, found one."

Evans scribbled frantically on a piece of White House stationery while his chief of staff watched, disbelief in his eyes. Evans pressed down so hard that the tip of the ballpoint tore the paper and put a long scar on the wood of the expensive desk.

David edged toward the door, opening it and motioning toward several secret service agents standing close. They watched in silence as the President of the United States mumbled and cursed.

"There, by God" Evans shouted, waving the paper in the air. "I've done it. Now the militias are through! I win! I win! I win!"

"He's babbling," a secret service agent whispered.

The president's face suddenly went slack and open-mouthed. One hand grabbed and clutched at his shirtfront, and he gasped as if in intense pain. He fell out of the chair, landing heavily on the floor.

"Call for an ambulance!" David shouted. "Alert the

hospital we're on the way. I think the president has had a heart attack."

It is the natural inclination of any decent, law-abiding citizen to obey the orders of a police officer, usually without question. But the thousands and thousands of militia members across the nation were in no mood to disperse, go home, give up their guns, surrender, or do anything else the police might tell them to do.

Outnumbered and outgunned as they were, the nation's police quickly realized that the best thing they could do—if they wanted to stay alive—was a one-eighty role reversal.

They found themselves taking orders both from the militias and from Baronne's people, and they quickly found that the militias were a hell of a lot easier to get along with than the Righteous members.

In the towns where the Righteous was in control, even people who had abhorred guns all their lives were attempting to arm themselves, then heading for the hills or the swamps or the deserts or the woods to band together to fight the extremists of the religious right.

Meanwhile, the militias chose to work with the police and the citizens—when the police and the citizens would let them. In most areas, they willingly cooperated, for even the militias who were decidedly racist stood firm for law and order.

Through it all, Americans not directly involved in the coup persevered, doing their best to ignore the events taking place all around them. They went to work in factories and offices, had babies, attended funerals, preached sermons, taught school, ministered to the sick and frail, and did a thousand-and-one other things that made life normal and bearable. The stock market faltered badly for a couple of days, then recovered and struggled on; to everyone's amazement and contrary to what the experts had been solemnly intoning, the markets began a slow progression upward, although overseas investors were naturally cautious.

All over the nation, right in the middle of an undeclared guerrilla war, life went on.

"Told you," Janet said to Jim.

Terry had managed to pull together dozens of small militia groups all over the northeast and then dozens of others in various locales across the nation. But Baronne's people could still lay claim to about half of the towns.

And unlike Terry's people and most of the other militias, Baronne's people were making drastic changes.

Eight

"Putting it in layman's terms, President Evans has had a mental breakdown," the doctor informed the White House staffers, secret service agents, and members of Congress who had crowded together in the hospital waiting room. "He did not have a heart attack."

The press had been told that Arthur Evans had been hospitalized for an as-yet-undisclosed ailment.

"Then why did he clutch at his chest and gasp as if in pain?" David Waymon asked.

He probably suffered from sudden heartburn or indigestion," the doctor replied patiently. What he really wanted to say was *How the hell do I know? What am I, God?*

"The prognosis, diagnosis?" AG Stella Newton asked.

"Ms. Newton, the President of the United States cannot even tell me his name," another doctor said. "He doesn't know where he is; he doesn't even know that the woman sitting beside his bed is his wife. We should know more about his condition in a few hours." The doctor wanted to add, *Which is horseshit. We probably won't know any more next week than we do right at this moment.* Instead, he said, "The president has been stabilized and is resting comfortably." *Now that we have a catheter up his dick and he isn't pissing all over himself.*

The team of doctors left the room.

The secretary of state said, "I have taken the liberty of notifying Vice President Potter. He is on his way back to Washington."

"You had no right to do that!" AG Newton flared at him.

"I had every right to do that, Ms. Newton," the unflappable secretary of state replied bluntly.

"My God, what are we going to do now?" a young White House staffer fretted, after adjusting the volume on his Walkman and digging in his jacket pocket for more bubble gum. "What is going to happen to this nation with Art Evans away from the helm?"

The secretary of state gave the young man a pitying glance and suppressed a caustic reply. He reached down and turned the volume of the Walkman wide open. The White House aide jumped about three feet into the air as screaming heavy-metal music shrieked into his ear.

In complete control, the secretary turned to a secret service agent. "Take me out to Andrews. Fred will be here shortly."

"Our first order of business is to make sure the savages are under control," Baronne told the gathering of cell leaders. When he had seen that the militias in the state were rapidly coming under Terry's command and that they would soon be in complete control of most of the rural areas of New York State, he had quickly moved his base of operations to a location on the Alabama-Georgia border. "We must deny them access to liquor and guns. We have officers on every force and department in the nation. When I give the word, our people who are still waiting to surface will do so and work with the officers. But for now, I want a dusk-to-dawn curfew for all Negroes in place beginning this evening."

"How long must we wait?"

"Not long. Be patient. And always remember this: God is on our side."

Huey Clark, the commander of the GBM—the Georgia Black Militia—had reluctantly put his forces on high alert when he saw that the citizens' uprising was nationwide. Huey didn't think it could be stopped either. Not even if the military got into it, and Huey knew something about the military. He was a retired Army sergeant major and had served with distinction with the Seventh Special Forces for ten years.

Huey knew guerrilla warfare. He had pulled five tours in 'Nam with an A-Team and had taught guerrilla tactics at the John F. Kennedy Special Warfare School at Fort Bragg. Huey had been raised on a Georgia farm and loved the land, but knew that making a living at farming was chancy at best; so upon his retirement after twenty-six years in the military, he had started what had become a successful landscaping business in and around Atlanta. He was well-liked and respected by all, and he still got to work the soil, but without a lot of the risk of farming.

Huey was an intelligent man, possessing more than his share of uncommon common sense. He knew that while some militias were racist to the core, many were not, welcoming blacks into their ranks. He also knew that there was a lot of racist feeling against whites in the black community, and it was because of this that he screened every applicant for his militia very carefully.

Most of his people were ex-military and most were in their forties—solid, steady, family men with all the youthful wildness gone.

He told his people to gather their guns and get ready to fight, for hard times were on the way . . . and hard times went by the name of Dr. Gene Baronne.

The secretary of state met VP Fred Potter at Andrews Air Force Base and brought him up to date on the ride to his residence.

"Art Evans is around the bend," the secretary told him. "Privately, the doctors told me they feel his recovery—if he recovers—will take a long, long time. I have a meeting scheduled for tomorrow with the top leaders of the House and Senate. I believe you will be sworn in as president within twenty-four hours after the meeting."

"Hell of a way to assume the office."

"We can't afford the luxury of time. Negotiations have to start with these . . . revolutionaries immediately."

"The First Lady?"

"She told me she saw signs of a breakdown several weeks ago. Said her husband had been acting, well, strangely."

Fred snorted derisively. "Ask me, he's been acting strangely ever since he was first elected to Congress."

The car phone rang and the secretary picked it up. He listened for a moment, then hung up. He sat in silence for a few blocks.

"What?" Fred broke the silence.

"The president has just suffered a series of small strokes. His personal doctor, that was him on the phone, said the First Lady told him to tell me to get Chief Justice Hullett and swear you in. Evans is through."

"We've got a chance to settle this peacefully now," Janet said, after watching a segment of the news the next morning. "Fred Potter is a moderate. Fiscal conservative and a law-and-order man, disliked by liberals but liked and respected by conservatives."

"I hope the first thing he'll do is get rid of all of Evans's advisors," Terry said.

"You can bet he's doing that right now," Janet replied. "He didn't get along with any of Evans's people."

The three of them were sitting in the office behind Terry's house on the outskirts of town. Jim hadn't seen so much electronic gear since leaving the service.

"That's how the militias around the country stay in touch," Terry told him. "We had a former CIA cryptology expert who was sympathetic to our cause work up a code for us. The feds never did break it."

Jim nodded, but his mind was busy working at something else. "Then . . . for all intents and purposes, this uprising is over, right?"

Terry laughed outright. "Oh, hell, no, Jim. It's just moved into another phase, that's all. Don't be too anxious to get back to the Big Apple. After the troops move out, that city, like many others, is going to be a battleground for a time."

"What the movement needs now is a skilled salesman. Fred Potter is going to call for a halt to all hostilities and for everybody to sit down and talk." Janet smiled sweetly at Jim.

"Oh, forget that!" Jim said. "Terry, you've just been

named national commander of the militia movement. I saw the communiqué, remember? You want to talk to the president, fine, go talk to him. Leave me out of it."

"I'll gladly go, Jim," Terry said. "But I want you with me."

Jim held up a hand. "No way! I cannot argue a point that I don't believe in."

"Sure you can, Jim, you've been doing it for years. As an advertising man, you've been selling the public on people and products you don't believe in for most of your adult life. This is no different."

"As far as I'm concerned, there is a hell of a lot of difference. I've read your manifesto, Terry. There is a lot of it that I don't agree with."

"But some points that you do agree with?"

Jim hesitated. "A few," he admitted.

"Then you'll assist me?"

Jim sighed. He knew why Terry was so anxious: The longer this situation went on, the higher the chances of the military's actually intervening. And if that should occur, the nation would be embroiled in a lengthy civil war that might well topple the country. Also, Fred Potter was a reasonable man and an honorable man . . . two reasons why his party had never backed him for the presidency. "All right, Terry. I'll help you. I'll do what I can."

"Good man. I knew I could count on you."

Jim kept his expression bland, but he was wondering: Just how did you know that, Terry?

The United States is made up of hundreds and hundreds of towns. About half of those towns had been taken over either by Baronne's Sword-of-the-Righteous people or by militiamen. But in the towns where the residents had yet to see their first militiaman or Baronne follower, they were definitely seeing what happened when Baronne's people took over: Refugees.

Blacks and homosexuals were being driven from their homes and told either to leave town or face the consequences. Those who chose the latter were never seen or heard from again. The others got the message and left town as quickly as possible, many with just the clothes they were wearing.

Baronne's followers had taken a page from one of the worst moments in history and brought it back to life. It was obvious now that Baronne and his people were following the bloody path carved out decades back by a man called Hitler.

When the press broke the story, Baronne and his followers were quick to react.

"Show us the first body," they challenged the press. "I challenge you to produce anyone who can truthfully say they saw us hurt anybody. You can't, because the charges are false."

It is often said that history repeats itself, but no one ever dreamed the neo-Nazi movement was that strong in America, or that hate could run so deep.

But it certainly was happening. The only problem was, nobody could prove it.

"I've stepped into a snake pit, haven't I?" the newly sworn in Fred Potter said to the roomful of people.

"You have no choice now, Mr. President," a senator urged. "You have to use the military."

Fred fired up his pipe and filled the Oval Office with

fragrant smoke. One of the few aides left from the Evans administration said, "Ah, sir, there is a ban on smoking in the White House."

"Get me an ashtray," Fred said, putting an abrupt end to that discussion, "and turn up the damn air-conditioning. It's warm in here."

"It's set on . . ."

"I don't give a damn what it's set on!" Fred cut him off in midsentence. "Cool this place off."

Fred laid his pipe aside. "Now, let's get some facts out on the table. We know that Baronne's radicals have done something with those blacks and homosexuals who refused their orders to leave town. We also know that the majority of Baronne's followers have nothing to do with these . . . alleged atrocities and are appalled by the reports. We have confirmed reports from state police all over the country that the militiamen have harmed no civilian; indeed, they have cleared many towns of Baronne's people and are working with the police to keep order. Before I commit troops, I want to know exactly what is going on and where."

Fred picked up his pipe and relit it as everybody in the room started talking at once. He puffed until the babble of voices had died down.

"The military has agreed to begin sending in small teams of special operations people to eyeball some of the towns under Baronne's control," Fred said. "And if news of that is spoken aloud outside this office, I will personally find out who was responsible and shoot the individual myself. Male or female." Fred's hard gaze touched the eyes of everyone in the room. "Now then, I'm setting up lines of communication with this Terry

Warden and some of his people. That's in the works right now . . ."

Once again, the room erupted in a babble of arguing voices.

"Shit!" Fred muttered, and puffed on his pipe. He listened for a moment, then shouted, "Shut up, goddamnit!"

The office became as hushed as a country church at midnight.

"That's better," Fred said, setting his pipe in the ashtray just placed on the desk by a young aide. A very nervous young aide who had been hired to work for Evans and did not know if he would have a job much longer . . . or if he even wanted to work for this man whom he considered to be loud, profane, and not in the least urbane.

Fred eyeballed the group, many of them holdovers from the Evans administration. He didn't trust many of the men and women in the room. Too many of them had what he considered socialistic leanings.

Fred Potter was not a typical tax-and-spend Democrat. He had seen his own father work an eighty-hour-week for years, building a small company into a huge, highly successful chain of stores that stretched into a half-a-dozen states; the idea of the government soaking hard-working people for all the taxes they could irked the hell out of Fred.

Fred was fond of saying, "This is America. It isn't goddamn Russia, goddamnit."

Fred was also a highly decorated Vietnam veteran; a Navy pilot who'd been shot down over North Vietnam and then taken prisoner. He was one of only a handful of American fighting men who had escaped alone and unaided from captivity, and he had done so only after cutting a couple of guards' throats, stealing an AK-47, and eventually finding his way back to his own lines.

Fred listened to a few comments—which he ignored—and then dismissed the group. After the last one had left, he turned to his own newly appointed chief of staff, grimaced, and said, "Nitwits! No wonder Art had a nervous breakdown, listening to that pack of screwballs."

Reese Perkins laughed and poured them both more coffee from a silver service. "You didn't tell them about the major with Warden's militia group."

"Are you kidding? Hell, no! I took a chance just telling them about the spec ops people." He sipped his coffee and relit his pipe. "Well, it's all up to Terry Warden now. I just hope he doesn't blow it."

Nine

After reading only the first page, President Fred Potter laid the file aside and ignored the list of demands he'd received from the group known as the Sword of the Righteous. It was so filled with passages from the Bible it was difficult reading. He relit his pipe, adjusted his glasses—he'd just had to go to bifocals and was having trouble with them—picked up the manifesto from the militia groups, and leaned back in his chair. He read it through without changing expression; then with a sigh, he closed the folder and laid it on his desk.

"Holy shit!" Fred whispered. "Talk about changes they are a-comin.' "

Fred knew that on some points, the militia and their supporters would be willing to negotiate and compromise. But on others, they were set in stone and there would be no back-up.

Fred punched the intercom and asked Reese Perkins to come in. Seated, Fred handed him a copy of the demands from the militia and said, "You tell me how we're going to sell that to Congress."

Reese quickly scanned the pages and looked up, amazement in his eyes. "Holy Christ!"

"Yeah. We're probably going to need His help in dealing with Congress on this."

"Fred, some of these issues have to do with states' rights, not the federal government."

"States' rights, Reese? Don't hand me that crap. What states' rights? The states can't breathe without the federal government giving them permission to do so. Don't get me started on that. Anyway, have you settled on a place to meet?"

"Right here, Fred. Just as you wanted. This coming Friday. Commander Warden . . . General Warden, whatever his title is, was opposed to it, but this James Kincaide convinced him that you would guarantee their safety. . . ." He smiled. "Along with an assist from Major Shaw."

The president nodded. "Advise the Army that when this . . . mess gets settled, Major Shaw is to be promoted to colonel. Immediately."

"I'll do that. Still no press on this thing, right?"

"None at all. Not for the first meeting. I don't want a word of this to leak. I want to talk with this man in private first."

"Two men. Warden and Kincaide."

"You haven't gotten a file on Kincaide yet?"

"Bare bones. Decorated Vietnam vet. Medal of Honor."

Fred arched an eyebrow at that. "Indeed."

"Yes. The DOD says he took over when his outfit was pinned down and the platoon sniper was killed. Before it was over, he had forty-six confirmed kills and about ten or fifteen more unconfirmed. His ability with that rifle saved what was left of his outfit."

"Interesting," Fred muttered.

"And he's a millionaire, too."

"That is interesting. Have you had any luck setting up a meeting with Gene Baronne?"

"He will meet on their ground only."

"Sounds as though he doesn't trust us."

"He doesn't." Fred shrugged his shoulders. "Meeting with that bunch on their own ground is out of the question. We'll talk with Warden and Kincaide . . . then worry about Baronne."

Reese pointed to the file on the desk. "What about the militia demands?"

Fred shook his head. "I agree with most of what they advocate. Hell, I always have. But the liberals in Congress are going to have a field day with those demands."

"The world's press is having a field day as we speak."

"It's as I've always stated privately: America is not the most beloved nation on this planet."

AMERICA THE MIGHTY IS FALLING APART, read on Friday morning headline. CIVIL WAR RIPS THE UNITED STATES, read another. PRESIDENT EVANS BREAKS UNDER STRAIN OF INTERNAL PROBLEMS, read yet another.

Most of the major newspapers in America were even less kind. They called for the military to go in and restore order, showing their lack of knowledge of guerrilla warfare.

"But not a one of these papers is calling for a meeting to discuss grievances," Jim pointed out.

"Of course not," Janet replied. "Check out the masthead and you'll know why. All those papers are owned by the same crybaby, liberal company."

"I don't believe I ever looked at it in quite that light," Jim admitted.

"If it isn't in the *Times,* it didn't happen or it isn't true, right, Jim?" Terry asked, stepping into the den.

"I'm not going to dignify that with a response. But I do have a question for you."

"Ask."

"Why are there no blacks in your militia unit?"

"We tried to recruit blacks. They just weren't interested in joining. Speaking of blacks, where is all your company?"

"Back at the lodge. Except for Cynthia and her hubby and kids. They went back to Albany as soon as this area was clear. No black was interested?"

"Not a one. At least not that I'm aware of. But there are some black militia groups." He smiled. "Baronne's people are going to find that out the hard way, I'm thinking. Especially when they tangle with Huey's people down in Georgia."

"Huey?"

"Huey Clark. Retired sergeant-major; ex-green beenie. He's got one hell of a group behind him. I have a hunch they're gonna get real nasty when Baronne's people start their racist shit down there." He cut his eyes to Janet. "I imagine the intelligence people know all about them."

"We do," Janet said.

"Am I right?"

"You are."

"Tell me this, Major, if you can: Have Baronne's people infiltrated the military?"

Janet didn't hesitate. "We know they have people in all branches and in all grades. We don't know to what extent."

"Why, Terry?" Jim asked.

"Oh, just curious, that's all."

"You sure you don't want to come with us, Janet?" Jim asked.

"I'm sure. I'd better keep a low profile."

Terry grinned. "Translated, Jimmy-boy, that means she'll have the whole house to herself and she can call in to her superior officers whenever she likes without having to sneak around to do it."

"I've told you I was calling in daily," Janet said.

"Yeah," Terry grinned. "So you did." He glanced at his watch. "We'd better shove off, Jim."

"Washington, here we come," Jim said, kissing Janet.

"You be careful," she urged him. "Both of you."

"We will," Jim replied, then picked up his suitcase and headed out the door.

When they were out of sight down the road, she moved to the phone and picked it up, punching out a number. "They just left," she said to the voice on the other end, then hung up.

Going into the kitchen, she poured a fresh cup of coffee and returned to the den. She sat down, a smile on her lips. "I wish you lots of luck, boys." Then she laughed.

"What the hell kind of military plane is that?" Jim asked as they watched the twin-engine, propeller-driven plane settle down on the runway.

"Beats me. I know nothing about flying. You?"

"I took flying lessons when I was kid. My dad was determined to make a pilot out of me. After twenty hours, my flight instructor told me to give it up for the sake of public safety."

Both men laughed. "You're kidding?" Terry asked.

Jim shook his head. "No. Really. I just don't have the knack for flying. But I can tell you it's a twin-engine prop job."

"Wonderful." Terry watched as the plane taxied toward the hangar area of the county airport. "What's the range of that thing?"

"Don't fly much, eh, Terry?"

"I hate to fly!"

"Well, I imagine about fifteen-hundred miles. It'll get us to Washington."

"In one piece?"

Jim snickered at the expression on the man's face. "I hope so."

"Not as much as I do."

"Terry, you were Airborne!"

"Big deal. I never minded the jumping. It's those god-damn planes that bother me."

The pilot taxied close and motioned for Jim and Terry to come aboard. Jim opened the cargo door, and the men climbed in and stowed their gear.

"Have a seat, gentlemen." The pilot's voice came through the speaker. "And buckle your seat belts."

"There is no co-pilot," Terry pointed out.

Jim chuckled. "It's a small plane, Terry. Stop worrying and relax."

"Shit!"

"We'll climb to 27,000 feet and cruise at two-hundred-and-forty knots. We'll be at Andrews before you know it. So, just sit back and enjoy the flight."

"Easy for him to say," Terry muttered.

Terry was white-knuckled as the plane took off and Jim studied his friend as they climbed to cruising altitude. He imagined the man had taken a lot of ribbing from his fellow jumpers while in the service.

After a few moments, Terry said, "Jim, we're heading in a southwesterly direction."

"So?"

"We should be heading almost due south."

Jim glanced out the window and checked the sun position. He nodded his head. "You're right. But there are restricted areas pilots have to avoid. Relax, Terry."

They had not been up ten minutes before the pilot walked back into the small passenger area. Both men noticed he was wearing a parachute. He was also wearing a holstered sidearm. He smiled at the men as he walked to the cargo doors of the plane.

"You going somewhere?" Jim asked, jokingly.

"As a matter of fact, yes. Have fun, boys." The pilot shoved open the doors and stepped out.

"Jesus Christ!" Terry yelled.

"We've been had!" Jim returned the shout over the rush of wind.

"I can't breathe!"

"Pop your seat belt and get up to the cockpit. Take the right-hand seat and get on oxygen."

"What are you going to do?" Terry gasped.

"Fly this damn thing—I hope. Move before you pass out."

Seated and belted in, oxygen mask and headphones on, Jim let his eyes sweep the instruments. He had had about twenty hours in a small single-engine plane. He had never even seen one like this. He didn't know what the majority of the dials represented. He located the horizon indicator, the compass, the microphone button. He also found the fuel indicator. The needle indicated about three-quarters full.

He slipped his feet on the rudder and brake pedals as his eyes located the turn-and-bank indicator. Then a suspicion washed over him. "We have plenty of fuel, Terry. And that doesn't make sense."

"What the hell are you talking about?"

"There is no way they could be sure one of us couldn't fly. Maybe they planted a bomb on board. Hang on. I'm going to check in the back."

"Wait a fucking minute! What about the plane?"

"It's on autopilot. Just don't touch that switch right there," he said, pointing.

Jim unbuckled and took a deep breath before leaving the seat. He had seen a small emergency oxygen tank located back in the cabin area. He would use that while he searched. He looked at Terry. "Terry?"

"What?"

"Don't light a cigarette. The oxygen will blow us out of the sky."

There weren't many places on the plane to hide a bomb, and it didn't take him long to find it. It was a good-sized chunk of C-4 with a timer taped to a bulkhead in the rear. Jim pulled the tape off and tossed the explosive out the yawning cargo door. Then he made his way back to the cockpit.

"How fast are we going?" Terry asked.

"Just above stall speed." He pointed to a dial. "There is the speed indicator. I've got to get us down under ten thousand feet so we can come off oxygen."

"I thought you said you couldn't fly a plane."

"Oh, I never had any trouble keeping one in the air. I just never mastered the art of landing one. Hang on!"

Jim put one hand on the yoke and reached out to disengage the autopilot.

"Is there anything I can do?" Terry asked, his voice shaky.

"Are you a praying man?"

"I didn't used to be."

Jim disengaged the autopilot and the plane went wandering all over the sky.

"Whoa!" Terry hollered.

Jim got control—in a manner of speaking—and put the plane into a gentle descent, all the while keeping an eye on the altimeter and speed indicator. When he reached eight-thousand feet, he leveled off, cut off the flow of oxygen, and removed his mask. "OK, Terry. You can breathe normally now."

"I will breathe normally when I have both feet on the ground. How about using the radio?"

"It's been disabled. Look at it."

The switches to the VHF and UHF radios had been removed and the metal shafts broken off.

"Wonderful," Terry said.

"There is no point in wandering around in the sky until we run out of fuel. Look for a meadow that's reasonably flat."

"And then you'll do what?"

"Land. I'm going down to a couple of thousand feet so we can get a clearer view of the landscape."

"Hadn't you better put the wheels down just in case?"

"No."

"Why, for God's sake?"

"I think it would be better to belly in."

"You think?"

"I saw this movie one time. . . ."

"You saw a fucking movie!"

"You want to fly this thing?"

"Hell, no!"

"Here we go, Terry. Heading down."

Jim put the nose down, and Terry's face paled to the color of chalk.

"Not so fast, goddamnit, slow down!"

"Would you like to tell me how?"

"Well . . . lower the flaps or something!"

"I don't think that's the right thing to do just yet."

"Oh, shit!"

"I think we're going down too fast, Terry."

"I know we are! Do something!"

"What?"

"Hell, I don't know. Level this thing off!"

Jim managed to level off at just over four-thousand feet.

"I think I'm having a heart attack," Terry said.

"No, you're not. Now, listen. I've got to learn how this feels. . . ."

"I can tell you how it feels. It feels awful!"

"I'm going to try a gentle turn to the right now, Terry. Do you have any idea where we are?"

"In the fucking sky!"

Despite their predicament, Jim had to laugh. "Do you recognize any landmarks?"

"There's a lake over there . . . about one o'clock."

"What lake is it?"

"How the hell do I know? I'm not even sure where I am. Jimmy?"

"What?"

"Have you ever landed a plane this size?"

"I . . . well . . . no."

Terry moaned.

"Tell you the truth, I've never flown a twin-engine plane before."

"Jimmy?"

"What?"

"The next time I ask you a question like that, do me a favor, will you?"

"What?"

"Lie about it!"

Ten

Durant and his people watched the pilot float down and were at the site within minutes. There, they broke the bad news to him.

"The plane didn't blow," Dr. Durant told him. "Our spotters radioed that it flew straight and level until disappearing from sight. Miles from here. There was a small explosion in the timber not far from one of the spotter sites."

"Damnit!" the pilot cursed. "That means that one of 'em can fly. They must have found the explosives. I was assured that neither man had any flight training."

"It wasn't Terry," Phil LaBarre said. "I know that for a fact. And if Jim Kincaide is at the controls, I don't know when the hell he ever learned how to fly a plane."

"Shit!" the pilot said. "This really throws a monkey wrench into the works."

"We can't undo what's been done. So let's get out of here," Durant suggested. "We've got towns to retake."

"And some traitors to kill," one of his men said, a coldness behind the words.

"Power to the righteous!" several said simultaneously.

The men moved out, grimly determined that what they were doing was the right thing.

* * *

Terry held on, his eyes wide as Jim buzzed a flowering meadow at a thousand feet at just over stall speed.

"I think that's it, Terry."

"Can you rephrase that?"

Jim grinned. He was much more comfortable now, having located the aileron and rudder trim and learned how the plane responded to his touch. He didn't know if they were going to walk away from this landing, but he was going to give it his best shot.

"I think I might just take up flying again, Terry."

"I wish to hell you'd decided that several years ago."

"Check your harness. Make sure you're buckled in tight."

"If I make it any tighter, I'll strangle myself." Terry peered out the window as they buzzed the meadow again. "What if we end up in that little pond on the end?"

"Then we get wet. Terry? Listen to me. We're not going to have but one chance to do this right. So don't talk to me; don't get my attention off what I'm doing. OK?"

"Is it all right if I faint?"

"Might be easier on you if you did."

Jim banked and started a climb for altitude.

"What the hell are you doing?" Terry almost shouted the question.

"Getting some altitude for my approach. Just trust me."

"Do I have a choice in the matter?"

Jim had no way of knowing wind direction; all he could do was hope for the best. He had made two passes and couldn't spot any ravines or deep depressions in the meadows.

Now there was no point in delaying what had to be done. He was committed.

"Here we go, ol' buddy!"

"Are you sure you don't want the wheels down?"

"I'm sure. No more talking."

Jim had no idea if what he was doing was right. Crash landing was not something his instructor had gone over, thirty years back. Just a few meters—he hoped—off the ground, Jim went full flaps, cut his speed, and dropped like an anvil. He sensed, just at the last second, that he had somehow screwed up, but it was too late to correct it now.

The plane hit hard, bounced, touched again, bounced, settled down. This time it stayed on the ground. The howling and shrieking of metal against rocks was terrible. Pieces of the plane tore off as they impacted against larger rocks that had been hidden by the grass in the meadow.

I came in too fast, Jim thought. Too damn fast.

The tail began slewing from side to side; the propellers were bent in grotesque shapes. The tip of the left wing ripped off with a horrible sound. "Oh, what the hell!" Jim said and let go of the yoke.

"What the hell are you doing?" Terry yelled. "Grab hold of that thing, man!"

"No point!" Jim shouted over the awful noise. "I don't have any control now."

"Did you ever have control?" Terry shouted the question. "Whhhooooaa!" he hollered as the plane turned tail where the nose should have been and they went screaming along backwards. "Oh, shit! Cut the damn speed, Jimmy."

"I can't! There is nothing I can do now."

Jim remembered to cut the engines to lessen the chances of fire. And as he glanced out the window, he was aware their speed had been cut drastically; the plane was slowing with each second. The passing landscape appeared to be in slow motion. For the first time, Jim really felt as if they might make it out alive.

Several heartbeats later, the plane stopped moving. It took a few seconds for that to register in Jim's mind. They had actually stopped!

"Are we dead?" Terry asked, his voice a hoarse whisper.

"We're not even bruised."

"I can't believe we made it."

"Oh, ye of little faith," Jim chided him.

"Now you start quoting Scripture!"

"Let's get the hell out of this plane just in case."

"In case what?"

"It might blow up."

Terry was unbuckled, out of the seat, out the cargo doors, and standing on the ground before Jim could pop his safety harness.

Jim did a walk-around of the plane. The tips of both wings were gone; both propellers were bent and mangled, and part of the tail section was missing.

But they were alive.

Terry walked a few feet away and sat down abruptly on the ground. "My damn legs are shaking so bad I can't stand up."

Jim made another walk-around of the wreck. There was no smoke, no fire. He took several deep breaths, attempting to calm his racing heart and jangled nerves, but it wasn't enough. He, too, had to sit down on the ground to ease his shaking legs.

Jim reached over, plucked a brightly colored, spring meadow-flower from the earth, and smelled it. Nothing had ever been so fragrant. He handed the flower to Terry.

The commander of the nation's militia movement took the flower and held it to his nose. "Wonderful," he said finally.

"We're two very lucky people, Terry. You realize that, don't you?"

"With every fiber of my being and with every breath. You did a hell of a job flying and landing that thing, Jimmy. I owe you my life. And I won't forget this."

"I don't think either one of us will ever forget it."

Terry chuckled. "I gave you a smile or two while we were wandering around in the sky, didn't I?"

Jim laughed. "Yes, you did."

Terry looked all around him. "I wish I knew where we were. None of this country is familiar to me."

"I made several direction changes, but I remember the compass reading due south just before we landed. So that would put that last lake we saw to our west . . . if that helps any."

"Well, if we start walking thataway," Terry said, pointing, "I think we'll run into Highway 28—eventually."

"You think?"

"Yeah."

"You feel like walking?"

"Not at the moment, no. I'm not sure I can stand up."

"Me, neither. We'll just sit here for a few minutes and relax."

"Sounds good to me."

The men stretched out on the cool grass and sighed contentedly. Within minutes, both were, surprisingly, sound asleep. Their adrenaline had slowed, and when it did, nervous exhaustion overtook them.

They came awake to the sounds of a racing engine and frantic shouting. They sat up in the grass, rubbing the sleep from their eyes.

"That's Eddy driving," Terry said. "From sector five. I recognize his Bronco. Now I know where I am for sure."

Jim and Terry stood up and tested their legs, found they would support their weight and function properly.

"How the hell did you find us so quickly?" Terry asked.

"Hell, Terry," the militiaman said. "You're only about five miles from my house. Me and Dave here watched the plane come down. We got news, Terry. Bad news."

"What?"

"You know how a lot of the guys was against this meeting with the president and the peace talks?"

"Yeah. So?"

"Durant and his people just declared open war on the government of the United States. It came over the radio and the TV about forty-five minutes ago. You know how we all took down the license numbers of anyone with a bumper sticker advertising a Democratic candidate for office so we could come back on them later?"

Jim gave his friend a long slow look of incredulity. "You did . . . what?"

Terry met the gaze with a cold look. "It was nationwide. You have to know the enemy, ol' buddy."

"You've got to be kidding!"

"No. I'm not." He looked at Eddie. "What about it, Eddie?"

"Anybody who works for the IRS, the FBI—any

branch of Treasury and Justice—and all liberal politicians is fair game. They've sworn to kill them all if that's what it takes."

"Good God!" Jim exclaimed.

"Oh, the news isn't any surprise to me, Jim." Terry spoke as calmly as if ordering a burger and fries. "I saw it coming a long time ago."

This thing just keeps getting more and more bizarre, Jim thought. What next?

"Neither one of you guys is hurt?" the other man asked.

"Not a scratch," Jim said.

"It's a miracle," Eddie said. "Come on. Let's get into town."

"Damnedest thing I ever seen," Eddie's friend said.

"You should have seen it from my position," Terry muttered.

Jim and Terry were hours late for their meeting with the president, but they made it. They were driven to the White House in an unmarked panel van, hidden from the eyes of the press—and there were plenty of press types around, eager for a story, any type of story about the uprising in America.

"Sharks in a feeding frenzy," President Potter said, turning from the window to greet Jim and Terry. He shook hands with both men and waved them to chairs. "I heard about your . . . ah . . . close call, gentlemen," he said, sitting down in a chair, a coffee table between them. "That shows just how heavily Baronne's people have infiltrated the military." He looked directly at them.

"But that's no news to either of you. You have your own people in there as well, right, Commander Warden?"

Terry was all business. "You know we do, Mr. President."

"Yes. So I do. Well . . . let's get right down to it, boys. You mind if I call you *boys?* I don't mean anything derogatory by it."

"Not at all," Jim said with a grin.

"My movement is not exactly politically correct, Mr. President," Terry added.

"No." Fred stretched the word into two syllables. "I suppose not. Well, boys, I think it would be safe to say that with this uprising, you all have made your point that some drastic changes are due in this nation."

"Jim had nothing to do with it, sir," Terry pointed out.

"I beg your pardon, Mr. Warden?"

"Jim and a bunch of other New York City liberals came up to his lodge in the park to escape the violence and sit it out. I . . . ah . . . well . . . sort of pressed him into service. We were friends when we were kids, used to play together. When he wouldn't line up with Baronne's people, they attacked the group. Jim got his dander up. That's when my group stepped into the picture. Jim and his people were caught in the middle, you might say. He was forced to take a side, and he chose us. That's how Jim got involved. I just wanted to clear that up for Jim's sake. That's all."

Fred nodded. "I'm glad, Mr. Warden."

"How about calling us Terry and Jim, sir?"

"Suits me. All right, let's get to it. First of all, this meeting is not being recorded. The tape recorders are off and so are the cameras."

"Cameras, sir?" Jim asked.

"Yes. There are cameras positioned in rooms behind

the walls. They usually roll. That started after Nixon. So, you boys are free to vent your spleens, so to speak."

"And you, as well, sir," Terry said.

"Yes. That's very true. Now, I'm going to call in my chief of staff, Reese Perkins, a senator and representative, the senate majority leader, the speaker of the house, and a member of the joint chiefs. All right?"

"Fine with me," Terry said.

"Good. Very good." Fred picked up a phone and spoke briefly. Within seconds, four men, one in uniform, entered the room. Introductions were made and coffee and sandwiches were brought in.

"If meetings such as this one had been held a couple of years ago," Terry said, "the revolt might never have taken place."

"Your part in it might not have," Fred said. "But Baronne's people would have risen up regardless."

Jim nodded. "I agree with that, sir. May I ask a question?"

"You may ask anything you like, Jim."

"Where is the attorney general and the director of the FBI?"

"Both of them have resigned—at my request."

"Good," Terry said. "Do something with that goddamn ATF bunch, and we'll really be making progress."

Fred smiled. "Terry, they were taking orders from the president."

"I'm sure of that," Terry came right back. "Plus a number of senators and reps."

"True," Senator Pittman noted. "But their constituents have as much right to representation as you do, Mr. Warden."

"I agree with that, sir." Jim stepped in. "But these

past several weeks have opened my eyes to a degree I've never before experienced. Now, to clear the air, I'm a registered Democrat and I've voted the party line for years. Up until a few weeks ago, I was what Terry refers to as a raging liberal. I'm still liberal in many ways; but, and this might surprise you, so is he on many issues."

"I don't doubt that," General Coplin said. "I wouldn't want to be in the same room with a person who didn't have some compassion in them." He looked at Jim. "Sorry for the interruption, Mr. Kincaide. Please, continue."

"Thank you, sir. I really didn't realize how much discontent, unhappiness, disgust, mistrust of government and politicians, and just plain hate there was among so many American citizens until I got involved in this . . . movement . . . revolution . . . whatever word future historians will finally choose to call it. But I certainly have a better understanding of it now."

Jim took a sip of coffee and carefully returned the cup with the presidential seal to the saucer. "My childhood friend Terry asked me to be a spokesman for the group—a salesman, if you will. All right, I'll certainly try. Gentlemen, during the last few days I've spoken with people who are not wild-eyed fanatics, right-wing whackos, racists, or anything that even remotely resemble those labels that many members of the press have given them. That isn't to say there aren't those who fit the label scattered among the groups, for I'm sure there are, but I haven't met any. Instead, I met citizens who are drowning in a sea of government-mandated paperwork, an ocean of government-passed rules and regulations. I met citizens who are convinced—rightly or wrongly—that the federal government is their enemy, who believe the federal government is slowly turning socialist, or Marxist. They see what they believe are their constitutionally guaranteed rights being taken away from them. I will agree with those people that they are overtaxed and underrepresented. I will agree with them that Congress is full of hot air and bullshit . . ."

President Potter made no attempt to choke back his chuckle at that, even though he did receive a very dirty look from Senator Pittman.

". . . Our judicial system is on the verge of collapse," Jim continued. "I'll agree with that. Our courts are so concerned with dotting each *i* and crossing each *t* that they are missing the point of whether the suspect is guilty or not. Our judges seem to be more interested in technicalities than in a search for truth. Defense attorneys are allowed to confuse jurors and distort evidence. We've become a nation of bad laws that permit the criminal to have more rights than the victim." Jim folded the piece of paper on which he'd hurriedly jotted down a few notes earlier that day and put it in his pocket. He lifted his eyes to the steady gaze of the president. "Will that do for starters, sir?"

"I believe it does, Mr. Kincaide. You have any ideas where to go next?"

Jim smiled. "As a matter of fact, I do, sir. I sure do."

Eleven

Jim and Terry were put up in a nice hotel in town under assumed names, and both slept well. They were awakened just before dawn by a secret service man.

"Your town's been retaken by a unit of Baronne's men," they were informed. "The chief of police is dead; and as far as we can determine, so are what was left of his men." He cut his eyes to Jim. "We don't know what happened to Major Shaw, Mr. Kincaide. I'm sorry."

Jim and Terry showered and shaved and dressed and were driven back to the White House in what looked like the same closed van they had arrived in only hours before. The place was jumping with activity. They were escorted to the Oval Office and a harried President Potter waved them to chairs while he spoke on the phone.

The office was crowded with men and women; both Jim and Terry recognized most of them as members of the House and Senate, liberal and conservative. The conservatives gave them friendly, if curious, glances. The liberal members offered them distinctly hostile looks.

"The enemy has arrived," a woman said, making sure her words were heard by both men.

"Fuck you," Terry told the woman senator from California.

The woman's face paled and her eyes narrowed; her

lips pressed together until they were nearly bloodless under a light shading of lipstick.

"We've had a few setbacks, boys," Fred said.

"We heard," Jim replied.

"Thanks to gun-nuts and whackos," a congressman from Michigan said.

Terry looked at the president. "What about my people?"

"They took a real beating, Terry," the chief of staff answered for Fred. "According to the rather sketchy reports we've received thus far, they held out for as long as they could—and put up quite a fight—before pulling back. That's the story all over the country. Baronne obviously was holding a large force in reserve. Your people were simply overwhelmed."

The senator from California opened her mouth to speak and Fred, very unstatesmanlike said, "Shut up, Ruth."

Ruth Bergquist closed her mouth and glared undisguised hate at the president.

"Our electronic town meeting will have to be put off for a time, boys," Fred said.

"What electronic town meeting?" Michigan Representative Hatcher demanded.

"*What* meeting?" Brooklyn Representative Weinheimer echoed.

"I'll explain it all later," Fred told the group. He looked at Jim and Terry. "I can arrange transportation for you boys—wherever and whenever you like."

"Can you give us a car?" Terry asked.

A fast smile came and went on Fred's face. "Sure, Terry. And a safe escort outside the military-controlled sector. After that . . . well, you're on your own."

"We'll make it," Jim said.

"I'm sure they have friends lurking on the outskirts of the city who will supply them with all sorts of guns!" Senator Bergquist flapped her mouth.

The senator from California had loudly, and as often as possible, proclaimed her desire to disarm all Americans . . . and to hell with anybody who disagreed with her. However, for years she had had a concealed weapons permit from the State of California and, during the past eighteen-or-so months, had been surrounded by hired bodyguards (paid for by American taxpayers) who protected her precious body with guns. To say she was a practicing hypocrite would be to belabor a point.

"We'll be in touch," Terry said, rising to his feet. He stuck out his hand and Fred took it. "We can work this thing out, Mr. President. It'll just take a little time, that's all."

"I'm sure we can, Terry."

"I'll get my people together and see about dealing with Baronne. Just keep the military off our backs for as long as possible, please."

Fred hesitated. He had not lied to either of these men and did not want to start now. He sighed. "I'll level with you: The brass is getting restless about this situation. I urge you to wrap it up as quickly as possible."

"We'll do our best, sir," Jim said.

As they were leaving, escorted by the secret service, Jim heard Senator Bergquist say, "Right-wing whackos!"

"Shut up, Ruth," the president said wearily.

When conditions began going sour, the decay spread nationwide in less than twenty-four hours. White-supremacist groups began rising up and spreading terror all over the nation. The majority of those groups had gone hard underground back in the late seventies and early eighties due to government pressure and had done their recruiting carefully and clandestinely. One group, called The Storm, had started out with a membership of less than twenty-five and in fifteen years had grown to over a quarter-of-a-million hard-core members, nationwide. The irony of that was that its front group, The Wind, had operated openly and even had web pages on the Internet. After someone requested more information on The Wind and, after receiving the literature, expressed a desire to learn more, they were carefully checked out and, after a period of time, sometimes as long as several years, eventually brought into The Storm.

The Wind and The Storm hated Jews, blacks, and homosexuals; and their agenda was to rid America of them. It was one huge, powerful, and dangerous group. And it had reached gale proportions nationwide.

"That military guy said Janet would be on one of these frequencies," Jim said, glancing at a piece of paper. "And she's probably with some of your people . . . if any of them got away," he added grimly.

"They made it, Jim. Janet's tough and so are my people. They're trained to hit and run and get the hell gone. Not die needlessly."

"I keep hoping."

"It's this Storm bunch that has me worried."

"You knew about them?"

"Oh, yes. But I didn't think they were this big."

"You think they've hooked up with Baronne?"

"I'd bet on it. And if they have, you can believe the military won't be long in getting involved. My people are game, but they can't fight hundreds of thousands of neo-Nazis."

"They're that big?"

"Put Baronne's people with them, and they'll number half a million, nationwide."

Jim shook his head as the men sped north, rapidly putting the nation's capital behind them. "How did it ever come to this?"

"Because Washington wouldn't listen," Terry replied.

Of Terry's original bunch, only a handful had escaped the fight in the town. Karen, Judy, and Rose, Johnny Burnette and Al Milner had managed to survive the assault, Major Janet Shaw with them. They had made the lodge, picked up the group there, including the FBI agent Pat Monroe and his wife Claire, and within the hour, after throwing together some supplies, were heading for the safety of the timber.

In order to make his plan work, Baronne reluctantly agreed to step up and shake hands with the devil, agreeing to join forces with The Wind and The Storm. After all, the two organizations shared many of the same views. And to make matters worse, across the nation, a major race war was on the verge of exploding.

In Los Angeles, police and federal troops were hard pressed to keep the lid on the boiling race pot, but so far they had managed to keep the killings down to a minimum. Other cities, despite the presence of troops, were not as fortunate as residents, with real or imagined grievances, loaded up rifles and shotguns and dug out pistols and took to the streets and the alleys to settle old grudges.

In many areas, blacks (man, woman, or teenager) took their lives in their own hands just driving through white sections of town. Walking there was out of the question. Whites got the same treatment in black neighborhoods.

Around Atlanta, a group of cross-burning nitwits flapped their sheets and made the mistake of going up against Huey Clark's Georgia Black Militia. The fight was short and brutal, with Huey's group walking away victorious.

The nation soon found—in some areas very violently—that the militia movement had not been solely confined to whites. In addition to the black militias, there were Indian and Hispanic militias. The entire Southwest, including parts of Texas, was threatening to blow up in everybody's face.

Still, President Potter hesitated to turn the military loose full force. He felt that at this time, that would serve only to harden the positions of the militia and Baronne and his allies. But neither could he openly support the militias against Baronne's fanatical ultra-right-wing, religious followers . . . even though many people had already guessed that was the case. He was, as the saying goes, caught between a rock and a hard place.

Jim and Terry planned to drive straight through, stopping only for food and gas—and one more stop that Terry refused to say more about. The car that had been provided for them had a full police package under the hood and a beefed-up suspension. Jim and Terry also had passes, issued them by the White House and signed by the president, allowing them to pass through any road-block manned by federal troops or the nation's police.

Just about an hour outside of Washington, D.C., Terry cut off the highway onto a secondary road, followed that for about fifteen minutes, then took a winding county road that got Jim thoroughly lost in a matter of minutes.

Terry finally pulled into the driveway of an isolated farmhouse and cut the engine. "Let's get armed, Jim. Come on."

In the basement of the house, Jim stood in awe. The large room was filled with cases of field rations, cases of ammunition, boxes of hand grenades and mortar rounds, and racks of weapons.

"Take your pick," Terry said with a wave of his hand.

Jim didn't hesitate. He chose the weapon he was most familiar with—an M-16, with a selector switch that could enable him to go to full auto. He filled a sack with full thirty-round magazines.

"How many places such as this do you people have, Terry?"

"Several hundred, located all over the nation. We've been stockpiling for years, ever since we saw which direction the country was heading."

Jim let his eyes sweep the gun racks: AK-47's, Chinese SKS's, N&K fully automatic 9mm submachine guns, American M-60's and Stoners, chain guns and several .50 caliber machine guns. There were MAC 10's and 11's, in 9mm and .45 caliber. Several racks of semi-automatic AR-15's and Mini-14's.

"That rifle you picked out at the lodge might be long gone, Jim. Better pick out another one. There's a Heckler & Koch competition rifle over there in .308 with one hell of a scope on it. It was donated by a friend. Damn thing cost about ten-thousand dollars."

"At least," Jim muttered, after opening the hard, plastic gun case and inspecting the rifle. He added several boxes of hand-loaded ammunition for the weapon and waited for Terry to finish packing rucksacks full of supplies.

"Overwhelmed by the size of it all, Jim?" Terry asked casually.

"You could say that. You people have been preparing for war for years."

"Oh, yes. But you can believe this or not, Jimmy: Damn few of us ever wanted it to come to this."

Jim nodded slowly. "I believe you, Terry. I wouldn't have, a month ago, but I do now."

"What changed your mind?"

"Talking to some of the militia members, then seeing what Baronne and his nuts have in mind for the future of America."

"Baronne has to be stopped . . . if it's the only thing we accomplish. We've got to stop him."

"I'm surprised the military hasn't already stepped in."

Terry smiled. Rather strangely, Jim thought. "That would be the worst thing the president could do. If he moved against Baronne and left us alone, that would pull Baronne's fence-straddlers off the fence and solidly into his corner. If he moved against us and left Baronne alone, that would pull a lot of people who are undecided over to us. If he moved against both of us, he'd have a full-blown, nationwide civil war that would last for years."

"Is there an end in sight, Terry?"

"Sure. My people will compromise. We never expected *all* of our demands to be met." He grinned. "That is, we'll compromise on most issues."

"Yes," Jim said drily, picking up his load. "I know. Let's get back on the road."

"Jim?" Terry's voice stopped him, and he turned around. "Have you considered that Janet might not be all she claims?"

Jim put down the rucksack filled with full magazines and grenades, then set down the gun case containing the sniper rifle. He sighed heavily. "Yes, I have."

"And? . . ."

"I guess that's something I'm going to have to play by ear, Terry. Hell, she's been an Army spook ever since she got out of college. You remember those people from 'Nam. They're weird anyway."

"You can say that again. All right. But, Jim, and please don't take this the wrong way: Until you're sure about Janet, play your cards close to the vest, will you?"

Jim laughed. "It's probably good advice, Terry. But there is only one hitch to it."

"What's that?"

"You're the only one with any cards to play."

"Things moving pretty fast, Fred," Reese said.

The two men finally had a few moments alone. Fred had noticed that Reese had been carrying around a sealed file folder for more than an hour but had not revealed its contents while the office was full of people.

"Too damn fast," the president concurred. "According to the reports I've read, this Terry Warden was commander of a militia unit in upstate New York one day, then the next day, he was elected or appointed or however the hell they do it, national commander of all militias. It doesn't make sense."

Reese held up the folder. "This will clear it up, I think."

Fred took off his glasses and tossed them to the desk. "Read it to me, Reese. I can't get used to these damn bifocals."

"I don't have to read it. It's so brief I can quote from memory. Terry Warden has done contract work for the CIA since his days in Vietnam."

"Son . . . of . . . a . . . bitch!" Fred swore. "The DCI was just in this office, sitting right there—" He pointed. "—not thirty minutes ago and he didn't say a damn word about it."

Reese shook his head. "He probably doesn't know. Hell, Fred, you know as well as I that the DCI is not much more than a figurehead. Besides, that isn't the point."

"Well, what the hell is the point?"

"I was just on the phone with State. Their intelligence people believe that rogue agents from all federal enforcement agencies, including the CIA, have been secretly supplying the militia movement with arms for several years." He held up a hand. "That's not all. So has the military. And State has proof of that."

Fred leaned back in his chair and rubbed his eyes. "OK. Now it makes sense to me. It's finally beginning to come together The military hated Evans and he hated the military. Some in the Bureau felt Evans was using them to harass people who talked against him—which he was. And he was wrong in doing so. Others in government didn't like him because he was an overbearing prick—which he was. Still others didn't like the attorney general and the director of the Bureau—among others in the Evans administration." Fred sighed and shook his head. "Aw . . . shit!"

"It's a hell of a mess, Fred"

The president nodded his head in agreement. "But where does this James Kincaide fit in? According to the FBI report, there isn't a blemish on his record—solid citizen type. Big contributor to the party. Then all of a sudden, he's Warden's second in command. What the hell's going on?"

"He makes the militia movement look respectable, Fred. Warden was smart enough to see that and grab him while he could."

Fred drummed his fingertips on the desk. "Is there a power play going on among the military's top brass, Reese?"

"Not to take over this office. No one believes that. But any military man who sucked up to Evans is going to be in deep shit among his fellow officers, you can bet the farm on that."

"I'll tell you something else that sucks, Reese. . . ."

"What?"

"This damn job!"

Twelve

Dr. Gene Baronne had carefully planned his every move . . . but he had not taken into consideration that the majority of the nation's militia members would turn against him. Weeks back, he would have laughed at the suggestion.

But they *had* turned against him; and to make matters worse, the government was quietly backing *them.* And now Baronne was sure that some in the military, and probably middle-level personnel in government enforcement agencies as well, had been secretly supporting the militia movement for years.

Who would have believed that a bunch of niggers would have formed their own militia and would be as well-trained and disciplined as Huey Clark's people? That had astonished Baronne. Had to be a fluke . . . the exception rather than the rule. Couldn't be anything else. A purebred, blue-gum nigger just wasn't capable of outthinking a white man. Sure, they could jump higher and run faster because they were closer to animals than whites. Everybody with any sense knew that. They could last longer in a boxing ring because their skulls were thicker than a white man's. Right there was walking, grunting proof a nigger's first cousin was an ape.

Take a fool to deny that.

Baronne called a meeting of his most trusted people and told them, "We can't win the way we've been fighting. God is on our side—I don't want any of you ever to doubt that—but sometimes God needs our help. This is one of those times. Oh, we could drag this out for months, even years, but in the end, *ZOG** would win. We have to strike at the very heart of government. We have to force the hand of government. And I know how."

"Baronne's forces just up and pulled out," a New York highway cop told Jim and Terry when they stopped in a rest area to use the men's room. The patrolman had driven in behind them, and Terry and Jim had identified themselves. The letter signed by the president put the highway cop at ease.

"Pulled . . . out?" Terry questioned.

"They quit every town they'd taken over," the trooper told them. "And not just in this area. All over the country. They just up and pulled back."

"Back where?" Jim asked.

"No one knows. It started early this morning. Baronne's people just faded out of sight. But you can bet something is in the wind. If this is a civil war, it's got to be the freakiest civil war ever fought."

"How do you mean?" Jim matched the intensity of the cop's gaze.

"Well, hell. The government hates the militia movement; they tried to put them out of business for years. Then along comes this Gene Baronne and his whacky group. For some reason or another, the military won't get

---

* Zionist Occupation government

involved. Now we've got the very groups the government tried to put out of business taking the side of the government *against* Baronne. It's a great big mess is what it is."

Back on the road, Jim said, "You know a lot more about this Gene Baronne than I do, Terry. What do you think he's up to?"

Terry was keeping the speedometer steady at seventy. He shook his head. "Damned if I know; but I can tell you this, he's got some real fanatics with him. And he's smooth. He can convince people to do things they ordinarily wouldn't even think of doing. That highway cop was right. This is a damn weird civil war."

After Baronne's forces pulled out, what was left of Terry's local militia left the timber and moved back into the Kincaide lodge. Janet felt the lodge would be the first place Jim would check out, and it was.

"We've got people scattered all over the area, Terry," Al Milner told him. "But of the local bunch, what you see here is all that survived the fight with Durant's bunch just after you left."

Johnny Burnette, Karen, Rose, Judy, and Al.

"We've been in contact with other groups around the nation," Al said. "They're hanging fire until they hear from you."

"Where's the base radio?" Terry asked.

"We set it up in one of the outbuildings. It's ready to go. What are we going to do, Terry?"

Terry did not immediately reply, and it occurred to Jim that the man didn't have the vaguest idea what they were going to do next. "Still keeping an eye on us, Pat?"

Terry asked the FBI man, who was sitting off to one side of the den, his wife, Claire, by his side.

"I'm still around, Terry."

Jim looked at Steve Malone, the minister who had supposedly lost his calling. "I had no other place to go," the man said quietly.

Terry walked outside with his entourage and left Jim with the others.

"What do you hear about the city?" Don asked.

"Still pretty much shut down. Emergency traffic only on the bridges still passable. The initial reports about all bridges being down were wildly exaggerated. But the city is a long way from being back to normal. Where're Donald and his girlfriend?"

"In the basement. Our bunch is all right."

"What is happening in the nation?" Shirley asked.

Jim looked at Janet. She shrugged her shoulders. "You probably know as much or more as I do," she said. "How was the president?"

"Harried. Tired. Worried. Any idea what Baronne's up to?"

"How would I know?"

"You still report in every day, don't you?"

"Yes." He met her gaze directly. "Not to give you a short answer."

Jim looked at the FBI man, who shrugged his shoulders. "I was told to take it easy until I'm back to a hundred percent. I don't know what's going on. But I am curious as to why the military hasn't stepped in and done something."

"You and me and about two hundred and fifty million other Americans," Jim replied.

"Did you hear about Huey Clark's black militia down in Georgia?" Janet asked.

"On the news coming up. We heard they kicked the crap out of some white-supremacist group."

"That they did. Now they're assisting the Atlanta police in keeping order. It just came on the radio news. Huey's group has already shot several black looters. Huey was quoted as saying if the L.A.P.D. had been allowed to shoot looters on sight out there, the Los Angeles riots could have been contained in a matter of a few hours, not days."

"If more blacks were like Huey—" Terry spoke from the screen door. "—and less anxious to scream police brutality every time the cops make an arrest, the races wouldn't be so far apart in this nation . . . and getting further apart."

"Oh, hell, yes!" Donald screamed from the stairwell. "Sure!" The young man stepped into the den. "And maybe it might help if the cops would stop picking on African-Americans."

"Oh, horseshit!" Terry said. "The law is the law. We can't have one set of laws for whites and another set of laws for blacks." He stepped into the house. "Grow up, boy."

"You don't call me *boy,* you mother-fucker!" Donald yelled.

Terry was across the room in a heartbeat, his eyes flashing danger signs and his face hard with anger. He decked Donald. The young man bounced to his feet and Terry hit him again, a left and right combination, then planted a solid right fist in Donald's belly. The air whooshed out of Donald and he hit the floor, gasping and gagging.

Terry backed up and stood, looking down at him. "I'm forty-five years old, *boy.* So that makes you a *boy* to me. There is nothing racial connected with it. And if you don't like it, *boy,* you can go right straight to hell!"

Terry wheeled and left the lodge. The screen door banged closed behind him.

Don helped his son to his feet. He turned and faced Jim. "I'll take my son's side in this issue, Jim."

"Your option, ol' buddy. But a nineteen- or twenty-year-old has no business calling a grown man a mother-fucker."

"I think it might be time for us to head back to the city," Don replied stiffly.

"That might not be wise on your part, Don. Think about it. You're ticked off now. Wait. Cool down. You know you're among friends here."

"Are we?" Don asked softly.

Jim and Janet sat on the front porch and watched as Don and Shirley left in one car, Donald and LaShana in another. Jim lifted a hand in farewell. Only Shirley returned the gesture.

"It's natural for a parent to defend his child," Jim said.

"Not when the child is wrong," Janet countered.

"Our group is shrinking," Pat Monroe commented, stepping out onto the porch, Claire beside him.

"Our group?" Jim questioned.

"Well, I feel a part of it, anyway," the Bureau man replied, "whether I am or not. Hell, you people saved my life."

"And the objectives of the militias?" Jim prompted.

Pat shifted in the chair, his brow furrowed in thought. "Off the record, of course?"

"Naturally."

"The country was drifting to the left, no doubt about that. Drifting, hell! It was racing to the left. Had to be stopped. I'll agree with the militia movement on that point, and a couple of others. The criminal justice system was screwed up. Too many criminals were in and out of that revolving door of justice. And people have a right to defend themselves, loved ones, and property without fear of going to jail for it, or losing everything they have in civil court. On those points, you people . . ." He gestured toward Jim. "Well . . . I know you got pressed into this . . . Terry's people, that is, are right on the money."

"AG Newton would have a heart attack if she knew you felt that way," Janet said.

"Stella Newton is an idiot," Pat said flatly. "I'm glad she's gone. But it might surprise you to learn that a lot of Bureau people share my opinions about this uprising."

"By the way," Claire interjected, "I just made a fresh pot of coffee. I'll pour us some."

"I'll help," Janet said.

Jim grinned. "Getting domesticated, aren't you?"

"You bet," she came right back. "You'd better watch out, boy. I've got my sights on you."

Laughing, the women entered the house.

"Jim," Pat said, when the women were out of earshot, "I wouldn't trust Terry one hundred percent . . . not yet, anyway."

"Why?"

"I have good reason to believe he's still heavily connected with the Company. He's been doing contract work for them for years. Did you know he speaks Spanish, German, and can get by in Russian?"

"Terry?"

"Yes. He was recruited in 'Nam. But he wasn't a team player and didn't fit in with the ol' boy network that was so prevalent within the Agency at that time . . . probably still is. They gave him the boot but still use him occasionally. That's firm."

"Jesus Christ! Terry. Next you'll be telling me not to trust Janet."

"Did Terry warn you about her?"

"Well . . . in a way, yes."

Pat chuckled. "I thought he would. Forget that. Janet's all right. We've worked with her a number of times."

Jim sat in silence, absorbing all that Pat had just told him. Janet shoved open the screen door and said, "You guys had better come in and hear this. It's started all over again. With a bang—literally."

Thirteen

"What is it?" Pat asked as they returned to the den.

Janet pointed to the small TV set she had brought from town to replace the wide-screen that had been hit by gunfire several days back. "Baronne's letting out all the stops. It came on as a news flash. They're going to a field correspondent now, but they're having some difficulty."

"There it comes," Claire said as everybody took seats.

". . . expected anything like this to happen," the network correspondent was caught in midsentence. "It's terrible! Except for the obvious devastation, about all we can tell you for sure at this time is that an elderly gentleman drove his car up to the roadblock at the same time a National Guard convoy was preparing to exit, heading in the other direction. The old man then detonated what must have been a massive amount of explosives packed in his vehicle. Some are saying hundreds of pounds of high explosives. All the guards at the barricades, all the troops in the first two trucks, and a number of people in buildings on either side of the street are dead. Blown to pieces. Preliminary figures are several hundred dead and wounded. My God!" the correspondent blurted, momentarily losing his professionalism. "I've never seen anything like it. There are body parts scattered all over a two-block area. What?' Yes." He put a hand to an earplug. "Oh, my God, no! All right. Yes. I'm sorry about that. This is Rick Perkins, on the scene in Chicago. We have another report coming in from Portland. Here is Vicki Walters from our affiliate station K. . . ."

The last bit of his transmission was lost in switching and a young woman appeared, standing in a light rain. Behind her, the remains of a ruined building. Several mangled bodies dangled from ruined floors above street-level, caught in grotesque positions amid the twisted metal support rods and concrete. "This is Vicki Walters in Portland. Behind me . . . what is left of the federal building after a suicide bomber drove her pickup truck past the barricades, past the guards, and into the lobby on the ground floor. Initial reports indicate an elderly woman was behind the wheel of the truck and loud religious music was playing from the radio or tape deck. Probably no one will ever know for sure about that, since the pickup truck was totally destroyed in the blast. When the woman turned the corner, right there—" She pointed. "—she accelerated. Eyewitnesses report she was traveling at least sixty miles an hour when she smashed through the barricades, jumped the curb, and roared into the lobby of the building. Eyewitnesses also report that the woman was smiling and appeared to be singing along with the music. Casualty reports are sketchy at this time, but we do know that the building was at least partially occupied by government workers. A spokesperson from the Portland bomb squad told me that it would take several hundred pounds of high explosives to cause devastation such as this. But he could give me no indication as to what type of explosive might have been used. This is Vicki Walters on the scene in downtown Portland. Peter? . . ."

"Yes," the familiar face filled the screen. "We have yet another report coming in from Atlanta. Gerry Watson is standing by. Gerry?"

"Peter, this is Gerry Watson in Atlanta. Behind me, twisted metal and broken concrete is all that is left of the IRS regional center. The building was fully staffed due to the relaxing of hostilities in this country. We know now that relaxing was a ruse. First reports are that several hundred people are dead and at least that many more injured—to what extent, we don't know. Many of the wounded are trapped amid the rubble, and rescue crews are going to have to be very cautious in any attempt to free them due to the instability of the building. What we do know for sure is that it was an elderly man who drove the pickup truck past the troops and police manning the barricades and into the side of the building. We also have interviewed several people who told us the man was smiling and waving as he drove to his death." The reporter paused, frowned, and then said, "Yes. All right. We're going to go to San Francisco now, for a report from Chick LaRue. This is Gerry Watson in Atlanta. . . ."

"I'm standing in front of City Hall, Gerry," Chick said. "Just about twenty minutes ago, a massive explosive device went off inside the building during a meeting of concerned citizens. The mayor and several other city officials are among the known dead. The large room in which they were holding the meeting was completely destroyed, and the building has suffered structural damage from the blast. Bodies and parts of bodies were hurled out of shattered windows. Rescue workers are still unable to reach the meeting room, which—I'm told—was filled to capacity. Moments before the blast, police received a call from a man who said he was suffering from inoperable cancer and wanted to die doing God's work. The call was tape-recorded, of course, and a police spokesperson said much of the caller's message was confused and filled with bits and pieces of Scripture intermingled with hateful words concerning homosexuals. I . . ."

A huge booming sound shook the ground, and the camera trembled. Several blocks behind the reporter, the entire front of a building blew out. Seconds later, before the reporter could regain his composure, the street where he was standing blew up; Chick and his cameraperson vanished. TV screens all over the nation went dark for a moment. The face of a badly shaken anchorman appeared, his tie loosened and shirt collar open.

"Ladies and gentlemen, we are now going to switch to the Emergency Action Notification System. . . ." He paused, brushed a hand across his face, cut his eyes away from the camera for a second, and said, "Oh, all right. Or whatever the hell it's called!" He threw a pen down on the desk and glared at the camera. After a moment, he said, "Well, do something! I feel like an idiot sitting here!"

The room seemed to move from side to side for a moment. The anchorman paled and grabbed onto the edge of his desk as his chair started to slide and the room tilted. In the background, there were screams of fright and shadowy figures ran in all directions. Others could be seen picking themselves up off the floor.

"The building has been . . . *what?*" The anchorman yelled the question at someone behind the scene. "Bombed!" The usually unflappable anchorman cleared his throat, brushed at his hair, looked at the camera, which was now at a definite angle, tilted to the left, and said in a very calm voice, "Well, shit!"

The next day there were fifty attacks on federal buildings, city buildings, black churches, Jewish synagogues, and military barricades. Fifty attacks and forty-nine explosions. One of the massive charges failed to detonate, and the elderly woman driving the truck was taken into custody. She was in her mid-eighties and dying of cancer.

Baronne had called for the old and the dying to sacrifice their lives for the cause in suicide runs. The faithful had volunteered in droves, happy to die for Christ.

"Monstrous!" Jim said, taking a break from watching the television.

"And you can bet he's got a lot more willing volunteers waiting in the wings," Pat noted.

"Several of those bombers were teenagers," Janet added. "Just kids, according to witnesses."

Terry had disappeared, and no one had seen him or any of what remained of his local militia force for over twenty-four hours. Everyone in the den of the lodge looked up at the sound of many vehicles pulling into the drive.

"Terry," Steve Malone called from the porch. "With militia leaders from all over the country."

"You know these people?" Jim asked, walking to the screen door and looking out.

"Most of them," the minister acknowledged. "This would account for all those small planes we saw this afternoon."

"Jim," Terry said, stepping up to the porch. He waved his hand at the men and women who were standing near the drive. They were dressed in civilian clothing and looked like any other group of accountants, small-business owners, salespeople, doctors, lawyers, and just plain folks. "These twenty-one people represent militias from fifteen states. We've been meeting over at the VFW Hall in town. They wanted to meet all of you before heading back to their units."

"Even me?" Pat asked, taking his place beside Jim.

"Especially you," Terry said. "I wanted them to see a real live FBI man and show them that you don't have horns and a tail."

Pat smiled—rather thinly, Jim thought—and said, "All right, Terry. What's your game plan this time? What the hell are you up to now?"

Terry cut his eyes to Jim. "Did Pat tell you all about me, Jimmy-boy? Did he tell you I've been doing contract work for the CIA for years? Well, I have. The Company recruited me twenty-five years ago . . . in 'Nam. Being a self-employed small businessman I was a natural for contract work. I made a nice piece of change every time I went out. Hell—" He waved his hand at the militia leaders. "—all these people know I worked for the Agency."

"And the CIA has been helping to supply the militia movement with weapons for years?" Jim questioned.

Terry placed his index finger to his lips. "Now, Jimmy, you don't expect me to give away all my secrets, do you?" Without waiting for a reply, he looked at Janet. "I guess this revelation doesn't come as any surprise to you, does it, Major?"

Janet shook her head. "No, Terry, it doesn't."

Terry chuckled. "Well . . . what's in the past is over and done. Let's talk about now. We've got to stop Baronne before the military has no choice but to get involved. The public is going to demand it. And if that happens, that will be the beginning of the longest-running guerrilla war in the history of the world."

"You have a plan?" Pat asked.

"Not much of one," Terry admitted. "And I don't know whether anyone in Washington will agree to go along with it. But we can't sit around and do nothing while this nation sinks in guerrilla quicksand. And that's what's going to happen if we don't come up with something and do it damn fast."

"Well," Janet offered offhandedly, "you and Jim have a pipeline to Washington."

"Jim does," Terry replied.

"What do you mean?" Jim asked. "We both met the president."

"Yeah, but by now President Potter probably knows that I'm heavily involved with the Company. I've got a hunch he might not trust me as much as he would you. It might be better if you talked to the man."

Jim sat down on a step and stared at Terry. "I wouldn't know where to begin."

Terry shrugged his shoulders. "You're an ad man, Jim. You've been taking ideas and turning them into successful sales campaigns for years. I'll tell you my idea and you take it from there."

"I guess it won't hurt to listen," Jim agreed. "Is this a big dark secret or do you tell me now?"

Jim laughed. "It's no secret and it isn't much of a plan. All you have to do is convince President Potter to agree to a meeting and to give Baronne some power in the new government."

"A coalition government?"

"I suppose that's the word."

Jim shook his head. "The people won't go along with it, Terry. America is based on democracy. Majority rule."

"Which obviously hasn't been working to the satisfaction of millions of Americans, Jim," Terry shot back. "Maybe it's time to try something else. Hell, it's worth a shot, isn't it?"

"Maybe. Go on."

"The president sets up a huge bank of toll-free numbers for people to call in and air their grievances—that's for people who don't want to appear on camera."

"On camera?"

"Sure. A huge link-up with every TV station in the nation. Those who want to can step up and say what's on their mind. Jim, you know as well as I do that for years Washington has been out of touch with the populace. This would give everybody, over a period of . . . hell, I don't know—five days, a week, a month, as long as it takes, a chance to say their piece. And the president could guarantee complete anonymity for those who wish it. It would be the biggest town meeting in history. That's the way it used to be done. Jesus, Jim, it's better than shooting at each other, isn't it?"

"Even if the president would agree to go along with it, in the end, Terry, what would it solve?" Jim asked.

"Maybe nothing, but it would give everybody some breathing room, some time to cool off. But Baronne would have to agree to stand his people down during that time." He waved his hand at the militia leaders. "We've all agreed to it. Unanimously." He cut his eyes to Pat Malone. "Pat, I know you don't like me or trust me, but could you convince your bosses to sit back and not snoop around or infiltrate during this time—if everybody agrees to the plan, that is? The first sign of a double-cross could blow the whole deal."

"Terry," the Bureau man said, "like or trust doesn't have anything to do with it. I don't have any special stroke with the powers that be. What you're asking is something that only the president of the United States could guarantee."

"But would you put your weight behind the plan?" Jim asked, twisting around to look at Malone.

"Well . . . sure. I agree with Terry on at least one point: It's better than shooting at each other."

Terry looked back at Jim, staring steadfastly at him until he had to reply.

"I'll help in any way I can," he pledged.

"Well . . . let's get the ball rolling, then. You call the president." Terry clapped his hands in anticipation of the work ahead.

"Me!" Jim was flabbergasted, and his expression clearly showed it.

"Yeah, you. Use the cell phone in one of the cars." He jerked his thumb toward the vehicles in the yard. "Come on, Jimmy, come on. Time's a-wastin'. Is this how you used to sell Kotex?"

"I never handled that acc—Oh, never mind!" He stomped toward the line of cars and pickups, muttering, "How in the hell did I ever get involved in this?"

Fourteen

"It's the damnest thing I ever heard of," President Potter said. "It's crazy. I like it, but it won't work."

His chief of staff visibly relaxed. "I was hoping you would say that. But tell me your reasoning."

"It would enflame the nation even more."

"Agreed. Then why would Kincaide, who seems a moderate sort of fellow, suggest such a thing?"

"He didn't. This was Terry Warden's plan right down the line. You can bet the farm on that. The man's up to something; but because of their friendship, Jim can't see it. I don't trust Terry Warden."

"And when you turn down the request for a nationwide town hall meeting? . . ." Reese let that dangle.

"Jim Kincaide will shrug it off, and Terry Warden will suspect that I don't trust him . . . which certainly should come as no surprise to the bastard."

"Have you considered . . . ah . . . eliminating that problem, Fred?"

"Yes," the president replied without hesitation. "I've already discussed it with . . . well, let's just say people who know how to get the job done. But that would lower me to the level of Warden and Baronne. I don't care to stoop that low, Reese."

"Every president since Washington has had that option, Fred, and most of them, if not all of them, have used it. You know that."

"I haven't. And I hope to God I never do."

Reese realized he was about to step off into deep, dark waters. Fred Potter was not only a moral man, but an unusual politician who actually put the country ahead of his own ambitions. Not many politicians could truthfully make that claim. Reese plunged ahead.

"Baronne?" the chief of staff asked.

"He's insane."

"That doesn't make him any less dangerous."

"I'll call Kincaide and tell him I don't think a nation-wide town meeting is a good idea at the moment. And Reese?"

"Yes, sir?"

"We'll talk no more about . . . eliminating. Understood?"

"Yes, sir."

"The president nixed the idea," Jim told the group at the lodge.

"No surprise there," Terry said.

"Why do you say that?" Pat asked.

"Mustn't do anything to upset the minorities in the country," Terry replied. "And you can be damn sure any number of programs that benefit or affect them would come up for heated debate."

No one in the lodge spoke for a full half-a-minute as they discreetly exchanged glances. Finally, Jim said, "Terry, do you blame all the ills and woes troubling this nation on the blacks?"

"A lot of them, yes. Oh, I know that some of you in

the room think I'm a terrible person for saying that, but you who feel that way just won't look at facts. I got a buddy down south, lives in a medium-sized southern city. 'Bout two years ago he went out and bought himself three scanners: one for his house, one for his car, one for his office. He started keeping a chart on all the trouble-calls the cops had to answer. Then, after a few months, he called some friends of his in other cities, told them what he'd discovered, and asked them to do the same. Pretty soon there was a whole network of people, nationwide, keeping charts on trouble-calls the cops rolled on. You know what they found, folks?" Terry looked and pointed at the FBI agent. "He does. But the government is reluctant to release those facts, aren't they, Pat?"

Pat shrugged his shoulders. "You've got the floor, Terry."

"I sure do. Sixty-eight percent of all the crime committed in the United States is being committed by a group of people whose overall numbers make up only about fifteen percent of the population. It's costing the rest of us billions and billions of taxpayer dollars. And what do the blacks do about it? They boycott, they march, they file lawsuits, they whine to the FBI's civil rights division, and they call anyone who has the guts to point out the facts a racist. Well, I've had a gutful of it, and so have millions of other Americans."

Terry turned on his heel and strode out of the lodge. The door banged shut behind him as if to emphasize his words.

"That is one very angry man," Claire said.

"He points out the problem, but offers no solutions," Jim said. "Except more violence."

"Well, I thought the town meeting was a good idea," Steve said. "At least it would have cleared the air and let everyone know where everybody else stood."

Jim stroked his chin. "It certainly would have done that."

"I guess the next move is Baronne's," Pat said. "God help us all."

"But we're all still stood down, right?" Jim asked.

"For the time being, yes," Janet replied. "But that's not going to last. Nor will it bring an end to the trouble."

"What will?" Claire pressed.

Those left behind in the lodge fell silent. Finally, Jim said, "Maybe nations within a nation, all answering to some degree to one central government. I've been giving that some thought lately. Hell, I feel as though I've been caught up in a whirlwind; everything happened so fast. But then, really, it didn't. We had plenty of warning signs. The problem is, people like me didn't pay any attention. The militias, the survivalists, the hate groups, the far right religious faction, all the fringe groups, why, they weren't really any big problem. Just a pesky mosquito, that's all. Swat at it a couple of times, and it will go away. Then if that doesn't work, we'll just pass more legislation and that will certainly take care of the problem." He shrugged his shoulders. "Big Brother will take care of us. Right. Sure. I never realized just how damn serious these groups were, how well organized they'd become, or how deep the resentment ran among them."

"And now, Jim?" Janet probed.

He shook his head. "It just might be too late to pull this nation out of the hole we all helped dig."

* * *

The nation seemed to pause for a day and a night to catch its breath while a badly shaken populace wondered what was going to happen next. Many could not believe all that had occurred had really taken place. This was America, wasn't it? There wasn't supposed to be war on this soil—we were too civilized for that. If we had a grievance, we talked it out, right? If we had an issue that affected us all, we went to the polls and voted—right? That had worked for two hundred years, right? So what had happened?

The nation's press pondered those same questions. But like the man who stares so long at the forest he can't see the trees, the press never had been able to understand basic human nature.

"You can't legislate morality," Terry said to the group. "The government can pass legislation until they fall over from exhaustion, but they can't force me to like someone I choose to dislike and they can't force me to respect someone I have no respect for. And it isn't right for them to order me to hire someone I don't want to hire. And millions of people feel the same way I do."

The more Jim listened to Terry speak, the uneasier he became. Not so much for what his old friend said, but for what he didn't say.

Maybe I'm being silly, Jim told himself.

But he didn't think so.

Terry was hiding something, keeping something from his friends and followers. But Jim didn't have the vaguest idea what it might be. Only that he was sure he was correct.

He glanced at Janet. Her eyes were narrowed, watching Terry as he paced the den. Jim looked at the Bureau man. Pat was keeping his face expressionless, but his eyes appeared cold and hard.

They both think Terry is holding back from us, Jim thought.

"The truth be known," Terry said, turning to face the group. "Before long . . ." He paused, then waved off the comment. "I'll see you kids. Got some things to do." He walked out the door. A moment later, they heard the sounds of a truck starting and the crunch of tires as it pulled away.

Now what the hell was all that about? Jim mused.

During this twenty-four-hour period of calm, the government, the militias, and Gene Baronne's people were moving as fast as they could. The government was working feverishly and as secretly as possible, putting together several hundred rapid-response teams from all branches of service, ready to go into action. The militias were mapping out new plans, getting reorganized, re-supplied, and making ready for a prolonged fight. Baronne was shifting around small teams of people all over the country. He had people in every state, working around the clock, making bombs and readying small teams of sick and old to die for God in suicide runs, should that again prove necessary.

The once-mightiest nation on the face of the earth was on the verge of disintegrating into open civil war.

All this had been predicted, more than a few times, by more than a few people. But not many had had the foresight to take those prophets of doom seriously.

Now it was too late.

* * *

"I spoke with the military about an hour ago," the president said, turning away from the window.

"And? . . ." his chief of staff asked.

"We have some teams already in place, watching from good cover. They're under orders to take no offensive action unless fired upon. But," he sighed, "a lot of those guys don't like the idea of going up against other veterans, many of whom were highly decorated for service to this country. They especially don't like going up against a Medal of Honor-winner like Jim Kincaide, who really backed into this militia situation. And I understand their position all too well. A lot of militia members are 'Nam vets and also veterans of the Gulf War, Grenada, Somalia, and Bosnia. To make matters worse, there are a number of ex-SEALs, Rangers, Green Berets, Marine Force Recon, Delta Force, and Air Force Commandos, and Combat Ground Controllers in the movement. These people have a brotherhood that most civilians don't understand. But I do. I served over there." He shook his head. "I don't know, Reese. When push comes to shove, the military is saying five to ten percent of these guys just might, they stressed might, go over to the militia side. That's a guess, sure, but still a strong possibility."

Reese had served in the military, as had most men his age, but he had never left the States and had not been a part of any line outfit. He did not really understand special ops people and what they were capable of doing. "And should that percentage actually go over to the other side?"

"We would be in a world of hurt, Reese. Take my word for that."

* * *

"Did you call in and make your daily report today, Pat?" Terry asked the FBI man cheerfully.

"I did."

Jim and Janet, Claire, and Steve Malone listened to the exchange from the den.

"Did you have glowing things to say about me?"

"To be perfectly honest, no."

Terry laughed. "That's a good agent, Pat. You haven't disappointed me yet."

"Oh, I wouldn't want to do that, General."

"Commander will do just fine," Terry corrected, sitting down with the group.

"I have a question," Pat said.

"Ask."

"What are your plans when all this is over?"

"Return to running my business. It'll be easier then and a lot more fun."

"How?"

"For one thing, I'll be free of the ATF. For another, there will be less forms to fill out. And taxes will be a lot simpler."

"You plan on doing away with the Bureau of Alcohol, Tobacco, and Firearms?"

"You got that right."

"How about taxes?"

"There will either be a national sales tax or a straight across-the-board income tax of about ten percent of gross earnings for everybody above a certain income. Either way, the IRS will lose much of its power."

"What about the forms you mentioned?"

"They'll be cut by about ninety percent."

The Bureau man nodded his head in comprehension.

"You'll do away with a number of government departments?"

"Either that or they'll be cut back drastically."

"Well, you may find this hard to believe, Terry. But in many of your endeavors, I wish you luck."

"Oh, I believe you. I think you've discovered—probably to your surprise—that most of us in the movement are not raving lunatics or heartless monsters. But the give-me-something-for-nothing days in this country are about to come to a halt."

"The people you're going to throw out of public housing, Terry. Where are they going to live?"

"We're not going to throw anybody out onto the street—although many of the people in the movement would like to see that done. But requirements for living in projects are going to be tightened up, with the elderly and physically challenged getting top priority."

"What about Baronne?"

"He'll have to be dealt with."

"By you people?"

"Maybe." Terry chose his words carefully. "Or perhaps Baronne and his followers will have their own section of the nation. That has been discussed."

"And you and your people with your own section?"

"Possibly, but I don't think it will come to that with us. All we want to do is get this nation back to dead center, politically speaking. We believe in the Constitution, Pat. But over the years, that document has been shaped and reshaped to suit the whims of both liberals and conservatives. We're either going to have to adhere to the Constitution as it was originally written, the frame of mind of those who agreed to that document at the time, or do away with it altogether. We can't keep molding it to suit our whims."

"That document was written about two-hundred-and-fifty years ago. A lot has changed since then."

"Not the basics. Right is right and wrong is wrong. What is moral and immoral in the eyes of God hasn't changed. Gene Baronne is right on the mark about that. And that point is about the only thing we agree on. We've got to pull this nation out of the toilet—and somehow do it without resorting to censorship."

"And your way is the best way to accomplish that goal?"

Terry stared over Pat's shoulder into the distance. "We won't be alive to see how history records this period. But in my opinion and in the opinion of millions of other Americans, it damn sure can't be any worse than it is right now."

Fifteen

Canada was not spared, but its citizens' revolt was minor and short-lived compared to that of its southern neighbor. Canadian officials thought they knew where all the guns were in the provinces.

Canadian officials were wrong.

Hundreds of thousands of Canadians, many of whom were in the western provinces, rose up armed to the teeth and told their elected and appointed officials to take their newly enacted gun restrictions and stick them where the sun don't shine. And if they didn't like that, they could get ready for a civil war.

Canadian officials, showing a great deal more intelligence than their American counterparts, quickly assessed the situation and agreed to sit down and discuss whatever issues were bothering the armed resistance groups—more than that, to do something about those grievances. Immediately.

"I think that might be what is going to happen here," the president muttered, studying a huge map of Canada.

"What, dear?" his wife asked, looking up from her newspaper.

"When all the smoke settles, this nation will be broken up into sections, provinces, if you will, much like Canada."

"It probably should have happened a long time ago,"

his wife replied. "Nations within a nation, all answerable to some small degree to one central government."

Fred stared at his wife. "Are you serious?"

"Very."

"You want to explain that?"

Helen Potter carefully folded and laid aside the *Washington Post.* "Put all the liberals in one section, or nation, or province . . . whatever. All the conservatives in another, all the moderates somewhere else. Give the race-baiters and hate-mongers and rustic rednecks their section—and the blacks their own section, of course; some have been calling for that for years. The Hispanics, too, should they want it. But they probably won't. And don't forget the Indians: They'll want a place to ride their ponies and paint their faces and wear feathers in their hair—from endangered species, of course—and beat on drums. . . ."

Fred stared at his wife in open amazement.

". . . . When all that is done," Helen continued, "the first thing that will happen is that all the people who want something for nothing will crowd into the liberal section, knowing that liberals will give them everything they want if they whine enough. That section will soon be in bankruptcy.

"The conservative section will look good for a while, but they'll eventually go under because they're too damn cheap to pay anybody.

"The bigots and hate-mongers and various morons who gather in the nitwit section will grumble for a while and then declare war on the black section, and those two parts of the country will wipe each other out.

"Ah, but the moderate section, made up of men and women of all political stripe and race, those people who can actually think about the consequences before they enact legislation, those people who know the law must apply equally to all . . . that section will prosper. Those people know that sometimes a child needs his little bottom spanked and that a spanking does not constitute child abuse. They know that when a punk shoots somebody it isn't the fault of the gun, it's the fault of the person holding it. They understand that there will always be rich people, poor people, and a working middle class . . . and to leave that system the hell alone, because it's worked for several thousand years. Those people know that without discipline in schools, teachers cannot teach; and they know that no nation can be all things to all people all the time. Do you get my drift, Fred?"

"Yes." The president reached for his first lady's hand. "You know, Helen, I love you."

"Of course, you do. I've known that for thirty years."

Fred stuffed his pipe, lit it, and leaned back in his chair. "Tell me this, what happens to the Indian section?"

"Oh, they'll ride their ponies around for a time and then come to the conclusion that the old ways really weren't worth shit."

"And then what?"

She gave him a sideways glance. "If they're as smart as I think they are, they'll declare themselves a sovereign nation and apply for foreign aid."

On a peaceful and warm Friday morning, Jim drove into the town he had helped Terry and the militia members defend and bought a 35-inch TV set. He then went to a supermarket for supplies. All the stores were open, and the community went about its business as if nothing special were going on. Chief Brocato and his men had been buried, and the militia were acting as police until a new force could be hired.

Jim wondered if this were the way it had been during the first civil war. Probably, he concluded.

Life goes on.

"Any further trouble?" he asked a militiaman standing outside the store.

"Not really," the young man replied. "Some local punks roared up and down the streets last night, playing the radio as loud as it would go and burning rubber until a citizens' group stopped them about midnight. One of the guys on duty last night said those were three scared teenagers."

"Were they hurt?"

"Oh, no. But their radios will never play again. Twelve-gauge shotguns at close range will do that. Sure made a mess out of those dashboards."

"I'm surprised the parents aren't suing."

The militiaman smiled. "The boys' parents can't find a single attorney to take the case. All the local lawyers seem real edgy about it." His smile widened. "I can't for the life of me imagine why."

"Me neither," Jim said, only slightly sarcastically. "Any state police around?"

"Not a single one. Nothing for them to do here. We have the situation well in hand."

"Seems that way." Jim went into the store and got a cart. As he wheeled up and down the aisles, he overheard customers chatting about last night's incident.

While pretending to read the label on a large can of beans, Jim heard one say, "This town is nice and peaceful now that the militia has taken over. My neighbor's boy used to work on that damn motorcycle of his until all hours of the night. Baaroom, baaroom, baaroom until two or three o'clock in the morning. Well, I called the police station two nights ago and some nice young men dressed in Army clothes came out. I don't know what they said to that boy, but the noise has stopped and I can finally get a good night's sleep."

Jim put the can of beans back on the shelf and wheeled his cart away, thinking, "I know what they said to him. *If you want to stay healthy, cut out the noise. If we have to come back, you're going first to the hospital, then to jail.*"

Not exactly following Constitutional guidelines, he thought, but it's certainly effective.

While waiting in the checkout line, Jim spoke to a man wearing a nametag that indicated he was the manager. "Having any problem getting fresh vegetables and milk delivered?"

The manager shook his head. "Not a bit. I've talked with store managers all over the state. Things are about as normal as they were before the trouble. Even in New York City. The tunnels weren't as badly damaged as we first thought and traffic is moving. It's slow, but it's moving."

Jim wondered how Don and his family were doing . . . and whether Don had gotten over his anger.

". . . Terry's friend, aren't you?" Jim caught the last of the manager's question.

"That's right."

"He's a good man. We need more people like Terry."

Jim nodded in agreement, not really trusting his voice.

"You find everything you were looking for?" the manager asked.

"Oh, yes."

"Good. Come back and see us again." He moved along, chatting with customers as he walked.

There is a damn civil war going on, people, Jim thought. A war that could forever change the direction of this country. And you're discussing the price of kumquats and kiwi fruit.

Following the bag boy out to Janet's truck, Jim thought: Janet and Terry were right. Millions of people don't give a damn who runs the country as long as their lives aren't turned topsy-turvy.

And those who hold views opposing the uprising are smart enough to keep them to themselves, he added. At least for the time being. Then he got the strong impression he was being watched. He looked around him as customers filed in and out of the store. No guns were visible on their belts, but several men wore their shirttails out and he could see the telltale bulge of holsters.

"No one will ever succeed in disarming this nation," Jim murmured as he got into the pickup and closed the door. "And we, and I certainly include myself in that group, were wrong to support legislation calling for gun control."

No! he amended. I'll never admit that we were wrong. Then he chuckled. I'm still a liberal at heart.

As he pulled out of the parking lot, the young militiaman in front of the store snapped him a salute. Instinctively, Jim returned it and headed back to the lodge.

While the citizens of America were wondering what was going to happen next, the militia members, Baronne's forces, and dozens of special ops teams were shifting around, ready to move into action should conditions go from bad to worse . . . as everyone expected they would.

None of the three main players in this modern American tragedy trusted the others. Both Terry and Baronne had agents planted deep in the military and both men knew about the spec ops teams. So, they reasoned, if the government weren't going to keep its end of the agreement, why should they?

At the lodge, Jim and Janet, Pat and Claire, and Steve Malone had gotten up early for their ritual morning coffee.

"Anybody have any idea where Terry went?" Jim asked, munching on a piece of buttered toast.

"He didn't tell you?" Pat asked, surprise in his voice.

Jim shook his head. "No."

Steve studied his coffee mug and, when he spoke, seemed to be addressing its depths. "Do you ever get the impression your friend doesn't trust you, Jim?"

"From the very first moment," Jim replied. "I'm no more the executive officer of the militia movement than President Potter is the Czar of Russia. Terry is using me the same way he's always used people. That isn't to say he isn't sincere in his desire to improve this country, for I believe he is. But Terry is a user; he's always been a user. He'd get us into trouble as kids, knowing I could talk our way out of it. Terry wanted me involved in this movement to lend some legitimacy to it. He needed my reputation, plus the fact that I'm a known Democrat liberal. As soon as he saw me that night out in the timber, his mind started working overtime." Jim met Janet's questioning gaze. "Hell, I knew I was being used from the outset. I know Terry. But I just figured I'd play along with him, see where it all led."

"And where is it leading?" Pat asked, his coffee and sweet roll forgotten.

"I don't know. But I strongly suspect Terry doesn't want this war to end, but, rather, to escalate. That's why he wanted that town meeting. He figured on hard words that would enflame already smoldering passions. He was one step ahead of the rest of us. Terry is buying time until he can get his people into better positions; he *wants* a war. Terry's smart like a fox, as the saying goes. He deliberately goaded Donald. Think about it. Think about the times he'd say things with a double meaning, banking on our taking it one way and Donald another. I can think of a half-dozen times he did that. We started out with a nice-sized group here. Now we're down to five people. Easily managed. *Controlled* might be a better word. And I'll go a step further and say that we can't leave this area. Oh, I can go into town whenever I want to. But I'm being watched the entire time. I could feel it this morning."

"What would be the purpose of keeping us contained?" Janet questioned.

"I would guess so Phil LaBarre and his people can . . . eliminate us," Jim said softly.

"What?" the Bureau man asked, and Jim repeated his hypothesis.

"Sure," he went on. "That's how Terry's mind works. He gives us sanctuary. I'm with him during a meeting with the President of the United States. We're the good guys, the peace-makers. But the bad guys, Baronne's forces, kill us. Terry and his followers are outraged. President Potter is outraged and turns government troops away from Terry and against Baronne—full force."

"And when Baronne is dealt with and the smoke settles," the Bureau man said, "in a final act of desperation, President Potter will be assassinated."

Jim nodded his head. "Yeah. But not by Baronne's people—although it will appear as if they'd done it."

"And that leaves Terry in the catbird seat," Janet summed up.

"That it does."

"But we can't prove any of this," Pat pointed out.

"Not a word of it."

"So what do we do?" Claire asked.

"Don't let ourselves be taken by surprise," Jim whispered—and drained the last inch of coffee in his mug.

Sixteen

Jim sat on the front porch of the lodge most of that morning. The others, including Janet, left him alone with his thoughts. Occasionally, he would go into the house for coffee or a drink of water, but always he would return to the chair on the porch. At noon, Janet brought him a sandwich and a glass of milk and sat down in the chair next to his.

"Fitting all the pieces of the puzzle together?"

"Most of them, but I still can't prove any of it."

"And when you get it all figured out, how will it affect what is happening in America?"

"It won't. There is going to be a war, Janet. You know that. For how long and to what intensity is anybody's guess, but this . . . matter . . . I've been mulling around in my head is between Terry and me. It's . . . personal. I guess that's the best way of putting it."

"And you and Terry are going to settle it, mano a mano?"

Jim looked at her. "That's right."

"Testosterone at work. Are you sure you're not from the Deep South?"

Jim shook his head. "Positive. Why?"

"Oh, I read somewhere that testosterone levels are higher in southern men."

Before he could reply, Claire pushed open the screen door and joined them. "Some 'experts' on the television are talking about a race war in this country," she told them, sinking into a weathered Adirondack chair. "They're saying it can't be avoided."

"I agree with them," said Janet.

"There will be terrible trouble between the races before this is over," Jim predicted. "Trouble that will make that skirmish down in Georgia look like child's play. But maybe that's what it's going to take. Liberal that I am, I know that blacks have got to stop blaming whites for all their troubles and woes and stop making excuses for blacks who break the law. It's got to come to a halt. Terry is right about that: We can't have two sets of laws and two different codes of morality. And yes, I will admit that morals in this country have gone downhill over the past couple of decades. Morals that the majority hold to be true, that is."

Hard words with considerable heat behind them drifted out of the TV speakers to the cluster on the front porch. ". . . You think it's normal for two men to fuck each other up the ass?" a voice from somewhere in the nation shouted. "And then suck on each other's dicks? That is normal behavior in your mind? If it is, then you are one sad, sick son of a bitch."

An angry roar drowned out the reply, and Steve Malone left TV and den in favor of the porch. He stood beside the railing, staring out at the quiet woods. "In my mind, God is very clear on homosexuality," the self-defrocked minister finally said. "I'm not saying He won't forgive them for those acts if they are sincere in asking for forgiveness, but it's still a sin. And I will support no society that openly condones this evil."

"The gay community in this nation is in for a rough go of it." Pat spoke from the doorway. "That is one point the religious right—moderate or radical—will never compromise on. Race is another."

"Sad, but true, I'm afraid," the minister agreed.

"And that leaves what?" Claire asked.

"More trouble," Pat said.

"Prognosis for the nation?" Janet asked, looking up at the Bureau man and minister.

"Violence. The military will be forced to get involved, and then it's really going to get messy."

"Well, before that happens, Jim and Terry have their own private little war to settle," Janet said, making no effort to hide the disgust in her voice.

"I saw that coming," Pat replied, turning his head toward Jim. "Terry's good, Jim. Don't sell him short for a second. You're going to have to take him out from long distance. And when you get him in the crosshairs, don't hesitate to pull that trigger . . . because he won't pause when it comes to killing you. He's seen the subtle changes in you over the past few days, and—to his mind—your usefulness is at an end."

"I think," Jim said, "we'd better get off this porch and into the house. Stay away from the windows. Come the night, I've got some prowling to do."

"Shit!" Janet said. "Testosterone at work."

"Do we turn the military loose, Fred?" Reese asked his boss.

There were four men in the Oval Office: The president, the White House chief of staff, the national security advisor, and the chairman of the joint chiefs.

Fred carefully filled the bowl of his pipe and lit it. "Not yet," he said.

"Goddamnit, Fred! . . ." Reese flared.

"I said *not yet,*" Fred spoke softly. He looked at the military man. "You concur?"

"Yes," the general said with a sigh. "If I give the orders for the military to start restoring order around this nation, almighty hell is going to break loose."

"My God!" Reese said. "If? When you add the force of the military to the millions of cops in this nation . . ."

"There are approximately six-hundred-and-thirty-five-thousand police in this nation," Fred interrupted. "Or there were, before the trouble started. Fifteen to twenty percent of them came out on the side of the militia movement. Another ten percent lined up solidly on the side of the religious right. About five percent went over to Gene Baronne. And we know the military is split on this issue, but not, thankfully, to that large an extent." Fred waved a hand. "There are only God-know-how-many thousands and thousands of American citizens out there, heavily armed, and ready for a fight. And I don't want that, Reese. We've got to buy some time. . . ."

Fred answered the buzzing of the desk phone, listened for a moment, then barked a vulgar word and hung up. "We may be all out of time," he said wearily. "Across the nation, in dozens of locations in every state, armed and organized elements of the religious right have warned school boards to dismiss every teacher who is a known homosexual. They're also telling homosexuals to get out of town or suffer the consequences." Fred looked at the chairman of the joint chiefs. The general crossed his arms and returned the gaze, hard and steady. Fred sighed; that look was a clear message that there was no help forthcoming from that sector. Besides, the general had already made his position on that subject known . . . bluntly. And so had the general's wife . . . at a small cocktail party . . . in a cruel jest about gay love. "Who is the fuckee?" she'd joked. "And who is the fuck-or?"

Fred again looked at the general, who sighed and uncrossed his arms. "What do you want me to do, Mr. President? You want my people to start shooting at citizens who are only trying to protect their kids from a bunch of queers?"

"I don't like that word, General," Fred said, perhaps a bit too harshly. "The term is *gay.*"

"I don't see anything gay about a bunch of queers and lesbos," the general objected. "I agree with the citizens who want to keep the goddamned perverted, degenerate bastards away from their kids."

Fred was openly shocked. "I'll want your resignation on this desk in the morning," he said fiercely. "I hate to . . ."

"I'll do better than that, Mr. President. The joint chiefs knew about the actions of the concerned citizens yesterday, and we discussed it at length." The general reached into the breast pocket of his uniform jacket and pulled out half-a-dozen white envelopes. His face hard with anger, he threw them on the president's desk. "Those are the resignations of every member of the joint chiefs. I'll not have a hand in seeing my people committed to a damn civil war over a bunch of fags!" He jumped from his chair and stormed out of the office.

"It's coming unglued, Fred," his national security advisor said. "The nation is coming apart at the seams."

"We've got a little time," Fred said, scooping the unopened envelopes into the center drawer of his desk.

"The JC's won't go to the press with the real reason they're resigning. They know the majority of the nation's press are sympathetic toward gays . . . or at least profess to be. As much turmoil as we have going on inside the Beltway, the JC's won't be missed for twenty-four or more hours. . . . I hope."

"What can we do in twenty-four hours?" Reese asked.

The president of the United States sighed. "Well, it certainly wouldn't hurt if we started with prayer."

Jim had sighted in the rifle the same day he'd picked it up at the weapons cache outside Washington, at Terry's suggestion, and then thought no more about it. He had not put the rifle in the gun vault, choosing instead to keep it handy . . . where anyone could have access to it. Now, he carefully took it down, piece by piece. He could find nothing wrong with the rifle. He turned his attention to the boxes of hand-loaded ammo. None of the cartridges appeared to have been tampered with.

"What's your plan, Terry?" Jim muttered. "I know you're up to something. My tragic death has to be part of your overall scheme. Nothing else makes any sense."

To be on the safe side, Jim laid the expensive rifle aside and picked out an older model Remington autoloader in .308 caliber that had belonged to his father. The scope was old, but still in fine shape. The weapon would do. There was plenty of ammunition. Jim locked the gun vault and then started a careful inspection of the basement. He found what he was looking for in a closet: enough C-4 to bring down a structure ten times the size of the lodge. It was to have been detonated electronically. Working carefully, Jim rendered the charge harmless and then called the others downstairs. He showed them the C-4 and the triggering device.

"I don't know who Terry was going to blame for my death," Jim said, "but I've got a hunch it was to be laid at the doorstep of the government."

"Makes sense," Pat Monroe agreed. "Then his militia would have been so outraged that nothing could have stopped an all-out civil war."

"It's kind of thin thinking on his part, but yes, that's the way I figure it."

"Not so thin," Janet said. "He may have planned to lay the entire breakdown theme on your shoulders."

Jim shook his head. "It's still thin. Who would believe that? I run an advertising agency, not a militia movement."

"Who could positively disprove it?" Pat pressed. "All of us would be dead, and the dead can't speak. You can bet Terry has given this some thought. All he'd have to do is announce that the grand planner of the takeover movement, the mystery man who played a dual role for years, has been assassinated. Terry can be a smooth talker. Believe me, I know. It all fits, Jim." He pointed to the massive charge of C-4. "Why else would he want us all dead? Hell, other than your friend Don Williams, we're the only ones who know the truth."

"Don!" Jim exclaimed, heading for the stairs and a cell phone.

Janet stopped him. "No time, Jim. We've got to get packed and clear of this area."

"No way," Phil LaBarre's voice came from the bottom of the stairs as he stepped into the light of the basement rec room.

The group turned. The caretaker held an M-16 in his hands.

"I told Terry you were smart," Phil said with an ugly grin. "He thought he was smarter, but I finally convinced him that a few of us ought to take shifts out in the timber to keep an eye on you . . . just in case." He cut his eyes to the charge of C-4 on a table. "How the hell did you figure it out, Kincaide? A candy-ass like you?"

"Just lucky, I guess," Jim said.

LaBarre laughed unpleasantly. "Well, your luck's run out. The rest of the militia are on their way, so we'll just stay down here and chat until they get here. Then we'll see about finishing what Terry started."

"I don't think so, Phil." Al Milner's voice echoed from the top of the stairs. "Lay that rifle on the floor. Do it, *now!*"

"Do what he says, Phil," Karen urged from behind Al. "We've neutralized your friends outside. You're all alone in this."

"Traitors," Phil hissed. "You're all a bunch of goddamn traitors."

"Put the rifle down, Phil," Al warned. "I won't tell you again."

"And if I don't?" Phil challenged.

The caretaker's head blew apart as the hollow-nosed .357 round from Al's pistol ended his sour life. Phil's brains splattered against the wall as he slumped to his knees and stayed there, his eyes wide and staring, his mouth open, leaking crimson. Jim grabbed the M-16 before it could hit the floor and discharge.

Al called down from the landing. "Grab your things and get out of here. We're runnin' out of time."

Seventeen

Only the largest cities in America had been placed under martial law and had troops helping the police patrol the streets. Only towns with a population between five thousand and twenty-five thousand had been seized by factions of the many movements. Midsized cities were virtually untouched. The only news the residents of those cities heard about the uprising came from radio, TV, or CB radio, something that thousands of people purchased when the mini-revolution began. The run on CB radios was still on. Factories were working around the clock, seven days a week, and still could not keep up with demand.

Before meeting with the president, the chairman of the joint chiefs had met with the joint chiefs, well away from the Pentagon. They had agreed to make several phone calls, explaining what they were about to do, and to ask a favor of the military commanders. Of the generals and admirals contacted, almost all responded favorably to the request, since the military does not look with great affection on the gay and lesbian community. The order soon went out to troops not already deployed: Stand down.

President Potter learned of the orders within minutes. A great sadness washed over the chief executive as he hung up the telephone and leaned back in his chair. He was alone in the Oval Office; he had never felt so alone in all his life.

"Damn!" he whispered. "DamnDamnDamn!"

Phil LaBarre's body was carried outside and dumped in the timber beside the bodies of those men Terry had assigned to watch the lodge. Now they stared only at death's cold eternity.

"Where is Terry?" Jim asked.

"We don't know." Rose replied.

"What's the plan?" Pat asked.

"We don't have one," Al said with a boyish grin. "We were hoping that Mr. Kincaide would."

A dozen other militia members had joined them in the timber. They all looked in hopeful silence at Jim.

Jim shifted his gaze to Janet, who stared back at him, a faint smile on her lips. His first inclination was to admit that he hadn't a clue what to do. But that was not what his supporters wanted to hear.

"Have any of you been in touch with other militia?" he asked instead.

"A lot of them," Al replied. "And some of Baronne's followers as well. The moderates are really pissed about that Aryan group, The Storm, and other whacko organizations becoming aligned with them. They want as far away from that bunch as they can get."

"Still others, maybe twenty-five percent, although that may be high," Karen said, "were sickened by the suicide bombings and the way members of the gay and lesbian community are being treated. And minorities."

"That's not what we had in mind, Mr. Kincaide," Judy

said. "We wanted government out of our lives, but we didn't want a return to Nazi philosophy. It's all turned upside down on us."

"We don't know what the hell Terry stands for." Al's tone held a note of real anguish. "I guess we never really did. He conned us all the way."

"Well, you're not alone," Jim confirmed. "He conned me, too." He chewed on his lip for a moment. "How about the town?"

"Terry's people are still there. 'Bout a dozen of them."

"Think they could be persuaded to join with us?"

Al shook his head. "Not a chance. They're hard-line. And Dr. Durant is with them. He's running the entire park area."

"It's past time for the military to get involved in this," Jim said to no one in particular.

"I don't think they will," Janet disagreed. "Small units might, but not the military en masse. I think we can count them out."

"We going to retake the town, Commander?" Al asked.

Jim smiled at the title. Promotions came quickly in this outfit. "I guess so. Sure!" Verbally, he toughened his decision and watched as silent resolve strengthened the men and women around him. "We have to start somewhere. I've got to get to a phone and make some calls into the city . . . see about some friends of mine."

"You talkin' about that black fellow and his family?" Karen asked.

"Yes."

She shook her head. "I doubt if they even made it out of the park. Terry hates black people."

In the back of his mind, Jim had been steeling himself

for those words. "Then I've been lied to right down the line," he said flatly.

"Yes, sir," Al said. "You sure have. And by us, too. But the lying and deceit is over. I don't know what else we can do to prove that."

"Why do you think Don and his family were killed?" Janet asked. *"If* they were killed," she added quickly.

Al, Rose, Judy, and Karen exchanged glances. Judy said, "They're dead. Believe that. Terry had us all convinced, for a long time, that he didn't have any part in the burning down of black homes and businesses or the running out of black families in this area. But there were some of us in the outfit, mainly the ones you see here, who never fully trusted him. Terry said he tried to recruit blacks into the militia. We recently found out he was lying when we intercepted a message from The Storm that was intended for Terry's eyes only. He's up to his ass in the Aryan Nation movement. That's when we—" She waved her hand. "—decided it was time to pull out and get away from him. Think about it, sir. Terry would never let those black people leave this area knowing as much as they did about the strength of his group." Her eyes shifted to Steve Malone. "The minister was the first to see through Terry. That's why Terry tossed him out of the movement and started a smear campaign against him."

"Lots of hate in America, Commander," Al said, "and it runs much deeper than the government ever knew or suspected. Lots of whites hate blacks; lots of blacks hate whites. There's hate toward the gay and lesbian community, hate toward the government, hate toward people on welfare. . . . A lot of people who preach redistribution of wealth hate rich people. You can see it on their faces when they're on television spewing their crap. I know people who live out west near Indian reservations who call Indians *prairie niggers*. People who are not like us, who have different lifestyles and customs, are viewed with suspicion and distrust. This nation is tearing apart at the seams, sir. And I don't know if there is a big enough needle and thread to sew it back together."

"Are you willing to try?"

"Ah . . . sure. But what can we do?"

"You know how to get in touch with every militia unit in the United States, don't you?"

"Yes, sir. By shortwave. I have all the frequencies."

"When we get the town back to normal, then we'll go to work on the radio and get organized nationwide."

As they were leaving, Jim riding with Janet in her truck in the center of the small convoy, he said, "I pray Karen is wrong about Don and his family."

"Don't get your hopes up."

"You think they're all dead?"

"Probably. What Karen said made sense. Terry couldn't take a chance of their talking, even though they really knew very little."

"That is one cold-blooded son of a bitch."

"And when you two meet, you had better be just as cold-blooded, baby."

"Ambush," the words screamed out of the CB radio. "Pull off and take cover."

Janet cut the wheel hard to the right and went bouncing off into the timber. Jim's M-16 was in the back of the truck, piled among other gear. He jerked the gun case containing the .308 from the small passenger area in the extended cab and bailed out as soon as the truck came to a halt. Janet joined him on the ground, some fifty feet away from the pickup.

Jim opened the case and took out the Remington, removing the protective caps from the scope.

"Now would be a good time to sight in that rifle," she whispered, her lips scarcely moving.

Jim grimaced at the coldness in her voice. "That's one way of looking at it, I suppose," he muttered. He checked the four round mag and jacked a round into the slot, then popped the mag and fitted another round into it, just as his father had taught him. "Dad probably had this sighted in for a hundred yards," he whispered. "I'll soon know."

The rattle and boom and crack of weapons' fire died away for a moment and Janet lifted her handy-talkie. "Al . . . you copy?"

"Right here, ma'am."

"We're on the right side of the highway. Where are your people?"

"On the left side. Everyone on your side is hostile."

"That's all we needed to know."

"I heard," Jim said, pulling the rifle to his shoulder. The magnification was slightly out of focus and he quickly corrected that. He did not have to tell Janet to keep her eyes open for trouble. She was off to one side and slightly behind him, her M-16 ready.

Jim scanned the terrain until he found a spot of color that was slightly off. He blinked his eyes a couple of times to relieve the strain and looked again. The splash of color lining up in the crosshairs was definitely wrong. Jim moved his finger to the trigger and gently began his pull. The butt of the rifle slammed against his shoulder, and he quickly relined the target in the crosshairs. Definitely a man . . . who was now thrashing around on the ground.

Jim did not waste another shot on the downed man; he was out of action.

He lined up the crosshairs on another target: a startlingly vivid splash of red hair among the earthtones. The scope pulled the target in, up close and personal. The side of the man's head blossomed in crimson and then was gone.

"Somebody get that shooter over there!" He heard a man's voice rip through the newly flowering vegetation and leafing trees.

Jim slipped fresh rounds into the mag and sighted in. The scope showed him what he thought was a mans hip clad in camouflage. A .308 round knocked the image sprawling and yelling in pain.

Janet's M-16 stuttered out a three-round burst and he heard her say, "Got the bastard."

Jim spotted movement as several men made their way toward the two casualties who had been hit but were still alive. One paused behind a bush, and Jim put two rounds into the dubious cover. The man staggered out, both hands holding his belly. He sat down on the ground, bellowing in pain. Jim shifted the crosshairs away from him to the hip-shot target.

Ground-movement caught his attention. The scope pulled in a man's face smeared with cammo paint. The crawling man paused, and Jim squeezed the trigger. The .308 round took the man in the center of his forehead and made a mess of his head.

Janet's M-16 rattled again and she cussed. Jim did not ask if she'd hit her target; he assumed not.

The enemy was becoming wary of Jim's shooting. No

one moved and the gunfire had all but ceased from his side of the road since no one wanted to give away his position.

The gut-shot man still screamed for help, and one man made the mistake of going to his aid. Jim put him down, stopping the man cold, then filled the magazine and waited.

"Fuck this shit!" someone yelled. "I'm outta here."

He didn't get far before Jim's rifle boomed one more time. The .308 round cut the running man's spine, and he dropped with all the grace of a ragdoll thrown by a child.

The sound of running boots in front and behind the man and woman drifted through the timber and brush, then all was silent except for the moaning of the wounded.

"Tell them our area is secure," Jim said, his voice distant to his momentarily hearing-impaired ears. "Crops the road low and fast and take prisoners for interrogation."

"Yes, sir," Janet responded automatically. This time there was not a hint of sarcasm in her voice.

Eighteen

Fred Potter was no longer paying any attention to the news reporters on TV. He had seen and heard enough from his own sources to know the country was ripped apart, fragmented, although not beyond repair. He was optimistic enough to believe that—but realistic enough to know the nation would never be the same. "And that's probably the understatement of the century," he muttered.

He did not want to be embarrassed by ordering out the military and having them refuse publicly. When millions of Americans were armed to the teeth and many of those spoiling for a fight, all the federal agents combined could do little against such a force.

There were dozens of teams of small military special operations teams deployed throughout the country, and they were the eyes and ears of the president. But what they had observed and reported back was anything but good news.

Many parts of the nation had been virtually unaffected by the citizens revolt, as some were now calling the uprising. But many, many more were under the gun, literally and figuratively.

His secretary opened the door to the Oval Office and said, "Mr. President, Jim Kincaide is on the line."

Fred nodded his thanks and grabbed up the phone.

"Jim! I heard that you were killed. Thank God, you're alive. And Terry? Is he all right?"

Jim talked and Fred listened, his face growing harder as the mostly one-sided conversation continued. Finally, Fred said, "You're sure of this, Jim?"

"Yes, sir, Mr. President. I'm sure."

"And the town you're calling from?"

"It's secure, sir. We had a pitched battle out on the road coming in and that seemed to take most of the steam out of Terry's forces. The town was a walk-through."

"This plan you've outlined . . . you think it will work?"

"Frankly, no. I'm sorry. I don't. But what choices are left?"

"I'll be just as frank with you. Our options are limited. When can you have some numbers for me?"

"In the morning. Midmorning."

"I'll keep this line open for your call. And, Jim?"

"Yes, sir?"

"Good luck."

Fred called in his chief of staff and laid out the gist of the conversation for him.

Reese shook his head. "We know very little about this man, Fred. How do you know you can trust him?"

"Oh, shut up, you liberal son of a bitch!" the speaker on the television yelled in frustration. Mini-summits were going on all over the nation, most of them degenerating into name-calling, and worse. "You people are the reason this country is in such lousy shape now—financially and morally!"

"You fascist pig!"

Fred sighed and jerked a thumb toward the TV. "Doesn't show any signs of letting up, does it? One network executive told me the ratings are high, so they're happy about that. Jim Kincaide? Hell, Reese, what choices do we have? The military has thumbed their noses at us. The cops are outnumbered. Millions of Americans are armed and ready for war. I have to trust somebody; and of the two men we met with, my instincts lean toward Jim Kincaide. Has the Bureau come up with any black marks against him?"

The chief of staff shook his head. "No. Not a one. He appears to be straight-arrow all the way."

"The agent stuck up there with Jim . . . Pat Monroe? He reports in almost daily. He likes Kincaide . . . says he's a good, honest, and fair man who is trying to do what's right. What more could I ask for?"

Reese spread his hands in truce. "All right, already!" he said.

"That's what I mean. The worst Kincaide can do is fail."

"And he really can't be connected with us, can he?"

Fred gave his friend a dirty look. "No, Reese, he can't. But I didn't take that into consideration."

"I didn't mean to imply . . ."

"The hell you didn't!" Fred softened his hard response with a gesture of friendship. "I understand. Damage control is part of your job, Reese. But this time around, I don't care about that. It's far too late to worry about popularity."

"You don't know what in the hell you're talking about!" someone shouted from the TV. "All you people care about is money, money, money. What about the poor?"

"What about them?" A woman returned the shout. "We're talking about *my* money. Money I work for. Why shouldn't I get to keep as much of it as possible?"

"Good question," Fred muttered.

* * *

"Terry is now firmly aligned with The Storm and Baronne's Sword of the Righteous," Al said. "But no one seems to know exactly where he is."

Jim nodded. "You've confirmed that, except for the troops deployed in the cities, the military is out of it?"

"Yes. Most of them. They've been ordered to stand down and remain on base. But there are dozens of special ops teams observing the movement in towns all over the nation."

Jim waved that aside. "That's probably all they're going to do unless attacked. So . . . everything is at an impasse?"

"More or less," the Bureau man said. "But the nation is still functioning . . . chugging right along. Which has to say something about, or perhaps for, the spirit of the American people."

"Yes, it does," Jim agreed. "But it doesn't solve the problem. . . ." His face suddenly developed a curious expression. "Or does it?"

"What are you talking about?" Steve asked.

"That's just it. Talking to the American people. Not a politician talking to them, but an ordinary citizen."

"Who?"

Jim studied his hands. "Well . . . how about me? Will I do?"

Before anyone could speak, one of the breakaway militiamen entered the room. "There's something you need to see, Commander. It's important."

"All right. What is it?"

"We found a grave just east of town. It's your friends from the city. Some of them, at least."

* * *

The bodies had begun to decompose, but the weather had been cool and the process slowed. Jim could easily recognize young Donald, LaShana, and Lori. Donald's body was riddled with bullet holes and fully clothed. The young women were both naked and had been shot once in the back of the head. The bodies had been dumped in the woods and hurriedly covered with a tarp, then with a loose layer of dirt.

"I figure they took turns raping the girls," a militiaman whispered close to Jim. "They were beautiful girls . . . even with their faces all puffy and bruised. They must have fought pretty hard."

"Can you get someone from the local funeral home to come out and get the bodies?" Jim asked. Where were Don and Shirley? Had they managed to get away?

"Yes, sir. Right now. Ah . . . well . . . something else. The county sheriff is dead. The chief of police is dead. Should I call the highway cops?"

"Yes. Yes, by all means. Do that before you call the funeral home, please."

Two state troopers were at the scene in less than half an hour and took charge. Jim stood for a moment, looking down at the bodies, then turned and walked slowly to the road.

In the pickup, driving away, Janet said, "It wasn't your fault, baby. If you're thinking that, put it out of your mind."

"I'm not thinking that."

"What are you thinking?"

"I'm thinking that for the first time in twenty-five

years, I want to kill somebody so bad I can almost taste it."

Whatever else the uprising did, it gave the networks a chance to put on mini-summits featuring citizens who were not afraid to speak their minds, and that brought home to those in power—local, state, and federal—the fact that millions of people of all races, creeds, and colors were weary of criminals not being punished severely enough, tired of lack of discipline in public schools, tired of cops' hands being tied by court decisions that—on the surface, at least—appeared to give more rights to the criminals than to the victims, and harbored a whole host of other complaints—large and small, many having nothing at all to do with the federal government. The people finally had a chance to air their gripes, and air them they did. When Jim called the president the day after finding the bodies, the mini-summits were still going on, hot and heavy, with no signs of letting up.

"I am sorry about the kids, Jim. You think the parents are still alive?"

"I hope so. If Don is alive, those responsible had better hunt a hole, 'cause he's going to be looking for them with blood in his eyes."

"There's certainly enough of that to go around." Potter's reply was dry.

"Yes, sir."

"Hang tough, boy. This mess can't last forever."

"I'll sure do that, sir."

"You know the private number, Jim. Don't hesitate to call."

"I won't, sir."

"You and the president are becoming big buddies, aren't you?" Janet commented, her eyes twinkling with good humor.

"You like Potter?"

"He's a good man. Nothing extreme about him. He should have been elected President instead of that nitwit Evans."

"You think the uprising would have been avoided had that been the case?"

She shook her head. "No. I think the country was too far gone for any one person to have made any real difference." She touched his arm. "What about the kids, Jim? I mean, funeral arrangements?"

"The city is in such a turmoil, getting any information out of there is nearly impossible. I told the funeral director to bury the kids in the local cemetery . . . when the state police release the bodies. And I have no idea when that will be."

"Want me to see if I can pull a string or two?"

"No . . . but thanks. The kids have stopped being impatient."

She stared at him. "That's a damn cold way of looking at it, baby."

"I guess. But I think everyone directly involved in this uprising has turned colder, emotionally. I damn sure have."

She put a hand on his arm. "You're wondering why, if Don is still alive, he hasn't tried to contact you, right?"

Jim tried a smile. "What did you major in, Janet— mind reading? Yes, I was thinking that."

"You two didn't exactly part on the best of terms, remember? He might think he's not welcome back here."

Before Jim could reply, Al rushed into the room. "Commander! You'd better come see what's on TV."

Jim caught just enough of the news flash to cause his stomach to do a slow rollover. ". . . and the credit for this cowardly attack on a government facility located just outside Washington, D.C., which has killed dozens of people and injured dozens more, was just now claimed by the militia movement headed by James Kincaide, a prominent New York City advertising executive turned leader of one of the largest of the government hate groups who call themselves militia. . . ."

Jim headed for a car cell phone. He dialed the special number President Potter had given him. When the call was answered, he said, "This is James Kincaide. Let me speak to the president, please."

Nineteen

"I had nothing to do with this bombing," Jim told the president.

"I know you didn't, Jim." Potter sounded tired, his words almost slurred. "But the damage has been done."

"But I've got an FBI agent and his wife with me!"

"Yes. There willingly. You get my drift?"

"Unfortunately. You realize that Terry probably did this?"

"That was the first name that popped into my head. What are you going to do, Jim?"

"I don't know, sir."

"Want some advice?"

"Certainly, sir."

"Stock up on supplies and head for the deep timber. This situation is going to get out of control . . . very quickly. And take Major—correct that, I just saw to it that she was promoted to colonel, it's official—Colonel Shaw and Special Agent Monroe with you."

"I'm sure she'll be glad to hear that, sir. Have warrants been issued for our arrest?"

"Not yet. But they will be. There is nothing I can do about it."

"No. Of course not. I wouldn't ask you to do anything. Mr. President? I hear something in your voice that tells me you've about given up hope for this country. Tell me I'm wrong."

"Oh, I haven't given up, Jim. Not yet. However, it just might be time to let matters run their natural course."

"The military is finally getting involved?"

"To a greater extent than before, yes. They have reluctantly agreed to take a hand in enforcing martial law. I have taken the appropriate steps to call out the Reserves and federalize the National Guard. Nothing is going to move between 6:00 P.M. and 6:00 A.M. without the proper travel papers. I'm closing down the interstate system between those hours. Take care, Jim. I'm sorry about all this."

"So am I, Mr. President. So am I."

The connection was broken on the Washington end. Jim turned to face the small group gathered in the room and laid out the situation for them.

Al Milner was the first to speak. "We've got supplies cached over the park area, Commander. All the way up into Canada, for that matter. Food and water to last small teams for several years. And there are militia up in Canada who would help us. All we have to do is ask."

Jim nodded, anger threatening to boil over inside him at what he was sure Terry had done. "Get our gear packed up and get ready to move. But I tell you all right now, I will not fire on the American flag."

"Neither will most of the militia members who have agreed to follow you, Jim," Steve Malone said. "I'm certain of that. At least, they won't fire unless fired upon."

"Al, contact the other groups. Tell them to hunt a hole and stay put. Baronne, Terry, The Storm, and all the rest of those bastards will have to either fish or cut bait now. And if they tangle with the special operations groups, those guys will feed them to the sharks. I have no intention of our becoming shark bait, so let's get cracking."

The Navy and the Air Force went on high alert to guard against possible terrorist attack from beyond the nation's shores. The Army, Marine Corps, the National Guard, and the Reserves were issued orders to spread out all over the nation in key locations in an attempt to put a lid on the growing civilian unrest. None of the military commanders believed they could contain the violence, but they reluctantly began committing troops.

Closing the nation's interstate highway system was much like the little Dutch boy with his finger in the dike. Those who wanted to travel during the curfew period just shifted over to secondary roads and kept right on truckin'.

The nation's several hundred unaligned government hate groups, which varied in size from half a dozen to five hundred or so and now included every whacko and nut who could pick up a gun, began surfacing. During the first night of full martial law, black churches and—to a much lesser extent—Jewish synagogues, homes, and businesses throughout the nation went up in flames of hate.

All bands of the shortwave were filled with talk of hate, revolution, and takeover. In Los Angeles, police shot half-a-dozen looters, and only the presence of tanks and Marines kept the situation from escalating into a full-blown riot. That did nothing but fuel the hate talk on shortwave.

"Niggers don't want justice!" hate-mongers shouted.

"They want to be able to loot and burn and riot and rape white women. Those savages are the real enemy."

And sadly, only a few prominent black leaders stepped forward to express full support for the troops and police handling the situation.

"And therein lies part of the problem," Pat Monroe said after listening with the others to a news report on a portable radio.

The militia members of Terry's old command had broken up into small teams and scattered to the far reaches of the park and beyond. Those who sided with Pat had been staying at the lodge: Janet, Claire, Steve Malone, Al Milner, Rose, Karen, and Judy.

They had found the first body, which Al identified as one of Durant's men, hanging from a tree limb.

"What the hell? . . ." Pat muttered, looking at the body.

"Don at work," Jim said. "Bet on it. He's stashed Shirley somewhere safe and is on the prowl."

"That makes me nervous," one of the militia-people said, glancing around uneasily. "Don might think we had something to do with the kids' deaths."

Jim shook his head. "Not unless he's gone completely nuts. And I don't believe that. He's just pissed-off . . . and hunting."

"You want to cut the body down, sir?" Al asked.

"No. That would be a sure sign we're here. Leave him. Let's go."

The nine of them were camped in a heavily wooded area deep in the park, miles from the nearest town. They had left their vehicles at the lodge and walked in, taking two days to reach the spot Al knew about. The location was just about perfect for concealment. Less than a mile from where they were camped was a large cache of supplies, buried there almost two years back.

"Won't the others know of the buried supplies?" Jim asked.

"Only four of us knew," Al said. "The three others are dead. One killed when they attacked the lodge, one killed in town, the other killed during that ambush on the road. No one else knows the location."

"Not even Terry?" Jim asked.

Al shook his head. "That was the way all, or at least most, of the militias around the country planned it. There are weapons there . . . among other things. This way, if I'm captured and forced to talk under torture, I can't disclose but two or three caches of supplies."

The Bureau man wore a look of absolute incredulity. "Al, do you really believe the United States Government employs agents who would use physical torture on you?"

"Yes, I do," Al answered without hesitation.

"Jesus," Pat whispered. He cleared his throat. "Did Terry feed you that crap?"

"No. He didn't have to. Not after Waco and Ruby Ridge. Not after all the reports of you people kicking in the wrong doors and rousting innocent people in the middle of the night and stomping little kittens and puppies to death, all in the name of looking for guns that weren't there and never had been. Not after listening to all the whiny liberals in Washington make speeches about how they wanted to disarm America. No, sir. He didn't have to say a word about it."

Pat shook his head. "How in the world did it ever get this bad?" he murmured.

"We could talk for the rest of the day and night about that, Pat," Karen said. "But I think you know the answer to your own question."

The Bureau man fell silent, then slowly nodded his head. "Yeah. I guess I do, at that. Being close to you people these past weeks has opened my eyes quite a bit to the problems facing America." He winked. "But not as much as you seem to have opened Jim's."

"Well . . . I've learned there are two sides to every issue, that's for sure," Jim conceded. "And I've certainly learned that if democracy is to survive, both sides have to be taken into consideration." He held up a hand, then placed a finger on his lips, listening. "I think we've got company, folks," he whispered.

The group slipped into pre-arranged positions around the camp area and went belly-down on the ground. All of them had but one thought: Please don't let this be the military.

None of them wanted to fire on any member of the U.S. military.

Al whispered to Rose; she whispered to Claire, and Claire whispered to Janet, quietly passing the word around the defensive circle. "Tom Durant and some of his people," Janet informed Jim.

Jim nodded and waited.

Faint bits of conversation drifted to the group as Durant and his people edged closer.

". . . around here someplace."

". . . supplies buried all over this damn park, Tom."

"But Hoot said it was in this area." Tom's voice came through clearly. "He was firm on that."

Jim lifted his rifle, his face hard and his eyes cold. He had learned from several break-away militia members that Tom Durant had given the orders for his father to be killed. "When I fire," he whispered to Janet, "Take them all out. Pass the word."

She nodded her understanding. Of all the people present, Janet had witnessed the most change in Jim. The man who had once believed that taxpayer money could solve all the nation's ills was gone, and more than likely would never return. Jim would probably never lose all his liberal beliefs, but many were gone forever, winging away under the hard light of reality.

Jim's order passed around the camp, and they waited.

". . . like to bend that Shaw woman over and get me some of that." A man's voice reached them. "I'm thinking that would be some fine pussy."

"Those light-skinned nigger girls wasn't bad," another said. "But they sure put up a fight."

"Had a mouth on 'em, though," yet another voice interjected. "One of 'em told Bert he had a dick like a flea."

Laughter filtered through the brush and flowering bushes.

". . . never seen Bert so pissed."

". . . She sure stopped her smart mouth when Bert pronged her up the ass though, didn't she?"

"Yeah. She got to bellowin' and squallin' like that deer I shot a couple of seasons ago."

"Tom? I don't think they're here. I think they left the park area."

"No," the doctor disagreed. "We've got the park covered. They didn't get out. They wouldn't have left their vehicles behind. They're here somewhere."

Tom stepped into clear view. The entire group was no more than fifty yards from the hidden campsite. Jim sighted Durant in and squeezed the trigger. The rifle roared and Durant slung his weapon off to one side as he went down, shock on his face and his shirt front bloody.

Jim's team opened up, turning the lovely, quiet woods into a killing ground. The firefight lasted only a few seconds, with Durant's forces able to get off no more than a dozen shots that hit no human target.

The team waited before cautiously slipping from behind cover and over to the sprawled and bloody bodies. There were three people still alive, Tom Durant one of them. Jim knelt down beside him.

"You son of a bitch!" Durant hissed. "How could just one man . . . manage to fuck everything up?"

"Just lucky, I guess," Jim replied, ice in his voice.

"Did you shoot me, Kincaide?"

"I sure did."

"A fitting end, I suppose." Durant closed his eyes, struggled for breath, then opened his eyes and stared at Jim. "You think I killed your father, don't you?"

"You gave the orders. Same thing."

Durant sighed. "Your father . . . well, I had high hopes for him. I wish things could have been different."

"I'm sure he would, too," Jim said.

Durant tried a bloody smile. "Just like your father. Same strange sense of humor." He suppressed a groan by gritting his teeth, then sighed as the waves of pain momentarily subsided. "You've managed to screw things up, young man. But you will never stop the revolution. It's too big for any one man to stop it."

Janet was kneeling down just behind Durant, a small tape recorder in her hand. She was getting it all. "I don't think you have to worry about that," Jim said. "Not after

Terry bombed that government facility outside Washington the other day."

Durant chuckled and coughed up pink frothy blood. "Ah, yes. Unfortunately, I can't accept any of the credit for that. That was a stroke of genius on Terry's part."

"I call it murder on his part."

"But the public believes you did it, Kincaide. That's all we were after. Now your name is sullied right along with the rest of us."

"The president doesn't believe I had anything to do with that bombing."

"Fred Potter is nothing." Durant coughed up more blood, and his body trembled with pain. "The liberals don't like him because he's too moderate. The conservatives don't like him because he's too liberal. And even should you again gain the public's approval, they will view you in the same light. You're nothing but a damn fence-straddler."

"I want what is best for the entire nation, Durant."

Durant fell silent. Jim looked down at the man. The doctor was dead.

"I got it on tape, Jim," Janet said. "I believe that should convince the networks to put you on the air."

Jim rose to his boots. He looked at Al Milner. "Now that Durant is dead, what will happen to his militia?"

"They'll fade, commander. There isn't a person in his bunch who can step up and lead."

"Well, let's take a chance on this tape recording and head back. What do you say?"

The team members began packing up.

That was answer enough.

Twenty

Jim's team found the vehicles that Durant and his people had used, piled in, and took off for town. On the way, Jim used the cell phone and talked with the president, bringing him up to date, then handed the phone to Pat Monroe to call in to his headquarters. When Pat clicked off, there was a faint smile on his face.

"Good news?" Jim asked.

"It might be winding down. At least part of it. A military spokesman just informed the director that they've come in contact with a lot of militia units, but so far no shots have been fired. As the president ordered, the military is making no attempts to disarm the units."

"That's wise," Jim said. "I think that, after this, the liberals had better forget about any attempts at gun control. That's not going to happen in America."

"I assume you were in favor of gun control before the trouble?" Pat asked.

"Yes. Still am to a somewhat lesser degree."

"He's still a hopeless liberal, Pat."

"I suppose there are worse things to be," the FBI man joked.

Janet rolled her eyes and grinned.

Jim took the kidding good-naturedly and said nothing. But it bothered him that he had just killed another man and felt nothing. He also recalled it had taken only one patrol and firefight in 'Nam to feel the same way. On the other side of the coin, he had known men in 'Nam who would not fire at another human being. They would fire their weapons, but never at a human target. Jim had been instrumental in getting two of those types out of his platoon. He did sympathize with them, but damned if he'd put his ass on the line for their feelings.

Jim was certain that, by now, the lodge would have been put to the torch by what remained of Terry's followers. But the old lodge was still standing, proud and strong in the sunlight. There were four vehicles parked in the drive and a number of men sitting on the porch.

"Oh, hell," Jim said. "Now what?"

"Relax," Pat reassured him. "Those are my people."

"That's supposed to make me feel better?"

Pat laughed. "You don't see them reaching for any guns, do you?"

Everybody was introduced, and the smiles of the Bureau men were genuine. "We've been waiting here for a day and a half," an agent said. "I hope you don't mind. We made ourselves at home."

"Not at all," Jim said. "Would somebody please tell me what in hell is going on?"

"President Potter had to let you think you were under suspicion, Mr. Kincaide," another agent said. "He wanted you and your people to head for the timber and stay out of sight while Terry showed his hand."

"And did he do that?" Jim asked.

"Oh, yes," said Inspector Williams, the agent-in-charge. "At least a large number of his followers did. The biggest bunch made the mistake of tangling with a contingent of paratroopers from Fort Bragg. Others, including some of Baronne's people, tangled with Marine patrols, and still others with a contingent of Air Force Commandoes. None of the regular militia has been involved with any firefights with government troops. As a matter of fact they . . . ah . . . have been quite helpful in ferreting out many of Baronne's more radical followers, as well as Terry's hard-line people and a number of the racist groups. It looks like the country had many of the militia people pegged all wrong right down the line." The SAC shuffled his feet on the porch floor in embarrassment. "Myself included, I have to say."

"Well." Rose spoke up. "You can lay much of the blame for all the misunderstanding right on the doorstep of the nation's liberal press and a bunch of asshole left-leaning senators and representatives."

The SAC cleared his throat while some of his men tried to hide their smiles. "Yes," he said. "Well . . . perhaps that's true."

"Tom Durant and his A-team are dead," Jim said, unfolding a map of the park. "There," he placed a finger on the map. "We didn't remove the bodies."

"I can lead the recovery team right to the spot," Al Milner volunteered.

"Thank you," the SAC said. "Is there a clearing close by where a chopper can land?"

"Yes. Only a few hundred meters away," Al replied.

Inspector Williams handed the map to one of his men. "Get with Mr. Milner here for details and then call it in."

"Yes, sir."

"No sign of Terry or Baronne?" Jim asked.

The SAC shook his head. "No. Unfortunately. They have both dropped out of sight . . . gone underground

probably. Along with a large number of their more fanatical followers. The leader of The Storm has also vanished."

"Then this uprising is far from over," Jim ventured.

"It's not over," the SAC concurred. "But I wouldn't
use the phrase *far from over.*"

"I would," Janet countered. "The taking over of towns
might be at an end. Probably is. I personally think the
citizens who have been caught up in the middle of all
this won't put up with much more of that. I think they'll
start arming and shooting back. But the fighting is going
to continue as long as there is one person out there—"
She waved a hand. "—who believes in what Baronne or
Terry preached. And our estimates show there were several hundred thousand of those . . . not counting the men
and women who were silent and/or underground supporters."

"You paint a dismal picture, Colonel Shaw," Williams
replied.

"Who was the person who said, 'I calls 'em as I sees
'em'?"

Williams smiled. "I've heard the phrase."

"I agree with Colonel Shaw," Jim said. "This uprising
might well have peaked, overtly, but it isn't over. The
radical movement has lost a battle, but not the war. Not
yet. Not by a long shot. I've gotten to know the mind-set
of those people over the past month. They're determined,
if nothing else. And they truly believe that God is on
their side."

Claire brought out a tray holding a pitcher of iced tea
and glasses. "Judy's making some sandwiches. I don't
know about the rest of you, but several days of those
dreadful field rations is quite enough for me."

"Any charges against any of us?" Steve Malone asked.

Williams shook his head. "No. None that I'm aware of. I don't know of any forthcoming, either. The president was firm on that." He glanced at Jim. "You made quite an impression on The Man. When you get cleaned up and rested, he wants to see you."

"What about?"

"I think he wants to offer you a job, Mr. Kincaide."

Jim and Janet were flown to Washington in a United States of America jet they caught at a military base west of the park area. Both pilots laughed at the expression on Jim's face as he looked with some trepidation into the cockpit upon boarding.

"Relax, Mr. Kincaide," the pilot said. "We're legit. We heard about your last effort at flying to D.C."

"That is one experience I do not wish to repeat," Jim told the crew.

"Ever flown a jet, sir?" the co-pilot asked.

"Hell, no!"

Both men laughed and waved Jim and Janet to seats in the small but luxuriously appointed plane. They climbed to their assigned altitude and landed at Andrews Air Force Base in what seemed to Jim a very short time. The base was on full alert, with armed troops everywhere one looked.

A limo whisked Jim to the White House, and another took Colonel Janet Shaw to the Pentagon. They would be staying at a hotel not far from the White House.

President Potter waved Jim to a seat in the Oval Office and, after coffee was served and the butler gone, said, "Sorry I had to keep things from you, Jim. I'll apologize to Pat Monroe as well. It was just one of those things that had to be."

"Perfectly all right, sir." Jim sipped his coffee. Excellent, just as he remembered from the last time. "This is marvelous coffee, sir. What is it?"

Fred smiled. "Cuban. But you don't have to repeat that."

Jim laughed. "I won't. I promise."

"I want you to go to work for me, Jim. You won't make as much as you would back at your ad agency, but I need you. What do you say?"

Jim didn't hesitate. "Sure. What kind of a job do you have in mind . . . as if I couldn't guess?"

"All right, guess."

"Public relations, more than likely."

"You're a pretty good guesser. You would be a big help to me at that, sure. But that's only a part of it. Jim, you've fought the extreme fringe elements of what some call the religious right and you've fought the racist elements in the militia movement and you've rubbed shoulders and made friends and fought side by side with the decent people in the regular militia. You know how they think. I want you to head up the commission I'm forming to investigate the why's of this uprising and to write recommendations to make sure it will never happen again. You'll hold hearings . . . lots of hearings with lots of people from all over this nation. The panel won't be made up of a bunch of damn eggheads, but with real people; and these hearings will have some weight behind them. Many of your recommendations will become law, and they'll become law pretty damn quickly—or I'm out of here. If Congress drags its feet on this, I'll chuck this job faster than a pig can get to slop."

Jim chuckled. Fred Potter could come up with some quaint expressions. "I'll be happy to serve on your commission, Mr. President. But you're forgetting Terry and Baronne, aren't you?"

"What do you mean?"

"This uprising isn't over. Just because the nation's military entered the picture doesn't mean that Terry and Baronne are going to jump up and surrender. They're still out there, with thousands and thousands of followers. According to the newspaper I read on the plane coming down here, both those men are wanted for murder. And so are many of their supporters. They have nothing to lose now. Nothing at all. What about them?"

"They're outlaws, Jim. I'm putting a price on their heads. A very large amount of money. Somebody will turn them in."

· Jim held up a warning hand. "Maybe, sir. And that's a *big* maybe."

"The good people of America are tired of this trouble. I have faith in the American people."

Jim felt the president was vastly overrating the American people and greatly underestimating Terry Warden and Gene Baronne. But he wasn't going to argue with The Man about it. "All right, sir. When do you want me to start?"

"Immediately. Today." He smiled. "Colonel Shaw is going to be assigned to the Pentagon for a time. She'll be liaison between the commission and the military."

Jim laughed. "You don't miss a trick, do you, sir?"

The president's eyes twinkled. "Why . . . whatever in the world do you mean, Jim?"

* * *

Terry Warden sat in a safe house in the mountains of North Alabama, drinking cup after cup of strong coffee and entertaining thoughts of killing Jim Kincaide. He now admitted, at least to himself, that he had sold the man short: Jimmy-boy was no pussy. Terry sighed, thinking, I should have killed the son of a bitch the first night I saw him in the timber outside the lodge. But it was a good plan to use Jim. It just didn't work out, that's all.

Terry knew his supporters had lost their momentum, but it could be regained. They would just have to pull back, go underground for a time, and regroup. He also realized he had made a bad mistake in aligning with Baronne, The Storm, and the smaller but just as dangerous racist groups around the nation. Now it was too late to make any attempt at disassociating his forces from the lunatic fringe . . . not that Terry really wanted to do that, for he didn't.

Terry sneered. Jim Kincaide, the boyhood buddy who grew up to be a rich liberal, making a fortune peddling sanitary napkins and headache pills, now is heading up a commission to study why the uprising occurred. Terry laughed aloud, causing the men and women in the large room to turn and look at him, silent questions in their eyes.

"Incredible," Terry muttered.

Gene Baronne sat behind a desk in a safe house in the Rocky Mountains and entertained many of the same thoughts as Terry. But unlike Terry, Baronne had no doubts about the final outcome of the uprising. He knew that God was on his side. God would not let him down.

God loved His Warriors, and Baronne was certainly

one of them. It was just that simple. There wasn't anything complicated about it. Baronne had known for years he was God's Voice on earth. He knew that because God had told him so. Baronne had had visions. Visions were nothing new. Men in olden times had had visions, messages from God. Said so right in the Bible.

God's Army would just have to regroup for the next battle. His warriors would gird their loins and make ready to rid the nation of faggots and liberals and minorities.

Baronne had no doubts about his ability to whip them into a killing frenzy. But first they would rest for a time and make plans.

He ran his tongue over his lips, hungry for blood. It certainly would be a nice touch if he could catch this upstart Jim Kincaide and President Nigger-Lover Potter together and kill them both.

Baronne suddenly fell to his knees, threw back his head, and clasped his hands together close to his chest. "Oh, God!" he cried. "Give me a sign. Tell me what You would have me do! Do not forsake me, oh, my God. I am Your Arm and Sword on this wicked planet . . . Yours to do with as You please."

Lightning licking around the snow-covered peaks of distant mountains caught Baronne's eyes. "Yes!" he shouted. "Yes! I see Your sign and I understand. Fire and smoke and destruction. Sodom and Gomorrah have arisen from the ashes of Your wrath and must be destroyed anew. Oh, my God, I will not fail You. You have given me new strength to continue on with the good fight. I am Your sword of retribution, my God. I will cleanse this land and make it pure of inferiors."

Baronne rose to his feet, his heart and head feeling filled with new strength. "Yes—Yes—Yes!" he shouted.

He and his followers would continue the fight. And this time, they would not fail.

Jim lay awake in bed long after Janet's breathing had deepened and slowed, signaling her gentle slide into a deep sleep. For him, sleep was elusive. His thoughts were not about the upcoming presidential commission he was to chair, nor were they about Terry Warden or Gene Baronne or the sorry state of affairs into which the United States had fallen. Even though Jim was certain that someday—probably much sooner than he realized—he would have to fight his childhood friend, and the fight would be to the death, he would overcome that obstacle when he reached it.

Jim had but one thought on his mind as he lay in the darkness of the luxury hotel room in Washington, D.C. He had pondered that same thought many times since Day One. As he sighed heavily and muttered aloud, Janet turned in her sleep and put an arm across his bare chest.

Jim stared up at the dark ceiling and whispered, "Why in the hell did I ever let myself get involved in this mess?"

Twenty-one

Before the first member of the commission could be chosen, Baronne and Terry struck again.

Small federal buildings in several dozen locations around the nation were hit with rocket attacks, the main targets ATF, FBI, and IRS. For a week the attacks went on, always at night, with no deaths or injuries on either side.

"They're getting smarter," President Potter remarked to Jim. "No one hurt or killed, no great public outcry."

"There goes my theory about the majority of the public having had enough and rising up to take arms against Terry and Baronne," Jim replied. "What about this?" He held up a flyer, one of hundreds of thousands that had been distributed throughout the nation during the night.

The flyer urged that all Americans who wished a return to government that was truly "of the people, for the people, and by the people" stop paying taxes immediately.

President Potter's face grew sad. "I'm surprised something like it hasn't surfaced long before this. Oh, whoever wrote this is right. If five-million citizens stopped paying taxes, this government would grind to a halt. And they're right about the government being unable to arrest millions of citizens for refusing to pay taxes. We certainly don't have the agents to even think about doing that and, even if we did, no place to put those we arrested. Furthermore, should we start arresting Aunt Molly and Uncle Harry and Cousin Bob and Grandmother and Grandfather for refusing to pay taxes, we'd have a civil war on our hands that would topple the government."

"What's been the reaction thus far?"

"We've received thousands of phone calls, telegrams, and E-mail from citizens informing us they will no longer pay taxes under the current tax system."

"And? . . ."

"I've instructed the agencies and departments involved to take no action. I won't play into the hands of Baronne and Warden. I have further asked Congress to start work immediately on a flat tax of ten percent across the board on all income, both earned and unearned, for all working citizens."

"And? . . ."

"Congress has refused to act, saying they will not be blackmailed by thugs. They say the government cannot run on a flat rate of ten percent."

"But they're wrong, Mr. President," Jim dissented.

"Of course, they're wrong. We'd have to tighten up on some budgets and eliminate some departments, but that needed to be done years ago. Of course," he added grimly, "we might not have to worry about public housing much longer, since Warden and Baronne have threatened to start blowing it up. Do you think they would do such a thing, Jim?"

"Yes, sir. I do."

"You answered that without hesitation."

"Even the most moderate of militia members I talked with don't believe that anyone with the exception of children and the elderly and disabled should be given a free ride. Public housing is a sore spot with them. Especially public housing that is built right in the center of middle- and upper-class neighborhoods. That really sends them ballistic."

Potter grunted and shook his head. "Any word from your friend—what's his name?—Don?"

"No, sir. Not a word. But Janet talked to Pat Monroe this morning. He said an even dozen of Durant's supporters are missing. And they were alive and well when we took to the timber. I think Don's been hard at work."

"I can't blame him. Well, if you can get in touch with him, tell him it's time for the killing to stop and for people to get back to the business of living."

"No charges against him, sir?"

"Not if he stops now."

"I may be able to find him. I'll bet he's within a ten-mile radius of the lodge."

"You may as well go look for him, then. Our citizens' commission just went out of business before it got started."

Janet stayed in Washington. Jim drove back to the timberland after calling Al and arranging for a Jeep to be left at the lodge. Before leaving the camp, Jim had secretly left some supplies behind. He had had a hunch all along that Don had been aware of their presence. At the lodge, Jim changed clothes and packed several days' supplies, a pup tent, and sleeping bag. He took a rifle and several boxes of ammunition. The knowledge that Terry would someday be back here looking for him was never far from Jim's mind. Al had also included two full five-gallon gas cans.

Jim headed out into the silent timber, taking barely passable old logging roads. He drove slowly, stopping often and cutting the engine, listening to the sounds of nature in midsummer. Occasionally he would get out and prowl both sides of the ancient roads, looking for any sign of Don.

About an hour from the lodge, Jim caught a flash of movement in the brush. He quickly cut the engine, grabbed his rifle, and bailed out. He hit the ground and rolled into the timber on the opposite side of the road. Unless his friend had somehow managed to change color, he knew he had not spotted Don. Jim pulled the stock of his rifle to his shoulder and slipped off the protective caps covering the front and rear of the scope.

A rifle cracked several times, the bullets whistling and howling through the leaves and brush, the last slug gouging out bits of bark from a tree just to Jim's left. Jim lay still, knowing the shooter was guessing at his location. He sighted in, slowly scanning the terrain across the old weed-grown road. The powerful scope pulled in leaves with such clarity he could see the veins among the green. He steadied the rifle as the scope pulled in a dirty face. Jim recognized one of the militiamen who had gone over to Terry from Al's group. Jim steadied the crosshairs and squeezed the trigger. The butt slammed his shoulder and Jim immediately pulled the rifle down and sighted in again. The green foliage now dripped with crimson.

"Under that lightning marked tree!" The shout came from across the road. "It's Kincaide. This time, kill the bastard. Terry said . . ."

The sentence ended in a horrible choking sound.

"Otis!" another called. "Otis?"

"No!" A third voice shouted, followed by a scream of pain and terror.

What the hell! Jim thought.

"Matt!" Someone shouted. "What is it, Matt?"

The woods were silent.

"Kincaide's not alone!" The shout reached Jim. "I'm gettin' the hell outta here!"

"Well, who the hell else could it be?"

No one answered the last question. Jim heard the sound of running boots. He waited for a long sixty count.

"It's all clear on this side of the road, Jim." Don's familiar voice sprang out of the brush.

Jim stood up, cradling his rifle, and stepped out onto the old road just as Don stepped out of the brush on the other side. The two men stood for a moment, staring at each other.

Don looked rough. He had not shaved in days, and his clothing was stiff with dirt and grime and dried blood. Jim did not think the blood belonged to Don.

"It's good to see you, Don. I mean that."

"Good to see you, Jim. You know about my son and daughter?"

"Yes. I arranged for the services. I'm just as sorry as I can be about them."

"The people responsible for it paid."

"I know. Now it's time to put that behind you and come on back to the land of the law-abiding. It can't last forever. It's got to wind down."

"Three dead over here. What about them?"

"Leave them. We'll call the authorities from the lodge."

"I could sure use a bath."

Jim grinned. "Yeah, I can see that. I'm glad the wind's not blowing in my direction."

Don smiled for the first time. "Jesus, I'm tired. I'm really whipped out."

Jim walked to the Jeep and got behind the wheel. "Come on, Don. Let's start putting the bad days behind us and concentrate on the living."

Don walked slowly to the Jeep and got in, sighing as he leaned back in the seat. Jim put the Jeep in gear, turned around, and headed for the lodge. Behind them, flies began gathering on the cooling bodies.

Twenty-two

Don took a long shower and a careful shave. While he was scrubbing away days of grime and most of the stench of hate, Jim called Janet.

"Don's with me. Both of us are all right and Don's agreed to end his vendetta. President Potter said he could guarantee no charges would be filed against him."

"I'll get word to him. When will you get back here?"

"Day or two. Why, you miss me?"

"Oh . . . a little bit. Your cooking mostly."

Laughing, Jim hung up.

Don walked into the den, dressed in some clothing he had left behind in his rush to leave days before.

Jim had made coffee and sandwiches. He drank coffee while Don attacked several of the sandwiches.

Jim waited until Don had devoured the first sandwich, then asked, "Where is Shirley?"

"Across the border in Canada. We have friends up there."

"You took her up there personally?"

"Yes. Our friends met us at the border."

"Is she? . . ." Jim's question trailed off.

"She's holding up." Don drank half a glass of milk and took a bite from another sandwich. He sighed and set the glass down carefully in a coaster. "We got separated leaving here. But we had the CB on. Donald warned us what was happening to him. Begged us not to stop, to keep on going, save ourselves. Lori screamed that by the time we got to them, it would too late, anyway. Shirley was crying, but she told me to keep going and heed the kid's wishes. Hardest decision I ever made in my life. I drove about four or five more miles, then parked the car in the timber and told Shirley to stay put. I was so rattled, I didn't even take a gun with me. I followed the road but stayed in the brush. Fell down a dozen times and got lost once. Stupid of me, I know. The damn road was always to my left. But I still got turned around. By the time I reached . . ." His voice broke. ". . . where it happened—it had taken me well over an hour—it was done. They had shoveled dirt over them. It was then I realized I didn't have a gun. Good thing, I guess. I would have surely been killed. All I could do was memorize their faces and get out of there. But I swore I would be back and kill them all." His face hardened. "I got about a dozen of them."

"It's over now. I think I can arrange to get Shirley and you two can go on back to the city."

Don shook his head. "Shirley doesn't want to come back. She doesn't want to return to America, says there is too much hate here. I don't know what we're going to do."

"Stay in Canada?"

"Maybe."

"But they had their troubles, too."

"Not like down here. Oh, hell, Jim, I don't know what we're going to do. I don't want to move out of the city. This is my country. I was born here. I'm just as much an American as anyone. But . . ." He shook his head.

"You're worn out, Don. Go get some rest. Sleep through until morning. We can make decisions then."

"Will you drive me up to the border?"

"You know I will."

Don wandered off to a bedroom, leaving Jim alone in the den with the television. There had been incidents of violence reported that day around the nation, mostly between the hard-line revolutionaries and the military, but no more bombings of federal buildings.

The national news over, Jim switched over to local programming and listened to what had been happening in the area. He had to smile, for this news reporter was decidedly conservative and made no effort to hide his delight in what was taking place.

In towns located within the park and in those just outside the park, crime had dropped to near zero. There had been a number of shootings of punks and thugs caught in the act of stealing; and with no one charged in the shootings, criminals had ceased their activity—just as anyone with half a brain had known would happen if law-abiding citizens were allowed to protect what they had worked for. Civil libertarians all over the nation were screaming about what they called a *gunpowder society.* Certain liberal democrats were, according to this anchor-person, moaning and having snits about the poor criminal's rights being abused by homeowners and business people with guns.

Jim applauded the openness of the man's opinions and fixed another cup of coffee during the commercial break between news and weather.

Rain was predicted to move into the area that night, with low clouds and occasional showers the next day.

The temperature would be unusually cool for this time of year.

Jim fixed an early supper and then sat outside, enjoying the coolness of the evening. He checked on Don, who was in a deep sleep, locked up the lodge, and went to bed. He dreamed of Janet and woke up smiling.

Don walked into the den stretching and yawning just as Jim was pouring his first cup of coffee.

"I slept like a rock, Jim. I'll bet I didn't turn over two times the entire night."

"I sawed some logs myself. You feel better?"

"A thousand percent."

The men took their coffee and went outside to sit on the porch. It was cool, but not unpleasantly so. A very light rain was falling, almost a mist, and fog clung to low pockets. Jim estimated visibility at seventy-five yards, at best.

"I'm going to call Shirley this morning, Jim." Don broke the silence. "I hope I can convince her we should stay here in America. Hell, New York is our home. It's where my job is. What would I do in Montreal?"

"Well, for one thing, you'd learn to speak French."

Don laughed. "Shirley speaks French. I have enough trouble with English." His smile faded. "It won't be easy convincing her to return. But we both need to visit the kids' graves and accept their deaths. That's got to be number one on our agenda."

"Will you have them exhumed and moved closer to the city?"

Don slowly shook his head. "I'd rather not. But that will be up to Shirley—if I can talk her into coming back. On the plus side, she loves her work and it won't be long before it's time for school to start." He sighed heavily. "Wanna go inside and watch the early news?"

"Yeah. Let's see who blew up what last night."

Jim entered the den first and headed for the TV. Don paused in the doorway. "You find the channel," he said. "I'll get us more coffee."

"That's a good deal."

A rifle cracked, the sound muffled by the weather, and Don pitched forward, his head bloody. He landed bonelessly on the floor and did not move. Jim jumped for the corner, where his gear was stacked, and hurriedly slipped off his house shoes and pulled on and laced up boots. He cut his eyes to Don. Don's head was bleeding copiously. That meant his heart was still beating, but there was no way Jim could check on how bad the wound was because the front door was wide open and offering an ample field of fire to whoever was outside. And Jim had a pretty good idea who that was.

Terry had returned.

Jim struggled into a shirt, then pulled an unlined field jacket over that. He buckled a web belt around his waist, the web belt holding a holstered pistol, a sharp sheath knife, and full ammo pouches for his rifle and pistol. Jim had six full ten-round extend-mags for the Remington model 742 and an ammo belt with all the loops full. His Beretta held fifteen rounds in the clip, and he had two more in a pouch on the web belt. His father had taught him to keep plenty of ammo at the ready, for he never knew when he might need it. Well, he sure needed it now.

"Oh, Jimmy-boy!" Terry's taunt was faint but audible. "You want to come outside and play with me?"

Jim made certain that his boots were laced up tight

and that the laces would not dangle and catch on anything.

"Come on, Jimmy-boy. Big hot-shot war hero. Let's see if you've still got the right stuff."

Jim crawled to the kitchen and drew a glass of water and drank it, then duck-walked to the rear door and opened it, slipping out. He rolled off the back porch to the ground and belly-crawled to the edge of the lodge.

"Come on, Jimmy-boy!" Terry called. "You either come on out or I'll burn you out!"

Jim pinpointed Terry's location. Keeping the house between them, he headed for the woods. There, he caught his breath. He began slowly working toward Terry's voice, hoping Terry would call out once more.

But this time, Terry called out with a bullet.

The bullet knocked bark from a tree near Jim's head, splattering his face and stinging. Jim hit the damp ground and lay still. He put a hand to his face. No blood.

"This is going to be too easy, Jimmy-boy," Terry taunted. "You're gonna have to do better. I could have killed you then, boy."

"Why didn't you?" Jim called.

"Cat and mouse, Jimmy-boy. I'm the cat and you're the mouse."

Jim gave the man who used to be his friend five rounds of .308s and then was up and running. He headed into the timber, then cut to his right and began another slow circle.

"Not bad, Jimmy-boy." Terry's voice was distant, but coming from the same location. "You surprised me with that burst. That sounds like a .308."

Jim bellied down on the ground, with thick brush in front of him, and waited. While he waited, he thumbed rounds into the magazine, filling it, then muffled the metallic click of the magazine seating in place.

"Not going to talk to me, Jimmy-boy? Aww, what a shame. I guess you haven't heard the news this morning, huh?"

Jim waited, motionless.

"Well, let me bring you up to date. Baronne got his stupid ass captured last night. Some of his own people turned him in. That has a familiar ring to it, doesn't it, Jimmy-boy? The latest round of federal-building bombings got to them. But no jury will ever convict ol' Doc Baronne of anything. Hell, he's nuttier than a road lizard. My own militia decided it was time to take to the hills, so to speak. Dig in and stay low. Not a bad idea, I guess, but it really doesn't appeal to me. I'm a marked man. The Company's got a contract out on me. Besides, I don't think I'd like prison. So that brings us full circle, Jimmy-boy. Now it's down to you and me."

Baronne turned in by his own people. Jim mulled that over. Terry was right about Baronne, though. He'd heard Pat Monroe often say that Baronne would never be sent to a regular prison, much less be put to death. He'd be confined in a mental institution.

"Then the war is over, Terry?" Jim chanced a shout.

"There you are. Oh, hell, no, Jimmy-boy. This war will never be over. The president can throw every man and woman in uniform he's got into the field; it won't stop us. Too many Americans want change. Too many Americans are willing to put their lives on the line for that change."

"Change is coming, Terry. Some federal departments are going to be eliminated or drastically cut. The nation is going to have a flat tax or user tax. The IRS will be virtually out of citizens' lives."

"Did your buddy, the president, tell you all this?"

"Yes, he did."

"Oh, Jesus Christ, Jimmy. The man's a politician. He'd tell you a giraffe shits on a flat rock every third day precisely at noon for a vote. Politicians lie."

"I believe this one is telling the truth."

"All right, Jimmy, what if he *is* leveling with you? What about Congress? Do you really think that bunch of liberal assholes is going to go along with him? The liberals' goal is to turn this nation on the road to socialism. Look at what they've done over the past three or four decades. Open your eyes, boy. Take off the blinders."

"Terry, I never said you and those who follow you didn't have a valid point—several valid points. But you went too far. Al and Rose and Judy and Karen and Pete and all the rest of the militia members I've worked with for the past weeks . . . they've turned on you. *They're* willing to compromise on issues, but not *you.* You said you'd compromise, but you lied, Terry. It has to be all your way or no way. You're unreasonable."

Terry laughed, the sound just reaching Jim. "If my plan to kill all the liberal senators and representatives had been put into effect, you'd have seen unreasonable."

Jim wouldn't have believed anything Terry could say could shock him. But that did. "What?" he called.

"I had a good plan, boy. We'd just rid the nation of all the liberals in power. I had snipers and bomb squads all set to go. Some of them are still out there. But federal agents nabbed most of them after Baronne was taken and his people talked. We'll still be able to kill a few of the bastards and bitches. It won't be a total loss."

Jim put his forehead against the wet earth and for a moment savored the coolness. His face felt flushed, as though he had a fever.

"After I kill you, of course," Terry called.

"Never happen," Jim muttered.

"Then I'm gonna kill that turncoat bitch you took up with," Terry shouted.

Jim raised his head. "Janet's not a turncoat, Terry. You just thought she was playing in your ballpark. She's a good operative. Had you fooled, didn't she?"

Jim thought he heard his old friend chuckling over the distance, but couldn't be sure. "Well, she had me fooled, for sure, Jimmy-boy."

"You were going to use Baronne for a time and then kill him, weren't you, Terry? You would have laid the blame for the killing on the government and that would have pulled your forces closer together, right?"

Another long pause. "You're smarter than I thought. I underestimated you. You can't fly a plane worth shit, but you're smart as hell."

Despite Terry's radical views and the fact that Terry was determined to kill him, Jim still could not help but like the man. That was part of Terry's charm, he supposed. "So what happens now?"

"I kill you, that's what happens. It's a damn shame, but I don't have any choice. You see, many of my followers don't think I can, or will, do it. I've got to show them they're wrong. That will help unite the organization. We'll lay low for a time, then resurface, stronger than ever."

"You're wrong, Terry. The uprising is over. The people

who wanted change are going to get some of their demands, and this nation will survive. It might even be stronger and better for it."

"This nation will be stronger and better when the people rise up and control the niggers, stick 'em back in their place, and keep them there until we can educate the savage out of them. That's what's going to happen. Bet on it."

Jim could now detect real anger in Terry's voice. He suspected the time for talking was just about over. He had taken the protective caps off his scope when he'd bellied down to give the glass time to adjust to the temperature change and not fog over. Slowly, he pulled the rifle to his shoulder. He adjusted a bit for range and the magnification lost its fuzziness and became sharper.

"Fuck it!" Terry shouted. "Nobody can talk sense to a goddamn liberal. I thought you might have changed, but you haven't. . . . Answer me, you son of a bitch!"

Jim waited.

"OK, hotshot. Play time is over. Now let's see how good you are."

Jim detected movement and chanced a shot, the booming of the rifle shattering the stillness.

"Not bad, Jimmy-boy. But close only counts in hand grenades and horseshoes. It's been nice knowing you, Jimmy. I will bury the body so the animals won't eat you."

"That's very big of you," Jim muttered, then saw a flash of movement and knew his old friend had shifted positions, moving to Jim's right.

While Terry was moving, Jim changed positions, moving to his left and sliding into a slight depression in the earth. Terry's rifle cracked, the bullet cutting a hot path low and through the center of the brush Jim had just vacated.

"Knew where I was all along," he murmured. "Very good, Terry."

"It's really too bad, Jimmy-boy!" Terry shouted, and Jim caught just a bit of color that was slightly off in the midst of the damp foliage. He put the cross-hairs on it. "We could have made an unbeatable team, you and me. You could have been my right-hand man."

Jim squeezed the trigger and the rifle slammed his shoulder. He quickly pulled the scene back into view and steadied the rifle.

Terry rose up from behind his scant cover. Through the scope, Jim could see a strange expression on his face. The front of Terry's jacket was staining rapidly with blood, and he had dropped his rifle.

"Why . . . you son of a bitch!" Terry shouted; and as he did, his lips turned crimson through the heavy magnification. "You really did it." Terry smiled grotesquely and then pitched forward and was still.

Jim slowly got to his boots, took several deep breaths, and jogged to the rear of the lodge. He paused, then ran the short distance to the timber, staying in the timber until he reached Terry. Jim had seen enough dead men in his life to know that Terry had reached the end of his. But just to be sure, Jim poked the man in the buttocks with the muzzle of his rifle. A man feigning unconsciousness will always tighten his buttocks at the touch; the buttocks of a man unconscious or dead will remain slack.

Terry was definitely dead.

Jim looked toward the lodge, a smile creasing his lips.

Don was sitting on the steps, a bloody handkerchief pressed against his head.

"Where do you keep the aspirin, Jim?" Don called. "I've got a hell of a headache."

Twenty-three

According to the press, Terry's organization fell apart when the news of his death spread nationwide. But Jim knew better. Only a few had turned themselves in; the rest went underground, as did the remaining members of Baronne's Sword of the Righteous, The Storm, and other lesser-known but just as dangerous militant and racist groups around the country.

The uprising was by no means over; it was just taking a breather.

President Potter awarded Jim the nation's highest civilian honor: the Medal of Freedom. Jim tossed the medal into the same box that held his other decorations, including his Medal of Honor. He knew what all his medals were really worth; he'd heard too many other highly decorated combat vets voice their opinions: Put them all together with a dollar and you might be able to get a cup of coffee.

Don had convinced Shirley to return to the United States and was back working at the ad agency.

Jim and Janet were quietly married in a civil ceremony in New York City and were living in the city until they could find a house in the suburbs.

As the summer wore on into autumn and then into winter, crime across America's rural sections fell to almost zero as more and more citizens armed themselves and began taking back the streets, occasionally by shooting it out with young hoodlums, usually just by their presence and past reputation and the punks' knowledge that the police simply were not going to interfere.

In dozens of cases around the nation, local DA's had tried to bring charges against people who used deadly force protecting their lives or loved ones or property, and an equal number of civil suits had been filed seeking damages for the families of the dead or crippled criminals. Not one had yet to make it to a courtroom. It had reached the point in almost all rural areas where sheriff's deputies just refused to serve subpoenas if they involved a law-abiding citizen shooting a criminal caught in the act. Civil libertarians were outraged and threatened legal action, which for the most part was ignored by those law-abiding citizens who felt they had a right to protect what was theirs against criminals who would rather steal than work.

Crime did not lessen that much in the cities once the military pulled out . . . to no one's surprise since the nation's cities, for years, had been filled with people who were quick to make excuses for any type of criminal behavior.

Millions of Americans were also very much opposed to what they perceived as the indiscriminate use of deadly force against criminal types and the newly proposed system of taxation, feeling a user tax would hurt the poor and a ten- or twelve-percent flat tax rate would not hit the rich hard enough. But those people, while many were organized, were not armed and didn't believe in violence anyway. So there was little they could do about the new system of justice and taxation, except bitch.

The nation's cities did not immediately turn into battlegrounds as some had predicted they would.

"That will come later," Jim said. "When the full impact of all the government cuts hit home and those who have made a vocation of being on welfare suddenly find themselves with no place to live and no money . . . that's when the rioting will take place."

"And that's when a lot of people are going to get hurt or killed," Janet added.

"You're right."

Jim knew that millions of citizens who lived outside the major cities were waiting with guns loaded for the rioting and looting and burning to start.

The nation's press harped and carped and wrote and broadcast editorials about the rights of the criminals being violated but, to their dismay, found their opinions ignored by the majority of citizens who were weary to the bone of hearing them.

As far as the mini-revolution, as it was now being called by some, it looked like the worst was over.

Twenty-four

On the first Monday in November, as the winter's chill was just beginning to touch the Northeast with a frosty hand, Jim and Janet woke up after spending their first night in their new home in Westchester County. Jim showered while Janet caught another ten minutes of sleep, then went to the kitchen to make coffee. Janet's coffee, unless it came in a premeasured packet, still tasted as though something had crawled up and died in the pot.

He clicked on the small kitchen TV and sat down in the breakfast nook to watch the news.

"Jim!" Janet called from the bedroom. "Turn on the news!"

"I've got it on." He returned the shout. "I can't believe it's started all over."

He watched and listened in stunned silence for a few moments, until Janet appeared in the archway. "I've been watching the 'CBS Morning News,' " she said. "It's . . . unbelievable. I thought the government had a handle on things."

"We all underestimated what was left of Baronne and Terry's militias. Some of Baronne's people just busted him out of jail. All hell's broken loose all over the nation."

"I was watching the riots in Los Angeles a minute

ago. But that's a different city on the screen now. How many cities are experiencing trouble?"

"About a half a dozen. They're showing Houston now. The city is burning. . . . What is that sound?"

"That's the doorbell, honey."

Jim slid out of the booth. "I'll get it. You have some coffee."

Jim opened the front door. Two grim-faced men stood on the porch, both of them holding their I.D.'s. Secret Service. "Mr. Kincaide?"

"Yes."

"The president would like to see you, sir. We have a plane waiting."

WILLIAM W. JOHNSTONE
THE PREACHER SERIES

WILLIAM W. JOHNSTONE
THE BLOOD BOND SERIES

BLOOD BOND   (0-8217-2724-0, $3.95/$4.95)

BLOOD BOND: BROTHERHOOD OF THE GUN (#2)
(0-8217-3044-4, $3.95/$4.95)

BLOOD BOND: SAN ANGELO SHOWDOWN (#7)
(0-8217-4466-6, $3.99/$4.99)